City of Slaughter

City of Slaughter

a novel

_____

Cynthia Drew

2012
FITHIAN PRESS, MCKINLEYVILLE, CALIFORNIA

This book is a work of fiction. Any reference to historical events, real people, or real locales is used fictitiously. Other names, characters, places, and incidents are products of the author's imagination, and any resemblance to actual events or locals or persons, living or dead, is entirely coincidental.

Cover photograph: "The twisted fire escape after the Triangle Waist Company fire, 1911" courtesy of International Ladies Garment Workers Union Archives, Kheel Center, Cornell University.

Published by Fithian Press
A division of Daniel and Daniel, Publishers, Inc.
Post Office Box 2790
McKinleyville, CA 95519
www.danielpublishing.com

Distributed by SCB Distributors (800) 729-6423

LIBRARY OF CONGRESS CATALOGING-IN-PUBLICATION DATA
Drew, Cynthia.

City of slaughter : a novel / by Cynthia Drew.
    p. cm.
 ISBN 978-1-56474-514-9 (pbk. : alk. paper)
1. Pogroms—Russia—Fiction. 2. Jewish orphans—Fiction. 3. Immigrants—New York (N.Y.)—Fiction. 4. Jewish women—New York (N.Y.)—Fiction. 5. Self-realization in women—Fiction. 6. New York (N.Y.)—Fiction. 7. Jewish fiction.
I. Title.
PS3604.R485C58 2012
813'.6—dc22
                  2011031456

For my sisters

Arise and go now to the city of slaughter;
Into its courtyard wind thy way;
There with thine own hand touch, and with the eyes of
    thine head,
Behold on tree, on stone, on fence, on mural clay,
The spattered blood...

    Hayyim Bialek
    "In the City of Slaughter"

City of Slaughter

— 1 —

Cheshvan 14, 5661
(November 25, 1899)

A FULL moon washed over the Pale of Settlement, lighting Eisig Ginter's work. He swept against a stiff north wind, his old arms pushing drifts of fallen leaves off the synagogue's stone steps: *cha-whish, cha-whish, cha-whish*. It did not matter that the leaves blew back after each thrust; the mean worry of cleaning his *shtetl* was Ginter's great joy.

He paused, listening to the wind howl through the newly-bare birches surrounding Lucava's cobblestone square, feeling as grateful now for peaceful streets as he had earlier for the hum of a busy market day. Lifting his eyes, he opened them wide and wider still to the moon's icy shimmer, then dropped his broom and cupped his hands over the moon's glow as though he protected his face from a white fire.

He shook a finger at the heavens. "Late you come, eh, frost moon?" he mumbled in the fricative melody of Yiddish. "Last year you took my Lidiya. Who will you take this year when you go?"

AT THE back of a print shop three blocks away, thirteen-year-old Carsie Akselrod sat with her mother and nine-year-old sister in front of the rusty iron cook stove, her feet warm at last.

Her father read to them from a story by Mendele Sforim:

"'Sendrel!' said Benjamin. 'Do you have any idea what's beyond Tuneyadevka?'
"'Of course I do. A tavern with first-rate vodka.'
"'I mean beyond that...'"

———

NO ONE in Lucava had any idea what lay beyond that night: five men who approached from the north, appearing first as dark smears against that moonlit stretch, their horses saddled without bit or bridle. They rode west along the rutted road out of Kishinev to the edge of the short-grass plain and south on the Bessarabian steppes, their eyes narrowed against the wind, their whistles and shouts flying like dried leaves on the cold night air: "*KAHzak SLAHvaaah!*" And again, "*KAHzak SLAHvaaah!*" Cossack glory.

"'BEYOND THE tavern?' Sendrel shook his head wonderingly. 'No, I don't know what's out there. Do you?'

"'Do I? What a question! Why, the whole world!' said Benjamin. 'Sea monsters, basilisks. And the Land of Israel with all its holy places. Wouldn't you like to go?'

"'Would you?'

"'What a question! I not only would, I soon will!…'"

The coals ebbed; Carsie's head nodded. With her sister, she retired to the next room, to a bunk cushioned by a straw mattress. She pulled up the rough wool blankets and closed her eyes—the only time she found a few minutes to think. Another Russian lesson that morning—*Gott im himmel,* was any language more maddening? Why did Mama insist she study Russian? Did they speak Russian in the Land of Israel? In America? Didn't everyone speak Yiddish?…Did Mama have to make turnip latkes so often?…How long would winter…

Her parents snuffed the wick in the oil lamp and huddled in a bed only slightly wider on the far side of the room, against a cold outside wall. Almost at once, Reuven Akselrod snored heavily, his jaw slack. Yona stirred, frowning over her shoulder at her husband. He always snored after a big meal, and tonight's had been bigger than most. Today, Lucava's market day, Yona had made the turnip latkes, Reuven's favorite; he had eaten more than his share. She dug an elbow into his ribs. He smacked his lips and rolled onto his right side, moving as close to the edge of the bed as he could, hoping to avoid any more of his wife's jabs.

A HARD freeze blackened the Pale. Rabbits scuttled to the warmth of their burrows, red stags nestled in thickets of goose-foot and mallow.

Eisig Ginter finished his chores, latched the synagogue door, and turned, frowning. Yisvi Kossov's violin *kaddish* echoed as it always did late at night from a window at the end of Zdunska Street, but beyond the violin's plaintive song, Ginter heard a call on the north wind. He spoke Russian; he knew the words.

THE AKSELROD family wakened to a knock on the kitchen door—one long, two shorts, and another, hurried, and a weaker one, the same rhythm lower on the door, and a fourth in the cadence, tap…tap-tap. When the knock came, they pulled on shoes and coats and ran with the others, their path lit by the same cloudless moon that guided the approach of their tormentors. All but Lucava's soundest sleepers ran, knocking the cipher on neighbors' doors as they fled.

Shivering, they tucked themselves under the Byk River bridge or hugged together in the darkness of the stables or flattened themselves under horse troughs or hid in the crawl-spaces of the shops around the square. Eisig Ginter covered his frail body with birch leaves.

Stories rang in the villagers' ears of Jewish women sold by the Cossacks to whore in Turkey, of children used for target practice, of men chained and buried alive on the steppes. Many swayed back and forth, *davening*, beseeching, whispering prayers that they would lose few to the Czar's foreign slave markets.

Sabers whirling, their cloaks spread like wings, the Cossacks screamed from a grove of stunted oaks into Lucava in full fight. Banners flying on fixed bayonets, they ransacked storefronts for anything of value until the youngest of them urged his gray Orlov up the steps of the synagogue. He spurred the horse and pulled at its reins, rearing the gray to kick at the synagogue's front doors until the hinges gave way. The four behind him pushed through the portal on horseback.

From their hiding places, the villagers heard noises erupt inside the synagogue—metal against metal, glass breaking. A vodka bottle flew through the window, shattering its inlaid Star of David. A gunshot rang, and another. Laughter rumbled, wood split. Wisps of smoke floated out the splintered doorway, along with maudlin songs in off-key harmonies. The Cossacks yelled and wept, swore and danced, and shouted, "*KAHzak SLAHvaaah!*" as dawn colored the sky.

THE SUN broke faint as a memory of summer over the riverbank, thawing the scab of ice on the Byk. Shadows faded, revealing the Jews in their hiding places. Inside the synagogue, all fell quiet.

Spent and boozy, the squad rode out the front doors and down the street. They did not look up through the trees to gauge the sky, skinned now in a scrim of winter, nor did they stop at the stables to see what might be worth stealing. They left Lucava by the bridge, their horses' hooves hammering over the heads of those huddled under its pilings.

Shifting in their hiding places, they watched the Cossacks retreat, waiting until they heard silence. Hugging their children to them, they scrabbled out from under the bridge, from the shadows of the stables, from damp crawl spaces. None of them noticed the young ringleader who watched from the far side of the bridge, circling his gray, seeing the people of the *shtetl* collect in the square. Then he turned to follow his comrades, glancing over his shoulder as though he itched to return.

THE JEWS went home, all but the men who could help with repairs, and one woman who stood apart from those men— Rabbi Shulman's wife. Shivering in the cold morning, they stared numbly at the synagogue, every one of them fearful of what damage waited inside. Rabbi Shulman mounted the steps first and edged through the doorway; others followed.

Shulman sank to his knees and cried out a single, bottomless syllable, retching at destruction more devastating than he'd imagined it might be. Behind him, Eisig Ginter keened in anguish. Tearful, the men of Lucava sorted through the vandalized remains of their temple: the Ark's splintered doors dangling loose, its light above—the Ner Tamid, the eternal flame—extinguished, the chain that held it bent and broken. In the middle of the prayer hall a pig's snout bled on the *Torah* scrolls, now charred at the edges. Their silver candlesticks were gone, the carved benches lay cloven. Three walls bore large holes and slurs written in feces. Embers of a fire sparked in the center of the sanctuary.

Still, though the Cossacks had defiled the synagogue and stolen the candlesticks, a few scrawny chickens and Natan Mikarsky's silver *kiddush* cup, they had taken no one in the raid. Three days until *Shabbat,* they had little time to clean up and rebuild.

Smells of ash and horse dung stung Reuven Akselrod's nostrils. He scratched idly at the shoulder of his black gabardine coat, trying to swallow a feeling of frailty that welled in his stomach, blinking heavy-lidded eyes that stared at the damage through thick round glasses. His lower lip pouted above a tidy beard. Printer's ink had permanently stained his knuckles. He nibbled at a blackened fingernail.

An assault on their *shtetl* had been inevitable, he knew. A routine trade stop on the route from Kishinev to Bialystok, Lucava's customs house and some of the surrounding stores did more business in a month than the shops in many *shtetls* did all year. In recent weeks the Czar's forces had menaced settlements closer to Kiev. Lucava's isolation, close to the western border, had helped to protect her people from the Czar's reach; but now, it seemed, they had been discovered.

He looked to the sides of the square, seeing the people of Lucava begin their day as though the Cossacks had never come, because they could not imagine what else they might do.

Eisig Ginter, leaf scraps still hanging from his skullcap and gray smock, broke from a group of men who talked in wispy breaths that rose on the early-morning air. He walked through the burned rubble toward Reuven, his shoulders heaving. "The Ark," he mumbled, his voice tight with grief. "Did you see? I remember when it was blessed—how long ago? Seventy years? Our poor synagogue, like a rock it has been to me…a tabernacle. Now? Defiled, dirty, torn like a rag in the wind." He doubled over, sobbing.

Reuven put an arm around the old man's shoulders. Ginter straightened, wiping away his tears with the sleeve of his smock. He patted Reuven's shoulder. "Go home," he said. "Guard your women. Write about what's happened here." He shook a finger in Reuven's face. "But be careful what you print."

Reuven understood. The Elders called for a broadside. He trotted past the home for the elderly on Mikolaja Street, hearing beginnings of the volley in his ears, seeing the layout, hoping he had enough ink.

He wove through the clutch of porters that talked of the raid while they waited for work in front of Yisvi Kossov's fabric shop, the ropes of their trade hanging loose on their shoulders—sturdy men buttoned into black greatcoats though the temperature had warmed to near freezing. He stumbled on the cobblestones when he ducked a water carrier's yoke and, crossing Zdunska Street, dodged a street vendor's wagon full of potatoes—old ones, soft and wrinkled and sprouted—as he hurried into Tamozhny alley and up the stone steps at the rear of the print shop.

He stopped in the doorway, listening to Yona school the girls in the next room, the room they all slept in. Carsie read reluctantly but Lilia seemed more interested in learning, despite her eyes, which were so crossed that she must press a book to her nose to see even its pictures. Still, she was a fast learner by ear alone; her command of Russian surpassed her older sister's.

Yona sat in a dim corner, the girls opposite her, facing the morning light from an east window. She nodded her head in cadence while Carsie read from a fashion magazine brought to Lucava from Moscow years back and handed now from neighbor to neighbor.

"*Vilstu té?*" Yona whispered to her husband. "*Vilstu té?*" Would you like tea?

"Yeh, *ikh bet dikh té,*" Reuven answered. He needed tea and quiet time to compose his proclamation. He kissed Yona's forehead and smiled down at his daughters.

"Dressmaking is one of the most highly skilled trades for women," Carsie read in faltering Russian. "The other being mi-mill-millinery. What's millinery?"

"Millinery is the making of ladies' hats," Reuven said.

"Hello, Papa." Lilia turned, her face always alight whenever she heard his voice.

Grateful for a break from the reading lesson, Carsie handed the magazine to Lilia and went to hug her father. Lilia pressed her nose to the magazine's open pages, trying to see its illustrations, scanning both sides of the spread for pictures and text.

Reuven looked at his youngest and sighed. It pained him to watch her read. *Beser a krumer oygn eyder a krumer kop,* he recalled the rabbi saying. Better a crooked eye than a crooked mind. Except for Lilia's eyes the girls were youthful likenesses of their mother, their long lashes, their fine noses and pink mouths set on olive faces. They wore dark stockings and gray wool homespun smocks, the same as their mother, who had added a black weskit for warmth. His wife, it seemed to him, was always cold, yet she did not cover her head like the other women in the village, preferring to wear her shiny dark hair knotted firmly in back while the girls wore circles of braids atop their heads.

Yona went to the kitchen. Lilia followed, still searching the magazine at close range for illustrations.

"The bastards had quite a time of it last night," he called from the bedroom. "There's little left of the synagogue."

"And Mayim Shulman? She stayed behind to see the damage?" Yona gently pried the magazine from Lilia's grip and placed it on the kitchen table.

Reuven sank onto the bed, his forearms on his knees. Through the door he looked at Yona. He raised an eyebrow and shook his head. He thought Mayim Shulman, the rabbi's wife, should not have been at the synagogue that morning. "*Balabusta,*" he spat.

"Hold mercy in your heart for her today, Reuven—everyone is grief-stricken over the damage to the synagogue. We women are no different. *Danken Gott,* we all are safe." She dropped a spoonful of currant preserves in the bottom of a glass cup and filled the cup with tea.

Reuven shrugged. "The Elders have asked me to write a broadside. I think it should call for intervention from the Czar. In heaven's name, they sent us out here to the Pale to get rid of us. Can't *we* be rid of *them?*"

He moved to the kitchen, watching Lilia pat the tabletop, feeling for the fashion magazine. Outside the kitchen window, Monday morning business stirred at the block-built customs house next door on Tamozhny Street.

"Hush, Reuven. Be careful what you say." Yona reached for Lilia, holding the child against her leg.

He sat. Yona set his glass of tea on the table in front of him, along with a letter.

He shook his fists in frustration. "I mean, it's in the *Rosh Hashanah* prayer, but I wonder if people hear themselves say the words: 'For you shall…remove the reign of evil from the earth and wickedness shall vanish like smoke'?"

She rested a hand on his shoulder. "I don't think the 'you' in that prayer referred to the Czar, though."

"It means us, doesn't it, Papa?' Carsie asked.

He stroked her hair. "Yes, Carsie, but we pray for *all* of us. Including the Czar."

"I'm sure the Czar doesn't think so," Yona said. "This kind of talk makes me nervous, Reuven." She pointed to the envelope on the table. "Read the letter—it's from Davora Isyanov. Her husband was taken last week by the Cossacks, sent to the Baltic to work in the Czar's shipyard. If we left now, went—"

He frowned at his wife. Here it was again—one of their long-simmering arguments had just rekindled. He took her hand. "The time for caution is past, *mayn shayneh.* Jews in the Pale need to unite against our Czarist enemies." He paused to sip at his glass of hot, sweet tea.

She tried again. "They will come for us, you know they will. If we went—"

"I need to print something people will read. Something to make them think. A broadside they will truly remember."

Yona shook her head. "But most Jews in the Pale are too tired to think and too busy trying to scratch out a living to even look at a paper, Reuven. Besides, most of them *cannot* read. Even those who can, don't."

Carsie stamped her foot. "Huh. Even *I* can read,"

Her mother looked at her, saying nothing.

"Well, I can read…some."

"Ha ha!" Lilia squealed. "I can read *and* I speak Russian."

Reuven considered the dollop of melted preserves in the bottom of his glass. He held the glass out to Yona, knowing she relished the syrupy finish at the end of a *glozell té.*

Yona took the glass and smiled her thanks. "Nezavisimaya must be looking for a typesetter to replace Davora's husband." She waited. "We'd all be better off in Kiev," she said. "Maybe you should go talk to them. We could stay with my mother until—"

"Typesetter?" he said. "How shall I inspire these people to stand up to the Czar if I am in Kiev working as a typesetter?"

Yona pointed the girls to the front room and closed the kitchen door. She spoke with her back to him. "We are fortunate to have my father's money, Reuven—not to have to scratch for food like others do. Will you endanger us for the sake of your…your *cause?*"

"*Endanger* us? You want to return to Kiev? To the same place Davora Isyanov's husband was taken? Are you trying to get us killed? Remember, Moishe and Selig fled Kiev to America, to escape what they feared the Cossacks might do."

She turned and sneered. "Your brothers would run from a pigeon. You know too little about being a Jew *or* how it feels to starve to write this! A broadside could put us in jeopardy with the Pale *and* the Imperialist government. We *belong* in Kiev." She took his shoulders. "Think, Reuven! Try for the job with Nezavisimaya, for the girls' sake."

"Carsie and Lilia know nothing of how to live in a city as big as Kiev—all they know is Lucava. Carsie doesn't even speak Russian well enough to go to school up there. And what about my work?"

"Is there nothing more important to you than writing pamphlets?" Yona pleaded.

"Who is the voice of the Pale if I shut the print shop to work for Nezavisimaya?" he retorted. "Our duty is *here*, Yona, to our people."

HER BACK against the door, Carsie clamped her hands over her ears; her parents quarreled again. She had heard these angry words countless times since the family left Kiev ten years ago—Papa wanting everyone in the *shtetls* to understand the importance of living a life free from rule of the Czar, Mama wanting only to leave this place, not to gamble on a threat that had become real last night. Carsie didn't know which of her parents was right, if either of them was. To inspire courage in your people—to get them to think? Or to protect your family from violence? They had moved to Lucava so Papa could take his passion for Jewish independence to those who needed to hear it, but he had trouble getting the people out here to listen. They were too busy trying to feed themselves and keep roofs over their heads.

She frowned. If they went to back Kiev, she might work in what her fashion magazine called an atelier in a couple of years, as an apprentice, learning to make beautiful clothes and splendid hats. If they stayed here in Lucava, what chance did she have to live among fashionable people like the pictures in her magazine? She wished Mama could convince Papa to leave, she prayed for it. She wanted, wanted more than anything, to live in Kiev or somewhere women dressed with style—not like they dressed here in the *shtetl*. She could learn Russian better if they moved to Kiev. Still, she loved her father and wanted him to be happy, and it seemed the only place that could do that was here, among the Jews in the Pale.

DURING THE week, Reuven drafted and redrafted his broadside, overstating his case, disregarding Eisig Ginter's warning to be careful what he wrote. Each revision became more zealous, pushing for the people of the Pale to understand—this was their call to act! He demanded Jewish autonomy from the Imperialist government, derided the Cossacks for their brutality, railed until what he wrote went too far. Only then he thought the tone of the broadside just right.

He printed hundreds of copies and sent bundles of them out on the workers' wagons and in the freight lorries on the next market day.

And though mightily angered by the destruction of the

synagogue, the Elders condemned the wrath of Reuven's broadside. They reacted too late. By *Shabbat,* the broadside had been plastered on walls and lampposts and tacked to fences as far south as Odessa and north to Minsk; it blanketed the *shtetls* closest to Kiev.

The Czar disregarded Reuven's ultimatum that Jews in the Pale be granted reprieve. Instead of reprieve came reprisal.

REUVEN AKSELROD had crossed the line before. The Elders had warned him then, but this! This broadside—the
words he used, the scare tactics! Reject the Czar as their leader? The people of the Pale should expel the Cossacks or kill
them where they stood? Reprehensible. Still, they forgave him
for the sake of his family. Reuven endured a few days of gossip
about his peculiar combination of indifference to the Pale's
safety and his zeal for the cause before everyone forgot the
matter in their preparations for winter and the repairs to the
synagogue.

The people of Lucava scraped together enough lengths of
lumber to splint the synagogue's pews and board the broken
window. A carpenter, out of work for seven months, mended
the holes in the walls against the coming cold weather. Midyan
Choresh lent his *Torah* for *Shabbat*. The sense of peril subsided.

Just before December's full moon had drunk the last light
of day a wind came up from the north. The night closed in
cold, but clear and dry, yet this near to the Byk River, snow
would fly before morning. No gaslight burned in the street;
no oil lamp lit a window.

Reuven covered his printing presses and went to the bedroom. Even in the cold, dark room, his daughters smelled
to him of green apples and hay—the sweet, eager smell of
young adolescence. He bent to kiss Lilia, already asleep, and
took Carsie's hand in both of his, struck by the contrast: her
young, clean hand had never clenched in a fist while his, ink-
stained and aging, he could not remember carrying any other
way.

He sat at the edge of the narrow straw mattress. Carsie smiled up at him drowsily. He kissed her forehead and whispered, "Remember well, remember right, goodnight, goodnight..."

"...goodnight, goodnight," Carsie finished. She yawned. "Papa? When the weather warms can I go to Kiev to see Bubbe Esther? To live with her, maybe?"

"Carsie," he chuckled. "Where did that idea come from? Your place is here, with your family. Think how your mother and I would miss you. And Lilia would be lost without you, you know."

Carsie yawned again. She fingered the gold kopek that hung from a chain around her neck. Her mother and father had given her the pendant, engraved at its edge with her name, at Chanukah. "I love my necklace. *A sheynem dank.*"

Reuven struggled to his feet and brushed a lock of hair from her face. "*Tsu gezunt.* So you should never be without money." He smiled. "*Zis chaloymes,*" he whispered. Sweet dreams.

Fully clothed against December's chill, he snuffed the kerosene lantern and crawled under the blankets to lie close to Yona. He huddled first on his right side, his arm around his wife until she brushed him away. He sighed and turned over, snuggling his back against hers. From beyond the bedroom wall he heard the glass lights break on the front door of the print shop, and he knew the Cossacks had come.

Once more the Cossacks used a bright full moon to find their way through town, riding over the cobblestones of Gypsy Street, through Butcher's Alley and down Tamozhny past Choresh's pharmacy and the customs office. This time they did not chance a war cry carrying on the wind; their horses beat no thunder on the street. The villagers heard nothing until the Cossacks began to tear wood sheathing off the print shop's walls. They piled it in the road atop pieces of the press and set the pyre ablaze. Acrid smoke billowed, flames licked high off the heap of newsprint, cans of ink, rollers and dry wood. The Cossack's chestnut and black mounts reared away from the fire.

Yona cowered in a corner of the main room, clutching her daughters. Carsie broke free of her mother's grasp and ran into the street after her father.

Reuven pulled in rage at his hair, gaping at the fire as it reduced his lead type to molten lumps and warped the metal plates. He pounded on the withers of a soldier's gray horse.

The young Cossack's whip cracked, slicing into Reuven's left shoulder. The whip pulled taut around his neck and away, cutting deep. The horseman reared and struck again. A blow hit the backs of Reuven's calves, buckling his legs. He fell to the cobblestones face up, cowering. The next crack tore at his hands and arms. A cut on the right side of Reuven's neck hemorrhaged.

Carsie ducked the whip to kneel at her father's side, taking his hand. "Papa!" she screamed. "Why are they doing this?"

"Because they say I do not know my place," he gasped. "Remember…" He paused, struggling to stay conscious, not remembering what he had started to say.

"Remember what, Papa?"

"Remember well, remember right," he mumbled. "Go."

"I want to stay here, with you."

"No, don't give in to them. Never let them know you're afraid."

Carsie heard Lilia shriek and looked from her father's face to see, by the light from the fire's glow, that Yona and Lilia had been separated. Yona, carried by a Cossack from the shop door into the street, bawled and fought. The soldier threw her to the ground and pushed up her nightdress.

"Mama!" Carsie cried.

Lilia, clutching the fashion magazine in one hand, grasped at the air with the other, feeling for her mother's hand.

Reuven moaned, trying to pull himself to Yona. "*Run,* Carsie…" he choked.

Yona's screams came again. The young Cossack had dismounted and cut off her breasts. Carsie dove for Lilia, pressing the magazine to her sister's face to block the horror, dragging her sister to the alley before she dared to look back: the Cossack had stuffed one breast into Reuven's slack mouth and tossed the other on the crackling fire.

Gagging from the stench of burned flesh, Carsie pulled Lilia down Tamozhny alley, running. She tugged at the cellar door on the customs building. Locked. They ran half a block farther on, to the coal bin on the side of Choresh's pharmacy.

She pushed Lilia into the small bin, climbed in and pulled the door closed. They gasped, breathless, gulping coal dust, knowing they must not cough—that silence might keep them alive.

Lilia could not have seen the horrors in front of the print shop, but she sobbed, terrified by the heat and smell of the fire, the thundering sounds, and a sense that her mother and father had been torn from her. She heard soldiers in the alley, bashing their guns against crates and rain barrels.

The tumult came near and nearer still: yelling, water troughs splintering, boxes slamming to the dirt or splintering against buildings. The girls felt tremors of horses' hooves pound the ground outside the coal bin. They squeezed their fists tight to their eyes, pressed their lips together and waited to be discovered. They heard angry voices but could not make out what was said.

The sound of Cossack horses returned to the cobblestones of Tamozhny Street, the beat of hooves faded, grew fainter and silenced.

Lilia unfolded from her corner and felt for the coal-bin door.

Carsie hauled her back. "No, Lilia, wait more."

"I want Mama and Papa!" Lilia snuffled.

A cold wind blew between the coal bin's doors. Carsie shivered. "The Cossacks took them," she said in a deceit she wished were true. Better to think of their parents begging in Romania than what she knew the people of Lucava would find. An ache twisted in her heart, a pain so real she wanted to cry out.

Wind whistled again between the coal bin's boards, and with it, quiet flakes of snow. Their hands and feet curled into their bodies, Carsie and Lilia hunched together, not expecting the night to become as wintry as the sky promised it would be.

— 4 —

EISIG GINTER washed and wrapped Reuven and Yona for burial and pulled their bodies into place on litters tied with ribbons. The men of Lucava cleared Tamozhny Street, flinging burned bits of metal plate and file boxes back into the gutted print shop. They cleaned Reuven's and Yona's blood from the cobblestones with snow.

Wrapped in a heavy headscarf and dark coat, Mayim Shulman, the rabbi's wife, patted at her arms and flexed her fingers, feeling the wind's bite as she moved from building to building—opening doors, peering under carts, questioning shop owners, moving on. She stopped in Choresh's pharmacy. She and Midyan Choresh emerged, headed for the coal bin. They pried open its doors, calling out in surprise and alarm— they'd found what Mayim had sought: Carsie and Lilia, asleep in the coal bin, blue with cold, slipping toward coma.

Men from the street detail lifted the girls from the smudgy box, wrapped them in greatcoats and hurried inside the customs house to warm them by the stove.

Feeling returned to her face and limbs, rousing Carsie with the throb in her fingers and toes. Her hands and feet ached; her ears hurt. She did not want to move. She mouthed the word, "Mama."

Mayim Shulman, still wrapped in her dark coat with its yellow armband, spoke to her husband at the back of the room before she came to the front of the pharmacy to kneel in front of Carsie. "Do you know me?"

Carsie nodded vaguely.

"Your parents are gone, Carsie," Mayim said. She wiped streaks of coal dust from under Carsie's nose and reached for her hand.

Carsie pulled away, frowning, not ready to be touched. What did Reb Shulman mean, they are gone? "Where, gone?"

"They are dead, don't you remember? They've been taken to the edge of town—behind the home for the elderly. For burial. Do you want to go? To say goodbye?"

Lilia stirred, choking up coal dust. "What does she mean, Mama and Papa are dead? You told me the Cossacks had taken them."

Mayim turned to the younger girl. "I mean that your parents will not wake up or feel anything or talk. Anymore."

"But last night Carsie said…" She searched Reb Shulman's face. "Will they stay dead?"

Mayim brushed coal dust from Lilia's face. "Yes, darling girl, they will stay dead. No one can hurt them now."

Rabbi Shulman leaned over Mayim's shoulder. "It is not right for them to go to the cemetery, Mayim, they are too young. I spoke with Kalev Yisrael. He has agreed to take them away tomorrow, when the next worker's wagon comes through. They should get warm and prepare for the trip."

Carsie sipped at a glass of hot tea. Her hands and face hurt less now. She unbent to slip from the lap of the man who held her, testing her feet on the floor. Mayim folded a blanket around Carsie's shoulders.

She stumbled toward her sister, her feet still numb at their core. "Lilia?" She held the tea to Lilia's lips.

Lilia turned away. "Mama wouldn't have run to the door if you'd stayed with us, Carsie."

Carsie saw the scene again—a Cossack carrying her mother from the door of the print shop into the street. "Drink this, Lilia. It'll make you feel better."

"I don't want to feel better. Mama and Papa are dead—not taken, like you said. This is your fault."

"I can be your Mama now, if you want."

Lilia pushed at Carsie. "Go away. I don't know what I want."

Mayim Shulman took Lilia up in her arms. "What you

both need is a warm bath. That will do you the most good. Come with me."

THE BURIAL legation hurried through the *taharah* of Reuven and Yona Akselrod—their purification. They hoisted the litters on their shoulders and carried the bodies to the cemetery, trotting down Tamozhny Street, across Zdunska, and along the sidewalk outside Yisvi Kossov's fabric shop to two hastily-dug graves in the cemetery beyond the home for the elderly. A professional mourner or two chased after the pall bearers, trying to keep up the pace.

Eisig Ginter trailed along behind the group, occasionally looking over his shoulder or glancing down alleyways or checking the road behind the little cortège as he sang funeral songs. He *davened* as he walked. A waste to lose such a one as Yona Akselrod—she had been a good Jew. Ginter wished her husband had listened when he warned him to be careful what he wrote. He wished everyone would listen to him. He had the benefit of years—they should only know what he knew. Their lives would be easier if only they would listen to him.

At the burial site he mumbled the only elegy that would be said over the couple: "Reuven and Yona, our son and daughter, we ask forgiveness if we did not treat you respectfully, but we act in accordance with our custom. Go in peace, rest in peace, and arise in your turn at the end of days."

KALEV YISRAEL, from the Jewish Workers Party, pored over a map, debating the best route to Palestine: to the east of town lay a new Cossack encampment; to the south, Odessa and the Cossack-held port of Tuapse. A route through the passes at the southern end of the Carpathian Mountains and down to the Kuban where they could join other refugee caravans would be too long. They might try to reach Palestine alone—sailing across the Black Sea, through the straits at Istanbul and, hugging the shoreline, working south, across the Mediterranean Sea to the Promised Land. Yes, he thought, perhaps that would be best. Yisrael was anxious to leave at first light, but these girls had to sit a *bissel* bit of *shiva* before they left.

Rabbi Shulman looked west from the customs house window to the burned-out shell of the print shop next door. Through a broken window he saw charred bits of the carved and decorated chairs Yona had brought from Kiev. "There is no *shiva* house over there—no place to mourn."

Mayim nodded and pulled chairs around in front of the window—enough for several mourners—placing two low stools at the center in front. "The girls can sit here."

The Shulmans brought Carsie and Lilia to sit at the window facing the print shop. Carsie could recall little of her life before yesterday, remembering only the sounds and smells of last night. "They say I do not know my place," her father had gasped, but her mother thought their place was somewhere other than where her father saw it. She stared numbly, feeling empty, unsure how to go on without their nurture. "They say I do not know my place," she heard Papa say again. She did not understand what that meant; all she had understood was that in the next moment the Cossacks had killed her mother. The only one left to care for now was Lilia. Yes, she had to be brave for Lilia. She would not cry.

Before Yisrael and the girls left for the stables, Mayim Shulman fed them bits of cheese, dried apples, and skewers of lamb *shashlik*. Then she wrapped a heavy, dark coat around each girl's shoulders.

"Ida Kossov sent these over—they belonged to her girls when they were about your age. Wear them in good health." Mayim kissed Carsie and Lilia. "Be careful and travel safe."

"*GORNISHT HELFN*," Mayim Shulman remarked to her husband as she watched Yisrael and the girls walk to the stable. "Beyond help, that girl. Did you notice? She didn't cry."

"What? Who didn't cry?"

"Carsie Akselrod, that's who. The little one, she cried.

But Carsie? Not a drop. She's too young to hold that dreadful night in her head." Mayim tapped her husband's breastbone with a knuckle. "You cry to let the misery out. A memory of that kind can eat you up."

CARSIE RAN to the coal bin on the far side of Choresh's pharmacy. She struggled to lift one of its heavy doors—how had she done it without thinking the night before, she wondered. She reached to the far corner, shook soot from the fashion magazine and, tucking it under her shawl, caught up with Lilia and Yisrael in the stable.

Yisrael tucked the girls back under the buckboard seat and covered them with a heavy gray blanket. Carsie whispered to Lilia, "Remember well, remember right. Goodnight, goodnight…"

Without response, Lilia rolled away from her.

"Goodnight, goodnight," Carsie finished, and sighed. She could not close her eyes, knowing, if she did, what she would see and hear.

Yisrael buttoned his coat around his stout body and bent himself into the haystack in a corner, pulling the hay around him for warmth. He slept restlessly, knowing it would be months before he could return to Kiev, already yearning for the touch of his wife and a smile from his infant son.

He wakened near dawn to the sound of distant gunfire.

Veiled by snow, hundreds of mounted Cossack soldiers broke from the blackness, their artillery rumbling as they advanced, a roar of burning bridges blocking all passage out of town.

Their leader held up his forces near the cemetery. "I am Pokrovsky," he called out in Yiddish. "Send me the printer's daughters! Send them out *now*, or you'll all find yourselves working for the Czar."

Pokrovsky's men dragged Eisig Ginter into the street, a knife to his throat. The general chuckled at the sight. "Can you see this?" he snarled. "Send out the girls or we come in after them. Turks like the young ones—the girls will make fine whores. If you force us to burn them out, we will kill any who get in our way."

Rabbi Shulman and his wife huddled at the customs house with the others who had come to mourn Reuven and Yona Akselrod.

"Let them have the girls," Natan Mikarsky offered. "Two little *maydele* are not worth losing our lives and the lives of our families."

"They would not stop with those two *kinder,* Natan," Yisvi Kossov answered. "We give them up, we lose all our children. And,"—he looked at Mayim—"our women."

Rabbi Shulman nodded. "God will protect us in this fight. We will not give in."

"Then we are dead," wailed Natan. "*I* am dead."

"Dead or not, Natan," Mayim said, "the children of Lucava might live to see tomorrow."

At daybreak the Cossacks came at the village from Mikolaja Street. The body of Eisig Ginter, thrown at the front of the customs building, bore the word *sveeñya*—swine—carved into his chest.

"Eisig," Mayim wept.

Led by Rabbi Shulman, the men of Lucava dumped trunks and freight from the back of the customs house in a haphazard barricade across Tamozhny Street, ducking machine gun bursts fired over their heads while they worked.

Drunk on vodka, a Cossack searched the stable as all of the buildings of Lucava would be searched that morning, on horseback. Carsie and Lilia heard a horse ride into the stable. Yisrael froze where he lay covered in the haystack. The Cossack's horse clopped over to feed, nosing aside enough straw to expose Yisrael's coat.

"Out!" the horseman shouted, spotting the dark fabric. Yisrael did not move. The Cossack reared his mount, landing the horse's front hooves on top of the haystack. Yisrael jerked from his hiding place, howling in pain, clutching his left side where the horse had cracked his ribs. The Cossack drew a short pistol, firing one shot into Yisrael's forehead.

The Cossack scanned the stable, squinting into its shadows. He rode toward the buckboard, pulled his sword, and pushed at the hay in the wagon bed. The shadows of early dawn concealed the two girls hidden under the lumpy gray blanket beneath the seat, and the soldier rode out of the stable.

He paused for another swig of vodka before he moved on to Choresh's pharmacy, to ride along the aisles of the store on horseback, sending beakers of curatives crashing to the ground behind him as he plundered.

VALENTIN MIKHELADZE caught movement out of the corner of his eye—a young woman fled, running toward the customs house. Unescorted women, he knew, could meet with calamity in situations like this one. With the slightest move of his body, he urged his chestnut stallion, Agripin, down the alley, caught the young woman's arm, and braced in his saddle to swing her up behind him.

She ducked Mikheladze's grasp and ran into Tamozhny Street. Agripin followed, unbidden, knowing Mikheladze sought only the woman's safety. She ran between the buildings and along the wall of the customs house. He and Agripin cornered her. She spun on him, yelling out in Yiddish. He shook his head, not understanding what she yelled out to him. It was she who misunderstood, he thought. He was trying to help her, not take advantage. She cried out again.

Two men from Pokrovsky's troop grabbed her from behind and pulled her into the alley. One pinned the woman's arms. The other shed his coat and unbuckled his belt, worked his pants to his thighs before he punched the woman's face. She fought against the man who held her, kicking at his legs, twisting in his grasp. Mikheladze jumped from his horse to wrestle the woman away from the two drunken soldiers. He scooped her into his arms and ran into Tamozhny Street, Agripin following behind.

Fires burned on both sides of the street. Pokrovsky rushed back and forth trying to bawl orders above the clamor. His men cursed and whooped, burning buildings collapsed, barrels and bottles thumped and rolled in the street as the Cossacks stormed through town. Still, Pokrovsky knew how to get his men's attention. He drew his pistol and fired at a metal horse trough. The bullet ricocheted and found another mark— deep in the chest of Mikheladze's chestnut stallion, Agripin.

FROM THE front windows of the customs house, Mayim Shulman watched the Cossacks' search, fearing each time one of the soldiers reappeared that she would see the girls dragged with him. But no, it seemed they had not yet been found. She watched a tall soldier in a fine hat run into the street carrying Liba Gendel in his arms. She saw Pokrovsky fire his weapon. A horse fell to the ground. The soldier cried out when he saw the horse fall. Gently, he laid Liba in the shelter of a nearby doorway and rushed to the animal. He shouted out in Pokrovsky's direction before he drew his own sidearm. He covered his eyes with his arm, pointed his gun at Pokrovsky, paused for a moment, dropped his arm and shot the horse between its ears.

THE SHOT rang in his heart. His hand trembled as he tucked away his pistol. Oh, the things he and Agripin had done together! He had trained the horse so well he could stand in the stirrups at full gallop. He could shoot from under Agripin's belly in a dead man's mount and the horse would not flinch. The chestnut had meant survival to Mikheladze; Agripin had been his warmest friend.

In the silence following the gunshots, Pokrovsky walked to the door of the customs house and knocked. "Rabbi," he called out. "Come out here with those girls in hand. You know what will happen if you do not," he warned in Yiddish. "What you have seen this morning will be nothing compared to what will come."

The soldiers waited. Cossack nostrils flared; veins stood out in their temples. The cavalry charged once more.

The men of Lucava *shtetl* pushed forward: those from the home for the elderly advanced shoulder-to-shoulder with porters from Yisvi Kossov's fabric shop, teen-aged boys from the school, and the wounded who had fought through the early-morning hours. The persecution would get worse, they knew, but they saw no choice. Perhaps Reuven Akselrod had been right after all. Still, they trembled. Each of them wielded what they could find, though their hands shook as they gripped their weapons—sticks, pipes, pitchforks—and marched into the advancing Cossack surge.

5

CARSIE AND Lilia felt the wagon bed bounce as though something had landed in it, something heavy. Smoke filtered under the gray blanket. The girls stifled their coughs—last night's coal dust had stung their lungs and now, once again, all the smells of hell. They heard flames crackle. Horses' hooves stamped. The buckboard swayed and lurched. They felt the wagon move.

Behind them, all of Lucava burned. Under cover of a dense scrim of smoke, the buckboard crept out of the stable just as the roof collapsed at the far wall, inched down a shallow embankment to the riverbed of the Byk, across and north toward Cossack territory.

In the afternoon light, their wheels left the only set of tracks in fresh snow.

From under their blanket, the girls dared not look to see who drove the wagon or which direction they went, knowing only from the fading smell of smoke that they were leaving Lucava. Nor did the voice they heard urging the dray horse up the far bank sound familiar.

Carsie pushed the gray blanket away from her face. An ornate saddle lay in the wagon bed. That, she thought, must have been the thump they felt and heard. A saber in its scabbard leaned against the saddle. She stretched her arm, trying to reach for it but realized she could not move without giving away their hiding place. She struggled to see the buckboard's driver—hoping to find Kalev Yisrael's bulky bottom sitting on the seat, knowing as clear as this cold blue sky that she would see someone else, but what she saw surprised her—a man dressed in a fine blue wool coat trimmed in gold braid and epaulets. He wore a black curly lamb hat. A gun and whip rested on his right hip.

Carsie retreated under the blanket.

"Where are we going?" Lilia whispered.

Carsie put a finger to Lilia's lips and the little girl held her breath. Remnants of smoke and coal dust inhaled over two nights overtook Lilia's breathing; she began to wheeze. The wagon paused. Lilia gasped. The rocking movement resumed once more. Carsie uncovered Lilia's head, hoping a breath of fresh air might calm her sister's urge to cough. The cold blast helped for a moment before Lilia's irregular rasps mounted. The little girl looked at her older sister, desperate tears welling in her crossed eyes. She reached for Carsie's hand. Her lungs could not hold back despite her efforts and a throaty cough racked her body.

The wagon's rocking motion halted. The driver lifted the gray wool blanket from the girls' faces. From under the seat Carsie gaped wide-eyed at a Cossack. Lilia shuddered and coughed.

"Well." The soldier raised an eyebrow and stared. "It seems I have found what we came for last night." He thought while he studied the girls.

Carsie wailed, her cries echoing on the snowbound steppes.

"Hush, you'll draw wolves. I am Valentin Mikheladze, a Cossack officer."

Carsie moaned. He spoke in Russian, but she understood well enough.

Mikheladze jumped down and pulled a fistful of hay from the wagon bed to feed the dray horse, still glaring at Carsie and Lilia. His boots crunched on the dry snow. Lilia's coughing subsided.

"Hmmm...so I have traveling companions," he said. He snatched away their blanket. The girls clutched at their coats, the fashion magazine, and each other, hugging together as they had in the coal bin. Mikheladze wrapped two corners of the blanket around his fists while he stared at them, his jaw flexing. He sprang forward, tucking the blanket tightly around them once more. "Well, you will make the trip trickier, but Pokrovsky, that bastard, deserves this for shooting Agripin." He laughed. "I have made off with his prize."

A wolf bayed in the distance. Mikheladze climbed back onto his seat and flicked the reins. The wagon rolled slowly.

"Why on earth don't you people feed your horses? This beast can hardly move, it's so weak. My mother's village is not far off—a couple of days' ride—more if this damned creature doesn't get moving. Yaaah!"

The wagon lurched forward and slowed again. Lilia and Carsie pulled the blanket over their heads, the rocking motion lulling them to sleep. When the sway of the wagon stopped, Carsie wakened, but lay still. She heard men's voices, and five shots. Then they rolled onward.

Lilia wakened. "He seems kind enough," she whispered.

"Is he? What did he say?"

"He's taking us to his mother's house. That's nice, don't you think?" She pushed back under the buckboard seat, pulling the blanket over her back. "I'm so tired," she sighed. "Ouch. There are itchy things in this hay."

"I'm hungry," Carsie said. Peeking from under the blanket, Carsie watched the landscape inch by: forest all around them. Trees, silhouetted by an amber sunset, spread long fingers of shadow across the snow.

Lilia slept again.

Carsie pushed her head out from under the cover, seeing Mikheladze slumped on the buckboard seat, the reins slack in his hand. He slept too. The horse trudged on, wandering off the road.

Ahead, beyond the trees, lay a shallow cliff and a bridge over a stream. The old dray ambled toward the rocks. Carsie scrambled from under the seat and tugged hard at the reins, jerking the horse to a stop. Mikheladze started, reaching for his sidearm before he realized how soundly he had slept.

Carsie frowned at him and took her spot again beside her sister in the wagon bed. The Cossack and the girls rode on in the darkening afternoon, passing a road sign directing them to the town of Trusheny.

"Are you cold?" he asked. She did not answer. *Ah,* he thought, *she probably does not speak Russian. A girl of the provinces might not.* He mimicked shivering and pointed to her.

She shook her head.

He mimicked eating and pointed again.

She nodded.

Ahead, lights winked on. The wagon rolled toward Trusheny, a settlement of bent cottages surrounded by crooked fences.

Mikheladze cocked his head in the direction of the *shtetl.* "We should stop while we can still see the road and who approaches. We'll eat here and spend the night."

At the head of a cobblestone street market day wound down. People milled about inside a brightly-lit drinking house. A man in the corner, his greatcoat buttoned to his neck, wrote letters for others. Men dressed in layers of dark clothes, each wearing a yellow armband on its right sleeve, sat with beer and herring or kvass and kielbasa in front of them.

All conversation stopped when Mikheladze, in his Circassian coat and curly lamb hat, Carsie, clutching the fashion magazine, and Lilia walked in.

Mikheladze nudged Carsie toward the bar. "These girls are hungry."

The saloonkeeper looked at Carsie's face and then at the armband on her coat. "These girls are Jewish. Why do they travel with a Cossack?"

Mikheladze looked puzzled until Lilia said, "They want to know why we are with you."

"You speak Russian, little girl?"

"*Da.* Yeh. I speak it pretty well, too," Lilia said in Russian. "Tell me why we are here, and I will say it in Yiddish."

He set Lilia down. "Their parents were killed by my…comrades."

She translated to the saloonkeeper before she looked again at Mikheladze.

He pulled a bag of coins from inside his coat. "Please, do you have something to feed these girls?" He held out money from the bag.

Lilia turned to the man behind the bar and spoke.

The saloonkeeper studied the Cossack from behind the bar. "Are you the deserter they hunted today?"

Mikheladze shrugged. "General Pokrovsky shot my horse. I left Lucava in that wagon, not knowing these girls had hidden under the seat. But I am no deserter."

Lilia spoke again, talking this time at length. Mikheladze wondered if she translated his words exactly or said something more.

Two men, their gray heads covered in skullcaps, leaned close to consult with the barman in whispers, nodding. "Pull the wagon around back, so it can't be seen," one of them said. "Pokrovsky's men stole chickens, ducks, and a goose from our market. They're camped not far off from here—outside of town—probably having a fine meal."

The barman nodded toward a door. "You can stay back there tonight. You'll find Grober Dragutski sleeping off a drunk in the corner, but he doesn't snore. I'll bring food for the three of you, and someone will feed the horse. And we'll get you a plain coat to wear so you don't stick out like *goyim* at *Shabbat*."

Mikheladze slid a generous number of coins onto the bar. "You are a good man, saloonkeeper," he smiled. "May God grant your greatest wishes."

6

GROBER DRAGUTSKY wakened early in the windowless back room of the public house. He opened the back door to urinate, not noticing the two girls and the Cossack until the dim first light of morning fell across their sleeping faces. Dragutsky knelt, studying the fine blue serge coat decorated in gold braid, closed by metal buttons, lined in curly lamb. He glanced at the sleeping girls. The bigger one slept the lovely slumber of children, the smaller one looked pallid. She moaned and coughed. He stroked a lock of hair from her face and gasped. The little girl burned with fever.

Dragutsky trotted to the front room looking for Max Siegel, the saloonkeeper. "Siegel! There are people back there! A Cossack!"

Max chewed thoughtfully on a piece of bread, wiped his hands, and smiled. "Yes, yes, Grober, two girls and a *former* Cossack—the deserter Pokrovsky's men sought yesterday. They came in after you fell asleep at the bar last night."

"Ahk, I'm not the man I used to be, Siegel. There was a time I could hold twice that amount of beer *and* an eloquent conversation." He sighed. "Now?" He thought a moment. "Now I could use a drink before I face Kefira." He leaned on the bar across from the saloonkeeper.

Max pulled back. "Feh. Wash yourself, my friend, once in a while you should wash and…" he moved his finger in toothbrush fashion. "And better you go home clear-headed to deal with your lovely wife. Shoo."

Dragutsky waved him off with a grimace. "See to the little one back there. She burns with fever. I'll watch the front while you tend to the child."

Instead Max opened the front door and pulled at Dragutsky's coat sleeve. "Grober, Kefira waits. Don't make her come down here angry again. Her furies do neither one of us any good. Go!"

Max shoved Dragutsky out the door, the old drunk pleading: "Please. I can't go home. Kefira has sworn to kill me for my drinking. Don't turn me out—my blood will be on your hands." He pulled his smelly coat around him. "Anyway, it looks like snow."

The saloon door closed behind him, and locked. Dragutsky glanced heavenward, then kicked at the door of the bar.

Curse Siegel's righteous heart, Dragutsky grumbled to himself as he stumbled up the cobblestones. How fortunate to be unmarried. He should only know how it feels to suffer with a wife. And now he believed the old saying, *Hostu khasene blind, vet dayn vayb dikh firn bay der noz,* marry blindly and your wife will lead you by the nose. He had discovered that too late—after he'd married Kefira of his own free will, it had seemed to him then. He'd become the same sort of prisoner he'd been whenever the sheriff locked him in a stable all night.

He scratched at his beard. Ah, but Siegel hid the Cossack deserter! And if Dragutsky had a way to let Pokrovsky's men know the turncoat was here, they'd take their man away to Kiev and leave Trusheny. Perhaps they'd trade a beer for the information.

He spotted an unfamiliar wagon in the lean-to shed behind the saloon. A scrawny horse bridled to it munched on a bale of hay. In an instant he untied the horse, threw a saddle out of the wagon bed, and sprang onto the seat of the buckboard.

MIKHELADZE AND Carsie stirred when Max slid a tray of tea and bread onto a beer barrel; but Lilia lay still, her breathing labored. Max lit a kerosene lamp. He leaned over, hands on his knees, and smiled at Carsie. "Good morning. I hope you slept well. Grober is gone, praise be. And he tells me this little *kinder* is ill?"

"Lilia," Carsie touched her, drawing her hand back in shock. "Yes! She is fevered!"

The barman bent to feel Lilia's forehead then straightened, frowning. "I will go for help. Get bar towels, soak them in the horse trough, and bathe her. Let's see if we can break this."

While Carsie ran to the bar for towels, Max slipped out the back door. Mikheladze stood, shook out his serge coat and laid it across Lilia's trembling body. He pulled on the black serge coat a sympathetic villager had left for him, its right sleeve striped in yellow. His wrists hung exposed and the coat would not button, but no matter. He did not plan to leave until he knew Pokrovsky and his men were well away.

In her sleep Lilia pulled away from Carsie's cold, wet towels. "Lilia," she pleaded, "Can you hear me? What's wrong? Where do you hurt?" She felt tears well, unshed in the rush of events three days ago, but her eyes would not shed them.

Lifting an arm to shield her eyes from the glow of the lamp, Lilia struggled to ask for water and to answer Carsie's questions, her parched tongue thick. She lay back, trying to sleep once more, seeing grisly images of her mama and papa standing at her feet each time she closed her eyes.

Max returned with a man in a white coat and pushed him forward. "This is Lavan Barchai, our apothecary," he said.

Barchai looked at Mikheladze's Circassian coat spread over Lilia, then to the only man who might fit that coat. He nodded. Mikheladze returned his nod. The pharmacist bent to his work, feeling the child's head, neck, and limbs, checking her chest and back.

Sounds of pounding came from the front of the bar. Glass broke.

Max glanced from the Cossack to the doctor. "Stay back here," he said, closing the door.

They heard a woman's screech, faint at first then louder, coming from the bar: "Where is Grober? Where do you hide that *putz*?"

The voices neared.

"Kefira, he left an hour ago! Stop! I do not hide him—there is no one back there!"

"Siegel, you *mamzer*! You bastard, if you are lying to me I will rip your balls off with my bare hands and feed them to you."

Barchai took the Circassian coat off Lilia, rolled it inside out so that the braid did not show and propped it behind Lilia's head. He motioned to Mikheladze. "Until we get a blanket give me your coat. Siegel has other problems just now."

"Mama," Lilia moaned.

The pharmacist looked at Carsie. "Is your mother nearby?"

Carsie shook her head, looking up at Mikheladze.

"Their parents were killed several days ago," Mikheladze said, handing his coat over to the pharmacist. "Just before the battle at Lucava."

The pharmacist scowled at the Cossack, not understanding what he had said. He gestured toward Lilia. "This is typhus," he said to Carsie. "Probably started by fleas."

"From hay in the wagon," Carsie said. "The wagon we came in. Something was biting her, she said."

"Possibly. We must not speak of this to anyone outside the bar," the pharmacist continued. "She will probably die. Perhaps best for her if she does."

"No!" Carsie screamed. "Not Lilia, too!"

The back room door flew open and a heavy, red-headed woman filled the doorway.

"Who are these people?" She turned to Max, who peered helplessly over her shoulder. "Why is Barchai here with them?" She glanced at Mikheladze and caught her breath. "And who are you?"

The pharmacist stood, shrugging. "The little *kinder* has a cold, Kefira. Her sister is concerned."

Mikheladze stepped forward and silently took Kefira by the elbow, smiling down at her, leaning close. She leaned on Mikheladze's arm, sighing, tipping her chin up to his face. He steered her from the back room to the bar.

Siegel pulled the door closed, chasing after Kefira and her Cossack officer.

Barchai looked at Carsie. "You should not stay back here. It may be too late, but if you have not caught typhus from your sister or the wagon you should be careful not to expose yourself now."

Carsie frowned. "Then who will take care of her?"

The apothecary looked at the closed door to the front of the bar. He stood, slipped into his coat and opened the back door to leave. "I think your uh…'uncle' should do that, don't you?"

Mikheladze and Kefira sat at a table, sipping at glasses of hot tea Max had set in front of them. Kefira Dragutsky laid her hand over Mikheladze's and smiled coyly.

Numbed by the possibility of losing Lilia, Carsie stumbled into the front room to tell Mikheladze of Barchai's suggestion.

Behind the bar, Max admired Carsie's dark hair, her slender, chaste body. The girl had possibilities, he thought. She was different from.…

The roar of horses' hooves thundered down the cobblestone street. Kefira looked up and ran, cowering in a corner at the sight: Cossacks on horseback following a wagon driven by Grober Dragutsky.

Siegel yelled to Mikheladze, "Behind here, quickly!"

Mikheladze sprinted across the room, diving behind the bar at the moment two Cossacks stormed the front door, breaking what glass Kefira Dragutsky had not shattered earlier.

Intuitively, Carsie ran to the back—to her sister's side—the Cossacks fast behind her. She spun on them. "Take her! Take us both. My sister is ill with typhus and I am sure to come down with it. We will die, but by then it will be too late. You will die our painful death too."

The two Cossacks snarled at the girl who gabbled at them in Yiddish. One soldier grabbed at Carsie while the other scooped up Lilia, wrapped in the peasant coat. The roll of Circassian blue serge lay unnoticed on the floor.

The second Cossack held Lilia at arm's length. "This child is fevered. I think that is what the girl was trying to tell us."

Carsie struggled against her captors, trying to understand what they said. "Typhus," she said.

The soldiers exchanged looks. The one that held Lilia laid her back where she had rested.

"And I am likely to get it. Be careful that you—"

The other soldier threw Carsie to the floor. Both men backed out of the room and turned to face Max Siegel.

"Tell us where the deserter is, saloonkeeper, or we burn this bar and all of Trusheny to the ground."

Max looked down behind the bar, seeing Mikheladze point at himself and shake his head, a finger to his lips. Shrugging, Max held his hands up, supplicant. "He is not here, I swear! Not here! The bastard dropped these diseased *maydele kinder* with me last night and left, riding east. He said he rode to Kiev...to see General, uh, General...somebody."

Once again, the Cossacks understood little of what the saloonkeeper said, except, "To Kiev?" The two soldiers look at each other again. "To see General Krasnov? He wouldn't!"

Max paused and looked down. From beneath the bar, Mikheladze nodded. "Ah, *da*," he said to the Cossacks. "That's it. *Da, da,* to see Krasnov. He said the girls needed to be with their own kind to die—so that we can bury them properly. Then he said, and he was quite clear on this, he said if you came looking for him, to tell you he was off to see Krasnov in Kiev. To clear his good name. To report Pokrovsky for shooting his horse."

Grober Dragutsky swaggered into the bar, not seeing that his wife cowered against the front wall. "You see? The girls you hunted are here—and the deserter too, no?"

Without a word, the taller Cossack drew his pistol and shot Dragutsky in the stomach.

Kefira ran to her husband. "Grober, my precious man!" She turned, spitting on the boots of the Cossack who still held his drawn gun. "You have killed the love of my life!"

The Cossack lost patience, listening to these people natter

in a language different from his own. Raising his weapon once more he fired a round into Kefira's head and wiped the spittle from his boot across her face. The two soldiers stepped over the Dragutskys' bodies, left the bar, and turned their horses in the direction of Kiev.

MAX SIEGEL posted a notice on the boarded-up doors of his saloon: CLOSED FOR REPAIRS. Villagers peered through the broken front window, trying to determine what repairs, aside from the glass, Max needed to make, until the following morning, when they buried Kefira and Grober Dragutsky. Still, no one discovered that Lilia lay ill with typhus in the bar's back room.

Mikheladze took Carsie's spot next to Lilia, sleeping next to the sick little girl on the thin mattress. Carsie slept on a wood bench under the window in the bar.

During the muddled days ahead, Carsie swept, dusted and washed the floor of the bar in exchange for their keep. She read the fashion magazine through a hundred times and grew bored with it. Trusheny confused her. Trusheny was smaller than Lucava. The *shtetl* had no customs house or doctor, and though she knew Mikheladze had not brought them that much farther north, it seemed colder here than in Lucava. More men than women lived in Trusheny, many more, and several of them seemed to rely heavily on the liquor and companionship they found at the saloon. This did not feel like her place. She saw no purpose in staying; these people seemed to wait for—what? Salvation? Death?

Whenever she took Mikheladze's meals to the door of the back room, she tried, from a distance, to gauge Lilia's condition. Her sister still lay languishing on her mattress. Carsie knew coming any closer than the threshold imperiled her, that she might contract typhus herself, but she missed Lilia's company. She felt she had failed her father—her mother was dead, her sister lay mortally ill. She had not been able to keep either one from harm.

But when Lilia recovered, Carsie thought, the two of them

could go to Kiev, to live with Bubbe Esther. Yes, that would be their lives now.

A SHORTAGE of women in Trusheny had left Max Siegel without a wife. He shared what food he had with Carsie and gladly—a slice of kielbasa, a loaf of bread—hoping to brush her hand or stroke her hair by chance. He tried to make her smile, this girl with no parents and soon, perhaps, no family at all. She would make a fine wife, and would give him as many children as they could afford to feed.

Mikheladze seldom emerged from the back room, where he stayed, applying cold compresses to Lilia's forehead, dripping water onto the little girl's parched lips, murmuring, "Good girl, good girl..."

Neither Carsie nor Siegel noticed a lethargy overtaking Mikheladze until it was too late. His movements slowed, his eyes glazed over. When he raised his head from tending Lilia he shielded his gaze against light that shone in the newly repaired glass window at the front of the bar.

The break of the following day found him slumped against a wall of the back room, confused and hard of hearing. He, too, had typhus.

Carsie nursed the two of them. Max despaired of losing her, should she fall ill, and if that happened he would be next to nurse the sick. His public house remained closed.

Carsie kept Lilia and Mikheladze as comfortable as they could be made to be, applying cold compresses, cooing to them, "It's all right, we are here, it's all right. Stay with us, stay with us..."

Four days later, Lilia opened her eyes. She mumbled, "Am I in heaven with Mama and Papa?"

"She is improving," Lavan Barchai decreed. "Now she must sleep to mend." He looked to Mikheladze. Abruptly he threw back the covers to check the Cossack's legs. "Siegel!" he called to the front room. "Get the rabbi."

Mikheladze roused, shouted out in Russian, and slumped back onto his pallet, his eyes staring at the ceiling.

———

ANOTHER THIN sun warmed the barroom, its reflection flashing in glass bottles behind the bar. Hearing movement in the back room, Carsie wakened.

She peered into the room. Her sister stared out the back door. "Lilia? What are you doing?"

"Looking at the snow. It is so beautiful."

Carsie guided her back to the mattress. "Rest. You have been very ill."

"But I feel better. I'm hungry."

"You can have something to eat later." She wrapped Lilia's fingers around a glass of water.

"Not water!" Lilia threw the glass down on her mattress, soaking it through.

"Don't be naughty, Lilia," Carsie scolded. "First you must show that you can keep water down before I give you food."

"Valentin will give me food—he's my friend. Where is he?"

Carsie looked at her for a long moment. "He got sick. He is gone."

"Gone?"

"You had an illness called typhus, Lilia. You nearly died."

"But I am well now, quite well! Where is Valentin? Where *is* he, Carsie?""

Carsie turned away, biting her lower lip. "He caught typhus from you, Lilia. We buried him day before yesterday."

— 7 —

CARSIE SUSPECTED Lilia was still angry with her for leaving Mama's side that night, for causing Mama to chase into the street after her. She had not cried for Mama and Papa when they were killed or afterward; she wanted to show Lilia how to be brave, show her that the Czar could not break every Jewish heart. By the time Valentin Mikheladze died of typhus, she had choked back so much sorrow that she had suffocated what she knew of grief. In its place she found nothing. Nothing.

EARLY ON a cold morning in January of 1900 Max Siegel paced outside the girls' bedroom door, eager to make his feelings known as soon as Carsie wakened. He did not know how to broach the inevitable question of what to do with Lilia when they married. He would prefer the younger, cross-eyed girl not live with them. Perhaps the rabbi's family could take her in.

Carsie's attachment to her sister was a bond stronger than he had observed in sisters before. Every night, before the younger one went to sleep, Carsie recited a poem: "Remember well, remember right, goodnight, goodnight…" and the younger girl would respond, "…goodnight, goodnight." Carsie would whisper, "*Zis chaloymes.*" All of it ritual, he knew, but he sensed it meant a great deal to the girls.

Carsie emerged from the back, yawning. Max handed her a glass of tea and set a plate of herring and a roll on the table in front of her. He watched her eat. "Carsie," he began, smoothing first his apron and then his hair. "You know, as everyone in Trusheny knows…" He gulped. These words were harder to say than he had thought. "I was wondering…"

When she spoke she did not look up, intent on the currant preserves as she spread them on her roll. "You have been very kind to Lilia and me in the many days we have been here, Max, but we have overstayed our welcome by a month. Do you have some idea what Lilia and I might do before we leave to show our gratitude to the people of Trusheny?"

He stopped stroking his hair. Leave? What did she mean, "leave"? Surely she didn't mean leave Trusheny? He plowed ahead. "Some in Trusheny think I am a wealthy man, but my parents died several years ago, so I have nothing to offer you other than this humble drinking shop, but... there are no girls in Trusheny interested in being my wife...that is, Carsie, uh, could we—you and I—it would be fine if..."

Her head jerked up. "Max—I am fourteen years old."

"I cannot afford more than what I offer you. And the Talmud says it is time you should marry. A man should have a proper wife. You know how my business works, people are comfortable having you here and I...well, I think you are very pleasant to look at."

Carsie felt a giggle well in her stomach. She stuffed part of the roll into her mouth, but the giggle erupted all the same. "I'm sorry Max, it just seems silly for a man your age to marry a fourteen-year-old girl, don't you think?"

"I am only thirty-one. And if you leave, where else shall I find a wife? Where would you go that you could find better than I offer? I admit you are young, but I am not that old. We would have many years together."

She said nothing.

"Please," Siegel sat, facing her. "Give me some reason to hope."

Carsie toyed with what was left of her roll. Finally she said, "Zirl spoke to me yesterday about leaving, and we are almost ready. Lilia is feeling better, and..." She chewed the bread and swallowed. "We brought you bad luck and soon you shall be free of us. There is your hope."

"Zirl? The postman, Zirl?"

"He knows of a caravan coming through in April. The caravan can take us away."

"Who is he to decide you would go with them? And where would they take you?"

"I don't know. Maybe to Kiev to live with Bubbe Esther, or maybe we'll go to America."

"Leaving is expensive. Staying here, in Trusheny, with me, is the right thing to do. Don't you know Kiev can be dangerous for people like you and me? And what would you do in America? And how would you get the money to go?"

She shrugged. "We will get the money somehow."

"I fear how that will be."

"Don't be afraid for us now, Max. The time to be afraid for Lilia and me is done. After the last two months we can tolerate anything."

"But wherever you go they might not keep kosher. Then what?"

"Zirl says the caravan comes with the thaw. Besides, you don't even know me. Marry someone else."

"I do not know any other woman who might marry me." He took Carsie's hand. "You have seen how it is here. What shall I do for a wife if you leave?"

Carsie shrugged again, pulling her hand away.

Max stood. "Will you show me no thanks for my food and shelter? For closing my bar while Lilia was ill? For running the risk of catching her disease myself? Do you not realize that you are in my debt?"

"I do, yes, of course. That is what I was wondering—how we might repay you for your many kindnesses. Your hospitality and generosity. That is, repay you…in some way other than marrying you."

"Carsie?" Lilia called from the back room.

Carsie stood, fingering her gold locket. "Mama and Papa grew up in the village where they were born, Max. They'd known each other their whole lives, and still they managed to disagree. Papa would say things that hurt Mama, and so she said things to hurt him. And all because they just didn't know anyone else to marry. That's why I don't think people should get married to each other just because they are there."

MAX REOPENED the bar that day, and each day from January to March, he placed tea at a table where he had set herring and a roll for Carsie. She was an indifferent creature, he thought. He had not seen her cry over her sister's illness or the terror of the Dragutskys' shooting, even though she had seen it happen. She had not cried when Mikheladze died, and she didn't seem to appreciate what he offered her.

When she emerged from sleep and slumped into her chair, he stood behind her while she ate. And each morning, when she licked bits of herring from her fingers and crumbs of her roll from around her mouth, she ignored him.

Whenever he moved to join her at the table she rose and went to the back, yelling over her shoulder, "Don't watch me, Max! Stop it!"

"I'd stand all day on a frozen lake to watch you, Carsie," Max would say.

Carsie passed her days in the dry goods aisle of the general store, stroking the fabrics, studying the trimmings and patterns. Lilia was not far off, reading the current magazines on the book rack.

And every evening, when Zirl Bakhtin came in, Carsie tried to sit next to him, to watch him write, and to read over his shoulder, as he wrote letters for the villagers. And every evening, Bakhtin would chase her away. It became a game for the two of them—to see who would prevail and for how long.

She did not sleep for several nights after Max proposed, lying awake in the dark wondering what to do, working the kopek coin back and forth on its chain while she thought, fearing she would never be loved again as Max appeared to love her. "Our place is here..." her father had said. Perhaps her place *was* here, in this little *shtetl*. Maybe she would be happy with Max Siegel…unless her place was somewhere else, somewhere at the end of a caravan's journey.

Lilia wept the morning Carsie told her she thought she would agree to marry Siegel. She pleaded with Carsie to return to Lucava, to the warmth of the *shtetl* they knew. What would become of her without Carsie's eyes?

On the day Carsie told Siegel she would marry him she said, "But it must be because you love me, Max. You know I come without a dowry."

"You have filled me with joy, Carsie—that is your dowry to me. And while I am not wealthy or handsome, I promise to return that happiness with a life rich in other ways."

Carsie rolled her eyes. "Can we wait until spring for the wedding?"

"I will wait," Max said. "Not gladly, but I will wait."

He arranged for klezmers to play during the wedding procession, and he found food enough for a feast. He bought fabric for Carsie's veil. He prevailed on the people of Trusheny, borrowing table linens and pieces of china, a tie from Meir the clerk, and a suit coat from Mendl, the general storekeeper, who also offered a pair of shoes that had recently arrived.

The first week in April, signs went up in store windows all over town announcing early closings due to the Friday nuptials of Max Siegel and Carsie Akselrod. Siegel built a *chuppah*—the wedding canopy—in front of the bar and decked it with ivy and winter iris.

Still, a vague skepticism hung behind Trusheny's festive mood.

IN THE early morning hours of April 4, 1900, Zirl Bakhtin, village correspondent and postman, his black greatcoat buttoned to the top, sat waiting astride a black donkey in the forest outside Trusheny. Only his yellow armband set him apart from the shadows. His pockets bulged with the enormous sum of sixteen hundred rubles—more money than the Federation had ever entrusted to him before.

He had seen Carsie and Lilia leave Max Siegel's bar that morning as he took the mail off the caravan. Now they approached the forest, clutching their fashion magazine and a basket of sandwiches. They leaned into a biting April wind, skipping between puddles of snow-melt. Some months back he had decided that they had to leave Trusheny. Carsie and Lilia could read. That was a problem for him—sometimes what he read to the villagers in their letters was, well, exaggeration: Nakhimov had been in no *real* trouble with the bank until Bakhtin saw to it, after the farrier had married the woman Bakhtin thought was his. For years now the Nakhimovs had struggled with their payments—always short when the postman mailed the coupon and the money to the bank.

And Demichev's son was not the fool everyone thought he was—Bakhtin took the rubles the boy sent every month from America and replaced them with American dollars that came on the Federation caravans. The Demichevs couldn't use that money—they had no way to change it until Bakhtin changed it for them, charging a hefty fee for his service.

He snorted. The Federation. Another bunch of dimwits—sending money to the *shtetls* so that refugees might leave. Money from the Rothschilds—wealthy Germans who knew nothing of how stupid these people were.

But Carsie and Lilia Akselrod could expose his connivances. The girls were orphans with no guardian, since the Cossack had died. They would go with the caravan, and Bakhtin would make a profit on that, too.

He urged his donkey out of the shadows. "Carsie! Lilia! Where are you going?"

Carsie frowned. She didn't like Bakhtin, and why was he here, in the middle of the forest this early in the morning? "To the house of Aoife Karpin, for her reading lesson," she said.

"I'm glad I found you. Come, I have somewhere else to take you, first."

"No," Carsie said.

Lilia gasped.

Bakhtin grabbed Lilia up in his arms, sitting her on the donkey's broad rump. "Stay there!" he ordered. He turned to Carsie. "Now—do I take your sister and leave you here?"

Carsie relented. Sullenly she walked to the donkey and waited for Bakhtin to offer her a boost. Off they clopped through the slush of an early spring thaw, the three of them bouncing back in the direction of Trusheny.

Day broke through the beeches; the streets yawned empty. At a corner near the synagogue they saw wagons—ten or more—and strangers milling around. Bakhtin urged his donkey to move faster as they approached the group.

Bakhtin pulled the donkey to a stop beside the lead wagon, murmured to the wagon master, pointed to the girls and handed the man a one-hundred-ruble note.

Carsie tapped on his back. "Zirl! No! We can't leave Trusheny now—remember? I marry Max Siegel on Friday."

Bakhtin turned to face her. "Yes, my darlings, you *are* leaving. The Federation has given you money for your passage— five hundred rubles to make the journey. A handsome sum, no? Besides, Carsie, no one has told you about Max Siegel because he is Trusheny's disgrace. Siegel has cuckolded almost every man in town—he gets them drunk, they pass out, and

Max takes advantage of their wives. Why, half the children in town were probably fathered by Max."

He looked around, spotting Rabbi Rubin's children standing nearby. The youngsters watched the caravan load.

"Tell me those children don't look exactly like Max, Carsie. Look at them."

"No, you're wrong. Max doesn't do that. Lilia and I have lived under Max Siegel's roof for four months and I have *never* seen him take another man's wife. You're lying."

Bakhtin shook his head. *Lying?* Carsie's name-calling had just cost her one hundred rubles. "Well, of course. He can't very well operate the way he did since you and Lilia came. But that is why they stay—the women of the village—Max is their lover, and the father of their children."

"But that's awful! When was I to find out about this?"

"Probably never, if left to others to tell. Didn't you wonder why Grober Dragutsky betrayed Siegel to the Cossacks? Why Kefira was so anxious to turn her husband out?"

Carsie thought for a moment. "Why do *you* tell me this? Has Max not had his way with your wife?"

"Carsie, you've seen me at Siegel's. I never, *never* drink alcohol with the others. My children are my own," he smiled. "Beautiful only to me—everyone else sees them for the scrawny pigs they probably are."

She looked again at the rabbi's children, remembering how her own parents had fought. She saw she did not belong—that she would always be an outsider to Trusheny's villagers, an obstacle to the desires of its women. She held out her hand. "Give me the money."

Bakhtin handed her a wad of bills. "There," he said. "Five hundred."

She tucked the money into her coat pocket.

"Do not be foolish with it," Bakhtin said. "You will need some for passage on the ship and more to get into America."

"They charge to get into America?"

"Like any other circus," Bakhtin chuckled, pleased with his own joke and the sizable profit he had just made.

Carsie and Lilia struggled down off the donkey, magazine and food basket in hand, and clambered into the lead wagon.

As Zirl Bakhtin rode away he heard the wagon master say, "Listen up! My name is Nikitin. We have rules...."

Max Siegel had just set a plate of herring and a roll on the table when Zirl Bakhtin walked in. "*Shalom*, Max." He pointed to the plate of herring. "For me?"

"For Carsie, when she wakens."

"Wakens? I saw Carsie and her sister walking in the direction of the forest as I rode into town."

"Ahk! Of course. I forgot—today she goes to teach the Karpin girl a reading lesson. Carsie is my gift from heaven, Zirl. I am a lucky man indeed to have found her. Friday cannot come soon enough."

"A happy day that will be, Siegel, *mazel tov*. Give me a shot of schnapps to warm my *tuchis* and I'll be on my way—the mail has come already and I have much to do. I've opened all the letters but I'll have many responses to write this evening. Nakhimov is in trouble with the bank again, I see, eh? And Demichev's son sent American dollars to his parents. What a pity."

"*Tsk*. 'Pity' is the word. Money they can't use here. That boy always was a fool. It's astounding he got to America in one piece."

"Too true." Zirl raised his glass to Siegel. "*L'chaim*." He tossed the schnapps to the back of his throat. "I'm off, Max." He threw a hundred rubles on the bar. "For your wedding, my friend. Use it in good health."

Siegel's eyes grew large when he saw the money. "This is most generous, Zirl. You are a good man, and good to our village."

"Eh," Zirl shrugged. "My duty to our people. We are in this together, aren't we my friend? *Shalom*."

THE GIRLS sat on a bench in the wagon, Lilia clutching the fashion magazine, Carsie the food basket.

"Back in a wagon," Lilia whispered. "But at least nothing's biting me."

Carsie fingered the money Zirl had tucked in her pocket and shuddered, thinking about what Bakhtin had said. She was lucky to have escaped the horrible Siegel. Still, she supposed she should say something to him—something about Bakhtin's accusation and a goodbye. She would write a letter. That would have to do.

The caravan moved out of Trusheny toward the hills slowly in the deep ruts of the muddy roads, their wheels and the horses' hooves slipping in the furrows. An opening in the canvas at the back of the wagon revealed fog settling across the brown hills to the north. Patches of snow lay in the shadows.

"Snow," an old woman said, pointing at the western sky. "That's more snow coming."

"Nah, snow," a white-bearded man leaned out to inspect the sky. "That's rain. Yeh, rain for sure."

"Eh? So, where do we go, do you know?"

"Straseni, I heard. We get on a train there."

"Train? Good, good. Better we should be on a train than in this drafty wagon."

The caravan rolled on, all eyes on the thickening clouds. Across the Dniester River the wagons worked along a ridge on a gravel trail. It was less muddy here, and easier to move, and they made faster time. Heavy white clouds mounded in the west but did not move in. The wagons climbed to the top of a gentle pass and into the wet, cold clouds.

Carsie's hand went to her throat, reflexively seeking the kopek necklace to work it in her fingers. A jolt went though her. "Lilia! My necklace! It's gone. *Mayn Gott, oy vey!* Where…" She felt the back of her neck, her shoulders, her waist. She searched the floor of the wagon at her feet and shook out her skirt. Nothing.

The wagons halted to rest the horses. Carsie scrambled down and ran back up the rutted road. She walked to the rear of the line of wagons and down the trail farther, scanning the rutted road back toward Trusheny. She had another reason to return, now. She owed Siegel a goodbye and she had to find her necklace.

It would be almost as fast to walk back to Trusheny as it was to ride this far in these ruts, she thought. We have survived a night in the cold before, we could be back in Trusheny by tomorrow. But that would not happen, she knew that, too. The way was fraught with dangers: wolves and Cossacks and cold.

Cloud cover followed the caravan, lowering, darkening the twilight sky. The air dampened. Lilia tucked the fashion magazine inside her coat to protect it from the weather.

The storm began as an innocent shower, quickly ratcheting to a downpour. Shivering, Carsie and Lilia climbed back into the wagon and glanced at their traveling companions: a blacksmith and his son, a pale-looking woman who tended two elderly people, a dark-skinned man with shiny black hair.

Rain dripped from every hole and corner of the wagon covers. Lightning flashed. Horses neighed, pulling at their tethers. The roar of rain and the sound of thunder echoed down the valley, swelling to a deafening din. Lightning crackled, close.

SIMCHA RUBIN entered the bar, staring wide-eyed at Max Siegel.

"What?" Max chuckled as the little boy gazed at him.

The boy continued to gape at the saloonkeeper. "Are you my father?"

"Why, no, of course not," Max ruffled the boy's hair. "Nahum is your father."

"Herr Bakhtin says you are."

"Herr Bakhtin is wrong, Simcha. You probably heard him say something else—I'm sure he said no such thing."

"He did, sir. On the street, I heard him tell that to Carsie Akselrod. He pointed to me and Nagida and he said, 'Max Siegel may be their father. Maybe he is father to half the children in Trusheny.' That's what he said."

Max laughed out loud. "That's not true! Where did you get such ideas?"

"That's what Carsie told him—that it could not be true. But Zirl says it *is* true," Simcha said. "Nagida heard it, too. Ask her."

Max hurried into the street, finding Simcha's older sister next door at the bakery with their mother. At the sight of him, the girl shrank to a far corner, behind a case of baked goods. The children's mother emerged from the back, a glass of tea in hand.

"Nagida!" Max peered around the bakery case at her. "What did the postman tell Carsie Akselrod today?"

"That you got our father drunk and took our mother to the back room. That you might be father of half the children in town."

Kyla Rubin chuckled. "Nagida, that is not true!"

Nagida nodded. "But Herr Bakhtin says it is. He swore to Carsie that Herr Siegel was doing that. He said Herr Siegel is taking the women of Trusheny after their husbands pass out from drink." She thought a moment. "Mama, what does that mean?"

Kyla Rubin wept with laughter, holding her stomach. "Oh, Nagida, you gullible girl! Zirl is a puffed-up old story teller. What a big fish tale! My daughter, I would never make babies with this man. I love your father too much. And one reason I love him that much is he *doesn't* drink! Not like Zirl, who drinks when he thinks no one is looking."

The baker laughed too. "Max, no one will believe Zirl's story. Relax. If you have trouble convincing Carsie, we will verify the truth. Come and see what I'm planning for your wedding feast..."

BY MID-AFTERNOON Carsie and Lilia still had not returned to the bar from the house of Aoife Karpin. Max paced, watching out the front window, waiting. At three he walked to the Karpin house, where Aoife and her mother assured him Carsie and Lilia had not been there at all that day.

He returned to the bar well past six in the evening, turned

up the gas lights, stoked the fire in the stove, and tied on an apron. He didn't know what else to do but open, like any other night.

Nahum Rubin, the rabbi, came in, shaking rain from his coat. "Eh, Max. I need to watch myself tonight, huh? Not get so drunk you can have your way with my wife?" He laughed.

Sitting at the other end of the bar, Hod Nakhimov, the farrier, had heard the story too, and he laughed. He rubbed his gnarled hands together. "And my children? If you are their father, Max, perhaps you should be feeding and clothing them!" Snickers rippled through the public house.

It went the same for an hour as the men of Trusheny came in—the hardware man, the grocer, the tailor—all of them teased Max about having the time and masculinity to father so many children. And every time the door opened he looked up, hoping to see Carsie and Lilia appear.

"Jumpy tonight, Siegel?" Nakhimov asked.

Max wiped his hands on a bar towel. "When Carsie and Lilia left this morning they went to instruct Aiofe Karpin in a reading lesson, but they did not get as far as the Karpin house, and they have not returned. They have vanished. Hod, I fear Cossacks have taken them. The last anyone saw Carsie and Lilia was when they spoke to Zirl. And what was he doing with them? When he was in here this morning he didn't mention that they had talked."

"Eh, I saw Zirl with the Jewish caravan just after daybreak. Getting mail off the wagon. I expect …"

Zirl Bakhtin walked into the bar. Max froze.

The room fell as quiet as it had the night in December when Valentin Mikheladze walked in with Carsie and Lilia in tow. Bakhtin settled himself at the corner table, spread out his writing paper and pens, preparing to write the villagers' letters for the following day's post.

Nakhimov climbed down off his stool, beer in hand, and walked to the table. Muscles twitched in his burly shoulders. "Bakhtin, ready to write my letter to the bank?"

"Sit, sit. Max," Bakhtin pointed at Max. "Bring me a schnapps."

Max stood rooted, staring at Bakhtin.

Nakhimov leaned across the table. "Shall we begin? Or would you rather apologize to Max and Nahum, first?"

"Apologize? For what?"

"For what you told Carsie Akselrod on the street today. Rabbi Rubin's children heard what you said about the rabbi's wife. They told our friend here. And while you're explaining, perhaps you can tell him where Carsie is."

Bakhtin's hands fidgeted in his lap.

Nakhimov leaned closer. "Will you apologize?"

"I apologize, Max," Zirl muttered.

"Louder, Bakhtin. 'I apologize, Max, for…'"

"I apologize, Max, for telling Carsie you laid with Kyla Rubin," he said weakly.

"How about apologizing to Nahum?"

"I apologize, Rabbi, for saying that your wife laid with Max while you were passed out drunk."

Max and the rabbi turned their backs on Zirl Bakhtin. Nakhimov grabbed Zirl's greatcoat, twisting it at the neck where Bakhtin had buttoned it tight. "And Carsie and her sister? Where are they?"

"Gone—with the caravan," Bakhtin coughed.

Max gasped as though he had been punched in the stomach.

"How much did the Federation give you to put them on the caravan?"

"One thousand rubles."

Nakhimov shook Bakhtin. "Again. How much did the Federation give you?"

"All right, all right. Sixteen hundred rubles. But I gave one hundred of it to Max this morning."

Nakhimov released the postman's greatcoat. He spoke to Max's back. "That right? He gave you a hundred rubles?"

Max turned. In the lamplight his cheeks shone with tears.

"He said it was for our wedding. He told me nothing about where the money had come from." He choked. "I should have asked. I can't believe he sent Carsie away."

"You gave him the hundred rubles saying it was for his wedding? Knowing a wedding would not happen?"

"I said nothing like that. He lies!"

"Max has tears in his eyes—I see none in yours."

"I am a man," Bakhtin sneered. "I am beyond sniveling like a child."

Nakhimov snarled, purple veins darting at his temples. He slugged Bakhtin, held him down with a knee, unbuttoned the black greatcoat and rifled the postman's pockets, throwing out everything: pencil stubs, old letters and finally a wad of paper money. He counted it. One thousand rubles.

He shook Bakhtin. "Where did you get this?"

"Get what?"

"This money in your pocket—where did you get this amount of money, Zirl?"

Bakhtin struggled against Nakhimov's grip. "How do I know you took that from me? I have never had that much money in the world. Perhaps you took it from Max. Perhaps I am surrounded here by liars and thieves. Everyone knows you're having trouble with the bank again."

Nakhimov punched him again. Blood spurted from the postman's nose. He cocked his arm a second time. "More? Do you want more?"

"No. No. It is Federation money."

"Federation money? Shouldn't you have given the Federation money to Carsie and Lilia to make the journey?"

"I gave them most of it."

"I am not good at math, postman, but I can do sums. The Federation gave you sixteen hundred rubles, you said—all of it meant to be given to those children for their journey. There is," he counted again, "a thousand here. And you gave one hundred to Siegel. How do you figure you gave most of it to Carsie?"

The postman whimpered. A foul odor emitted from his pants. Nakhimov dragged him out the front doors of the bar. Everyone watched through the plate glass window as the farrier said something to the postman, the postman replied and Hod Nakhimov slugged Zirl Bakhtin a third time. This time the postman fell to the street unconscious, his greatcoat soaking in rain.

Nakhimov returned to the bar and handed the wad of rubles to Siegel. "He says the caravan moves toward Brody, to the pass there. I have heard unhappy tales about what happens to children in Brody. Nahum and I will watch the bar. Take the money and the Cossack's wagon, my friend. Find those girls."

— 9 —

WELL AFTER dark on the first Wednesday in April, 1900, Max Siegel harnessed the sickly dray horse to the wagon Mikheladze had taken from the stable last December. He knew the way to Brody—his brother lived not far from there.

He had slept well the night before; he could travel until dawn if he needed to. *But,* he thought, *I could gain time and perhaps head off the caravan if I took a more direct route through the woods rather than along the road.* Riding that way presented no problem for him—he had lived in Trusheny his whole life. He knew the countryside, but he had not taken that route for years, now that he was tied to the public house. Though he had heard about it, he did not know exactly the site of the new quarry a mile and half to the west of Trusheny.

By nine that night he had arrived at the western side of the woods. Cold rain drove between his shoulder blades. He stopped at the forest's edge to button his greatcoat and squinted across the wide plain ahead of him, trying to spot the caravan's campfires through the sheeting rain. He urged the dray horse forward again, the wagon's wheels slipping in muck. The horse stumbled on stones as Siegel urged it toward the rough-hewn walls of the new quarry.

The dray horse stumbled once more, toppled with a jolt, and fell, pulling the wagon toward a hole into which the horse had tumbled. Water bit cold.

Siegel surfaced, gasping in icy shock. Beside him, the horse fought against the wagon's weight, which was pulling the animal under water. Max sprang upon the horse's back to release the harness. When the wagon began to sink, he held the bridle and urged the horse to what looked like solid ground, but again it was ice and the ice broke; he made another spring and ice broke once more; he made plunge after plunge until he had broken the pond open all around, clinging to the reins, trying to hold the horse's head up, to keep the deep water from drawing them both under.

Finally his shoulder bumped against the bank of the quarry pond and he heaved himself ashore, shivering with cold, rattling with icicles. He pulled at the bridle, urging the horse to jump, but the horse kicked at his hands and he dropped the reins. Exhausted, the sickly dray horse gave up its fight to stay afloat and slid to the bottom of the pond.

Siegel stood, saturated and freezing, and squinted once more through the rain. In the distance the lights of a cabin burned. Against the bitter squall he staggered toward it, pounded at the cabin door, called out. Nothing. He pounded again, drowsy now, beginning to freeze. After a long delay the door opened a few inches. A gust of warm air from inside the cabin hit Siegel in the face like a hammer. He sank to his knees in his ice-laden greatcoat, his eyes rolled back in his head, and he slumped to the ground.

WHEN DAWN broke, the blacksmith and his pimpled son rode at the back of the wagon on the bench where Carsie and Lilia sat. The blacksmith's nose bent to the right. He snarled more than talked as he told of escaping a Cossack five months ago and coming upon the caravan. "I grabbed my son and we ran. We ran over the bridge and after we caught our breath, we came out of the forest. We heard a wagon approach and we hid in a ditch, but when we looked up a Cossack stood over us. I begged for mercy for the boy. He aimed his pistol down at us, raised it and fired five shots at the tops of the trees. Then, like a miracle, he got back up on his wagon and left. After that we found the wagon train and joined up." While he told the last of his story, the blacksmith removed his shirt. He ordered his son to look for lice on his back.

Carsie had never seen a man so naked, his back blanketed in dark, curly hair. She wondered if her father's back had been like that—Papa was always cold, but she couldn't see how, if all men's backs were covered in hair, like this man's was.

Shortly before noon the wagon master rode down the line with a large bundle over his shoulder. He handed down loaves of stale bread to each of the teamsters, who tore off hunks for themselves before they distributed the rest to the passengers in his wagon. Carsie halved her portion and wrapped Lilia's fingers around the piece she held out.

Lilia threw the bread down. "No, I don't want it."

Carsie retrieved the bread and pressed it into her sister's hand again. "Eat some," she urged. "We don't know when we can eat again."

"No stale bread, Carsie. You know I don't like it."

The blacksmith leered at the girls. "You think you are better than stale bread? Perhaps you are not hungry enough."

"Leave her alone, Papa!" his son growled from the shadows. "Pick on me, but don't pick on little girls."

Farther on, the caravan passed a row of soot-blackened men marching alongside the road, each of them carrying a tremendous bag of coal. The men were guarded by two Cossacks—one in front, the other at the rear. Their wagon neared the middle of the row.

The blacksmith called out, "Run! Run, to save your skins!"

One of the coalmen frowned up at the blacksmith from under his enormous bundle. "Run?" he muttered. "I am so tired I can barely walk."

Crows flocked in a corn field, scavenging what remained of last autumn's harvest. The blacksmith's son tossed the last of his bread to the birds.

The blacksmith pitched forward, grabbing at the bread. "You fool! Don't ever waste food!" He raised a mighty arm and brought his fist down on his son's head, then pounded the boy a second mighty blow. The boy's shoulders shook and he fell sideways.

"You hurt him!" Carsie cried out.

The blacksmith shrugged. "He is my son, I can hurt him if I choose. He gave his food to the birds. If he did not want the bread he should have shared it with…with others here in the wagon."

"You mean, with you."

"Watch your mouth or I'll make sure you can't eat for a month. Then you won't need to worry who is sharing food."

The blacksmith's son groaned and rolled over.

"You see?" The blacksmith smiled at Carsie. "He is fine. Now, stay out of our affairs."

The caravan stopped at the outer reaches of Brody, where the wagon master ordered all the travelers down from the wagons. He led them, single file, through the town to a music hall. Several men in brown shirts stood outside the theater. The blacksmith cut to the inside of the line and walked faster, ducking his head, trying to make himself small. He reached the door, and almost inside before two more men in brown shirts forced him aside. "You," a brown-shirted man motioned to the blacksmith. "You'll come with us."

"Papa!" The blacksmith's son stopped, watching as the men prodded the blacksmith, herding him to a wagon. "Papa, wait! I am coming with you."

"No!" the blacksmith motioned to his son. "Stay with the group! Go on in, you will be fine—I'll be back in a moment. These men just want to tell me something."

One of the men chuckled and jabbed the blacksmith with a rifle butt in the small of his back. "Oh, yes, we are telling him something that will change his life."

Inside the theater, Carsie led her sister to seats near the front, where the blacksmith's son sat. "Hello," she said to him. "Did your father hurt you?"

The young man looked away, scratching at a pimple on his face.

"Are we going to get a musical show, I wonder?"

"I don't think so," he said. "It doesn't seem to me we're here for entertainment." He looked over his shoulder at the door in back.

"What are we doing here, then?"

"Just another step in the journey, I think."

"Oh." She thought for a moment and sighed. "My name is Carsie Akselrod."

The blacksmith's son said nothing.

"*Carsie Akselrod,* I said."

Silence.

"My name is Lilia Akselrod," Lilia smiled up at the ceiling.

The boy scowled at Lilia, but he answered her. "My name is Louis Levy."

"Hello, Louis Levy," Lilia giggled. She sang to herself, rocking back and forth in her seat.

Carsie studied the boy again, curious. "How old are you?"

"Stop asking questions. Leave me alone."

"I'm fourteen," Carsie persisted. "My sister is ten."

Louis Levy leaned over and stared at Lilia. "She's an odd one, your sister."

"She was sick, maybe that's why."

"Is she better, now?" Louis peered at Lilia again.

"Yes," Lilia said, still rocking back and forth in her chair. "I'm much better now, Louis Levy. I am much better, thank you. I had typhus."

Louis gasped and slumped back in his chair, quiet again. He twisted, checking behind him once more and to the sides of the theater.

"Still looking for your father?" Carsie asked.

"Yes. I hope he comes back before we have to leave."

Carsie pulled her coat around her. "Button up, Lilia. There's no heat in here."

"Seventeen," Louis said sullenly. "I'm seventeen."

Other men from the caravan left with the soldiers in brown uniforms. Afternoon stretched into evening. The travelers moved quietly, spoke softly, made no gestures. While Lilia pressed her nose to the pages of the fashion magazine Carsie squeezed her eyes closed and thought.

Her thoughts returned to her parents' argument in Lucava, to the Cossack raid, to the trip to Trusheny. Grief and anger and frustration made her stomach hurt, but still she could not weep. She could not grieve for her mother and father, and now there was more—Max Siegel had turned out to be someone other than the safe harbor she craved, and she had lost the only piece of her parents she had—her gold kopek necklace.

Carsie turned her back to the others and unbuttoned her inside coat pocket. She pulled the hundred-ruble notes out and counted them. One, two, three, four, only four notes… but the postman said he had given her five!

She tried to think who might have been close enough to reach into her coat pocket. "Lilia," Carsie whispered, "did you take any money from my coat pocket? It's okay if you did, but I need to know."

"Carsie, no! I didn't take anything. Zirl gave us five hundred rubles, yes?"

"That's what he said, but there are only four hundred rubles here."

"Only four hundred? Is that enough?'

Nikitin climbed the short set of stairs and walked to the center of the stage. "I have made new arrangements," he called out. "We go now to the train, but it is a different train from the one you might have taken. *Zol zayn mit mazel.*" He turned away and shook his head. "I am sorry. I tried. *Zol zayn mit mazel.*" Good luck.

— 10 —

THE QUARRYMAN and his wife pulled Max Siegel in the door and laid him in front of the fire. Worse than his face, his hands were white and blistered. Deep frostbite. Gently, the man pulled off Max's boots. His feet looked the same as his hands, white nearly to his ankles. He massaged Max's feet as far down as he dared, without breaking the skin on his blistered toes, while his wife went for blankets, and to quiet the baby. He unbuttoned Siegel's coat and laid it back, seeing he was wet to the skin. The quarryman opened the soaking vest and shirt and his wife covered Siegel with a blanket. Both of them worked on his feet, wrapping each toe in a strip of cloth torn from a diaper.

UNIFORMED OFFICIALS counted the travelers as they boarded the train. A young brown-shirted man motioned Carsie off the line. She pulled Lilia away with her. He motioned her closer.

"You have money?" he asked in Yiddish.

"No."

"Don't lie to me. You came from a Federation caravan. Everyone from the caravans has money—the Rothschilds send money for the journey. You are not going anywhere unless you pay me. Now."

"I need my money to pay for our passage. What does paying you buy us?"

"It buys your freedom. These people are not going to freedom."

"And you can get us freedom?"

"For a hundred rubles."

"But I told you, I can't pay. I need the money for our passage."

The man shrugged. "Passage will be less than a hundred rubles for both of you."

"But all I have is two hundred rubles," Carsie lied. "And we will need some money when we get to...wherever we are going to go."

The man shrugged again. "Suit yourself. But if you do not to pay me, let me tell you how life will be in the work camp. The children are pushed. They work at night, the young ones, so the adults can sleep."

"How do I know you can set us free?"

"I'll tell you what," the guard smiled. "Stay with the group, and watch what I can do. I choose who gets fed, who gets a bed and who sleeps on the floor, who works during the day and who works nights. Once you believe I have the power to set you—"

"Me *and* my sister..."

"It will cost extra for her freedom."

"How much do you want from me? I told you, I have two hundred rubles."

"Look me in the eye and tell me again how much you have."

Carsie pushed Lilia behind her and thrust her chin forward. "I have two hundred rubles."

The guard took an apple out of his coat pocket. "Would you like?"

Carsie snatched the apple from his hand and bit into it. "Look at my sister. With her eyes she cannot work."

"You will not spend your money to buy freedom? Well then, it's off you go to dig coal. Shoo." The guard waved her away.

"Wait. You don't know us—my sister and me. We are—"

"Lilia! Carsie! I've been looking for you," Louis Levy called from down the line. "That man can save us, Carsie! He can!"

"But Louis, how do you know?"

"Because Papa arranged for my passage—and for yours, yours and Lilia's."

"I don't understand—*your* Papa?"

The guard stood. "You are the girls the Jew spoke to me about? Too bad. You have been exempted—to go to America." He sneered. "But, you see, what you'll find in America is no better than our work camps. Thousands of children younger than you labor in those factories. Little girls whose hope is gone, babies tired enough to die."

Carsie glared at him. "What difference is there between that and your work camp? I think we will find out for ourselves. And if Mr. Levy has arranged our passage to America I'll keep my money."

"You'll stand in one spot all day, turning out cheap glass bottles or cheap cloth or cheap cigars! Your teeth will blacken from snuff while your lungs blacken from disease." His lip curled. "If you survive the voyage."

THE WESTBOUND train moved on for three days, stopping only for coal and water. Now its shadow fell in different directions from before—they moved north and west. Little by little the snowy fields and forests receded and the weather warmed. On the fourth day they started the climb into a mountain range that ascended gently, curling around precipitous peaks and up, higher still. The air chilled and a foggy rain pelted the roof. Then, their ears popping, they zigzagged down into a land of red tile roofs warmed by a yellow light. Carsie stared out the window of the train car at fields divided into green squares by fences and roads.

After five days the train stopped on a siding. Everyone climbed out of the car to change for a train on a narrower track. They moved off once more. In the distance a wide, blue ocean sparkled. People in the car whispered, "It's France. We are in France."

French officers in long blue coats issued them clean clothes as they clambered off the train. That night they slept on the scarred wood floor of the customs building where, they were told, they would be held for a week in quarantine. The following day an ocean liner came to port, taking and leaving passengers dressed in furs and silks before sailing away to places more foreign-sounding than Carsie had ever dreamed.

Before dawn, a week after they had arrived in France, a guard and his interpreter called people forward. In a low voice the interpreter asked each traveler a few questions, nodded at the guard and handed over a loaf of bread. Carsie recalled breakfast at Max Siegel's table and how little she had appreciated the bread he set down for her. She wished she could see Max again to apologize for her disdain toward him while Lilia and Mikheladze were ill, and for leaving him very nearly at the altar without a word of goodbye. "...covered with blue-black silk and lined, on its underside...," she mumbled. "The brim is bound by black velvet ribbon..."

A guard called them to the table. "Names?" The interpreter began a new form. "Ages? Parents?"

Carsie provided the answers and the interpreter gabbled to the guard in a language that lay soft on his tongue. He gestured to Carsie and Lilia. The guard responded in the same fluid idiom and the interpreter turned once more to the girls.

"How are you planning to get to...wherever it is you plan to go?"

"We have money."

"How did you come by the money?"

"A postman in our village gave it to us when we started our journey," Carsie said. "We came with a Federation caravan."

The interpreter nodded and straightened, mumbling again to the guard, who handed over a loaf of bread to Carsie. Carsie passed the loaf to Lilia, who hugged it close. "New York, Cape Town, London, Leeds, or Manchester?" he asked. Carsie paused to think. Their uncle, Moishe, lived in New York, she knew, with his new wife, Shalva. And New York had been mentioned in their fashion magazine. Perhaps they had an atelier there. The interpreter looked over the top of his glasses and asked again, "New York, Cape Town, London, Leeds, or Manchester?"

"New York, please," she said.

"How many traveling?"

"Two."

"Thirty-two francs, then."

Carsie looked at him, puzzled. "I should not have to pay at all," she said. "Herr Levy arranged our passage."

"Herr Levy *arranged* your passage, yes, but he did not *pay* anything toward your travel. What he arranged is that you should not be sent with the others to the work camp. That the two of you should leave on the *Marseilles* tomorrow. You should be grateful to Mr. Levy. He took your place in the work camp."

Carsie gasped. She had thought so little of the blacksmith. "But," she protested. "I thought we would be sailing on the *Statendam.*"

"That is not what we arranged with the blacksmith."

"What boat is it, again?"

"The *Marseilles.* A very safe ship. Passage is thirty-two francs for the two of you.

Carsie gave her head a short, insistent shake. "What are francs?"

"French money."

"I have only rubles." She pulled the roll of money from her pocket.

"Of course," the interpreter smiled. "You are from a Federation caravan. You have only rubles." He sighed and pinched the bridge of his nose. "Very well, there will be a surcharge for the difference between your rubles and the money we use here. Thirty-two francs comes to a little more than two hundred rubles. So you'll pay me three hundred."

"How much over two hundred does it come to?"

He shrugged. "It comes to two hundred nineteen rubles. The difference is for feeding you the past week, a change of clothes, and the inconvenience of having to change the money into francs before I give it to the bursar." He stood and held out his hand. "Three hundred rubles, total. For everything."

"Louis Levy," the guard called out. But instead of asking Louis the questions they had asked Carsie, two men took him by the elbows and pulled him outside, toward the water.

MAX SIEGEL rolled over in bed, dreaming fitfully about Carsie, and how far she might have traveled by now. He saw her walking out of Trusheny alone, on a muddy road. He saw her sitting on the bench under the front window of the bar. He saw her standing in the door of his bedroom. He wakened, and fixed a gaze on his right hand, minus three fingers he had lost to frostbite. To lose three fingers was nothing. He would risk more than three fingers to find her.

LOUIS LEVY leaned on a mop and watched from the deck of the *Marseilles* as Carsie and Lilia clambered up the freighter's gangway. He had come aboard earlier that morning, and already the crew had given him chores.

"Jew boy!" one of the dock men yelled from the wharf. "Show your little friends to the steerage hammocks."

Carsie smiled up at Louis. "The interpreter explained about your father, and what he did for us. We are indebted, Louis. I'm sorry for ever thinking…that is, I thought…"

"I know," Louis said. "Everyone thinks Papa is a monster, but when he is sober he has a good heart." He stared back at the customs house. "I shall miss him."

As they made their way down to the hold, a shrill whistle sounded noon. The ship lurched and nosed out of port, turned toward the Straits of Dover, and away from Boulogne sur-Mer.

Carsie stopped to watch the shoreline recede. "*Zay gezunt*, Papa and Mama," she said. "*Zay gezunt*, old life." Goodbye to all she knew. The date was May 25, 1900.

11

IN THE cargo hold Carsie and Lilia shared one hammock. Louis sat in another, nearby. Mounded between the hammocks, caged guinea fowl, Muscovy ducks, and pigs rutted and snorted and fouled the air. Carsie pulled the few extra clothes given them by the French customs officials from the picnic basket and hung them on pegs behind the hammock.

The freighter slipped out of the bay, its mighty engines grinding as it turned and headed into the sea. Pushing into open water, the ship rocked from side to side, riding the waves up and down. Up again and down. Side to side. And up. And down. And left to right. Carsie's stomach churned. She and Lilia rode out the afternoon in their hammock, breathing the stench of barnyard gases emitted by the animals. Carsie gulped, trying to keep her stomach in place as the ship pitched and rolled from the Straits of Dover to the southern end of the North Sea.

The ship stopped moving. Carsie struggled from the hammock and climbed to the top deck. It was night—still and dark and warm. A rat scuttled across the deck and jumped into a coil of rope on the wharf. Steamships sat farther out in the harbor with all but their running lights dimmed.

A crewman approached. Carsie waved to him. He nodded to her and slowed.

She pointed to the glitter of lights in the southern sky. "*Vos shtot?*" What city?

The man cocked his head and thought. "You're speaking Yiddish?"

Carsie tried to puzzle out what he said, recognizing only the last word, "Yiddish." Now there was no interpreter. Would people in New York speak Yiddish or...something else?

The crewman motioned for her to follow. He led her to the galley, doled out a dish of lentils, and offered a spoon. Carsie held up two fingers. The crewman smiled and nodded. He spooned more lentils into the bowl and handed her two spoons. As he bent with the bowl and spoons he pointed outward, to the city spread around them.

"London," he said. He pointed to the bowl. "Lentils." Out again to the city. "London." And to the bowl again. "Lentils."

"London," Carsie whispered to the city. "Lentils," she said, looking down at her dinner. She smiled up at him. "*Danka.*"

He smiled at her. "Thank you."

She raised her eyebrows. "Tank you?"

"Th…th…" He put his tongue to his front teeth. "Thank you."

"Thank you," Carsie said and nodded. "Thank you…lentils."

The crewman smiled and patted her on the back. "Thank me if they stay down, young lady. If they stay down, thank me then."

When Carsie sat, the hammock's movement wakened Lilia. She struggled to a sitting position and peered closely at the contents of the bowl Carsie carried.

"Ugh," she wrinkled her nose. "*Chechevitsa.* I'm not hungry enough to eat *chechevitsa.*"

"Lilia, you must eat something." Carsie lifted a spoonful of lentils to her mouth. She settled back, self-satisfied. "A man on deck showed me where the food is. *Mmmm…*they're very good."

"No, they're not."

"Well, no, they're not good," Carsie said. "But they're not bad."

"Really?"

"Really. Try some." She held out a spoonful.

Lilia chewed, felt for the second spoon and dipped into the bowl herself. "Who was the man on deck?" she asked.

"He works on the ship, I think. He told me the name of the town where we are now. London."

"London? That's in our magazine!" Lilia took out the

magazine and scanned, the pages pressed to her nose. "Yes, here it is. We are in London?"

"Finish your *chechevitsa* before we go up to find Louis. I haven't seen him all day."

In their brief search for Louis topside they did not spot him. The girls returned to their hammock in the foul steerage cabin.

"Remember well, remember right," Carsie whispered to Lilia.

"Goodnight, goodnight, goodnight, goodnight," Lilia whispered back.

Louis Levy, afflicted by seasickness so severe he dared not move, slept curled in a lifeboat where the air was fresher.

CARSIE AND Lilia stood at the railing, Carsie describing to her sister how people busied themselves on the docks: bringing aboard boxes and large cloth bags stuffed with goods, crewmen removing a man in handcuffs from the ship's hold and handing him over to a guard in a strange black hat, unfastening big coils of rope from around metal cleats, pulling up the gangway, preparing to get under way once more.

The freighter floated free of the dock, started its engines, and turned away from the dock. The captain called out his orders: "Half full, Mr. Krukov, half full for now."

"Aye, Captain," a crewman called. A bell rang twice. "Half full it is."

Moving down the Thames the ship creaked pleasantly, sighing with the wind. Carsie spotted the crewman she had met the night before and waved him down. Clutching her coat around her, Lilia stepped behind her sister.

The crewman smiled. "Good morning."

"Gut mor-ning," Carsie repeated.

The crewman looked over Carsie's shoulder and pointed to Lilia cowering behind her.

Carsie pulled her sister forward. "This is Lilia," she said in Yiddish.

"Lilia?"

Lilia nodded without looking up at him.

"And what is your name?"

Carsie frowned.

The crewman thumped his chest. "I am Marek." He waited. "Mar-ek," he said again.

She brightened. "*Ikh heys Carsie.*" My name is Carsie. Beyond the crewman she saw Louis Levy tumble from a lifeboat and stagger to the rail. He leaned over and gagged.

"Carsie and Lilia," Marek said. "Good mor-ning Carsie and Lilia."

"Good mor-ning, Marek," Lilia mumbled.

"*Wohin gehen wir?*" Carsie asked. Where are we going?

Marek shook his head.

Carsie pointed at a distant shoreline approaching off the starboard side of the freighter. "*Vu?*" Where?

"Oh. France. Now we go back to France."

"France?" Her mind reeled. Had the French decided she and Lilia and Louis should work in the camp after all? Had they rethought Herr Levy's arrangement because he hadn't paid? "France?" Carsie backed away from him. *France? Neyn! Neyn!*"

Marek held up a reassuring hand. "No, no! Not Boulogne-sur-Mer, Carsie. We take on freight in Cherbourg." He held up a finger. "One day. It's okay. Okay. See?" He put on an exaggerated smile and pointed to his face. "O-kay."

Carsie looked past Marek, seeing Louis Levy heave. They ran to his side. Bumping heads and elbows, the three of them carried him down the two steep ladders to steerage. His hands and face felt pale and clammy. He shouted out rambling nonsense syllables. Marek brought him tea and sugar water, and Louis took enough of each to calm his stomach, quieting his rant.

The ship docked in Cherbourg that afternoon, and the lack of movement helped quell Louis's seasickness. Carsie and Lilia hid in steerage the following day, unwilling to chance a French change of heart about being sent to a work camp. Late that afternoon, an older couple descended the ladder at the far end. The man began unpacking a carpet bag.

The woman wailed, "Aaron, talk to them. We can't travel in this...in this squalor."

"Miriam," the man pleaded, "I have talked to them. They have nowhere else to put us."

Meticulously, he laid out their clothes, shoes and books, took a tea pot and left the cargo hold for the galley. The woman followed, a handkerchief over her nose.

The ship departed Cherbourg at dusk that evening, entering the Atlantic. Louis moaned again as his stomach churned along with the engines, but Carsie's fears about being sent to the work camp stilled.

Plowing against a strong head wind the next morning, the *Marseilles* navigated into open ocean. Louis remained in his hammock, asleep. Marek wakened him and tried to get him up and moving. Louis resisted.

In the days that followed Lilia thrived on the ocean air and starchy food. Color returned to her cheeks for the first time in six months. Marek showed Carsie how to walk on deck in time with the waves and against the ship's next pitch. She enjoyed the peace and promise of the journey and tried to ignore doubts and worries that eddied in her mind: their likely inability to speak the language of New York, how they would find Aunt Shalva and Uncle Moishe once they arrived, and the uncertain value of the remaining one hundred rubles in her coat pocket. She could not guess what that equaled in American money, but she knew that the U.S. charged an entry fee.

Just after first light on June 1, ocean waves swelled from six to eight and ten and fifteen feet in front of the *Marseilles*. The ship keeled from side to side, over hard left and hard right, sliding down the face of one wave and fighting up the back of another. Throughout the day the little porthole over the stinking animal pens dribbled water from the waves that broke over the freighter. Seawater flooded the decks and into the engine room, and took the ship's only life boat when it receded. The sky remained as black as night, lacking the night sky's clouds of stars.

They all clutched at whatever they could to keep from rolling into the stinking stock pens. Louis twisted his fingers in the hammock's webbing, moaning and retching. Carsie belched and clutched at her stomach, but Marek's lessons in the days before helped keep her seasickness at bay.

The couple introduced themselves as the Count and Countess de Kelemen, from Kiev. The Countess once again held a handkerchief to her nose and read to Lilia from one or another of the books they had brought with them; the woman and Lilia stayed together nearly all morning, neither of them suffering any effects from the sea's ruthless pounding. The Count paced, impatient for the ship to move through the storm.

On Monday morning the storm subsided and the seas calmed. Louis lay in his hammock, weaker still from his last bout of seasickness. Lilia lay in the hammock, bored and restless. She hummed to herself, shaking a foot in time with the melody.

"Can you please be quiet?" Louis asked. "I'd like to sleep."

"If you slept at night, you wouldn't be sleepy now," Lilia replied.

Louis smiled to himself. She had nerve, this little girl. He liked that.

"Where are you from, Louis?"

"From Kiev, like everyone else."

"We aren't from Kiev. Oh, my mother was, but she's dead now. The Cossacks killed her. And Papa."

"I'm sorry to hear that." A wave of nausea struck him. He belched. "Was it awful, when the Cossacks came?"

Lilia stopped wiggling her foot. "Yes. Awful. Carsie and I ran from them, before they killed us, too. Would you like some water?"

"I need air. Could you help me up, please? Would you like to go topside with me?"

Lilia grinned. "I would like that a lot, Louis. I really would."

———

WHILE THE Count and Countess ate breakfast on the top
deck, Carsie studied the Countess's dresses hanging on pegs
in steerage. She fingered the crocheted edge on a sleeve—
filigreed threads woven with gold. The dress, lavender with a
striped overskirt, fell floor-length with no train or bustle—the
kind of dress Carsie had only seen in pictures. Its starched collar stood stiff and high, the mutton chop sleeves billowed like
those sketched in her fashion magazine.

"Carsie?"

She started, and looked behind her. "*Guten morgen*, Countess," she said, smiling.

"Do you know how do you say it in English, dear?"

"Y—yeh, I know how."

"Then, let me hear it."

Carsie's smile faded. "Gut mor-ning."

The Countess nodded. "You will need some English in
America."

Carsie smoothed a wrinkle from the lavender dress. "Such
pretty clothes. May I ask, that is I wonder…where did you get
them?"

The Countess smiled, stroking the lavender dress. "The
Count bought them for me in Kiev, after we met. He was a…
man with…privileges. His father had worked as an artisan for
Herr Fabergé."

"An artisan?"

"An artist who makes things. He worked in gold, making
pretty candlesticks and bowls and eggs for the Czar's wife. The
children of the artisans were permitted to go to school, so he
learned to read, and he learned languages—Russian, Hebrew,
French, English."

"Then he taught you?"

"Yes, that was how we courted. He was my tutor. Carsie,
why is it you take such interest in our clothes?"

"I don't know why, really, but I like clothes. I think perhaps
when I go to New York I will make them."

The Countess sniffed. "Clothes are not a purpose in life,
Carsie."

"They are purpose enough to those who publish the fashion magazines."

"When you're grown you will understand that making clothes is not a proper way to earn a living. The only thing clothes do is set us apart from the apes—nothing more."

"But, what better way could there be to earn a living than to make something beautiful? Wasn't that what...what your husband's father did?"

"At the expense of his eyesight, his lungs, and eventually his life, my dear. Do you think beautiful clothes are worth that?"

At the noon whistle on Wednesday the ship pulled into Saint John's harbor and dropped anchor. Crewmen scurried up and down the gangway, loading and unloading barrels and crates, taking and leaving mail and bags, signing papers, yelling, cursing, and finally hauling anchor and casting off.

The freighter turned for the outlet of the bay. They skirted a rocky shoreline, moving slower now, wary of icebergs that might lie hidden in the fog. Villages and farm land appeared before being shrouded once more in fog. Mountains, sheared off in straight walls, faced the sea. The water calmed. Lanterns of fishing trawlers and sailboats winked as the freighter made headway south. In the misty evening, a lighthouse here and there warned of danger. They found a cove and dropped anchor for the night. Navigating these waters in fog was treacherous enough—running at night was foolish.

LOUIS LEVY swung his feet off the hammock and pulled himself up. His head pounded, his mouth was dry. Even so, his stomach was still and he stood unaided for the first time in days. He could do that at least, though his knees shook. He worked his way to the ladder, climbing slowly, his breathing labored before he reached the top deck. He leaned against the bulkhead, panting for a moment, perspiring, even though the night was cool and still.

The moon, waning off full, fused out any stars, lighting

the shoreline in an eerie shimmer. Louis leaned once more against the rail, remembering the misery of his seasickness. He had thought he was dead. He had wished to die.

A rowboat advanced, two men aboard. Louis stepped into the shadows to watch its approach. At the bow of the freighter, Marek signaled the boat with a lantern, dropping a rope ladder over the side of the ship. Tying off the rowboat, the two men climbed the ladder to board the freighter. Without a word Marek led them down the forward hatch to cargo level.

Louis followed, inching halfway down the hatch ladder before he crouched to listen.

"Twenty cases," he heard Marek say.

The larger of the two men from the rowboat opened a case from the stack, pulling out a bottle labeled "Mrs. Winslow's Soothing Syrup." "And no tax stamps?"

"You give me a hundred dollars, you sell it for whatever you can get."

"We get two bits a bottle for it all over town. That's two hundred fifty bucks from twenty cases." He handed Marek a fan of ten-dollar bills.

"Then good for you, a hundred and a half in profit." Marek counted his money. "And good for me. Anybody figured out yet that it isn't the real Mrs. Winslow's?"

The man smiled. "Tastes like it, doesn't it? Packs a punch like Jack Johnson, though, this stuff. Got more opium in it than a Chinese den."

Stuffing his money in his pocket, Marek stepped forward, catching sight of Louis's feet. He stepped between the ladder and the two men, his hand behind his back, motioning Louis to move away from the cargo hold. The men from the rowboat prepared to load their cases of opium tonic.

Silently, Louis turned on the ladder, but stumbled, falling face forward at Marek's feet.

"*Ow!*" he howled. "*Agh,* my foot, my leg."

The larger man pulled a pistol from his waist. "Who the hell is this?"

"One of our passengers—harmless boy." Marek smiled. "Probably looking for a place to throw up. Seasick all the way across, this kid."

"Could be the first of many crossings for him," the man with the gun said. "I believe he's just been drafted to the Merchant Marines. We can get another fifty for him when we hand him over. They'll be happy to have him."

"But he speaks only Yiddish," Marek said.

"Don't matter a speck to me—or to them." The man stepped forward and grabbed Louis's arm. "What's his name?"

"I forget," Marek said.

"Neyn! Neyn!" Louis cried out as the privateers tied his hands behind his back.

"Shut up and stand still, 'I forget.' We have some people who want to meet you." The man trained his gun on Louis, as he bent to pick up a case of bottles. It took less than twenty minutes to load their captive and the cases of opium tonic into the rowboat before the two men, their booty, and Louis Levy headed back to shore.

12

"HAVE YOU seen Louis this morning?" Lilia asked.

Carsie shaded her eyes with a hand. The sun shone bright and hot, glittering harsh off the water. "His hammock was empty when we got up," she said. "I'm sure he's around somewhere."

"NO," MAREK smiled. "Not New York, not yet. Boston. We stay here two days," he held up two fingers. "Look," he pointed.

A three-masted Italian naval schooner pulled into the harbor, its sails furled loosely to the tall masts, the uniformed crew lined in white rows along the gunwales of the ship's dark blue hull.

Obscured by the schooner's shadow, two men in a rowboat struggled against the wake of the Italian ship, their skiff weighed down with twenty cases of opium tonic and a young Russian Jew bound for the U.S. Merchant Marine ship.

Marek understood little of what Carsie and Lilia told him as they stood at the top of the gangway, except the name Louis Levy. Carsie pointed to the wharf. He shook his head. "*Neyn.* No." He wagged his finger back and forth. "You must not get off." Letting two Jewish girls loose on Boston's Irish-run wharves begged calamity.

"Louis—" Carsie began.

"*Neyn,*" Marek said.

"Yeh," Lilia said, stamping her foot.

"*Neyn,* Lilia. We cannot wait for Louis. He is not coming back." He looked at the girls, his palms up, supplicant.

THE FOLLOWING day Louis Levy watched the *Marseilles*

depart Boston harbor from the deck of the Merchant Marine ship *M.S. Vincent* as a boatswain led him to his bunk. They had fed him rum that afternoon, his first taste. The first gulp had felt like fire, and then it warmed him, and with each sip he came to like his dram of rum better and better, and how it made him feel before he felt nothing more.

THE *MARSEILLES'* engines fought the current as the ship turned south out of the harbor, an onshore wind to its port side. The ship swung a wide right, the shoreline closing on both sides through a long narrows. City buildings crowded down to the water line until the bay widened. Ships crowded the bay to the west, around a tall statue.

Marek came up behind the girls and pointed at the statue which stood on a pedestal in the middle of a small island. "The Statue of Liberty," he said. "Just there. At the base it says..."

Carsie and Lilia turned their backs to him, glaring across the turgid water in the direction of the statue, unable to understand the words he read to them from the tablet etched onto its base.

"Means nothing?" Marek shrugged. "Suit yourselves," he mumbled, and pointed once more. "There's Ellis Island—the immigration building burned a few years back, so you won't be going there. It'll be open again by the end of the year, but..." He shrugged again. "Not yet." The freighter rumbled on without pause, turning again to the east toward a warren of docks on the opposite shore. Carsie caught her breath. This was New York City? It was big beyond her comprehension. Behind the docks rose ramshackle wooden warehouses and red brick buildings, and, towering over those, taller buildings—buildings of a size she had never seen. As they pulled closer she saw people, people everywhere, shopping for fish or fruit or working at their trades—but in a place more soaring, more hectic and more crowded than Carsie could understand.

Her stomach flinched; she felt her heart beat in her throat. *No,* she thought, *we can't get off here! Lilia and I aren't ready for*

this. We don't speak the language. We don't know how to get around.
This can't be New York.

The freighter stopped in the bay, within sight of the wharves, dropping anchor while boats and ships of every description navigated around them. The Countess came topside and urged the girls down to pack their things in the picnic basket.

"We get off here, I think," she said.

"Here?" Carsie asked. "Here, how? We are in the middle of the water."

"We have arrived in New York at last," Miriam de Kelemen said. "Another boat will come for us now—a special boat from the government—to take us to the immigration building."

"What about Louis?" Lilia asked. "How will he find us?"

Countess de Kelemen smiled sadly. "Lilia, I'm not sure you should plan on Louis finding you. Louis probably left the ship in Boston. Maybe he decided he didn't want to come to New York City."

"He didn't decide that," Lilia pouted. "Louis wouldn't leave me."

A tender bumped against the freighter's hull. Marek flipped the rope ladder over the gunwale and handed Carsie down without a word of goodbye. The Countess shepherded Lilia down behind her.

The turreted gray stone Barge Office, at the Battery's outer wall, teemed with people who looked as different from Carsie and Lilia as they looked the same—the set of their mouths betraying foreign tongues, their eyes telling of hardened hearts longing for a tolerant America.

Up the bay a few hours before, the *Statendam* had belched up its steerage passengers, an ill-assorted crowd of men and women, some of them holding babies as carelessly as they held their carpetbags, older children clinging to their skirts and pant legs. All of them milled in the main hall, confused and anxious, while immigration officers indifferently winnowed among them. Still, the mood among the immigrants was deliverance, the discomfort of their voyage already receding, their journey at an end.

Immigration officials divided the newcomers into groups of twenty without regard to family size, nationality or social status. Carsie and Lilia stayed close by the de Kelemens, shuffling along with the rest of their group until they stopped opposite a fenced area where a few men sat caged.

"Why are they in there?" Carsie wondered aloud.

"The sign says they will be deported," the Count answered.

"Deported?"

"Sent back. Returned to where they came from."

The group moved on, an immigration official quizzing each passenger as they shuffled by. Carsie played her fingers in the fencing as she walked, staring through the wire mesh at the men on the other side. It had never occurred to her that she and Lilia might be returned to Russia. "Why would anyone be sent back?"

"Some are paupers without enough money to get into America," Aaron de Kelemen explained. "Or because they have a serious illnesses or physical defects that will keep them from making a living here." He shrugged. "Some are returned for political reasons; others have no papers proving they are citizens of their native countries."

Carsie's eyes widened. She shivered.

"A few are returned because they are insane," de Kelemen continued. "All of them are there because the authorities don't want any of us to become what they call 'public charges'."

The door to the cage clanged shut, one more passenger isolated on the other side.

Carsie staggered, clutching at the Countess's skirt.

"What is it, dear? You look...shaken."

"Lilia and I have no papers to prove our citizenship," she whispered.

"But the French customs men...didn't you give them money for your passage?"

"I paid them three hundred rubles—they told me it was

just for our passage, nothing more. They said nothing about papers."

Miriam de Kelemen put an arm around Carsie's shoulders and reached back to take Lilia's hand.

Carsie whispered up to her, "And Lilia has been ill with typhus."

"She is well, now, isn't she?"

"Yes. That was months ago. But her eyes—they might think she cannot make a living with her eyes as they are. And Papa was... killed for his quarrel with the Czar. They might...put us in there, and...deport us."

The gate on the fence slammed shut once more. From inside the cage a well-dressed woman railed at immigration officials in the soft language Carsie had heard in France.

She gazed at the woman standing in the center of the cage. "What..."

"They think the lady is a thief."

"But, she isn't dressed like a thief—why, look at her coat, her beautiful hat."

Countess de Kelemen chuckled. "What better disguise for a thief than fine clothes and a high-minded attitude? You and Lilia stay close, Carsie. We'll work this out together—you won't be deported." She stepped forward and murmured something to her husband. He nodded. The Countess stepped back, smiling.

The de Kelemens advanced to the front of the line, Carsie and Lilia close behind them.

"Names?" the guard asked

"Aaron de Kelemen," he bowed to the guard and gestured with a nonchalant hand as he introduced them in Yiddish. "My wife, the Countess Miriam, and my daughters, Carsie and Lilia."

The guard rolled his eyes, wrote and continued his questions without looking up. "Nationality?"

"Russian, Russian Jews. From Kiev."

"Papers?"

Aaron de Kelemen pulled a packet from his pocket. The guard gave the documents a perfunctory nod and went on. "You have your entry fees?"

"We do."

The guard held out his hand. De Kelemen placed four thousand-ruble notes in the guard's palm. The guard unlocked a box, counted out five hundred dollars in American currency and handed it to the Count.

"Train tickets?"

"Yes. We will go to Schenectady."

"No," Carsie whispered to Miriam. "Lilia and I will stay with family here in New York City."

"Shush, dear."

"Have you had, or do you carry any diseases?" the immigration official asked.

"No, oh no. We are all healthy—a miracle after our voyage." De Kelemen rocked back on his heels, pushing Lilia behind him.

The guard pulled four slips of paper from his clipboard. Those that he pinned to Carsie and Lilia's lapels read: *Carrie de Kelemen, Kiev, Russia, June 15, 1900–555* and *Lily de Kelemen, Kiev Russia, June 15, 1900–556.* "Step to the doctor," he said.

Carsie's stomach tightened as they approached a man in a white lab smock. The doctor waved the Count and Countess past, but stopped the girls. He smiled at Carsie and then, with a stick of white chalk, marked the back of Lilia's coat with an *E*.

"What did he do?" Lilia whispered.

"He put a mark on your back with a piece of chalk."

"Will it come off, do you think?"

Carsie rubbed at the E with her elbow. The chalk lines lightened, but did not disappear. "It will come off, but it'll take some work."

"Then do it."

"They want the mark there for some reason, Lilia."

"I don't want it there. Rub."

Eight or ten yards farther on another man, all in white as

the first had been, waved the girls forward. He caught Carsie's chin in his chubby hand, running an index finger around the rim of each eye before he turned to Lilia. He pushed her head from side to side. "Can you see well enough to read, young lady?" he asked in English.

The Count stepped back from his position ahead of the girls and repeated to Lilia in Yiddish what the guard had asked.

"I can read," Lilia smiled. She pulled the fashion magazine out of the picnic basket, opening it to a page she knew well. "Dressmaking is one of the most highly skilled trades for women," she read in Russian, "the other being millinery."

"*Zeyer gut!*" de Kelemen beamed at the doctor. "She's a *good* reader!"

The doctor used a rag to rub the *E* off Lilia's coat. The girls shuffled on, led by the de Kelemens, to a room divided into lanes by bars and grates, each lane corresponding to the names and numbers on the ticket pinned to their coats. They waited again. And again officials questioned the family at the end of their wait.

"*Vo sie gehen?*" the guard asked de Kelemen. Where do you go?

"Schenectady," de Kelemen answered.

"*Hundert dollars.*"

De Kelemen counted out one hundred dollars. The guard handed him four slips of blue paper. "*Dort,*" he said. "*Auf der linken seite.*" Out there, to the left.

"Lilia and I have family here in New York City," Carsie said as they climbed the stairs to the train platform. "We will leave you here."

De Kelemen raised an eyebrow. "Yeh? Where is your family? They care so much, where are they?"

"They did not know we were coming. And I don't know how to let them know we are in New York."

"Immigration officials send a telegraph, telling them you are here. That is the way it works for those who truly have fam-

ily here and are not telling tales about their aunts and uncles."
He shrugged. "If no one comes within five days, you are deported. But you don't worry about that—I think you will come
with us."

Carsie looked at the trains, waiting on both sides of the
tracks, rising from their rails like gleaming metal steam-
breathing beasts. She groaned. "We cannot bear another train
ride. We'll stay here."

Miriam de Kelemen smiled down at the girls. "Aaron and
I know what's best. You'll come with us."

"We want to live here. We have come this far by ourselves."

With an exasperated sigh, the Countess sat down on a
bench. "You didn't get out of Immigration by yourselves, did
you?"

"No, and I am willing to pay you back for our train tickets,
but—"

The Countess frowned up at Carsie. "That's quite enough
kvetching. You owe it to us to come to Schenectady—to stay
with us for a while."

"Our Aunt Shalva and Uncle Moishe are here. Why do you
want us to go with you to Sh...Ska...why do you want to leave
New York?"

"We have business in Schenectady. And you can earn back
the money we paid to get you through Immigration. You can
clean, can't you? And cook? I would let you take care of my
clothes."

Carsie stopped to consider Miriam de Kelemen's offer.
The idea was tempting—taking care of the Countess's clothes
was a privilege, she knew, even if she had to cook and clean
to do it.

De Kelemen gripped Carsie's arm. "If you stay here, the
guards will put you in the detention cage until your aunt and
uncle come to collect you."

Carsie wrenched her arm away, staggering backward.

The Count continued, "You should know that if you make
a scene here, I will be forced to admit you are not our daugh-

ters. That would jeopardize all four of us. Likely we would be deported without delay."

From behind her Carsie heard Lilia whisper, "We have run before. This time it is warm, we have daylight and a huge city to hide in."

Courage spiked up Carsie's backbone. She gazed at the food stalls near the end of the platform. "In any case, we will need something to eat—either for our train trip or for our wait in the cage, and I have enough money to buy that. Lilia, let's go get some food."

"The train leaves in fifteen minutes," Aaron de Kelemen snarled. "Miriam, go with them. Don't leave their side."

While Carsie and Lilia browsed among the boxed lunches the Countess stepped to a newsstand to buy a copy of the *Jewish Daily Forward*. Carsie looked over the railing and out across a broad lawn in front of the building. Close by, steps led down to the rail beds and the grass beyond, through which a sidewalk ran out to a group of red brick warehouses. She bought two boxes—each containing a loaf of bread, a tin of cooked beans, sausages, beef, sardines, ham sandwiches, and four oranges—and glanced once more at Miriam de Kelemen, who had become absorbed by an article in the newspaper. Quietly Carsie slipped one of the oranges out of the box and rolled it down the stairs.

"Follow me," she whispered to Lilia. "If anyone asks, we are chasing an orange."

The girls slipped down the stairs, hewing to the inside of the staircase, against the wall, where they would least be seen from above. At the bottom of the stairs they turned a corner and paused, waiting, listening. They heard the Countess cry out. Other voices exclaimed, "They went that way, I think," and, "I didn't see where they got to," and, "Lady, they're your daughters, you worry about them."

Carsie peered around the corner and up the stairs. Empty. "Don't run," she said to Lilia. "Hold my hand and just walk— like we are going on a picnic."

Step at a time, the two of them crossed the rail beds. Carsie's hands trembled, her head buzzed, her breath came in short gasps. They clambered onto the grass and down to the sidewalk, Carsie mumbling, mechanically reciting sentences from the fashion magazine: "The lavish brim sweeps around the face creating an illusion of a hat suspended as if by magic on the head…"

With each step Lilia counted backward in Russian from five hundred to distract herself from the thought of a short, hard life in the coal mines.

A shout came from behind them. Carsie glanced over her shoulder, seeing a uniformed guard fifty feet behind them, closing in long strides. She pulled at Lilia. "Hang onto me and don't let go. Now, *run!*"

— 13 —

SHALVA AKSELROD bent to her work chalking coats, using the long light of a hot June afternoon to mark a line below each collar. Later, at Melnick's, she would sew a label at the chalk line. She hated working in the summer heat, breathing air that stank of open toilets, a stench that infused the Tenth Ward. The wool, hot and heavy across her lap, had, years ago, stained her hands black with the dye.

She had worked from before seven that morning, and now the clock across Bowery Street, outside Franck's Tailor Shop, showed just past five in the afternoon. Through one of the room's two windows overlooking the street, she watched Moishe emerge from Franck's, slip something inside his vest pocket, adjust his derby hat, and cross the street.

Soon she would bundle forty coats with rag strips and carry the lot of them to the shop to set in the sleeves and sew on the labels. She dreaded the humid seven-block walk to Canal Street weighed down by the load of wool, fighting, in the late-day heat, to protect the bundle from street thugs angling to steal one or two, or from toppling the entire load to the sidewalk.

She had fallen behind on the number of coats she produced. Melnick would slap her again and accuse her of performing vile acts instead of using her night hours to sew. Her gums throbbed while she worked, her face swollen and purple on its right side where Melnick had hit her the night before.

Shalva had spent her nights sewing at Melnick's Coat Company for nine years, knowing nothing but piece-work since she was five years old. She had married Moishe last year, at the age of thirteen, praying he might change something about her life. After the wedding, she moved from the room next door, a large, quiet room at the back of the building, a room she had shared with her father, to this smaller one, shared only with her husband and his brother. Certainly the furniture had not changed, sparse and ordinary in her parents' room, sparser here. What had changed? Still, she supposed she should count herself lucky—they had a place to themselves, while others had to rent space to boarders.

Her father had sent her off with a chair as her dowry, the chair she sat in now. The only thing that had changed was her view of the world—instead of overlooking dandies and thieves and drunks in the alley, she saw pushcarts and pulled wagons and old men in skullcaps and caftans, and whores elbowing newsboys, and rag-pickers jostling women in cheap hats packed together and shuffling down Bowery Street as though pushed from behind.

Garbage mounded on the cobblestones—moldy bread, rotted fish, slimy vegetables, meat turning from green to black—and a sweaty cloud from the teeming throngs that walked in the streets because they were too poor to rent a space to sleep and too restless to stop moving added to the stink that mingled with odors from the hallways: the sour tang of boiled cabbage, a smell of mold. The decay stung Shalva's nose.

She doubled over, laying her bruised cheek against the rough wool coat she held in her lap. She wanted to sleep; she had not closed her eyes for two nights, but her every nerve sparked awake as though the sun blazed in her head. She trembled. She had never hung so near the dizzy brink of the unreal, unsure whether the door to the room opened only in her imagination, or if Moishe had really come in until he took her shoulders and righted her.

"Shalva?"

"I am so tired." Her hand went to her right jaw. "And my mouth hurts where Melnick hit me last night."

Moishe could not risk Shalva losing her job. He set the wool coat aside and pulled her to the table, shoving a plate of stale brown bread in front of her. "Here. Eat, my love. You need strength." He wondered if Melnick hit her because she deserved it. His wife was not much of a worker. Still, she was young, and he felt that was in her favor. She was too young to nag. He understood nagging to be a habit of older women; he hoped Shalva would keep her patience with him for another few years yet.

"You talked to Franck about a job today?" she asked.

He sat opposite her. "I have been thinking. Instead of me getting a job, we'll take in a boarder. He can sleep in that corner." Moishe gestured to a bare patch of floor farthest from the window.

Shalva's head swam. Sharing the small room with a third person, another man, a stranger, would give her no rest even if it meant a few extra cents at the end of the week. She pushed the brown bread away. "He would eat with us?"

"Yeh, sure he would. We would charge him for his food."

"I would buy food for four of us, then, rather than three?"

"It's not like you eat very much anyway, my love." Moishe nudged the plate of bread toward her once more. She stood and groped under the bed, pulling out a bottle, staring at its label: *Mrs. Winslow's Soothing Syrup.* She stroked the bottle in her hand, its sweet elixir waiting to cast its spell.

"No, Shalva," Moishe said.

"I'm tired, Moishe. I want to sleep."

"No, you'll go to work. I will help you carry the coats tonight, but you must go. You can sleep when you come home."

"I can't bear the thought of a boarder—someone else in this place. Someone else to clean and sew and cook for. A stranger, at that."

"I've already told him to come around with his things." Moishe piled the load of wool coats over his arm. "Selig will let him in while you're at Melnick's."

"And where will you be?"

He gave her his most boyish smile while he baled the coats with rag strips. "Where I always am—at the men's hall."

"What's this man's name, this stranger who will live with us now?"

He hoisted the bundle of coats high over his shoulder and motioned for her to open the door. "His name is Velvel Kagan."

They walked down Bowery Street, moving with the rest of the throng.

"We have to bring in more money," Moishe said. "Your job only pays our rent and food."

Shalva stopped to peer in the windows of a rooming house. "Why don't you bring home some money, then?" she whispered.

Outside the rooming house a sign read:

TO LET — $3 A WEEK

NO JEWS, NO WOMEN

A boy darted from the doorway, punched at the stack of coats and grabbed at Moishe's pocket, trying for his wallet while Moishe wrestled the coats.

"Get out of here, you little *goniff.*" Moishe batted him away. "Or I'll call the cops!"

"No, you won't." The boy mocked. "They'd arrest you before they got me."

Moishe straightened his derby and grunted. He gave his wife another beguiling smile. "Wouldn't you like a new hat once in a while? How about money to go to a show?"

"What does he do, this Velvel Kagan?"

"He's a butcher, over on Allen Street. My God, it's hot, with these coats."

She took the load from her husband and wove quickly through the crowd. Moishe trotted along behind. She looked over her shoulder at him. "So, where did you meet him, this Velvel Kagan?"

"At the hall. Unless we have more money, my love, I…"

The crowd on the sidewalk pressed close, and she thought

about the days to come, cleaning and cooking for three men rather than two, before leaving for her job at Melnick's Coat Company seven nights a week. "There are other ways to make money, Moishe. You could take a job at Lord and Taylor, fitting shoes, maybe…"

"Lord and Taylor? Too far. You know I don't like to travel. The hotel and the theater—my God, I had to take a streetcar to get all the way up there." He supposed employment was inevitable, but he hoped to forestall it as long as possible.

She sneered in disgust. He'd held two jobs in the year they had been married, but held them both halfheartedly. The first, night porter at the Oriental Hotel, uptown at Broadway and Fortieth Street, he had held until he quit for better hours next door, selling tickets at the Empire Theatre. Neither suited Moishe's idea of what he should do with his life.

"But Lord and Taylor is only ten blocks from here," she said.

"That's too far, too, Shalva. At least Franck's is just across the street." He shrugged again.

"And how much did Franck offer to pay you?"

"Ah, that stingy Jew bastard…sure didn't offer enough to make it worth my time."

"So Velvel Kagan makes us rich instead? How much will he give?"

"A quarter."

Shalva looked at him wide-eyed. "A quarter a night? Why, that's wonderful."

"A week," Moishe said meekly. "A quarter a week."

She gave a scornful snort. "More, Moishe. Much more."

"What do you mean 'much more'?"

"He needs to pay more than a quarter a week, Kagan does. A nickel a night to sleep and two dollars a week for food, laundry, and lights. Make it two-fifty."

"But…that's ten times what I told him he could pay."

"No wonder he took the deal. He pays two-fifty a week or he doesn't move in."

Moishe stopped. "I told him different."

"Then you'll tell him different, still," Shalva said over her shoulder. "Two-fifty."

"No," he yelled. "No, I won't. If I told him different he wouldn't respect me."

Shalva returned to where Moishe stood. "Then I'll tell him. I won't go to work tonight for waiting on Kagan to show up, but I'll tell him." She walked again, carrying the coats back up Bowery Street toward their tenement building.

Moishe ran after her, catching her arm. The bundle of unfinished coats tumbled to the asphalt, toppling into a slurry of rotted vegetables. Shalva waved off the coats and continued on without them.

Moishe jumped into the street, snatching the coats off the pavement and out of the scrap heap, wiping as much garbage as he could off the black wool. He called after her, "You must go to work, Shalva. You'll lose your job."

She spun on him. "Yeh, probably. But you should have talked to me before you told Kagan he could move in, Moishe. You'll learn." She shook a finger at him. "You'll learn, one of these days." She turned again toward the tenement house.

Moishe stared. The forbearance he had counted on in his young bride had evaporated in the summer heat. He chased after her, burdened once more with the load of coats that now stank of garbage. "I tell you he won't move in with us for that much."

She stopped. "Yeh, he will. He has all his things with him when he comes? He knows a fair price for room and board. He'll pay."

Chaskel Grinberg sat on the front stoop of the building watching his daughter and her husband dart through the crowd with their load of coats, weaving among the pushcarts, dodging garbage thrown from windows along Bowery Street. Tonight, for some reason, Moishe helped her carry the coats. He should only do that every night, Grinberg thought.

He stood when he saw Shalva take the coats from Moishe

not a block down the street as the two walked back toward Canal Street. *If he leaves her to walk to work by herself I personally will punch that guy in his worthless face,* Grinberg thought. *Thinks he's too good to work. If he doesn't find a job by the end of the month, I'll find one for him.*

A MERCHANT Marine ship put into Manhattan's west side ports on the afternoon of June 15, 1900 to discharge one of its crewmen, a young Russian Jew who clearly had no sea legs. He wobbled down the gangway and paused, grateful to see dry land, then reached for the coffin flask in his hip pocket. Around him, the docks teemed with donkey engines and derricks and scores of longshoremen hoisting bananas from Jamaica, coffee from Mexico, tea from China, wine from France, macaroni from Italy, spices from the Indies, sugar from Cuba, wood from Brazil and Norway, cloth from England, and cutlery from Germany. Dock workers rumbled here and there with boxes, bales and barrels, hand trucks, horse trucks and auto-trucks, and loaded departing goods as well—machinery, shoes, and large cartons of coats from Melnick's Coat Company.

Louis Levy passed into the city without examination by immigration authorities, as did every ship's crewmen. He stepped onto West Street pier half-drunk and at liberty, walking from the wharf across a cobblestone street before he stopped a second time, steadying himself against a lamp post as he stared goggle-eyed at the city spread out in all directions. The jolt of drays, freight trucks, mail wagons, furniture vans, butcher carts, and garbage bins rumbling on the streets thundered in his ears. People scurried, ducking carriages, hansoms bumped along next to clanging trolley cars, and in the center of the street, the tracks of a long freight train of the New York Central Railroad.

Cabbies and truck drivers yelled to make themselves heard, their faces purple from trying to out-roar the rumble. Shipping agencies, supply stores, warehouses, factories, mills, markets, lumber yards, and cubbyholes no bigger than closets selling food or drink or clothing to the longshoremen dotted both sides of the dusty street.

The races of the earth, it seemed to Louis, walked with him as he turned right and headed south, moving with the crowd into the city. Each of those in the throng around him seemed to speak a different language.

Waifs, stowaways, tramps, thieves, dock rats, thugs, and derelicts mingled with the refugees, all of them waiting for something or someone to turn up.

WHEN HE came around to Moishe and Shalva Akselrod's room on Bowery Street that evening, Velvel Kagan carried a box containing everything he owned: an extra shirt, another pair of pants, and three knives of varying sizes in a scabbard. During the day he wore the scabbard on his hip, an important part of his trade at the butcher shop.

Moishe told him what Shalva had said about the rent— that it was to be a quarter a night for room and board. Kagan was not happy with the price, but he had to leave The Bend after he'd stiffed Antonia Candia for three months' rent. He knew Shalva's price beat what the rooming houses wanted, and he needed a few square feet to himself. He set down the box containing his clothes and his knives and held out two dollars and fifty cents.

Moishe raised his hands and stepped back. "Don't give it to me," he said. "Shalva will want to see the money herself, believe me."

Repocketing his rent money, Kagan raised an eyebrow. Moishe Akselrod was no more than a *kinigl*—a rabbit, afraid of his wife.

Women had become difficult for Kagan since his escape from Blackwell's Island last year—his pallor yellow from deprivation and contagion when he got loose, his collarbone broken in three places from his time on the island. That he had spent time in prison he ascribed to Hanae Donders' painted face. Kagan first saw Hanae's rouged lips and tinted cheeks when he'd gone with Moishe to Koster and Bial's Music Hall, on Thirty-third Street. Hanae danced in the line there. After that first show, he had gone back countless times to the revue, staring transfixed from the moment Hanae came on stage until the final curtain rang down, captivated by her pouty little mouth and milky throat. Oh, how she moved! He wanted to touch the lithe body that dipped and swayed in perfect time to the music.

After the show he would go around to the back of the theater to wait at the stage door, hoping to talk to Hanae. Most nights she came out with the other chorines and he felt awkward about interrupting, but one night she emerged alone. Kagan approached and asked if she would like to come out with him for a bite of supper.

Hanae began to laugh. Kagan laughed along with her, a self-conscious chuckle, puzzling, while he laughed, at why she laughed at all. He stared at her face: the pretty little mouth rouged too red, her cheeks too pink, her throat too white. Hanae turned on her heel and walked away.

He stood rooted, not believing she would snub him, that she refused his offer of supper without a word of thanks. He caught his breath, his mind reeling. "You're lucky I came around," he called after her. "You look like a whore, you know."

She glanced back at him, still smiling. "Coming from a pimp, that's quite a compliment."

Kagan's shoulder blades tensed with anger. He grabbed her by her white neck from behind and dragged her under the stage-door stairway. First he tried to kiss her, but Hanae gagged and spat, wiping her mouth with the end of her scarf, twisting away. Kagan grabbed her again, pulling one of his knives from the scabbard on his hip, thrusting it deep into Hanae Donders' back. He wiped the makeup off her face and severed her head with two clean blows from his razor-sharp knife. He left her body hidden by packing crates under the stairs.

Even he could not account for what he did next. Kagan packed Hanae Donders' head in a box, filled the box with building sand and walked seven blocks north to the Oriental Hotel where he checked the box in the luggage room on the last night Moishe Akselrod worked there as the night porter.

The following morning the Oriental's manager noticed a smell in the vicinity of the luggage room door. Two men from Tammany's police force questioned Moishe while others found witnesses who had seen Kagan talking to Hanae just before she was murdered. When they tried to question him, he bit one of the cops.

It had not been the murder so much as it had been Kagan's violent temper during the arrest that cost him nearly a year at Blackwell's Island before he stowed away on a supply boat, where longshoremen beat him and threw him in a barrel of sewer sludge. This time, the cops didn't bother looking for him. None of them wanted to be bitten again and all of them were loathe to admit they'd let him escape so easily.

— 14 —

SHALVA RETURNED to the room on Bowery Street after midnight. She glanced over at Moishe and Selig. With them sat a third man, all of them on the floor in the corner, marking racing forms. She spread a load of coats on the table, unpinned her hat, slipped off her gloves. She rubbed at a bruise Melnick had given her on her upper arm when she brought him the coats smeared with garbage.

"Shalva," Moishe said when he looked up from the racing form. "Meet your new boarder." He pointed with his pencil. "Velvel Kagan, my wife. Give her your rent money, Kagan, before you gamble it gone."

Shalva counted the money and nodded. "Breakfast is bread and coffee. Supper at four, before I leave for work. You're on your own for lunch, three pieces of laundry a week, you bathe and shave on Thursday."

She scrutinized her new boarder. There was something wrong with him: the whites of his eyes shone yellow; at their corners pink and watery. His complexion was gray, his features too sharp. He had no ear lobes.

Moishe stood, handing her a section of the *Jewish Daily Forward*. He pointed to an article, thumping at it with his index finger. "Did you see this?"

"I haven't seen a paper in weeks," Shalva said. "I've been busy."

"Says here somebody at the Sheltering Society is looking for us...our names right there. I don't like it, I tell you. You need to go down there and figure out what's going on."

Shalva snatched the paper from her husband and read the headline:

JEWS SEEK RELATIVES
FAMILIES IN RUSSIA ASK AID OF
HEBREW SHELTERING SOCIETY

She shook her head and shrugged. "I don't know, but I can find out, I suppose, after I do this load of coats tomorrow."

"You've still got your job, then?"

"I do," she said, working her right shoulder. "Though Melnick near broke my arm tonight."

She hungered for the touch of her pillow, so tired was she that she yearned to fall asleep at once. Still, she knew that after she had laid down Moishe and Selig and Kagan would talk, keeping her awake. She handed the paper back to Moishe, giving him a tired smile. "Goodnight. Please don't make noise. Better, come to bed."

Kagan nudged Moishe with a foot and grinned.

Moishe batted at him with the newspaper, but he resumed his spot on the floor, marking the racing forms once more.

To shut them out for a few hours, for that brief bath of oblivion, Shalva took a swig of Mrs. Winslow's tonic and slept.

MAX SIEGEL raised his head and looked around, recognizing the room as his own bedroom, behind the public house in Trusheny. He propped himself on his elbows and blinked. Had the visit from the Cossack and the two girls been a dream? What time was it? It was daylight, and that meant it was past time to open. He tried to sit up, but the world went dark. He fell back on his pillow, dizzy and weak. What had happened to him? How long had he been asleep? Was he ill?

He opened his eyes and tried again to sit up, this time more slowly, clutching his legs so he would not fall backward again. He pulled his body up, raising his head, taking in a deep breath. He looked down at his hands, the right one black and blistered at the end of his remaining two fingers. He had seen it before—frostbite. Then he remembered: A thin layer of ice had formed on top of the pond and, through the pounding rain, Siegel had mistaken the ice for solid ground. He, the horse and the wagon had dropped into the quarry pond. After that, he remembered nothing.

Nakhimov stood in the bedroom doorway. He smiled. "I thought I heard mice. So, my friend, you are with us once again."

Wordlessly, Siegel held up his frostbitten right hand.

Nakhimov held up his right hand by reply, missing the last two fingers. "Between us, we have one good right hand, eh?"

"How long did I sleep?" Siegel asked.

Nakhimov shrugged. "A month, maybe a little more. We turned you, we changed you like a baby. Best, we talked to you and you said nothing—oh, it was glorious."

"My feet?"

"Can you feel them?"

"What should they feel like?"

"They should feel like…feet. The far end of your legs. I don't know—can you wiggle your toes?"

Siegel thought about wiggling a big toe and saw the blankets move at the end of the bed. "What is it then, May?"

"The month? No, it's June. You can come out now—the weather is warm." Nakhimov threw off Siegel's covers and swung his pale legs around to the floor. He put a hand under Siegel's arm. "You want to try standing?"

Siegel shook his head as though clearing cobwebs from in front of him. He looked around and gasped, seeing Carsie's kopek pendant on the table next to his bed. "Carsie's necklace! Is she here? Did she come back?"

"I am sorry, Max, no. Simcha Rubin found it near the spot where the wagons loaded that day. He brought it to me on the evening you left."

All the memories flooded in, though Siegel tried to push them away: Carsie and the wedding and Zirl Bakhtin. He wanted to sleep again. He tucked his legs between the blankets once more. "Maybe tomorrow, Hod," he said. "Tomorrow, I'll try getting out of bed."

———

JUNE'S HEAT and humidity wakened Shalva at five the following morning. Moishe lay, fully dressed, on the edge of the bed, snoring. Selig slept on his mattress in a corner. Velvel Kagan had gone.

She rose and, while the water for coffee came to a boil, marked the label lines on her newest load of coats. She made coffee, set out the same stale bread Moishe had urged her to eat the previous afternoon, and, working quickly, set in sleeve linings, spending no more than fifteen minutes on each garment. By four that afternoon, Shalva had completed her lot, both index fingers thread-cut in her haste. She boiled potatoes and cabbage and dressed to leave, pinning on her finest fichu and hat. She had two hours to spare before her shift at Melnick's.

She turned south on Bowery to Delancey and walked east through brigades of cart pushers and pullers, past old shops and boys playing in the street, their jargon and dress betraying the Tenth Ward. She turned south again on Norfolk, worked her way through the construction of the new Williamsburg Bridge and down to Grand. The address was nearby now.

Trips like this one, she had heard, could change your life, and she trembled. Velvel Kagan's arrival at the Bowery Street room had been enough change for a while. She walked on, hesitantly, once more reading through the *Jewish Daily Forward* article Moishe had shown her last night:

JEWS SEEK RELATIVES
FAMILIES IN RUSSIA ASK AID OF
HEBREW SHELTERING SOCIETY

The Hebrew Sheltering and Immigrant Aid Society has received a number of appeals from Jews in Russia asking that their relatives here be notified that they are in want, or that they desire to join them in this country...

Here is the list of those sought:

MOISHE AND SHALVA AKSELROD

Address unknown, thought to live in the Tenth Ward...

"...that they are in want, or that they desire to join them in this country..." Shalva read again, this time out loud. How could she and Moishe help anyone?

She remembered what it had been to work as a five-year-old child. She was fourteen now, and she had worked for Melnick for nine years. She knew nothing else. She worked seven days a week and sometimes carried twice the weight of the forty coats she had carried home last night. In the summer, when demand for Melnick's coats was greater in preparation for the fall selling season, she often worked nineteen or twenty hours a day in order for the shipments to leave on time, sewing at the shop until one or two o'clock in the morning. There was no limit to a day's work, only to her physical endurance, her stamina beguiled by the promise of a Mrs. Winslow's tonic when she returned to the room on Bowery Street.

She would never call that room home. Home was what she remembered of Russia, where she had eaten black bread and played in the pure air. Now she ate brown bread in this stinking place and no longer played at all. She and her father had come to America ten years ago, when they fled the Czar's tyranny, but here they found the rule of sweatshop bosses and landlords no better.

She consulted the address in the article, squinting through the window of a storefront that housed the Hebrew Sheltering Society. She and Moishe had no money, and no relatives who planned to come to the U.S., but the trip out of Russia had been made by someone else—people who thought they knew her.

She slid the newspaper article across the desk and pointed to her name in the column at the bottom. "I am Shalva Akselrod. You advertised for me?"

The old Jew behind the desk regarded her warily. Shalva wondered how she would feel when she reached this man's age, knowing nothing but fatigue her whole life. At least what this man did was useful—pairing immigrants with their loved ones, while she simply made coats. And was often beaten for it.

"Do you have identification?" the old man asked.

"There is no one else standing here with the name Shalva Akselrod, is there? That is my identification." She glanced around the room, seeing a pair of girls sitting on a bench behind the desk.

"There are those who come in saying they are who they are not. They try to collect people, to take them away and use them."

"Use them? For what purpose?"

"Usually as factory workers."

"I am Shalva Akselrod and I live in the Tenth Ward. You asked to see me. I do not even know why, or what people you're talking about."

"There must be a hundred Shalva Akselrods in the Tenth Ward."

"Perhaps. But probably the only one married to Moishe Akselrod, the *mensch.*"

The old man chuckled. "Only a wife talks about her husband that way."

Shalva tapped at the article lying on the counter. "'Moishe and Shalva Akselrod of the Tenth Ward' it says here. But aside from my father and my husband's brother, we have no family at all, and both of them are here, with us. Just so you know. You have made a mistake, eh? I'll go now."

"Just a moment. We have another way to identify you." The old man motioned to the girls on the bench. Staring numbly at Shalva, they came forward. Shalva studied them, examining their sallow faces and dirty hair, their hollow eyes and dusty coats fastened with yellow armbands.

The old man patted Carsie's shoulder. "Do you recognize this woman? She has come to collect you."

"This is Shalva?" Carsie asked.

"She says she is."

"I have never met her—she and my uncle were married in America, some time back. My father received a letter that said so, but we didn't get a picture."

"Wait," the old man put up his hand to silence Carsie. He turned to Shalva. "Shalva Akselrod is your married name, yeh?"

"Of course," Shalva said.

The old man pointed a shaky finger at Shalva. "Aha. You claimed your husband's brother was with you here in the U.S."

"He is. But...it says here that someone..." Shalva sorted through mental images clouded by weariness and Mrs. Winslow's tonic. "Oh, wait. Moishe and Selig have another brother—he is ..."

"So, it goes this way? You say he is here, I say there is another, a man who is still in Russia. Suddenly you remember him, when you didn't remember before?"

"Yeh, I remember his name, now."

"Then who is your husband's brother? The father to these girls?"

Shalva lifted her chin, remembering. "His name is Reuven. Reuven Akselrod."

"Is Reuven Akselrod your father?" he asked Carsie.

"He *was* our father!" Lilia cried. "The Cossacks killed him. *And* our mother."

"*Oy!*" Shalva burst out, groping for the support of the railing. "*Oy veh!* Moishe and Selig will be grieved to hear this!"

The old Jew sighed and pulled a sheaf of papers from a file. "These girls have come a very long way by themselves, Mrs. Akselrod, and they are in your care now. They are Carsie and Lilia Akselrod—your nieces. *Mazel tov.* You have lost your brother- and sister-in-law, but your own family has extended by two—these girls are your *mishpocha.*"

THE RELATIVE quiet of the Sheltering Society gave way to sounds of the Tenth Ward. Peddlers sold bread and sausages from bags and cloth from pushcarts; *farkoyfer* yelled to sell, *yente* hondled to buy over the bawl of those at their elbows, money was passed and snatched. Children played in water spraying from stanchions at the corners of the streets. The clang of trolleys and rumble of carts on the asphalt and shouts from neighbor to neighbor out tenement windows rang between the buildings. Carsie covered her nose with both hands against the stench of horse dung and garbage and sweat, and yearned for two more hands to cover her ears. What a different place America was, and so dark—its people and buildings and all that happened on the street, every swath of it shades of rust and brown and gray and black. There was no green, little blue.

She kept one eye on Shalva, so not to lose her in the crowd, and the other on Lilia, for the same reason. Silently she mouthed the words, "Dressmaking is one of the most highly skilled trades for women…the other being—"

Shalva turned. "Take off your coats or you'll go faint from heat stroke. Here, I'll carry them." She darted left and right through the throngs of people.

Words in Carsie's head struggled down to the back of her tongue. "Masses of feathers … occasionally complete stuffed birds for those who can afford them," she mumbled, quoting from memory passages in their fashion magazine. "Or decorated with ribbons and artificial…"

Shalva called over her shoulder, "How long did you travel to get here?"

Carsie thought. How long *had* it been? "It…ah…a very long time, it seems."

"Since December," Lilia said. "We started from Lucava in December, after Mama and Papa were killed, but we had to stop when I got sick."

Carsie pulled Lilia up beside her, giving her arm a squeeze. "Yes, she had grippe for a while, but she's fine now."

Shalva turned, taking Lilia's chin in her hand. Her eyes narrowed. "Is that all it was? Grippe?"

"Oh, yes," Lilia said. "A bit of grippe. We stopped in Trusheny while I rested. After that we went on."

"We got on a freighter at the end of May, and here we are." Carsie wiped her forehead with the edge of her sleeve. "New York is very warm, isn't it?"

"It is very warm now, but it'll be very cold this winter."

"Cold, like Russian cold?" Lilia asked.

"Colder, I think. And not as pretty."

"I never thought Lucava was a pretty place," Carsie mused.

"But after a while, when you think back on it," Shalva said, "you will."

"No." Carsie frowned. "I would like to forget Lucava altogether. And I'm not even sure it exists anymore."

The three of them walked on, single file through the crowd.

Carsie began again, mumbling to herself, "Violet and crepe de Chine, trimmed in velvet…Who is the girl in the elegant gown?" she whispered. "I can make you look like a peacock…a rustle of silk petticoats…"

From the stoop of the tenement building where Chaskel Grinberg sat, he saw two girls close behind Shalva, the three of them scuttling up Bowery Street. His stomach tightened. He knew Shalva had gone to the shelter and he had hoped for an adult or two behind her when she returned, real help instead of little burdens. Still, the older girl looked to be about Shalva's age although…He sighed. The same age, maybe, but not as sturdy as his Shalva, that he could see, and not strong enough to work.

Velvel Kagan adjusted his derby hat when he spotted

Shalva working her way through the crowd with the girls behind her. He poked Moishe and pointed. "We got company, looks like. Wonder where *they're* going to sleep?"

Moishe watched his wife approach, but said nothing.

Shalva pushed Carsie and Lilia ahead of her, up the stairs to the top step. "Moishe, these are our nieces, Carsie and Lilia—Reuven's children."

Moishe blinked and frowned. "Reuven's *children?* But… where is Reuven? And Yona?"

Lilia hung her head. Carsie stared at the throng swarming Bowery Street.

Shalva bit her lip. "I am sorry, Moishe. The Cossacks got them."

Chaskel Grinberg rocked back and forth in place, moaning, "*Oy vey, oy vey iz mir.*" Woe is me. Behind his *davening* he smiled inside. So then, the girls were orphaned. Tonight Shalva would feed them crusts from the stale brown bread on her table and tomorrow he could take them around to the orphans' asylum.

Moishe looked at Carsie. "Let me see you." Yes, he thought, she was certainly old enough to work, as was the smaller girl, but the little one had an eye problem. Yet if they made half the money Shalva brought home, life could be quite comfortable. Reuven had been a fool to stay in Russia—The Voice of the Pale, he'd called himself. Well, the Czar had silenced the voice and little wonder. He and Selig had known to fear the Cossacks, but Reuven knew only his passion. That passion had gotten him killed and driven these little wage-earners to Moishe's doorstep.

Moishe checked the clock across the street in front of Franck's. "Shalva," he reminded, "you'll be late for work."

"Yes, I need to go," she said. "Come, girls. Let me show you our room."

Moishe smiled up at Carsie. "You are as beautiful as I remember your mother. Welcome to America, my daughters."

They followed Shalva into a hot, dark hallway that led, at

its other end, to a rusty water pump outside. Shalva pointed. "The toilets are out there. You'll have to come down to use them. Whenever you go that way, take a pitcher and bring back some water."

She guided them to a narrow stairway caked in layers of mud, and they climbed two flights to the third floor. Shalva pushed open the door. Carsie led Lilia into the room they would all share, a blast of stifling heat snatching her breath away. Dust motes danced in the afternoon sun. Carsie handed Lilia to the chair by the window, unpacked the food boxes, handing the remains to Shalva: a loaf of bread, two tins of beans, some sardines, and three oranges. Hungrily, Shalva sliced off a wedge of bread, laid some sardines on top and bit into her sandwich.

"Put the basket under the bed," she pointed while she chewed. "Heat up some beans for your supper. Do you mind if I have an orange?"

"Go ahead," Carsie said. "The food is yours now."

Shalva studied her out of the corner of one eye. "Yeh. Thanks. So, how did you do, getting through Immigration?"

"We did fine. We had help." Carsie stared out the window at the tumult of people on the street below.

"Help?"

"Some people we met on the ship—they brought us through as their daughters."

"Where are they, these people who claimed you as their daughters? Why didn't you stay with them?"

"Because they didn't really want two daughters."

"We ran!" Lilia giggled.

"Yes," Carsie nodded. "We ran away."

"And how did you find the Hebrew shelter?"

Carsie shrugged. "They found us. From our coats. A man in a carriage saw us running. There was an Immigration officer chasing us, because…because, as I said, the people that helped us through Immigration wanted to take us to Sh… Sk…Scheck…Schenectady with them."

"So, a man from the shelter came along in a carriage and spotted the two of you running, and you had yellow armbands on your coats."

"Yes, I suppose so. He pulled us up into his carriage, and we trotted away."

"It wasn't the first time we've run." Lilia said. "I'm good at running."

"Why didn't you want to stay with the couple from the ship? The ones who wanted you to go with them?"

"They wanted us to work for them," Carsie said.

Shalva sniffed. "It's all the same here in America, Carsie. You must work for someone—the only difference is who you work for. You might have been better off with the people in Shk...in...anyplace other than here."

MOISHE AKSELROD watched Shalva and the girls climb the stairs. "Shalva can get the older one a job with Melnick," he said. "The little one...that might be harder. Maybe she could sell newspapers or something."

"I'll take them both to the orphanage in the morning," Chaskel Grinberg said. "Shalva doesn't need the burden."

"The girls stay, Chaskel," Moishe said. "They are my brother's girls. My family. Mine. You won't take my family from me."

"Oh, no?" Grinberg stood. "My Shalva is the one who will worry over them, mother them."

"She is *my* Shalva now, and those girls are my daughters."

"Then act like it, Moishe. Help her with her load. A good husband gets a job, to support his family."

"Jobs are hard to come by, Grinberg. If you're so crazy for Shalva to have help, you help her."

"My feet, Moishe, my feet. I cannot stand, I cannot walk. You know that. You let Shalva work while you hang around with that worthless Monk Eastman."

"Eastman is a gentleman. More than I can say for any of us."

Velvel Kagan chuckled, threw aside his toothpick and

shambled down the stairs. "See youse later," he mumbled. "At the hall."

Grinberg waved Kagan away. "You're afraid to get your hands dirty, Moishe. You think you're better than work."

"You're not the only one who can't work on his feet, old man. Don't forget I wrenched my back slinging luggage at the hotel."

"Faw. You hurt your back. Go get a job, fart knuckle. A real job. And don't come back until you do."

Moishe stood, dusted off his pants and leaned down to whisper in Chaskel Grinberg's ear.

Grinberg fanned the air with his hand, his face contorted with hate. "*Shtick dreck*," he yelled. Piece of shit.

Moishe danced away, grinning. He turned the corner off Mulberry Street into the crooked alley called The Bend. Ruby Swink waited amid the boozers and thieves and garbage. She was good at her job. Being good meant being fast; Ruby could accommodate seven or eight men in a night. She knew what made them angry, what made them horny.

Angry with his father-in-law for suggesting he was lazy, and with his brother Reuven for not abandoning his ideals and his family to come to America, Moishe saw Ruby Swink waiting to comfort him.

She pulled him under a wood staircase where a pile of dirty rags sufficed for a crib, and there she laid back, gathered up her filthy skirts and smiled a tobacco-stained smile.

"Talk to me, baby," she croaked in a whiskey-soaked whisper. "Tell me what you want…why'd you come to see Ruby?"

He unbuttoned the top of his trousers and slid his hand inside the top of her dress. She pushed away his pants and looked at his penis. "Quarter more," she said.

"What for?"

"For this, Jew boy. Micks and wops ain't fixed like this. This costs extra. How bad do you want me?"

"After," he said. "I'll give you another quarter after I'm done."

"Now."

"You whore," Moishe mumbled, nuzzling Ruby's neck. He moved his hand between her legs. "Come on, let me in!" Moishe pushed inside her.

She pumped against him, insistent, hurrying him. He finished and rolled off. She wiped his genitals dry with a dirty rag and threw it back in the pile before she gave him another tobacco-stained grin. "Move," she said, seeing a man in the alley behind him. "I'll have that quarter and you get lost. I'm keeping another customer waiting."

"I'm not done," Moishe said. "I'll give you a quarter to put your mouth on me."

"Yeh, sure you're done," Ruby said. "You want a woman to put her mouth on you, you got to give her some reason other than a quarter. Every girl wants a man to like her, tell her things. I don't just go doing stuff to please you boys—I have my own kind of honor." She shoved Moishe away. "Forget the quarter, just take off."

OSHER MELNICK had fought all day with his wife, who yearned to go to Coney Island, where, she had heard, they showed a man who was tattooed head to foot, a woman with the head and arms of a spider, and a hunchback who could give you good luck. Melnick told her she had work to do; there was no taking time off for nonsense. He listened to her whine while he looked over the coats Shalva Akselrod had finished the night before. There were usually problems with Shalva's work, and he'd found plenty of mistakes in this batch. More than he'd seen in the coats she'd brought him before. Here, a neglected basting thread left on a coat sleeve, there, irregular stitches that would tear out when a lady pulled on the garment, a sleeve lining twisted where it was felled...

"...cooler out there, next to the water," his wife said.

Melnick threw the coats aside and kicked a chair. "We have work, I said."

His wife moved away from the ironing board where Melnick steamed a sleeve, trying to straighten the lining.

"Damn that girl!" Melnick yanked the coat off his sleeve board. "Another twisted lining. She *does not* pay attention to what she is doing."

"Perhaps if you gave her a day off to rest she would be better," his wife suggested.

"We make coats, Varda. The selling season is coming, along with winter. We'll rest at *Rosh Hashanah.*"

"But that's in September—Coney Island will be closed!"

"And after the holidays the work drops off. What do we do for money then?"

She wiped a lock of hair out of her face and a tear off her cheek. "The heat, Osher, the heat—I cannot breathe."

Melnick shrugged and returned to his pressing. He would dock Shalva Akselrod ten cents apiece for these coats—two with the sleeve linings sewn in askew and a third with a seam so poorly sewn that he had to wonder whether the girl watched what she did with her hands at all. Every night, after she settled in the front room to finish the coats, he could almost see her mind wander. She daydreamed—sometimes so far gone only a slap brought her around.

Besides, getting rough with Shalva made it easier to listen to Varda's whining. He kept her around to take the blows he wished on his wife, and Shalva would never quit. She needed the job. Her invalid father depended on her, and her lazy husband ran with Monk Eastman. Melnick wondered how long she would last before she fell victim to one of the illnesses circulating on the Lower East Side—jaundice or trench mouth from her diet, or French pox brought home by that lout she had married.

AFTER ZIRL Bakhtin left Trusheny, the *shtetl* used Max Siegel's bar as its post office. For two years Siegel worked at being both bartender and postmaster, and at healing his body. Although his feet and legs strengthened he found that his ache for Carsie Akselrod persisted. He cherished the ache, held it to him at night. He hated the ache during the day and pushed it away while he worked or exercised his legs. He knew that the only thing he could do to satisfy it would take even more time. Losing toes to the frostbite hadn't helped. Standing was still difficult, let alone walking any distance.

SHALVA ROUSED Carsie and Lilia after daybreak the following morning. She laid out bread and sardines for their breakfast from the food boxes Carsie had given her when they arrived. Already the heat in the tenement hung in the air. Selig Akselrod and Velvel Kagan snored on their mattresses on the floor in the two far corners of the room, their bodies slick with sweat. Outside, peddlers called out what they offered for the day: fish, ice, pickles. The first streetcar of the morning rumbled up Bowery toward the mansions of Washington Square. Women reeled out lines of laundry to dry over the steamy streets.

"We are going to visit a friend of mine this morning," Shalva whispered. "She is ill. I'll take her one of these oranges, if that's all right."

Carsie nodded. "The food is yours, I said. What ails your friend?"

"She has ague—chills and fever—and she cannot get well. I used to work with her, making coats, but she is too ill to work any more."

"Can we catch ague?"

"No—it is a kind of malaria. When she lived in Italy she was bitten by some kind of a beast they have there that gave her the disease." Shalva took a fresh bottle of Mrs. Winslow's tonic from a shelf over the table and tucked it into her handbag.

"Bitten by a beast?" Lilia gasped. "What kind of beast is it that bites and makes you ill?"

"She didn't notice when it was she got bitten, so it must have been something small. An ant or some such."

"Oh, yes," Lilia nodded. "I know about..."

Carsie prodded her from behind and put a finger to her lips.

Shalva pinned on her fichu and set her hat. "Carsie," she said, "how old are you?"

"Fourteen. But Lilia, you're ten now—you've had a birthday and we forgot all about it. Why do you ask, Shalva? How old are you?"

"Fourteen—I thought we looked about the same age, that's all."

"I'm ten?" Lilia squealed.

"Ssssh! Let's go." Shalva held the door.

THEY CROSSED the Bowery, turning south and west. The jabber of Yiddish gave way to the supple sounds of Italian. They entered a large tenement house from its Mott Street side and walked along a wide hallway lit only by windows at each end. Water dripped from a tap at the near end of the hall, pooling in a rusty pond that had rotted the surrounding floor boards and wall.

Three children in calico rag diapers scuttled into an open door when they saw Shalva and the girls approach. Behind the next door a man and woman yelled at one another and at the far end a woman dressed only in her underwear, her heavy breasts falling to her waist, stared numbly at the three of them walking to the stairwell where a door stood open on a foul-smelling common latrine.

Carsie spotted a pool of vomit in the doorway and gathered her skirts to avoid the mess. She breathed through her mouth to keep from gagging. An old woman scrubbed the threshold clean, creating a bright spot on the filthy floor. *Besser tsu shtarben shtai'endik aider tsu leben oif di k'ni*, Carsie reflected. Better you should die upright than live on your knees. Not in Lucava or Trusheny or on the train or even when they shared the steerage quarters on the freighter had she smelled such a stench. This was more than poverty. Life had battered these people so often they could not live any other way.

"What a difference a few good clothes would make…" Carsie mumbled. "…a gown of reticella trimmed in grosgrain…a day dress of wincey gaily decorated…"

They climbed the stairs to the second floor. Three rooms along one side revealed men and women sewing—the men on machines, women sewing buttons and making buttonholes.

She glanced behind her and thought she recognized the faintly-lit silhouette of Moishe Akselrod in his derby. She remembered he was not in bed when they left. He had not come in the night before.

A young man stood in a doorway, eating bread with no butter and he looked…no, he reminded her vaguely…no, he looked *exactly* like Louis Levy.

"You are imagining things, Carsie," she breathed. "This place is hell. It would make anyone doubt their sanity. I will never live in a place this bad. Never."

— 16 —

MONK EASTMAN stood in the open doorway of Silver Dollar Smith's saloon on Essex Street. He held a large wooden club he used to keep order around the Tenth Ward; his reputation had been built on it. Every time he hit someone, he cut a new notch, and the bat bore forty-nine notches. His merit as a brawler had spread to Tammany Hall, where the politicians found value in Eastman's gang. Especially during elections. His followers numbered more than a thousand, including Moishe and Selig Akselrod and Velvel Kagan. His boys were called the Allen Street Cadets because they used the brothels along Allen Street as their meeting places.

Eastman surveyed the main room of the bar: quiet. The morning barman wiped away the residue of last night's excesses while Moishe Akselrod slept in a chair, his derby hat tipped over his eyes. Eastman swung the club like a ball bat, bringing it down with a whack on a table near the chair where Akselrod slept.

Moishe jumped, his hat rolling along the floor.

"Go home, champ," Eastman said. "Ain't no good, sleeping in a chair like that. Give you back problems."

"I already got back problems, a wife that's a pain in the ass."

"Don't care," Eastman growled. "You can't sleep here. Straighten out those problems at home—you know how to do that, don't you?" Slapping the club against his palm, Eastman took another swipe at the air near Moishe's shoulder. Moishe ducked. Eastman chuckled and patted him on the back. "Fix it. You're a man—fix it so's you can sleep in your own bed, fer Crissakes. Take off."

Moishe knocked sawdust and bits of peanut shell off his hat and reluctantly headed for the Bowery, trotting the few cross-town blocks to the tenement room he shared with his wife, brother, boarder, and now his two nieces. His father-in-law wouldn't gimp out to the front stoop for another hour or so. Moishe had been up until dawn, collecting the night's take from the pimps at each of Eastman's brothels. He took off his shirt, lowered his suspenders and settled on the bed, his hat once again cocked over his eyes to block the morning light. He hoped Shalva had gone to do her marketing so he could get some sleep.

SHALVA SMILED to herself as they walked back to the room on Bowery Street. Carsie had seen the squalor, and she didn't like what she saw. This life scares Carsie, she thought. And well it should. She'll like it less when I am through teaching her about America. She will think it the hell I do.

They returned to the tenement near noon. Summer heat and noise from the street and the surrounding buildings flooded through the open windows at the front of their room. Shalva had not done any marketing, preferring to eat the food Carsie brought, hoping to use the rent money Velvel Kagan paid to buy a new pair of shoes. When the three of them entered the room, Moishe stirred.

Shalva glanced at her husband from her chair near the right window, shaking her head in quiet defiance. She bent her head and began marking coats for the labels. Carsie stood at her elbow watching. Lilia sat at the table a few feet away.

Carsie moved to the pile of coats and took up a stick of tailor's chalk. She marked the inside back collar as Shalva had done and marked another. Shalva checked Carsie's work and nodded.

Moishe studied Carsie and Lilia from beneath the brim of his derby hat. Pretty enough, he thought. Especially the younger one, despite her eyes. Too bad the girls didn't appreciate what they had now—their last hours before they went to work for the rest of their lives. He sat up, pushed the derby to the back of his head and scratched his chest.

Shalva threaded a needle to set in a sleeve lining. "Did you look for a job?"

Moishe swung his feet off the bed. "Yeh, yeh. I got a job, just to shut you and your father up."

"Where are you working?"

"Here and there. Nights again, like last time."

"Doing what?"

He stood and put on his shirt. "This and that."

"Who for?"

"Whoever."

"You didn't really look for a job, did you, Moishe?"

"What's the big deal about a job? Did you bring me a Coca-Cola from the market?"

"I didn't go to the market. Or maybe I should say I did, since you like lies better than the truth."

"Where have you been?"

"To see Alba Riccardi."

"Alba Riccardi? Your wop friend in the Big Flat?"

"Yes. She is very ill—too ill to do for herself, and in this heat I don't know who else will do for her what she cannot."

"You went to the Big Flat? You took my nieces to see that... that pile of garbage?"

Shalva bit off a strand of thread and continued sewing. "You're calling Alba 'garbage'?"

"I'm calling the place garbage. In heaven's name, Shalva, you belong over here, on this side of Bowery. Don't go over there—it's trouble of too many kinds."

"We didn't get into any trouble, Uncle Moishe," Carsie said. "We were fine."

He turned to the girls. "Carsie, tonight you go to Melnick's with your Aunt Shalva. To do what she did."

Shalva's head snapped around. "Oh? And what will I be doing, then, after today?"

"Velvel Kagan is working out as a boarder, isn't he? Maybe we can take in more."

Shalva reached behind her, under the bed and brought out a bottle of Mrs. Winslow's Soothing Syrup.

"No, Shalva. No tonic!" Moishe grabbed at the bottle.

She ducked away from his grasp, drank, recapped the bottle and put her arms around Moishe's neck, nuzzling her nose in his chest.

"Yeh," he sneered, pushing her away. "Lap up your hooch if it makes you feel better." A wife, he thought. What had he been thinking when he first spotted Shalva's pretty little body? Oh, he knew what. He hadn't been thinking at all.

"In this life," Shalva sighed, "Mrs. Winslow is the only one who makes me feel better." She turned to Carsie. "Now, when you tack down the lining at the bottom of the sleeve, it's called felling...."

OSHER MELNICK had new problems. She had brought in her niece, Carsie, to take her place, saying she had trained the girl as his new finisher.

Oy veh, Melnick thought. I know plenty of girls who need a job—do I want to trade one bad feller for another one? Does this girl even *know* how to fell a decent sleeve? Shalva's work was marginal, but her redemption had been her submission—whatever frustration had kindled with Varda during the day he could vent on her that evening. He would give Carsie Akselrod a try, and unless she had the same agreeable compliance and a minimum of skill she would find herself back on Canal Street looking for work the following day.

IN THE three months from the end of June to late September, three months when the heat rose and broke twice more, the Akselrod clan—all but Shalva's father—took two rooms in a tenement house on Orchard Street. Now they had space for more nickel-a-night boarders; and Moishe had made good on the threat he had whispered to Chaskel Grinberg the night

Carsie and Lilia arrived. He had taken Shalva away from her father.

The extra floor space filled quickly as immigrants continued to flood New York City. Nowhere in the world were so many people crowded together in thirty-odd blocks as they were in the Tenth Ward, and all of the Akselrod's boarders counted themselves lucky to have found floor space, though they shared the floor in shifts—some of them sleeping while the others worked or roamed the crowded streets waiting for their chance to use the same fragment of the room.

Since Shalva's trip to the Sheltering Society, Carsie and Lilia, Velvel Kagan, and seven new boarders had come to live with them. Thirteen of them shared the two rooms. Shalva cooked and laundered and marketed, and little else. After supper she was too tired to show any interest in Moishe. For his part, Moishe usually took his pleasures at one of Monk Eastman's brothels.

In the same three-month span Carsie found the drift of life on the Lower East Side and settled in. She proved too good a feller for Melnick to abuse. She sewed a seam as deftly as he had as a young man, her sleeve linings hung straight, and she worked fast enough for two Shalva Akselrods. She continued to learn his trade and came to the job willingly, seven nights a week if he could find work enough for her. At first, Shalva was proud of having taught Carsie her trade, but when she saw Melnick favor Carsie while he continued to abuse her, Shalva announced she was leaving. He wasn't surprised, but was in some sense bothered by her departure and in another way relieved.

Melnick had trouble keeping Carsie busy. She pressed the coats whenever his lumbago acted up and learned to operate a sewing machine so he could take a break to rest his back. She ripped and restitched any seam that wasn't perfect and bound a faultless buttonhole. Carsie was Melnick's gift from heaven. He couldn't risk losing her, and most frustrating, she had befriended his wife.

He had a problem around money, too. Carsie cost him more than Shalva had. Her work was good—he had no reason to dock her pay—and it put him in a financial bind. Another of the coat makers had talked to him about consolidating their businesses, moving them out of the house and uptown to a factory building. And with the end of September the Jewish holidays had come. The selling season slowed.

While Carsie worked, Lilia navigated the Tenth Ward by herself, developing an uncanny skill for finding her way around by smell and sound and feel. Moishe found a job for her not long after the girls arrived, carrying hats for the Brooklyn milliners who had discovered that a pedestrian could weave through the tangle of Lower East Side immigrants and peddlers faster than a wagon could. The milliners paid Lilia a nickel a trip to carry a load from the foot of Division Street up Bowery past store-front synagogues and mill-end vendors and fruit stands, her head bobbing left or right of her high stacks of round hatboxes, to Houston Street, where she met a wagon that took the load on to Fifth Avenue.

For her first few trips two of Monk Eastman's men escorted her. That kind of bodyguard put everyone in the ward on notice: give Lilia Akselrod any trouble and you invited Monk Eastman's club when you least expected it.

Lilia, too, enjoyed what she did for money. She loved trundling back and forth on Bowery in the warm weather, trusted to fend for herself. Her seven-block trip took the better part of a morning or an afternoon, and she could make two trips a day if she applied herself and the hats were there to carry.

On the Sunday night before *Rosh Hashanah,* while she chopped potatoes for latkes, Shalva bit into a slice of apple. Abruptly she stopped chewing, feeling something give way in her mouth. She probed the right side of her jaw with her tongue. Pain shot to the top of her head. She leaned over the sink and cupped her hand. Two teeth dropped into her palm. Her gum bled freely where the teeth had come out. She stared at the teeth she held and the pool of blood spreading in the bottom of the sink, trying to clear her mind. A knot of fear tightened in her stomach.

She had attributed her unrelenting headaches to the punch Osher Melnick delivered in mid-June, but the pain on the right side of her face had not dissipated and her cheekbone throbbed on days when the weather was humid.

Alone in the flat, she lay down on the bed and groped for her bottle of Mrs. Winslow's Soothing Syrup. When she sipped at the tonic a sting traveled from her gums up under her eye. After that, she felt nothing. No pain, no stinging, no headache. She took another sip and leaned back on the pillow.

THE CONSTANT undercurrent of sewing machines humming in the tenements had quieted for the day. Weary after a night's work at Melnick's, Carsie climbed the dark staircase to the third floor. She heard only the squeals of children playing. *Odd*, she thought, *it neared midnight—the Petrow children were still awake?* The door to the Petrow flat stood open.

"Mrs. Petrow?" Carsie called from the doorway.

"Yes? Who calls?"

"Carsie Akselrod, from across the hall. Is everything all right?"

Pearl Petrow came to the door holding a nursing baby to her breast. "Oh, hello, Carsie. Everything is fine. I'm just too busy with the new one to put the others to bed right now. Are the children bothering you with their noise?"

Carsie smiled. "No, no bother at all. I was just coming in from work and thought perhaps…you were ill or something."

Pearl clasped the baby to her naked breast. "Never better, Carsie. I was born to bear babies—they are my salvation. I never felt better in my life."

SHALVA SLUMPED half-off the bed, unconscious, a pool of dried blood on the floor beneath her head. Near her limp fingers, an open bottle of Mrs. Winslow's syrup lay on its side, seeping into the mattress in a thick brown blot.

Carsie dropped her bag. She took her aunt by the shoulders and helped her back onto the pillow. Shalva's eyes fluttered. Carsie felt for a fever, but Shalva's head and hands were cold rather than warm, her face so pale that blue veins showed around her eyes. *The tonic had finally done its worst,* Carsie thought. *Shalva must stop using it, or they would lose her.* "What is it, Shalva? Where do you hurt?"

"Give me my tonic," she moaned.

"It spilled into the mattress. There's nothing left."

Shalva struggled to sit up. "There's another bottle in a box under the bed."

"You don't need tonic right now. You need help—a doctor."

Shalva's arms hung listless, her head lolled from side to side. Carsie checked her eyes; the pupils had closed to the size of a dressmaker's pin. Shalva gasped, her breathing shallow. She slumped back on the pillow. Carsie took a hand mirror from the dresser and held it under Shalva's nose as she had seen the apothecary in Trusheny do when Lilia was ill. Shalva was alive; she slept. Carsie sighed with relief and whispered, "Remember well, remember right. Goodnight, goodnight... goodnight, goodnight."

Moishe came into the room and shed his jacket. He looked at his wife, snorted, and shook his head.

Carsie laid a hand on Shalva's shoulder. *"Zis chaloymes..."* Sweet dreams.

— 17 —

CARSIE STOOD at the kitchen sink the following morning, the first morning of *Rosh Hashanah*. She tied on Shalva's apron, arranged latkes in a pan to warm, filled the coffee pot with water, lifted it from the sink to the stove, and threw kindling into the firebox. Last night's embers ignited.

While the coffee water came to a boil she twisted her long hair in a loose knot on the back of her neck, as Varda Melnick had taught her to do, and stared into the mirror over the sink. Her face had lengthened during the summer, and her body had grown curves.

It had been almost a year, Carsie thought, since that deadly night in Lucava. She tried to recall her father's eyes without terror in them, ached to remember how it felt when she and Lilia sat in front of the cook stove in the kitchen while Papa read to them, and yearned to taste Mama's turnip latkes once more. She tried to see Valentin Mikheladze's smile and wondered for the hundredth time about Max Siegel's past. All those images had faded. She could scarcely remember her mother's face, yet that night—she could remember everything about that night....

Now she had family again, people to care for, and another kind of life. She and Lilia no longer wore their hair in braids like school girls. She took delight in making coats, and last week she had bought a hat with part of her pay—a modest black straw adorned with a large ribbon bow. Even before she laid down her quarter for that hat she knew more hats would follow, grander hats. The hats spoke to her—beckoned.

Lilia stirred.

"*Gut yontiff,* sleepyhead," Carsie smiled. "It's a fine day today, and no work."

Lilia stretched and yawned. "What then?"

"What then, what?"

"What do we do, if we don't work today?"

Moishe sat up in bed and belched. "This afternoon we walk across the Brooklyn Bridge," he said. "We cast our sins into the water."

The sun broke across an unusually quiet Tenth Ward, washing down Orchard Street.

Shalva stood in the doorway, clutching at her dressing gown, watching the boarders in her kitchen, all of them but Velvel Kagan, each wishing the others *Shanah Tovah* and *Gut Yontiff*—Good Year—while they ate warm latkes dabbed with applesauce.

"*Guten morgen. Shanah Tovah.*" Shalva managed a weak smile. "I'm not walking on the bridge with you today. I'll stay and rest." She felt her jaw where the teeth had fallen out.

Carsie paused. "You need the rest, Aunt Shalva, but a walk would do you good, too."

Shalva scanned the kitchen, then looked to Carsie. "Have you seen my tonic bottle, dearest? I know I had one that was open."

"Do you not remember last night? You were very...you scared me. I thought you were dying."

Moishe poured coffee for the boarders and a cup for himself. "Give her the tonic. She'll drink it while we're out this afternoon anyway." He went to the front room.

Carsie shook her head. "Aunt Shalva, that tonic—I've seen what it does to you."

"Let her drink herself to death, so what?" Moishe called over his shoulder.

Shalva clenched her fists at her sides. "I do not need to defend this to you, Moishe. Mrs. Winslow's is sold at the druggist's—it's for babies! What could it hurt if it's for babies?"

"You are not a baby, Shalva!" Moishe yelled. "Though you sure acted like one when you quit that job—"

"Melnick called me a piece of shit," she said, her lower lip trembling. "When I brought him the coats. When he found mistakes."

Moishe sat in her chair by the window. "Maybe he was right, Shalva."

Carsie looked away. "He didn't mean it, Shalva. He has a short temper, is all. He and his wife argue—you've seen it." Was this part of being married, the arguing? She tired of hearing it, and if she married—if she *ever* married—she would not argue. She removed the apron and hung it on its peg. "Moishe, Shalva needs to rest today. Perhaps some fresh air this afternoon, but she's weak. We'll walk the bridge while she stays here." She looked at Shalva. "But I'll take the bottles of tonic with us and I'll throw them in the river, because today we cast our sins into the water."

Shalva clutched the doorframe. "No! The tonic helps with my menstrual cramps, and it helps...when Moishe doesn't come home at night. I sip at Mrs. Winslow's to sleep, rather than sitting up worrying about whether I am a widow, or if he has found someone else."

"Or to feel better," Moishe called from the front room.

"To feel better when my husband comes home stinking of fornication and a guilty conscience," Shalva shouted.

Carsie looked at her aunt. "Shalva, I will throw the bottles away this afternoon."

"Then I will buy more."

"Not today. The druggist is closed today."

Shalva's face reddened, veins pulsed in her temples. "The day I collected you and Lilia at the Sheltering Society I knew it was a mistake." She slammed her hand down on the table, her face wet with tears. "This is how you thank me for all I have done."

"It is, yes. And someday you will thank me, too."

Shalva stood, trembling. "If you throw those bottles in

the East River, you are not my *mishpocha*, Carsie, and I am not yours. If you do that, you take your sister and go. I gave you my job and my board. But if you dump that tonic, you throw more away than you know."

While she drank her tea, Carsie stood at a window in the front room watching a constant stream of Jews walk reverently down the Bowery toward the Brooklyn Bridge, then she and Lilia ducked behind the dressing curtain. They had saved what they could in the last three months for the clothes they would wear this morning—new stockings and modest corsets, a petticoat for Carsie and a new white voile shirtwaist, while Lilia pulled on a dress of powder blue trimmed in white.

Carsie tied Lilia's hair back with a white ribbon bow and stepped out to the mirror to pin on her new black straw hat. A few of the boarders remarked on how lovely the girls looked in their new clothes, while Moishe Akselrod's only response was to raise an eyebrow.

His brother's reaction was quite different. Selig had seen two girls duck behind the drape, but what reappeared, ten minutes later was, to Selig's mind, a pretty child and a beautiful young woman. When Carsie stepped from behind the closet curtain Selig caught his breath. Her white shirtwaist set off her olive skin and brunette hair, and showed off her figure. The black skirt was properly modest, and her hat shaded her mysterious, sad eyes. How had he not noticed her, living in the same two rooms for the last three months? His head swam.

Nine from the Akselrod's flat joined the hundreds from the Tenth Ward who walked to the bridge that afternoon, a crowd that streamed hourly from Bowery and Allen to Centre Street and onto the bridge walkway. The day was warm; the breeze seemed to carry everyone's good spirits.

Selig matched his pace to Moishe's. "How old did you tell me Carsie is?"

Moishe smiled to himself. *Selig—interested in Carsie?* He

could keep her in the family, with no thought to a dowry. "Seventeen, I think," he lied. "Turning out nice, isn't she? Smart one, that. Smarter than to get involved with that damn tonic of Shalva's. More to the point, so far as I'm concerned, she earns more money than Shalva ever could. You'd do well to marry Carsie, Selig."

Today, Selig thought the same. Part of it was the fine weather, part of it Carsie's new clothes. And he had begun to tire of Monk Eastman's demands on his time—the ragged hours, Eastman's insistence on his being available without notice and for strange errands. Too, Eastman had begun to recruit outside the Tenth Ward to keep the gang's numbers strong—larger than the rival gang of Paul Kelly. The non-Jews in Eastman's retinue grew daily. It was time to leave Eastman, to get a job and settle down.

A loose-jointed boy walked toward them—all hands and feet, his head lolling forward and back as though he danced to a tune no one else could hear. Carsie tapped the boy on his shoulder and spoke to him. Selig stepped forward, behind the girls.

"...THOUGHT WE'D never see you again," Carsie said.

Lilia beamed at the boy. "I knew we'd find you, Louis. Knew it. Do you like my dress?"

"Yeh, I'm happy to see you, too. So...happy." Louis smiled a sloppy smile at the girls. He wore a white shirt, its sleeves rolled to his elbows, and pants not long enough to reach his ankles. He hid his hands behind his back, but not in time. His fingernails were dirty, his knuckles scabbed. He rubbed the toe of a government-issue shoe against the back of his pant leg.

Carsie and Selig stared at him for too long, not saying anything.

Lilia took his hand. "Walk with us. It's nice today, isn't it?"

"Yeh, I suppose..." He wobbled and stopped to look around. "Can I sit down?"

"Louis," Lilia frowned. "What's wrong? Why do you want to sit?"

"I don't...I don't feel well. Maybe it's the bridge—the water. It makes me dizzy."

"Then let's go back to land," Lilia said. "I'll show you the parts of town I know best. You can walk me home."

"I'd like that, Lilia. If you get me off this bridge, I'll walk with you anywhere you want to go."

Lilia smiled up at him and took his rough hand. "I know you will, Louis. I've been waiting..."

Midway across the bridge Carsie removed the bottles of Mrs. Winslow's Soothing Syrup from her bag. She looked left and right, realizing she could not throw them into the river from the walkway as she had promised Shalva she would. To fling the bottles either direction they might land on the roadway below—or worse, hit someone driving by in a carriage. She would pour the contents in the gutter when they returned to the ward, she decided, and throw the empty bottles away later.

She looked at Selig Akselrod. "He's a friend of ours, from the freighter we took over."

"I figured," Akselrod said.

"Seems to like Lilia."

"Yeh. Seems to."

Carsie turned, walking back the way they had come. Selig strolled along beside her. "Mind if I walk with you?"

"No, Uncle Selig. That's fine." She studied him out the corner of one eye. He was young still, and handsome after a fashion. Hollow cheeks, happy eyes, square shoulders, taller than Papa. Why hadn't he married? Papa had, and Moishe. Why not Selig?

"I can't throw Shalva's bottles from here," Carsie said. "I'll get rid of them before we get back to Orchard Street, though. She shouldn't drink that stuff." She looked at the city. *Someday, I shall live farther up*, she thought. *Up where the smell is different, maybe.* "I don't know where we'll live now that Shalva wants us out."

"Shalva will have forgotten what she said this morning by the time we get back. You won't have to leave."

Carsie stubbed her toe on a board in the walkway and grabbed for Selig's arm to steady herself. He tucked her hand in the crook of his right elbow, looking sidelong at her.

"Uncle Selig, may I ask——"

"No you may not. Not until you stop calling me 'Uncle Selig'."

They walked on in comfortable silence. Carsie began again. "Do you remember Papa at all?"

Selig watched the city skyline grow larger as they neared Manhattan. This was not the conversation he had hoped to have with Carsie. "He was ten years older. When he married your mother I was nine. I don't remember much about him at all….I was off doing things younger boys did. And then they—he and your mother—left Kiev for Lucava. After that, Moishe and I came to America and we never wrote except to tell him when Moishe and Shalva married."

She looked at him from under the brim of her hat. "And you? Why have you not married?"

Selig shrugged. "Too busy, too tired. Who would marry a man like me?"

"You are busy, always gone. What do you do, Uncle Selig?"

"It's hard to explain. I run odd jobs for someone and he takes care of his crew by, well, seeing that they—you know—do better than some around the ward. Carsie, could you *please* not call me Uncle Selig?"

"But you *are* my Uncle Selig."

He covered her hand with his own. "Yes, but…I was hoping you might try to think of me as someone other than an uncle."

LOUIS AND Lilia sat on a bench at the foot of the pedestrian walkway. He told her about the men who sold him to the Merchant Marines, but while he described his second awful experience at sea he closed his eyes and fell asleep, dozing in the warm afternoon sun. Lilia lifted his hand close to her face, studying his fingers, his weathered arm, the pallid color beneath his chapped skin. She smelled dirt on his skin, and behind that a musty odor and the scent of Mr. Hertz's fruit stand. "Pears," she said.

Louis roused. "Hmmm?"

"Pears. You smell like Mr. Hertz's fruit stand."

He smiled at her. "I'm glad to see you. Let's not lose track of each other again, okay?"

"No, we won't. Where do you stay, now?"

"There is a hallway on Allen that usually has room when I need to rest. I don't have anything other than these clothes, so I leave nothing behind."

"Louis! What about your uniform?"

"Stolen. All but what I have on—my shoes, my pants and this middy."

"But…the weather will cool now—you'll need a coat. And what do you do for food?"

He hung his head. "I haven't eaten much in the last few months. Soup kitchens, the garbage, what I could steal. And there are days when I can…" He looked at the river. "When I can manage to forget I should eat."

Lilia brightened. "You can stay with us. Aunt Shalva charges two-fifty a week, which is quite reasonable. You get a place to sleep, coffee and bread in the morning, supper at four, a bath and three pieces of laundry a week. Uncle Moishe will find you a job. He found one for me."

Louis glanced down at Lilia, his eyes glittering. He squeezed her hand. "But I am sick, Lilia. I don't know if anything will make me well. I wouldn't be able to hold a job until I felt better, so…how would I pay room and board?"

Lilia thought for a moment. "I'll get a job that pays better than the one I have now. I can pay your board until you get well. When Moishe finds you a job you can pay me back."

A tear fell from his eye, but Lilia could not see it slip down his face.

"Louis? Is that okay?"

"How old are you now, Lilia?"

She smiled. "I'm ten, now. I'll be eleven in January."

He studied her. "Pretty smart for ten."

She giggled. "Smart enough to know we are both thinking the same thing."

WHEN SHALVA announced she was pregnant, Moishe and Selig pushed the bed to an alcove off the kitchen. Shalva went to bed in October, and by the end of November she rose only to use a chamber pot or walk the two blocks to Bowery to care for her father. She did not bother to bathe or groom her hair. She left the boarders' cooking, cleaning, and laundry to Carsie and Lilia, directing what needed to be done from her bed.

The Akselrod's rooms faced toward the East River. When they had taken the flat during the summer, they had thought onshore breezes would keep the place cooler, but the surrounding buildings radiated more heat than breezes could diminish. Autumn was brief that year and insistent winter winds lashed early and hard from the east.

At dusk on December 17, the first day of Chanukah, a cold rain blew through the gaps between the window sashes and the walls of the tenement building.

Carsie packed scraps of cloth around the edges of the window frames to cut the sting of the weather. She crossed the room to cover Shalva, now three months pregnant.

Shalva trembled, eyeing her tonic on the shelf over the stove. "Hand me my bottle."

"No. No more tonight."

"Do it, Carsie."

Stepping to the stove, Carsie tied on an apron and picked potatoes and an onion from a box behind the line of laundry drying in the corner.

"You want me to beg?" Shalva said. "*Please.*"

Moishe rose from the kitchen table, folding an old copy of the *Daily Forward*. "She said, 'No,' Shalva."

Lilia came in, shook icy rain off of both her hat and coat

and hung them on pegs in the hallway. She peered into the front room. "Is Louis here?"

"No." Carsie frowned. "He went out late afternoon. I haven't seen him for awhile."

"Is he getting better, do you think?"

Carsie looked away. Varda Melnick had told her of a Chinaman on Mott Street named Qi Yin who, though it seemed improbable, spoke Yiddish and claimed to cure illnesses without the patient knowing. Though his cure for Shalva had not, so far, worked, Carsie kept buying his infusions, liniments, and fermentations designed to cure Shalva of her opium addiction. She had sought Qi Yin's advice again this morning, when she went out to do her marketing. They talked about Shalva, both of them baffled that she had not miscarried. Then Carsie asked for advice on Louis. His color had gone ashen, she told Qi Yin, most of his hair had fallen out, and his eyes were bloodshot.

"I asked Qi Yin what he thought was making Louis so ill," Carsie told her sister.

"And?"

"He says it sounds to him like liver-fire."

"But, that could be serious. How do you treat liver-fire?"

"Qi Yin says feed him dandelions."

"Carsie, it's winter. All the dandelions are dead. If we don't help Louis soon, I don't know what will happen."

"I pointed that out to him. Qi Yin will sell us a dandelion tonic…but it's expensive."

ON THE first afternoon of Chanukah, Louis Levy stopped in front of Silver Dollar Smith's saloon, fingering the dollar coin in his pants pocket. Just one couldn't hurt, and how it would warm him, that sweet, dark rum he had discovered during his brief tenure with the Merchant Marines. He had needed it then to calm his stomach; now he more than needed it. The mere thought of climbing two flights of stairs to the Akselrod flat exhausted him.

He lay down alongside the door of a storefront synagogue, his energy sapped, and dozed for an hour, protecting a banana he had stolen for Lilia's Chanukah gift. When he wakened he ate the banana himself. Feeling better, he pulled himself up and set off toward Mott to steal something else Lilia might treasure.

Aching with cold he paused at a pushcart of used coats on Bowery Street, fingering a heavy black worsted with a beaver collar. The peddler called over his shoulder, "Three dollars! A good price for such a coat," he said before he turned to another customer. Louis pulled the coat around his shoulders, running his fingers through the beaver fur collar. He put his arms inside the sleeves, buttoned the four buttons, snapped the collar high around his ears and slipped his hands into the pockets. He remembered he needed a Chanukah gift for Lilia. He couldn't think about a coat. But the coat, *this coat,* made him feel invincible. In this coat he could do anything. He inched to the far side of the cart, away from the peddler, stepped into the gutter, took one step and two, and he ran.

The peddler ran after him shouting, "My coat! That kid took my coat—little thief! Stop him!"

Louis knew he ran but could not feel his feet, numb with cold as they hit the cobblestones. His legs buckled, but he ran on as though in a dream, sluggishly, turning the corner off Delancey, stumbling up Eldridge, where he fell against a wall, panting. The thud of his heart beat in his ears, drowning out police whistles that closed fast behind him.

— 19 —

WHEN THE cell door swung open, Aaron Bender saw a familiar face. He frowned. How could this frail, timid boy, the boy who had disappeared in Boston, end up in jail here in New York? The jailer led Louis to a cot and handcuffed him to a ring on the wall. Bender swung into the upper berth, hiding, for the moment, not yet ready to explain to anyone why he was there too.

Louis had seen worse than the inside of the cell where he lay. The jail was not warm, but it was not as cold as the weather outside.

IN THE Akselrod's flat twelve gathered to light the *shamash*— the candle in the middle of the *menorah*. Lilia spun her wooden top while she sang the traditional song, "I Have a Little *Dreidel.*" Moishe tucked a piece of candy in her pocket, and others stepped forward to do the same. The smell of potato latkes filled the air throughout the building.

"I have something for you, too," Carsie whispered. She handed a paper-wrapped parcel to Lilia. "For your first Chanukah in America."

Lilia held the package to her nose, trying to work out how it had been sealed. Peeling back the paper, she pulled out a pair of kidskin gloves. She held them up and gasped, stroking the leather.

Carsie smiled. "Wear them in good health."

"These...these are..." Lilia stroked the delicate leather. "I've never seen anything this luxurious."

"We've worked hard, Lilia. You deserve them."

———

LILIA PINED for Louis. She refused to eat, slept little, lost her enthusiasm for work. Winter's hold on the city that year made her walk from the bridge to Houston Street, uncomfortable on warmer days, unthinkable on colder ones. She stood at the window searching the street below for Louis, or asked at the soup kitchen on Eldridge or at the Sheltering Society whenever she made her way north and south through the Tenth Ward carrying a load of hat boxes.

On a wet day in March, southbound from a Houston Street delivery, she stopped to inquire at the police station on Eldridge, just down the street from the soup kitchen. The police warmed immediately to her sweet face, to the plea in her voice. They checked their records for that first day of Chanukah last year. Yes, he had been there, arrested, they told her, for stealing a coat. He had been sentenced to three months on Blackwell's Island. He was due to be released in a week.

Lilia ate again, and slept, and trotted back and forth between the bridge and Houston Street, carrying her loads of hat boxes. A week later Louis came up beside her as she hurried home from her last round of deliveries.

"I'm sorry I missed Chanukah," he said.

"Louis! You're out! Was it awful? Velvel Kagan told me horrible stories."

Louis took her elbow and stopped. He studied her. She had grown more beautiful in three months—how was it possible? "It was the best thing could have happened to me, Lilia."

"What? Why?"

"Because I'm well now, and I can work. I ate and got warm and…and I didn't drink rum. I'm strong. I did calisthenics while I waited to get out. I have so much to tell you…"

Lilia giggled. "Such as?"

BACK AT the table in the Orchard Street flat Louis laid out the whole tale. "Guess who I shared a cell with at the Eldridge Street police station? Count de Kelemen—from the freighter."

Carsie set a *glozell té* in front of him. "Count de Kelemen?"

"And the Countess too, in the next cell. Imagine—the two of them arrested for cheating people out of their money. Rich folks, they said, not like us. Just the rich ones, people who could afford to lose money and not notice so much. Can you imagine not noticing you had lost some of your money?"

Carsie winced, remembering the hundred-ruble note lost somewhere between Trusheny and the French coast. Still… "rich folks…not like us." Louis's words resounded.

"But listen to this! The police didn't call them by the name de Kelemen. Didn't call them 'Count' and 'Countess' either. The cops called them Mr. and Mrs. Bender. They had come down from Sh…Sk…from upstate," Louis continued. "And they had read about a dance to be held at a grand house on Twenty-third—a house owned by a family named White. So they got themselves invited."

"A ball," Lilia gasped. "The Countess…I mean, Mrs. Bender went to a ball!"

"But they didn't go as Herr Bender and Mrs. Bender," he laughed. "Even with those people they called themselves the Count and Countess de Kelemen. They told everybody they were from Hungary."

Carsie nodded. "To account for the accent, I guess."

"I'll bet you're right—that would work, wouldn't it? There was a splendid orchestra, they said, and a fine dinner of many courses. Count DeKele—uh, Herr Bender presented a note of introduction from Mr. Vanderbilt. *The* Mr. Vanderbilt."

"But, how do the Benders know these people?" Lilia asked.

"The note was forged."

Carsie chuckled. "So, that's why they were on a freighter, rather than on the *Statendam*—they were hiding from someone, I'll bet. They couldn't afford to be spotted."

Lilia stared at him. "They wanted to be somebody other than who they are—other than plain old Russian Jews." She thought a moment. "Poor Miriam de—poor Mrs. Bender."

"Their scheme worked for a while," he said. "But Herr Bender needed more money to pose as a Count, so he borrowed it from his new chums' banks. And they lent it to him without too many questions. After all, the Count and Countess had been introduced by Mr. Astor himself…until the day one of them asked Mr. Vanderbilt…"

"Uh oh," Lilia said. "What happens to them now?"

"They are being deported."

OSHER MELNICK continued to negotiate with the two men who were interested in beginning a company uptown. They sought a silent partner, and Melnick suspected they had tried to hire him only to capture his prize finisher, Carsie Akselrod. But he had heard of their tactics—withholding the first week's wages from employees, claiming it paid for training and supplies. Carsie, he thought, was too good a worker to be treated that way.

Life had improved at Melnick's flat. Varda was happier, and glad to stay home now that she had a friend in Carsie.

For Carsie, the work had become tiresome in its repetition. When she had time, she sewed garments for herself or Lilia. She made day dresses for Varda and nightgowns for Shalva. Their Russian fashion magazine had fallen apart the first summer Carsie and Lilia lived in the tenements, but after they began to work and Shalva took to her bed, pregnant and addicted, they scarcely had time to read.

Carsie browsed *Godey's Lady's Book* for the latest styles; sought fabrics, thread, buttons and lace from pushcart peddlers. She devised her own patterns, cut from yesterday's *Jewish Forward*, and made adjustments until she became as adept at dressmaking as any in the ward. She learned to calculate costs and undercut the other dressmakers in the neighborhood. She lived with a tape measure around her neck.

A FRIDAY in April brought the first warm day of spring. Throngs of Orchard Street's residents tumbled out by eight in the morning, many to the Pig Market on Hester. Carsie joined the stream of people shuffling south. She needed horseradish and cabbage at the market, and if she was lucky she might find fresh bread before the baker ran out. There was enough money from the rent this week to buy eggs and a chicken and perhaps some fish.

Already women sat along the curb selling overripe tomatoes and soft oranges. Two old hags sold stale bread, baked not in loaves, but in the shape of a big wreath. A brawny butcher, sleeves rolled up above his elbows, a clay pipe clamped in his teeth, skinned a goat hanging from a hook. Men in black coats and black hats sat in doorways of the saloons, talking and gesturing as if forever on the point of coming to blows. Half a dozen banks worked out of storefronts in the block, sandwiched between steamship agencies and synagogues.

Carsie paused at a cart selling hats for a quarter, finding only unimaginative, faded felts from last winter, hats that needed reblocking because they had hung on the pegs too long. She moved on to an optician's shop where she inquired whether glasses could improve Lilia's eyesight. Yes, the man said, bring your sister around. Glasses might help and they were only thirty-five cents.

She went to the fish peddler who shouted over the din, "Fourteen cents a pound," when she asked the price on carp. The fish man reconsidered. "Fifteen cents," he said. "Not fourteen, fifteen."

"Not fourteen or fifteen," Carsie had learned to call back. "Thirteen."

"Feh, thirteen," the fishmonger yelled. "I have to live. Fifteen cents a pound or nothing."

"Nothing, then." Carsie turned for the door.

"Fine, fine, thirteen cents a pound...my poor children starve so you can eat."

Back on the street, Carsie stopped to look at a pile of used clothes on a peddler's cart. The peddler stood at her elbow holding a pair of pants, yelling at a man nearby. "Sixty cents? Fifty? Look at these pants. Quality goods. So help me, I'm losing money at fifty—"

The man waved him off. "I said, 'Thirty.'"

The peddler grabbed his sleeve. "Forty? Why not forty?" He threw the pants on the ground at his customer's feet. "Take them for thirty. Wreck my life."

ON THE gentle night of April 10, petite blonde Emma Goldman hurried from her room on Third Street down Rivington Street in a nurse's uniform. She hugged close to the buildings along the littered sidewalks of the Tenth Ward, darting from one shadow to the next, on her way to deliver a baby. The day had been tiring, but her speech had triumphed. Public speaking—especially as impassioned as Emma spoke—wore her out. After what she had said today, protesting against the outrages of the Spanish government, she knew the police would be on the hunt, eager to harass her. It had happened before—her anarchist views were not popular with Tammany Hall. And she knew tonight's birth would be as arduous as the day had been.

Shalva Akselrod's opium habit had made getting her through the last few months of her pregnancy difficult. Trying to withdraw the woman from her drug while she was pregnant would surely harm the baby, but seeing Shalva pregnant and addicted was heartbreaking—the girl had spent her entire pregnancy in bed, indiscriminately drinking contraband opium tonic, and though the baby still kicked within her, Emma had no idea how the child would fare once it was born.

She had never been to the flat this late in the day; the stairways were darker than usual. Most of the Akselrod's boarders had chosen to be gone while Shalva gave birth, but three men sat in a corner—one she knew as Shalva's husband, Moishe, the other two read newspapers that obscured their faces.

Shalva whimpered and moaned in her bed. Carsie and Lilia stood in the kitchen, readying rags and water. Emma pulled up her hair in a tight knot and dropped a white smock over her dress. She stiffened and gasped when the last of the boarders in the living room rose to leave—Jerome Jacobs. He stopped only for a second, stared at her, nodded curtly, and left, but she knew he would be waiting when she finished. How had he found his way to the Akselrod flat? Seven years ago he had brought her up from Philadelphia as a prisoner, and had attempted to persuade her, on their way to New York, to betray the cause of the working man. She used the alias of E.G. Smith when she performed nursing duties, but Jacobs would know better.

Shalva let out a scream. Her real birthing had begun.

Emma leaned over her. "Surrender, Shalva. That is the secret to this—surrender to what is happening. Your baby is coming down the narrow passage to the light."

Shalva screamed again, gripping Emma's arms. In the kitchen, Lilia moaned.

"Submit, Shalva," Emma whispered. "You must get to the other side of this—don't fight it."

Carsie handed Emma a cool, damp cloth. Emma sponged Shalva's face and mopped her own.

"Let go," Emma said. "Think that baby's going to stay inside you forever? One way or another it's coming…" She checked between Shalva's legs. "It's coming now."

Carsie watched as the baby appeared—head, shoulders, arms, its tiny body. A girl, thin and weak, but alive.

"You're done, Shalva," Emma Goldman cooed to her. "It's a daughter."

"A girl?" Shalva wept. "Please, no, not a girl. Look again—it shouldn't be a girl."

"But it is," Emma cut the baby's umbilical cord and bathed her. "And she will grow up to be a great lady someday."

"She can't," Shalva wept. "They won't let her, Emma. You know that."

Emma wrapped the baby in a blanket and laid her at Shalva's withered breast. "Who won't let her?"

"Them. Men."

"Men have less and less to say about what women do, anymore." She thought, and smiled down at Shalva. "Come to think of it, childbirth is about the only thing any of us has to submit to at all. And tonight you enjoy your daughter. Have you thought about her name?"

"Her name is Naomi, after my mother."

While Shalva dozed, Carsie and Emma rolled her over on her left side, pulled the bloodied sheets off the bed, and changed her gown. Lilia made a cradle for the baby in a dresser drawer.

Shalva stirred. "Hand me my bottle," she murmured.

"You've just had a baby," Emma said. "No tonic now. Once you've had some sleep we'll see how you feel."

Shalva whimpered before she dropped off again. Naomi began to cry, her little face red beyond the flush of a normal newborn. Emma watched the infant choke and scream.

"The boarders won't be able to sleep with this going on," Carsie said.

Emma raised an eyebrow. "The boarders will have to put up with it. Babies cry."

"But if they can't sleep here they'll find somewhere else to live."

"What would you have Shalva do, Carsie," Emma said. "You must see this for what it is, not what you want it to be."

"But, we can't afford…"

"That woman cannot get up right now to silence her baby."

Moishe came into the kitchen and looked at his new daughter, still screaming in the dresser drawer. "Maybe the *hintele* is hungry, eh?"

"Shalva can't nurse, Moishe," Emma said. "Someone else will have to do that."

Naomi's screams echoed throughout the tenement hallways. The flat's walls closed on Carsie. She felt for a chair, her breath coming in short gulps, her stomach heaving. She covered her ears. "A style that is dressy, stylish and becoming… the hat is constructed of navy blue satin braid…" she mumbled. "Make her stop crying, Emma," she wailed. "I don't want to hear it. This baby shouldn't have been born alive."

"But she was, Carsie."

"Not to this world…it's not fair."

"And the way you and I came to this world? Was that fair for our parents to let us see…this?" Emma pinned a diaper on the new baby.

Lilia took her sister's hand. "Carsie? Are you all right?"

"No, I am not all right, Lilia. I'm scared and angry."

"*Carsie!*" Selig shouted from the front room. "Settle down."

Carsie laid her head on the table in the crook of one arm. She wanted out of life. She wanted to spare Lilia and Naomi from what she felt. She wanted to forget, to run. "…feathers and a rhinestone buckle as well as artificial flowers at the edge of the brim…" she mumbled. The sounds in the room seemed as though they came from under water. "I will never be a mother. Do you hear, Selig? *I will never be a mother.*"

"And I said, 'Settle down,' my love."

She hugged her elbows to her stomach, mumbling to herself, "…a good quality embroidered net scarf caught down with ornaments…" Then she remembered—just across the hall, Pearl Petrow was nursing.

SUMMER HEAT had broken for another year, shepherding in September, a welcome month for those in the Tenth Ward. The autumn holidays arrived again, along with cooler weather for a while, before winter bit once more. On the second day of *Rosh Hashanah,* most of the boarders had gone to *shul.* An eerie silence settled over the Tenth Ward, broken only by a newsboy's call, shouting out an extra edition of the *Daily Forward.* Selig Akselrod sat at the window reading his copy of an Extra edition while Carsie peeled apples and set out honey.

"Hmmm. President McKinley died," Selig commented, not sounding much surprised.

Carsie frowned. "But I thought he was doing better."

"The doctors thought so, too. Apparently they were wrong."

"Did we like President McKinley, Selig?" Carsie asked.

Akselrod folded his paper neatly. He had no thoughts one way or the other about McKinley, nor did he have any opinions about the world at large beyond wishing women wouldn't talk so much. Like Moishe, he thought women walked in his world to support him in word and deed, and to do it quietly. "Decide for yourself who you like—don't ask me."

Velvel Kagan stood behind Carsie, massaging her shoulders. "You're wrong, there, Akselrod. Thinking gets women in trouble. All those free-thinkers out there make me sick—believing they should be allowed to go to school and vote and such—to live like men." He stroked her hair and the back of her neck.

Carsie shook his hands loose. "Please don't. You shouldn't do that." She set one apple aside and began to peel another.

"Do what? An innocent pat on the shoulders? And you watch your mouth—you don't tell me what I can do."

Selig bristled. "Keep your hands off her, Kagan."

Kagan ran his hands down from Carsie's shoulders to her breasts. Carsie shrieked and ran to the kitchen. He followed. "Don't run away like that!" he yelled, catching her elbow. "It makes me very angry when a woman pushes me away. I simply meant a man should tell you what's right to think and what's not."

"She should learn to think for herself, Kagan," Akselrod yelled from the living room.

"She shouldn't push me away like she did, and you have no right to tell me—"

Carsie slid the paring knife into the right sleeve of her shirtwaist and turned, shaking loose of his grasp. "Don't put your hands on me."

Kagan took her in his arms and leaned her over the sink, trying to kiss her. Once more, Carsie felt power rise up her back. She moved as though to embrace him. He smiled and dipped his face toward hers, his eyes closed. She pulled the knife from her sleeve, plunged it into his neck, just below his left ear, and pulled down. Kagan gurgled and slumped to his knees, clutching at the throbbing wound in his neck. His upper lip curled in a sneer. "You may have got me," he twitched. "But I know you. You can't..." He gasped, and fell to the floor.

THE BEAT cop's only reaction was a raised eyebrow and a disdainful sniff. "This guy has been trouble for years," he said. "Can't say I'm sorry to see the end he came to. He was bothering you when...this happened?"

Carsie stood gripping the sink, trembling, convinced she would be conveyed to Blackwell's Island on the next prison boat.

"Ma'am? I asked, was he bothering you?"

"Bothering...yes, he was. He made an advance and I tried to fight him off. Then...as you say, this happened."

"You defended yourself, did you? That's all it was?"

She nodded, whispering, "...a large bunch of violets on either side of a rosette of straw in the center..."

The policeman flipped his book closed and stepped over Kagan's body on his way to the door. "I'll send the mortuary wagon around to collect the body. Terrible shame about President McKinley, wasn't it?"

Carsie felt for a chair behind her and sat. "Gowns for the morning hours..." she mumbled. "...differ in lengths and fabrics from evening gowns...carriage dress and walking costumes are made of somewhat more sturdy fabrics..." She had killed someone, had done it knowing what she did. It had been easy, in the moment she did it, and she remembered the look on the young Cossack's face as he whipped her father— his lip curled, the disgust in his eyes. She was no better, she thought, than the Cossacks.

MOST EVENINGS Selig and Moishe sat in the front room, reading *The Jewish Daily Forward.* Carsie would sit by the kerosene lamp, pick up her sewing and say, "Read to me, Selig. Read to me like Papa used to. While I work."

And Selig would read. "Carrie Nation was arrested again, here in New York, I see. Seems she was getting a lot of attention at a rally and when the cops went to break it up she got feisty." Often he read somber bits and commented. "Queen Victoria's died. Well, well. I wonder how it will go for her darling Czarist granddaughter now?" And, "Oh, listen to this! A woman named Maud Willard tried to go over Niagara Falls in a barrel yesterday, it says here. But she took her fox terrier with her and the dog fell across her face as they pitched down. Killed them both—broke the dog's neck and suffocated poor Maud. I wonder what makes people do that sort of thing?"

On a hot, still evening, Selig looked over the top of his paper. "Was it not Emma Goldman who delivered Naomi last spring?"

"Yes," Carsie said. "I'll never forget her—or that night. But, why do you ask?"

He leaned to the glow of the kerosene lamp to study an article in the *Daily Forward.* "Because she's been arrested in Chicago for plotting with the man who shot McKinley."

"Impossible. That woman was far too kindhearted to do anything of the sort."

"You women," Akselrod sighed. "Always with the opinions. Once you start thinking for yourselves, you never stop."

Carsie smiled at him. "Remember, Selig. That I think for

myself was your idea. You helped the genie escape from her bottle."

IN JANUARY of 1902, Osher Melnick formed a partnership with Isaac Harris and Max Blanck and moved his business uptown, to the second floor of a building on the east side of Washington Square. He took a room at a nearby hotel in order to enjoy the company of Rose Freedman. Melnick's partners disapproved of his affair with Rose Freedman, a finisher at the shop, who electrified Melnick's soul. He insisted to Varda that the hours he put in at the coat factory demanded he be closer to his work than their flat on Canal Street.

For Carsie and Lilia, the day's work at Melnick's new coat company began each morning at seven-thirty. They left the flat at six-forty-five to catch the horse car, changed for the number five trolley that took them across Houston and up Sixth Avenue, where they walked across Washington Square, a peaceful residential area.

Stanford White's Washington Arch graced the eight-acre park at the foot of Fifth Avenue, and along Washington Square North town houses made up a row of red brick buildings with free-standing white marble porches supported by Doric columns. Facing the park to the east were the buildings of New York University, in the same block as the Asch Building, at the corner of Washington Place and Greene.

The girls entered the building from the Washington Place side, the foyer's elegant marble floor leading to an innovation neither girl had experienced before they came to business uptown—an elevator.

Somehow, the morning trek made their work more satisfying than doing the same thing at their flat or in Melnick's, and they felt a bond with the other women their age who worked at the coat company, immigrants who spoke Yiddish—many of whom had come from Russia, all of them somehow finding the same corner of America. The day's work was scheduled to end at six in the afternoon, but during most of the year

Carsie and Lilia stayed until nine each night except Friday and Saturday. To keep them there, Melnick fed them apple pie for supper.

Carsie worked as Melnick's assistant, Lilia as a cleaner—snipping sewing machine threads off the finished coats. She was the eldest of those working in the "children's corner" where she and three other girls sat, clipping the long bits of thread, folding the coats and placing them in large cases.

On a snowy afternoon in February, Carsie sat at her desk updating inventory numbers, when she smelled smoke. She ran to the back where Lilia worked, sweeping around the cutting tables, but the odor diminished. She watched Lilia for a moment, pleased at how her sister had changed since they had bought her glasses. Lilia could see a few feet in front of her and could read without holding the book so close to her nose.

The stench of smoke came again, and Carsie ran to the stairwell. The smell was stronger there, and mounting. "Lilia!" she called from the stairwell doorway. "Take the children and alert the cutters—we need to get out. There's smoke coming from below. Go." The employees of Melnick Coat Company watched the pumper wagon irreparably drench everything on the second floor.

Osher Melnick had not yet arrived when the fire company left. He had slept in that morning, after a night of dancing with his mistress. By noon the company he had built over the past ten years lay in ruins. He suspected the fire had been set by his partners' hired hands—probably Paul Kelly's men. He supposed Harris and Blanck had wiped him out to get rid of him as a partner, and to end his affair. Insurance would pay for his losses, but his reason to live uptown, near Rose, had been reduced to ashes.

But at that moment, the woman he needed to see was Varda, who knew more about his wrath than his joy.

———

THAT EVENING Carsie and Lilia talked with Selig and Louis about the future. Selig agreed to wait until the autumn of 1904 before they married. Louis agreed to wait for Lilia, too, and his wait would be long. Lilia would not turn eighteen for another six years. With the day's fire, the girls' jobs at Melnick's coat company had ended. Louis had taken a position as an apprentice at Lord and Taylor in the menswear department, and Selig realized the time approached for him to quit Monk Eastman's gang and find salaried work.

"Speaking nothing but Yiddish holds us back," Carsie said. "People uptown speak English, and I, for one, plan to live uptown."

"Yeh," Selig snorted. "How're we going to live uptown? You don't even have a job."

"You're the one who is always telling me to think for myself, Selig. Well, I've been doing some thinking this afternoon. I'm going to take English lessons and start my own millinery business. If there's anything in this world a lady will never be without, it's a hat."

AFTER ONLY a week out of a job Lilia found work with Melnick's partners in a company they owned on the eighth floor of the Asch Building, a firm called Triangle Waist Company. The firm made a new blouse called a shirtwaist and business had burgeoned in the last six months, as the shirtwaist—a sheer high-necked blouse worn with a tailored skirt—had become popular.

Lilia's newest job put her on the cutting floor at Triangle, sweeping fabric dust, collecting wicker baskets of scraps for the rag dealers, and distributing supplies to the cutters. Now that she had glasses she could see well enough to find her way around the shop with little trouble. Her starting wage was a dollar and a half a week—a long week, consisting, more often than not, of seven days, especially during season, which ran from April to September. On Saturday afternoons Isaac Harris posted a sign over the elevator that read:

IF YOU DON'T COME IN ON SUNDAY
YOU NEED NOT COME IN ON MONDAY

OVER THE following week the villagers came to wish Max Siegel well, pressing slips of paper into his hand, slips bearing proverbs he should remember on his journey. The baker, next door, brought "Every new beginning comes from some other beginning's end," and the general storekeeper, "While I can run, I'll run; while I can walk, I'll walk; when I can only crawl, I'll crawl. But by the grace of God, I'll always be moving forward." Nakhimov gave him this one: "If you live each day as if it was your last, someday you'll most certainly be right." That was his favorite—it cheered him, reminding him that he had come close to living his last had it not been for the kindness of these people. He would miss them, he thought, as he stitched Carsie's locket into the lining of his coat.

On April 4, 1902, two years to the day after his accident, he signed the bar over to Hod Nakhimov, who had begun to enjoy being publican more than farrier—hefting a keg of lager was easier than fighting a horse to stand still—and struck out, walking with a catch in his gait. Having lost the two biggest toes on his right foot to frostbite as well as three fingers, he was grateful to walk at all.

The trip over the Carpathians and across the continent took nearly six months in the warm weather, and towns along the way were hospitable. He paid the quarryman and his wife a visit on his second day out, leaving them with a hundred rubles of the Federation money for their trouble two years ago. In Romania he found a group of *Fusgeyers* aiming to board a boat to America. He walked with them for three weeks. They carried guns and lanterns and supplies for emergencies. Important to Siegel, too, they kept kosher, and he felt safe in their company. The thought that he might see Carsie before Chanukah was enough to keep Siegel putting one foot in front of the other.

———

"HATS," CARSIE said to the Frenchwoman who stood in front of her. "It's all I can think to do—to make hats."

"That," Madame Anya Pelletier said, "is the mark of a professional. When hats are all you can think, when they are all you dream, when you no longer want to clean or have babies or please a man, but only to make hats." She held a finger in the air to make her point. "Then you are a milliner. Let me see your fingers." She inspected the fronts and backs of Carsie's hands. "Yes. *Bon.* The hands, they will do fine—nimble and dry. Some rules, we have. First, I am Madame. It is the only thing you will call me. Then. You sit here." She scraped back a wooden chair at the foot of the table. "When I think you are good enough to move up, and there is an empty chair, you move up. It can take years. Are you willing to spend years to learn a fraction of what I know about the millinery?"

Carsie nodded. She had not thought the process would be as formal as that—that there would be social strata even here, or that she would start at its bottom.

SHE WALKED home from the Socialist Literary League in bad sorts. Her fifth English lesson had been difficult—the lesson on variations in pronunciation and meaning. An English word might be used in several ways: a bandage wound around a wound, and there was no time like the present to present a present. You prepared chicken in a kitchen—or was it the other way around? A hopeless tongue, English, she thought, impossible to learn. What other language permitted that kind of craziness? Not even Russian was this bad.

She did not feel like working on hats tonight or listening to Selig read his silly selections from the *Daily Forward*, or arguing with Shalva about doses of tonic, or taking Naomi to Mrs. Petrow for her feeding, or doing the boarders' laundry. None of it. Every day was the same dull routine in the same cramped flat in the same colorless neighborhood, and she wondered whether her life would ever be different.

She glanced around as she walked: men in doorways who

had sat there since that morning, women who looked so tired they might drop where they stood, and children who stole vegetables because the family couldn't afford to buy them. Who might save these people from the brutalities she knew lay ahead of them, she wondered. "...a wide-brimmed hat with heat-curled feathers...," she mumbled. "...velvet bows and ties and a beadwork top...the position of the collar seam at the back of the neck can be fixed by the eye and should be indicated by a light chalk mark...raise the arms of your client...in joining the pieces of the pattern care must be taken..."

When she arrived at the flat she unpinned her hat and put it on a hat stand as usual, tied on an apron, and stabbed at the embers in the stove, bringing them to life. Then she took out a piece of butcher paper and sat down to write.

She wrote what she had seen and smelled on the street that afternoon, telling of the poverty and how it made her feel, wondering whether life in the Tenth Ward would ever improve and questioning that the wrongs could be righted. When she was done, she folded the paper and addressed the outside to the *Jewish Daily Forward*.

Writing the piece improved her mood, and after she posted it, she took Naomi to Pearl Petrow's flat for her feeding, then boiled potatoes and cabbage for dinner, doled out a dose of tonic to Shalva, and tended to the boarders' laundry.

After dinner it occurred to her that writing a protest had started her journey out of Russia two years ago—the protest then had been her father's broadside to the Czar. Had it been only two years since the journey had begun? It seemed a lifetime. She took sad comfort in knowing America permitted people to speak as they felt. Poor Papa, she thought. He would have loved America. Here you could say whatever you felt, and publicly. This time there would be no aftermath to fear.

— 21 —

THE *RMS Carpathia,* Cunard's newest ship, set out on its maiden voyage in May of 1903, bound for Boston. Max Siegel quit his job at a rough Liverpool pub for a spot in the steerage compartment, where he sat on a wood crate or slept on the floor for most of the voyage. The floors had been painted, but little cargo accompanied him for the trip—few wanted to risk sending freight on a ship with no proven safety record. By halfway across the Atlantic, he had met a crewman who, for a hundred rubles, agreed to take Siegel through U.S. Customs at Boston with the *Carpathia*'s crew, and put him on a short-haul steamer bound for New York City.

ON SATURDAY Carsie's English lesson was in Conditionals—the ideas of time and probability, from "certain" to "impossible." She understood the concepts, and the lesson went better. *Fascinating language,* she thought.

She stopped at a fishmonger's to buy a whole cod on her way home from the Socialist Literary League. When she came into the flat, she laid the package of fish on the table next to a copy of the *Daily Forward* that had been folded back—a circle drawn on the editorial page. Inside the circle was her letter, with her name signed at the bottom.

Selig sat in the front room, in the dark, smoking a cigarette.

Carsie turned up the kerosene lamp on the table. "Sitting in the dark? Not reading?" she asked.

"Did you see? The *Forward* published your letter."

She smiled. "Yes. I never thought they would—I just wanted to say something about, well, about the way things are."

"You don't decide what's wrong with 'the way things are,' Carsie. That is not yours to decide."

"It is as much mine to say as anyone's, Selig. And if I think there are problems I will say so."

"No, you won't. There are boundaries to a woman thinking for herself—stepping over them will get you in trouble."

"Why do you care so much whether the *Forward* published my letter? Did it embarrass you?"

Akselrod said nothing.

She snatched the newspaper off the table and studied her letter. The paper had published it exactly as she had written, and she still felt as angry about conditions in the ward as she had then. "It did embarrass you, didn't it? Your friends didn't like it that you plan to marry a woman who thinks like this, did they?"

He continued to smoke, silent.

"*Did they?*"

Nothing.

"Selig, I am asking—your friends didn't like it that I spoke my mind, *did they?*"

"It's time you knew what I do for money, Carsie," he sighed. "My livelihood is made on the people of the Tenth Ward. I work for Monk Eastman, running numbers."

"But he's..."

"Eastman depends on these people living just as they do— if everyone started thinking for themselves we'd have no business at all down here. He called your letter treason. You've put me in an awful position—I had to agree with him or..."

"You *agreed?* Monk Eastman is a gangster and you agreed with *him?* That...bully?" She waited, staring at him. "What did you say?"

"That you're no better than Emma Goldman."

The front door opened. Two boarders came in, followed by Louis and Lilia.

"Carsie!" Lilia squealed. "Did you see? Everyone in the building's talking about your letter! It's really brought them 'round—the bits about landlords setting fires and people cheated by the numbers runners and…" She looked from Carsie's face to Selig's and eased toward the kitchen. "Whoops. Have you taken Naomi to Mrs. Petrow's yet?"

Despite Selig's concern that she had become an anarchist, Carsie did not stop thinking or writing. She became known in the neighborhood as the Voice of the Ward. When she was not making or selling her hats she wrote letters for people—letters to relatives in Russia or Eastern Europe for less literate men and women. And when she was not writing letters for others, she wrote to the *Forward*, signing her protests with fictitious names.

Selig continued to run numbers, though his business dropped by ten percent. Carsie feigned innocence and kept on writing her letters. Monk Eastman's men shadowed her.

Most days, Shalva lay staring at the ceiling with her hollow, dark eyes. She rarely dressed and went out except to buy opium tonic. She bought more, now, because she fed it to Naomi to keep her from crying. Both mother and child wasted. And though the two of them slept, the boarders could not, unwilling to live with the specter of Shalva lying in the alcove, staring. One by one, they moved out.

In the evenings, while Carsie worked on her hats and Lilia did the boarders' laundry or cleaned the flat, Moishe and Selig read the paper. Occasionally she and Selig went out to the Yiddish Theatre, if a musical was playing. Selig would not take her to dramas—plays that made her angry or made her think. He said she thought too much already.

She had begun to spend more money on her clothes, planning for the day she and Selig would marry and move to Union Square or farther uptown. Her business dictated that she dress well, and certainly—her favorite word in English, now—certainly that she wear a showy hat.

One evening in April Selig took Carsie to Weber and Fields Music Hall on Broadway to see Lillian Russell in the musical *Come Down My Evening Star.* Selig pointed to a heavy-set man in an opulent box to the right of the stage. "The man up there," he whispered, "that's Diamond Jim Brady. He and Lillian Russell, they, well, you know. And they're not married to each other." Selig patted Carsie's hand and smiled. "I think it's a grand idea."

"You do? But Miss Russell is not married—why doesn't Mr. Brady marry her?"

"Why does he need to?"

"Because, I think, he loves her. Don't you think so? Isn't that the reason you want to marry me?"

"If we married, what would be different? You would still have the same last name and the same place to live and the same relatives. You would go to business just as you do now. All that would change is the spot in the flat where you sleep. I am suggesting you could do that tonight and every night after tonight, and we wouldn't need to be married. After all, we're already bound by blood."

THEY STAYED in—Carsie blocking and decorating her hats while Selig read to her from the *Daily Forward*. He had a taste for unusual bits and sometimes for the morose: "A doctor in Paris has separated the Siamese twins in Barnum and Bailey's circus, I see," he mused one night as he thumbed the pages of the paper. "Not much of an attraction, now, I'd imagine." And, "An explosion up at Madison Square Garden has killed fifteen people and injured seventy more," he remarked. "Must've been blood everywhere." On another evening, "Some wop anarchist took a shot at the King of Belgium…friend of yours?"

On April 20 Selig read to her from The *Jewish Daily Forward*:

In the Bessarabian town of Kishinev twenty-four Jews were murdered and 275 seriously wounded in the most violent attack ever on a Russian Jewish community. An organized band of peasants and laborers set on the Jews with the goal of murdering them…but the Jews of Kishinev fought bravely, fearless and strong as iron. When the pogrom began young and middle-aged men came from all over and fought like lions…they fought bare-handed against attackers armed with knives and axes, ready to wipe out the Jews.

"The riots were worse than the censor will permit us to publish. At sunset the streets were piled with corpses and wounded. Those who could escape fled, and the city is now practically deserted of Jews. Both President Theodore Roosevelt and former President Grover Cleveland have spoken out against the pogrom and pressured the Czar for reform.

Carsie stared down at the wide-brimmed straw hat that lay in her lap, its blue cabbage roses hanging limp on its hatband. How unimportant the big blue hat looked, how foolish. She laid her hands on the straw brim and splayed her fingers. Her vision blurred but she did not weep for the people of the Pale.

FOR TWO seasons—fall and winter—Carsie sat at the foot of the table, last among the six who studied with the great French milliner, Madame Anya Pelletier. Frequently she delivered a hat, or purchased findings—the ribbons and trims and supplies. When she sat at the far end of Madame's worktable she made hat linings and bandeaux—bands that held feathers and flowers that might be worn in circumstances other than those where one would certainly wear a hat—at a party or on an evening out. Between Carsie's chair and Anya Pelletier's sat four "makers" and "trimmers," preparing shapes for Madame to trim.

In spring, a seat became available in the next rank up. But before Carsie could qualify to move toward the top of the table Madame asked her to create a bandeau without help. She fashioned a simple gray band affixed with a single ostrich feather on the left side.

Madame Pelletier took one look at the thing and threw it in the stove. "*Merde!*" she said. "A stupid piece of work. You disappoint me, Miss Akselrod. You will remain at the foot of the table for an additional two weeks. And while you are there,

I would suggest that you actually pay attention. Have you seen nothing in your time with me?" She turned to her makers. "Now to the veil—a symbol of the custom when women never showed their faces on the street…"

"HERE WAS one cop, and here was the other at this end of Eldridge," Louis explained. Three crumbs on the table marked a triangle where the three had stood the evening of his arrest. "I was here…too…ah…ill to see."

Carsie and Lilia sat with *glozell té* in front of them, and a dish of buttered bread. The talk had circled, as it often did when the three of them sat together, to Louis's time in prison, and how it happened. Lilia looked at him, finding it hard to imagine her gentle Louis on Blackwell's Island.

"But I did my time, and, as I said, it was for the best. Without that, I might have died in some doorway—frozen or beaten to death." He paused and thought. "The saddest thing was there were too many like me in the jail here in the ward, and at Blackwell's. Men and women addicted or desperate for a break—why, even the Benders had run aground—and all of us with no future to look to when we get out." He smiled at Lilia. "I am so lucky."

A current ran through Carsie. If the prisoners on Blackwell's Island knew how to read, or if they could speak English, they might hope for a better life once they left the penitentiary. She could teach them those things.

She knew Selig and Lilia would object to her idea. They would say it wasn't safe for a woman to go to the prison, but she had seen criminals of various sorts. She counted herself among those who had killed out of hatred. She knew of men who cheated their own people, and those who beat their children, and street bullies and thieves. And sometimes, when men stole coal in the winter to keep their families warm or hungry children stole fruit from the stand, there was good reason. She thought there might be occasions when people were helpless to avoid arrest, as Louis had been, and that there would be times when arrest was welcome—warm shelter or a meal or a six-foot stretch of floor on which to sleep.

Telling people to be good so they would get rich and be happy was ridiculous, she thought. Monk Eastman was rich, and he was worse than any she could think of, offhand. And the poor people of the Tenth Ward, good because their imaginations were not dark enough to be wicked, had not become any richer.

She was as sure of her convictions as she was sure the price of mackerel would go up at Passover. Some of those possessed by that evil lived on the Lower East Side. Too, she knew there was little danger of a rich man going to jail. So the people she needed to reach were poor and criminal and she wasn't afraid of them. It was the wealthy who scared her.

MAX SIEGEL disembarked the steamer on a warm June afternoon three years after Carsie and Lilia had arrived. He paused, one foot on the gangway, the other on the shore of... America. He had come.

He looked up and took a deep breath, filling his lungs with the stench of a nearby tannery. Fire bells clanged close by, adding to the clash and clamor of people disembarking from the ferry to find relatives, noises rising on air already thick with humidity and the stink of horse dung and garbage. Siegel removed his jacket and doubled it inside out, masking the yellow armband. Perspiration wet his shirt to his back.

Thunderheads rose from behind him, black and yellow at their bases, and lightning flashed against the moist cores. For the moment, though, the sky burned bright blue above him. He stepped into the street, jumping away from a carriage that pulled up in front of him and stopped. An elderly man looked down at Siegel and tucked a side-curl behind one ear. He smiled and said in Yiddish, "You need a place to stay tonight, no?"

A man in tatters ran by, wielding a stick, chasing a dog with meat in its mouth. Wagons trundled over the cobblestones, their wood wheels rumbling.

Siegel nodded. "Yeh, I need a place to stay tonight. Yeh." He swung his bag into the back of the wagon, hiked a foot onto the horizontal wheel rung and swung into the buckboard seat. "Where do we go?"

"Sheltering Society. You're a Jew, yeh?"

Siegel gazed at the scene passing on both sides of the wagon, scarcely believing he had arrived—even as they rode across town on this wide, busy boulevard. He checked the lining of his coat as he had a hundred times on this journey, feeling for Carsie's kopek necklace. The wagon bumped along, the old man whistling people out of the way, working his way through the maze of pushcarts and litters that lined the streets. They turned a corner into a narrower lane and stopped.

"Take a look around, son," the old man said. "These are your people."

If these were his people, Siegel thought, he could start looking for Carsie right away. A knot rose from his stomach to his throat as the heat drove garbage smells into his nostrils. He turned from the old man who drove the wagon, trying to stifle the gagging feeling by spitting onto the littered cobblestones.

SELIG AND Carsie walked down Essex Street to the market before dark on a warm evening in August, Selig once again trying to convince her of the folly of marriage, when a friend of his stepped out of Silver Dollar Smith's Saloon. The man had a disarming look about him, Carsie thought, his soft big eyes set in a slender, clean-shaven face. He smiled tentatively and touched his hat to her when Selig introduced them. This man worked for Monk Eastman, too. His name was Arnold Rothstein.

— 22 —

AT THE end of the week Moishe, Selig, and Shalva sat in the front room when Carsie and Lilia came in. Carsie unpinned her hat and set it on the stand, hung her coat on the peg, and tied on an apron. Lilia hung her coat over Carsie's and reached for a pinafore.

Moishe snuffled. "Come in here, please, the two of you. We have something to talk about."

Carsie glanced at her sister as they brought chairs from the table so that the five of them sat in a circle. She waited. Moishe rarely spoke—this was an event. "Yes?" she said, smiling. "What is it?" She looked from Moishe's face to Selig's and to Shalva's. Shalva looked away.

"It's your wages, is what it is," Moishe said. "Yours and Lilia's. You're not giving us all of it."

Carsie stared at Selig. He met her gaze and shook his head. "Carsie, are you keeping money for yourself?"

"Why, of course I am."

"No, that's not right. You give the money to Moishe, and he gives you an allowance."

"But we must have money to buy lunch and for carfare and clothes and such. Shalva? Do you give Moishe all your pay?"

Shalva remained quiet.

"How do you expect we would get on if we didn't have our own money?"

"That money is not yours," Moishe said. "You have no money of your own."

Carsie stood. "Today was payday for Lilia and her envelope is still sealed, I'm sure. I have already made a deposit at the bank, and I kept enough to give you what I have given you every week, and a little to cover carfare and my lunch."

"A deposit at the bank?" Selig asked. "But, what are *you* doing with a bank account?"

She had opened the account sometime back, after she changed the hundred-ruble note for a little more than fifteen dollars. Each week she added to that sum. The account wasn't large, but after she had lost the kopek necklace her parents had given her, having that small amount of money meant she was never broke. The account was talismanic, connecting her to Mama and Papa. "Why should I not have a bank account?"

"Because you are…" He caught himself.

"What, Selig? Because I am what?"

Shalva stood and turned away from her husband and Selig. "Because we are women, Carsie. We are not allowed to manage our own money. The bank should not have opened an account for you."

"Uncle Moishe," Carsie said, "how much do you put in the household account each week? Selig, how much do you contribute?"

Moishe sneered. "That's none of your affair."

"Selig?"

Selig said nothing.

Carsie turned to Shalva. "Do you think it's possible they are not putting anything in the household account and the three of us and the boarders are paying the rent and the grocery tab and buying the kerosene and everything else, and these two keep everything they have made during the week for themselves?"

Shalva did not answer.

"Shalva? *Do they keep all their money for themselves?*"

"Shalva," Moishe said. "Don't answer her."

She stared at her husband for a moment, squared her shoulders and stuck out her chin. "Yes, Carsie," she said. "They do. They take our money so they can keep theirs for themselves."

———

CARSIE SAT at the table, reading the *Daily Forward*. With the holidays coming on, the new novelty, teddy bears, were in short supply, and mothers all over the country were getting testy about the shortage. Russia's harvests had failed once more, famine lay ahead. Mr. Hershey had made his chocolate bars, once a luxury, available at a price everyone could pay. Painter Paul Gauguin had died of syphilis back in May, but the news had been slow reaching the world outside French Polynesia. Israel Zangwill had a new play titled *Merely Mary Ann* in rehearsals up at the Garden Theatre.

Lilia looked up from her dime novel, frowning. "Carsie, what's Norman blood?"

"What are you reading? Who's talking 'Norman blood'?"

"I found a new *My Queen* novel yesterday, *The Interrupted Wedding*. At the end Marion Marlowe says, 'True hearts are more than coronets, and simple faith more than Norman blood.' So, what does that mean?"

Carsie smiled at her sister. Lilia loved the *My Queen* novels—stories of the dauntless Marion Marlowe, a young farmer's daughter who had come to New York to find her way in the world despite every hardship. The story was always the same—Marion got herself in a bind, battling the great city or traveling as a member of an opera company where she worked, or, in this case, as a maid of honor, but in the end courage and virtue triumphed. Most interesting about the books, Carsie thought, was that Marion Marlowe herself never married in the final pages.

Carsie smiled and tapped a knuckle on a review she had just read in the *Forward*. "There's a new book out you should read. A book by a woman named Helen Keller…"

SHE BEGAN to do her marketing in the late afternoons at the Essex Street Market, hoping to see Arnold Rothstein again before she could forget his face. Four nights after they first met, she found him again, standing in front of Silver Dollar

Smith's. Again he tipped his hat when he spotted her. She smiled primly. After she reminded him of her name they made small talk about the weather and Enrico Caruso's sensational debut uptown at the Opera House. She learned Rothstein sold cigars and liked to play pool but little else about him other than that he claimed to be good at math. She suggested he might contrive a budget for the Akselrod flat that would include payments from Moishe and Selig, and they both laughed. Rothstein asked how she was related to Selig, and she said Selig was her uncle. She did not mention their wedding plans.

THE OLD man led Max Siegel to a room at the back of the Sheltering Society and flung open the door. "*Farshtunken,* yeh?"

"Yeh," Max said, wrinkling his nose.

"You stay only until you find a job or a relative that takes you in. *Farschtein?*"

Max nodded. He understood.

The old man closed the door. Siegel breathed a sigh, his first moment alone in America. He sat on a cot that smelled of sweat and tobacco smoke. He lay down. He sat up. He stood on a box intended to serve as a table and looked out a window high on the wall, then tried to open it, but water and time had warped it shut. He needed air.

He grabbed his coat and stepped out into the street, his senses assaulted once more by the sounds and sights of the lower Tenth Ward—butchers tossing offal into the gutters, the smell of whiskey and cigarettes hanging at the door of a bar, men shouting over a load of rotting cabbage in a cart.

He wondered how to begin searching for Carsie. By calling out her name? By asking for her? But where? This was going to be more difficult than he'd thought. He hadn't expected this...this chaos, this crowd. He didn't know how he thought it would be, but he knew now it would take time. The stubs of his frostbitten fingers swelled and ached in the humidity. He had never had much luck, and he needed all he could muster. He turned back to the Sheltering Society.

The old man smiled tiredly at Siegel when he came in. "It scares people, the first time they go out by themselves. You'll get used to it. But you'll wish for home a thousand times a day. I did, for many years, until I realized I would never see it again."

"I've come to find someone. If I find her, my home is here," Siegel said.

The old man stepped to his book.

JEWS SEEK RELATIVES
FAMILIES IN RUSSIA ASK AID OF
HEBREW SHELTERING SOCIETY

The Hebrew Sheltering and Immigrant Aid Society has received a number of appeals from Jews in Russia asking that their relatives here be notified that they are in want, or that they desire to join them in this country...

Here is the list of those sought:

CARSIE AKSELROD

Address unknown, thought to live in the Tenth Ward...

SELIG AND Moishe Akselrod sat in the doorway of Silver Dollar Smith's saloon on Essex Street. Selig finished reading the article, folded the newspaper down and handed it back to Moishe. "Who looks for her? How do we find out?"

Those ads were nothing but trouble, Moishe thought. He had seen the ads before—it was the same as the one that brought Carsie and Lilia into his life. "I say we don't mention it," Moishe said. "She doesn't need to see the paper today. Everyone goes about their business." He glanced across the street. "You have other things to worry about." He nodded in the direction of the Essex Street Market, where Carsie stood in front of the potato bin, talking to Arnold Rothstein.

Selig thought Rothstein stood too close to Carsie as the two of them laughed at a shared joke. Rothstein tipped his hat and walked on down Essex. He turned and waved. Selig watched from the doorway of the saloon as she lifted a gloved hand to her lips and waved back.

Selig's eyesight blurred, his temples pounded. He felt his feet move beneath him, running across Essex. He grabbed Carsie's arm and wrenched her to him. "Did I see you blow a kiss to Rothstein?"

"I don't know what you saw. I like him, is all." Yes, she thought, maybe someday I will love a man like Arnold Rothstein. "He's a nice man. Pleasant. Not like some."

"You and I are getting married. Rothstein is nothing to you."

"Are we? Are *you and I* getting married? I thought you didn't want to do that. I thought I was free to find someone who might be interested in marrying me. You've been talking about how we don't need to marry—but the first time you see someone else who likes me, it all changes?"

"You agreed to marry me."

She pulled her arm away and rubbed the spot where Selig had gripped. "You told me it was not necessary—that we were already related."

"You're planning the wedding."

"Was planning the wedding—until recently."

Selig's eyes narrowed. "When you met Rothstein."

"Yes, as a matter of fact."

"No, as a matter of fact. You'll marry *me*."

"Then here's the way I'll marry you, Selig. We'll marry only if you agree to contribute to the household fund the same as the rest of us do."

"But Moishe doesn't—"

"That's not mine to say, but your portion is. And I say you give us the same amount everyone else does. And there's one other thing."

"What? What else can there be? *Oy vey!* I'm to be a married man like this?"

"That's the only way it can happen if you want to marry me."

"Then...*what?*"

"You will not argue with me. If I am happy, you'll be happy—remember: happy wife, happy life. If I want to go somewhere or do something or want you to run an errand there is no discussion. Do you agree?"

Selig leaned against the market wall and looked at the sky, wondering how his advantage in this conversation had eroded so quickly, how Carsie had turned this marriage agreement into an unconditional surrender. He knew he had an argument ahead with Moishe. He gulped.

"Selig?" she said. "Do you agree?"

23

MONK EASTMAN did not live in the Tenth Ward; instead he lived at Bowery and Fifth Street, two blocks from his archrival Paul Kelly and Kelly's New Brighton Social Club. Eastman lived there to keep an eye on Kelly. But in the last two weeks of August 1903, New Brighton Social Club had fallen quiet. That made Eastman nervous.

By mid-September Eastman discovered where Kelly's Five Points Gang had gone—they had flanked the Tenth Ward from their original ground near Five Points on the south end of Bowery, and the north end, down from Great Jones. They spread east, enforcing their rule across Bowery nearly to Silver Dollar Smith's saloon on Essex—Eastman's own headquarters. They took over some of Eastman's whorehouses on Allen Street and encroached on the numbers racket along Delancey. They sold protection to the stores on Christie despite Eastman's extorting the same kind of money from the shop owners.

Eastman's gang decided it was war.

SEPTEMBER 17, four days before the beginning of *Rosh Hashanah*, dawned early for Moishe and Selig. The two men stopped at Silver Dollar Smith's for a whiskey and to pick up guns before they doubled back to the east side of the Second Avenue elevated platform to wait, joined by dozens of others who worked for Eastman in various parts of the ward. Just after daybreak, someone shot across Christie at Paul Kelly, and the battle began.

When Carsie lifted a window at the front of the flat she heard the first volley of gunshots, one and another and a third, and a barrage, roaring, battering, hammering. It seemed to her almost a dream that people in America shot at each other. *Surely,* she thought, *I am only remembering. Only remembering. Things like this do not happen here.* "The imported models..." she mumbled, "show a lavish use of flowers...the seal of approval on floral trimmings...as in past seasons the rose has the preference...made of velvet and in realistic colorings..."

She stepped out to do her marketing, her lips still moving. "The new millinery material called damas dentelle...a sort of silk damask...set in simulated lace...requires little trimming beyond a rich plume..."

At Stanton Street, policemen pushed her back, declaring that they themselves dared get no closer to the vicious gun battle. She gazed down Rivington, seeing a man set the barrel of his gun against another man's temple and pull the trigger. Others lay shot and bleeding on the sidewalk, blood pooling in the gutters for dogs to lick. She covered her ears, recalling vividly the sounds and smells of the Cossack attacks. Memories washed over her again of yelling and gunshots and the acrid smell of black powder in the air.

MOISHE CAME in alone late that evening. He glanced into the front room but said nothing and stumbled to the bed in the back room, where he lay down to sleep. Near midnight he rose and left again without a word to Carsie or Shalva, and without eating supper. He did not return until the following day.

Shalva had taken a job, selling ladies' garments and making alterations at Franck's Tailors, across the street from their old flat on Bowery. News of the gun battle reached the store in fearful whispers and knowing comments from customers and vendors all that afternoon, everyone saying it was the gangs. She knew in her heart that Moishe and Selig had been involved. And when Selig did not return to the flat that night the knot in her stomach told her what had become of him.

When she came in from work the following afternoon

Moishe sat at the table, reading an account of the gun battle in the *Daily Forward*. He looked up and closed the paper.

She set a basket of groceries on the table, raising an eyebrow at her husband. "You and Selig? Were the two of you involved in the…the thing under the El yesterday?"

Moishe shrugged and tapped the *Forward*. "Yeh. Cadets, they call us here."

"That's what they say out there too. The Allen Street Cadets they've named you. Faw. Cadets. You're working for Eastman, aren't you?"

Moishe stood, a finger in Shalva's face. "And proud to walk by his side."

"How about Selig? Is he proud to walk by Eastman's side too?"

Moishe slumped back into his chair. "Selig is dead. Gut shot. I buried him last night."

Carsie spent three days mourning with the family before *Rosh Hashanah* cancelled the balance of their *shiva* and all of *sheloshim*, the thirty-day period following. It was the first time she had felt relief when someone died, and on each of those days she sat on her stool in the circle thinking, *my life is mine, now. My life is mine. Lilia has Louis and her job at Triangle Waist Company, and I have found my place.*

Yet she felt odd because losing Selig had left not a void in her life. Was that wrong? Was sitting *shiva* a pretense when she did not grieve?

THAT FALL, she created twelve of the most elaborate hats New York had ever seen: plumed in long lengths and when one plume wasn't extreme enough she devised a way to join it to another, clustering groups of them low on the back of the hats so that they fell over a left shoulder in Cavalier fashion. Others bore wings and cock feathers or yards of purple velvet trim. Benjamin Altman bought every one of them for his store on Sixth Avenue at Nineteenth Street.

On New Year's Eve Carsie and Arnold Rothstein rode the

new IRT line uptown to Forty-second Street to see the fire-works. In the past three months they had gone to prize fights at Madison Square Garden, to horse races at Aqueduct race-course in Brooklyn, and to the theatre. Next week they had an invitation to a party at the Astor mansion on Fifth Avenue. The party was a night of gambling, and Rothstein was a superior gambler. He bet big. Betting big made him popular uptown.

He had brought her a sapphire-blue taffeta party dress at Chanukah, asking her to understand that the gift meant only that she should wear it sometime when they went out, nothing more. He didn't want strings, didn't need complications. He liked how little affection she showed him.

ROSE SCHNEIDERMANN sat at the table across from Car-sie, talking while she worked on a black felt hat trimmed in white plumes.

"...had to pay thirty dollars for my sewing machine," Rose was saying. "And they only paid me six! Six! That meant five weeks without a sou, because I had to buy that machine. So Mama says, 'Don't say a word, Rose. Men don't want a woman with a big mouth.' But I'm telling you, Carsie, this has gone on long enough. Do you know, there are children out there mak-ing the flowers we use? *Kinder!* Little strays with no education, and no hope for getting one."

Carsie finished tacking a plume to the underside of a hat brim and bit off the thread. "But that can be fixed, Rose. And you and I are the ones to do it."

"GOOD MORNING. How may I help you?" Carsie whispered as she walked home from English class. "That looks good on you, but this one looks better. May I wrap that or will you have it sent? Perhaps we can improve on the price, if you buy more than one." She dodged a pushcart and crossed Orchard Street. "Good evening, Alice," she called to a neighbor in English. "I hope you had a fine day."

———

AARON AND Miriam Bender did not bother to unpack their steamer trunks when they disembarked in Odessa. They took them, instead, to the train station and bought tickets on the Trans-Siberian Railway. Their journey across Russia lasted more than a month, transferring from train to train to accommodate the differences in rail gauge as they worked their way from Siberia to the Sea of Okhotsk. Once there, they boarded a steamship bound for San Francisco harbor. Aaron Bender had business in the U.S.

CARSIE'S HATS were in demand at fine stores all along Fifth Avenue, in anticipation of the annual Easter Parade. Her creations lavished flowers over their crowns, roses made of velvet, sprigs of wisteria or cabochons of mock coral, turquoise, and malachite encircled by crystals set at the center or to one side of the hatband.

Clutching her copy of the new issue of *Ladies' Home Journal,* Carsie strode up Sullivan Street, hoping Arnold Rothstein would ask her to the theatre next week. A happy show titled *Piff! Paff!! Poof!!!* had opened, starring Eddie Foy, and she could use a dose of happiness.

She paused at the entrance to the flat where she had bought fabric flowers when she worked for Madame Pelletier. Since she'd left Madame's atelier after a disagreement over the width of hat brims, her own millinery business had flourished.

She consulted her list. Hat brims had narrowed according to pictures she had seen from Paris; embellishments were stacked higher on the crowns rather than spread across a wide brim or radiating plumes from the back and sides as in previous years. She sighed. She did not like change.

Herr Macy had asked for her hats for his new store on Thirty-fourth Street, and others wanted them, too. Herr Bloomingdale had asked for an exclusive, but that was impossible now that she had so many customers. Orders had begun to stack up faster than she could produce.

Mercifully, the last of the boarders had moved on, having

found friendlier landlords than the Akselrods. She knew her family was not easy to live with, and apparently the boarders felt that way too, after she had stabbed Velvel Kagan. Some of them could afford a place of their own now, or found a bigger room that they shared with others or cheaper space in Hell's Kitchen.

She and Lilia and Shalva had no one to answer to now, but they paid a larger portion of the rent. She could work as late into the night as she needed, though Moishe got cross with her when she burned the lantern wicks down to nubs.

The workroom where she bought her feathers and flowers buzzed with the high-pitched voices of children, each of them leaning over a task—shaping velvet roses or poppies or lilies or grooming ostrich plumes, shaking out their cramped little fingers between projects. Children were ideal for this job, she knew, and some of them had true talent. A child saw a flower more completely than an adult did, and their agile fingers could mold the fabric or paper with an unfettered imagination.

In the back two men argued, one on each side of a desk.

"So? A penny more per flower—would it kill you? I can help these children. Give them lunch—something more than a cup of clear broth with a little piece of fish."

The other man waved him off and donned his beaver hat. "A penny more? Not on your life. I say cut your price by two cents or I take my business elsewhere."

She looked down at the imploring little faces that gazed up at her like baby birds. She knew they saw an adult standing in the doorway dressed in a gray basque-waisted coat, her black felt hat tied on with a large white silk scarf. None of them could imagine that it had been only four years since she sat in a place so like where they were now. She removed her gloves and pulled up an empty chair.

"Good morning," she said, smiling. "I've come for two reasons this morning. First I need gray ostrich plumes and the biggest purple roses you can make. And while you work, we will begin to learn sums, shall we? Yes. So, if I pay you six dollars a week and you need thirty dollars, how long—"

A boy stood, frowning, "Lady, six dollars a week? Who pays that kind of money to a kid?"

JUST AFTER the turn of 1904, Lilia was fourteen—as old as Carsie had been when their journey began, and as tall.

In February, two-year-old Naomi broke out in blisters on her arms and legs and stomach, and scratched the rash raw within a day. Shalva insisted on feeding her Mrs. Winslow's tonic to keep her from scratching, and indeed, the opiate made her sluggish enough that she stopped clawing at herself. Carsie checked on her hourly, concerned with the rash and how red Naomi's tongue had become. The baby ran a low-grade fever.

Carsie pulled on her coat and boots, wrapped Naomi in blankets and took her to a clinic she knew on Market Street, under the new Williamsburg Bridge.

A nurse led Carsie to the examining room, Naomi in her arms. The woman glanced sidelong at her as they walked to the examining room. "You are Shalva Akselrod's *mishpocha*, aren't you?"

"Yes, I'm her niece."

"I remember. From the night I delivered this child."

"You're Emma? Emma Goldman?"

"And you are Carsie Akselrod, aren't you? The one who writes letters to the *Forward?*" She smiled. "I know your letters—the words you use, your ideas. You may not sign your own name, but I know the letters are yours. I wish I had thought to do that, instead of..." She shrugged. "I might not be here tonight—hiding from the police." Emma Goldman nodded as she lifted Naomi's gown. "This child has scarlet fever. And you?" She looked over the top of her glasses at Carsie and shook a finger. "You have an obligation to your people. Naomi will probably not make it, and you must be sure others know why."

———

FIVE DAYS later, Naomi died of scarlet fever. Her death surprised none of them, including Shalva, who stayed in bed rather than sitting *shiva* for her dead daughter.

But by March, Shalva's father, Chaskel Grinberg had succumbed to diabetes. For him, Shalva rose from her bed and sat *shiva* for the full eight days. The first afternoon, sitting on her bench, her teeth chattered and she began to shake, and after three days of trembles and chills she shook off the first primitive grip of opium addiction. On the afternoon of the eighth day of *shiva* she went to the Williamsburg Bridge where she sat clutching the girders, her legs exposed to the bite of March winds off the East River. She tried to remember the last four years, seeing only flashes, knowing she had dozed through most of those months. She recalled taking Carsie to work at Melnick's. She heard the pharmacist say she should not use the tonic as often as she did. She saw her teeth lying in her hand, and the blood in the sink. She felt the doctor prod her belly and tell her she was pregnant. And she remembered childbirth. Beyond those events, she could summon nothing. Near sunset she stood, staring at the frigid water beckoning below. No, she thought. Too easy. She wanted a life—some sort of life—back. She threw five bottles of Mrs. Winslow's tonic in the river and turned back to Canal Street. But she knew she would always feel the bottle fairy sitting on her shoulder.

MAX SIEGEL found work at Silver Dollar Smith's Saloon on Essex Street, although as the weather cooled standing on his right foot had become gradually more painful. After his first week he had moved from his stained cot at the Sheltering Society to a small room in a tenement on Second Avenue, outside the Tenth Ward, where he could afford to live by himself. The place had provided him shelter from the bite of winter, but not by much. He had hoped to find Carsie by now—this was the turn of the year. Still, he wasn't giving up.

Occasionally, he ran a classified advertisement in the *Daily Forward*, seeking anyone who might have information about her. He had put aside the Federation's money to give to Carsie when he found her, using his meager tips from the saloon to pay his rent and for his lessons in reading and English at the Socialist Literary League. Between his work and the lessons he had little free time to search for her, but he had faith.

CARSIE PULLED on silk stockings, her first pair, attaching them at the top to her corset. She had never felt anything as smooth as those stockings against her legs. "I love your dress," she mumbled in English. "Tank, no, th- th-! Thank you, yours is beautiful, too. Thank you for the lovely party. Thank you for the lovely evening, Arnold."

Lilia sat on the bed, listening. "Who are you thanking in there?"

"Mmmm? Oh. I'm practicing. I hope I don't forget and use the wrong word."

Lilia giggled. "Try to remember everything tonight, Carsie."

Carsie smiled. "Everything, everything?"

"*Everything*, everything. Remember what Papa used to say when we went to sleep? 'Remember well, remember right.' So remember...everything."

"I will." She flipped open the closet curtain and kissed the top of Lilia's head.

"I mean, remember what the Astor house looks like and what the other ladies wore, and what food you ate. And the music. I'm sure there'll be music, won't there?"

"Maybe I should send you, rather than going myself. Lace me up, would you?"

Shalva came in, holding pink satin pads that Carsie tied around her hips and under her arms to accentuate her waist. She pulled up her bloomers and stepped into a petticoat. She sat when Lilia stood, buttoning her shoes, and then reached for the dress.

She paused and sighed. Ever since she first saw a blue taffeta dress in a shop window in Kiev one summer, when she had gone to visit Bubbe Esther, she had dreamed of wearing a dress like this one to a grand party. Blue taffeta was a summer fabric, but Rothstein had given her the dress and he wanted her to wear it. Here she was, dressing for a party she could never have hoped to attend had she stayed in Russia. Mrs. Astor would understand, she was sure.

She fastened Rose Schneidermann's pearl choker at her neck, hooked on pearl drop earrings and took up the long gray kid gloves she had received from Herr Altman in exchange for two of her hats.

"Perfect," Lilia said, beaming. "You look like a princess."

Shalva swept a high-necked bombazine cape around Carsie's shoulders, careful not to crush the bouffant dress sleeves, and pinned a wide-brimmed gray beaver hat into Carsie's hair.

"The cab is here! The carriage!" Lilia shrieked. "Oh, gosh, Carsie! Have fun, have fun! Just think! A party at John Jacob Astor's house!"

FROM THE corner of Houston and Orchard, Max Siegel saw a crowd, mostly women, clustered near the doorway of a tenement building halfway down the street. A hansom cab waited at the curb. A man in an overcoat with a fur collar handed a woman dressed in an elaborate blue party dress into the carriage. The crowd clapped and cheered. As the carriage turned onto Houston, Max caught sight of the woman in the blue dress. Though she looked older and more sophisticated, the woman's eyes reminded him very much of…he blinked….Yes, the woman's eyes reminded him of Carsie Akselrod.

24

CARRIAGES QUEUED in front of the Astor's limestone mansion on the corner of Sixty-fifth Street and Fifth Avenue at dusk, flambeaus standing on either side of the wrought-iron gate to light the guests' way up the drive. After a butler took their coats at the foot of a wide staircase, Rothstein handed the man a calling card.

"Arnold Rothstein and Miss Carsie Akselrod," the butler called up the stairs.

Rothstein offered his arm and he and Carsie climbed the marble staircase to a mezzanine, where Ava Astor stood greeting her guests.

Carsie's head swam. The ceilings were impossibly high and ornate—how did anyone keep this place clean? The house smelled clean and floral, different from the flats downtown.

Mrs. Astor wore a loose brocade smock, adorned with whorls of soutache braid and caught at the waist with a wide ribbon. Her short blonde hair curled around a headband that caught a fan of egret feathers. Long strands of pearls dripped from her neck. She carried an unlit cigarette in a black cigarette holder. Ava Astor winced when Carsie offered her hand and blew a kiss over Carsie's shoulder by way of welcome.

"What a clever dress," Ava Astor smiled. "How different to wear taffeta at this time of year. I can't wait for the others to see it."

"Thank you," Carsie beamed. "It was a gift from Arnold."

Ava Astor turned away. Carsie did not hear her mumble, "Egad, a gift? The damn thing screams, 'loving hands at home'." Mrs. Astor brightened and held out her arms to another woman. "Grace, how glad I am to see you." She turned a pirouette in her brocade smock. "It's Poiret! Do you love it?"

The party came angel-close to Carsie's dream: women in brown velvet gowns and dark green brocade and gray samite. Carsie's was the only dress there of taffeta, the only one in a shade as bright as sapphire blue. Of the few who wore gloves, hers were the only ones that were not white kid. Her hosiery was not as translucent, her shoes did not button on the side and the soles were not as thin as the other women's shoes. But she had something they did not, and could not buy: her hair was darker, shinier and thicker than anyone else's, her eyelashes longer, her neck and throat younger and smoother, her skin more radiant.

In the green salon, the women sipped sherry and worked jigsaw puzzles and talked in whispers all evening, turning their backs whenever Carsie approached. The men gambled in an oak-paneled smoking salon on the opposite side of the mezzanine. At nine o'clock a butler called them all to dinner. Carsie found her way to the dining room table by herself, which amused a few of the women, although Ava Astor was not amused.

"Arnold," Carsie said when she saw him come in. "Mrs. Astor has me sitting at the opposite end of the table from you." She began to struggle out of her gloves.

He pulled her into the picture gallery. "Let me explain how this works, Carsie. First, when we are called to dinner, you wait for me to take you in. Next, expect that we will not be seated together." He looked down and frowned. "Third, put your gloves back on. You do not remove your gloves to eat."

"Oh, please. What if I get them dirty? I'd never forgive myself."

"Leave them on. For my sake."

"What else?"

"I thought you knew these things. You always seemed so…I don't know, proper."

"What else do I need to know? Hurry—I'm starving."

"No one sits until Ava is seated. And with Ava, that will take some time. She will move around the table talking to one or another of her guests for a while before she sits down."

Carsie gulped. "But—I'm already faint from hunger."

He smiled. "You'll grow fainter still before you eat. When we're seated, we chat with our dinner partners while the servants bring in the first courses. When everyone is served, *and Ava has picked up her fork,* you may begin."

"*Gott im himmel,* Arnold! That could be an hour from now. Let's get in there." She started for the door.

"*With me,* Carsie."

"Oh. Yeh."

"And this crowd uses 'yes.' English, remember?"

"Yeh—*yes,* of course. Come on. I'm mad to eat."

Rothstein tucked her hand in the crook of his elbow. "Watch me, at the other end of the table. I'll give you cues, okay?"

"I didn't dream these people had such rules. Never mind they eat in the middle of the night."

"Hmmm? The middle of the night?"

"Our brood usually eats around four."

"In the afternoon?" He shook his head.

They walked back to the dining room, Rothstein coaching: "Okay, listen. Hands in your lap between courses, no elbows on the table—I don't care who else does it, you can't. Begin with the outer fork and work inward…the bowl of water to the right of your plate is a finger bowl.…"

Dinner ground through eleven courses over five hours: clams and oysters, a clear consommé, a liver paté, and dressed cucumbers. After the staff cleared the plates there was a lengthy pause.

She looked down the table at Rothstein, who sipped at his wine while he listened thoughtfully to the woman on his left—Mrs. Metcalf, who had bent his ear since they sat down.

These people, despite their penchant for rituals like eating late and how to do it, looked to her like any in the Tenth

Ward on a Friday night. She had been mistaken to hold them in awe.

Two maids brought out poached trout with potatoes, followed by roast beef with horseradish and cold asparagus. Talk at the dinner table turned to events of the day, both in the U.S. and overseas.

Ava Astor smiled down the table. "Tell of the news you heard from Russia, Reverend Sewell."

Sewell shook his head. "Appalling. Demonstrators gunned down by the Cossacks in St. Petersburg. Honestly, the Czar can't continue to slaughter people like..." he groped for a word.

"Rabbits." Carsie jabbed at a piece of rare roast beef with her knife. "He slaughters them like rabbits, like he butchered my mother and father."

The table fell silent, everyone's eyes focused on their dinner plates.

Rothstein broke the hush. "I heard sympathy strikes are going on all over the country, Reverend. Any truth to that?"

"Mmm," the cleric nodded. "The city has no electricity, no newspapers. All the public areas have been closed. I swear Russia moves closer to revolution every day."

"And about time," Carsie mumbled to no one. "About time."

After the roast beef, dinner seemed at an end. Still, no one left the table. Soon, the maids reappeared with a lemon ice, fruit and cheese plates, and a spice cake. She thought of the people back in Lucava, carving away rotted bits of a potato, trying to find enough to make their supper; of all the lentils she had eaten because they stored well; of the garbage in the gutters of the Tenth Ward because produce and meat would not keep. She put down her fork and sat back. This much food for so few people, and how much of this might the servants eat?

While many of the guests lingered over Marsala and brandy, two of the men drifted off to talk business and some of the women excused themselves to the second floor gallery. Carsie remained at table because Rothstein did.

"So, Miss Akselrod," the man to her right began. "How do you fill your time?"

"During the day, you mean?" She picked up her napkin and glanced at Rothstein. He dabbed with his at the corners of his mouth then replaced it in his lap. Carsie did the same. She smiled at her dinner partner, who had introduced himself earlier as Captain Tallmadge, up from Atlanta to visit relatives who lived on Madison Avenue. "I am a milliner," she said. "I have my own business. And I teach children."

She had surprised herself. It was the first she had spoken the words, "I am a milliner, I have my own business." She had her own business, that was true, but she worked out of the flat. Until she had a shop she felt like an imposter—no better than the Benders.

"Teaching," Tallmadge nodded. "Admirable. Where do you teach?"

"In the sweatshops. I'd like to teach the prisoners on Blackwell's Island, but my family is afraid for me to go over to the prison."

"Still," he chuckled. "In the sweatshops. You are a brave woman, Miss Akselrod. What on earth do you teach them—how to beg a bone on the steps of Tammany Hall?"

She stiffened. "I teach them to read. And to do sums."

"Reading and sums? To children in the sweatshops? But surely not, Miss Akselrod."

"Why not, Captain Tallmadge?"

"Well, first because knowing those things would bewilder a child, don't you think?"

Carsie smiled. "I learned those things as a child and the knowledge didn't bewilder me."

"Then this, Miss Akselrod: if those children find better jobs because they learn to read and do sums, we'll have to hire others to do the same work—probably older people who will want more money. The price of our products would go up. And anyway, it's above their station for children in the sweatshops to know how to read and do sums. People should learn first where they fit in…just as…well, just as most women should understand they cannot run a business, really."

Carsie thrust out her chin. "And if a woman wants her own business, what would be wrong with that?"

Rothstein cleared his throat. She glanced toward his end of the table. He frowned and shook his head. She turned again to Tallmadge. "I beg your pardon, Captain Tallmadge. I thought I heard Mr. Rothstein say something."

"Indeed I did," Rothstein said, standing. "It's going on two in the morning. The cabs stop running in a bit—I think we should find Mrs. Astor and say goodnight."

Carsie and Rothstein climbed a second set of marble stairs to a long gallery, where Ava Astor stood with some of her guests, her back to the stairs.

"…God-awful garish shade of blue taffeta," Mrs. Astor said. Though others saw them coming and put a finger to their lips, Mrs. Astor held forth. "And so *Jewish*. I mean, Rothstein is, but Jack likes his company." She raised an eyebrow. "Well, Jack would. Still, to bring that tarted-up shop girl into my home…"

When the guests stared wide-eyed at Carsie and Rothstein, now standing behind her, the doyenne paused and glanced over her shoulder.

Carsie stepped closer to the group. "Say your goodnights, Arnold. I won't be back, so it's not necessary for me to behave myself any longer."

The ride down Fifth Avenue began awkwardly quiet. Lit by gas lamps along the way, she stared numbly at her gloved hands in her lap, against the blue taffeta dress Mrs. Astor had deemed garish. She didn't know what she would tell Lilia, and her friends in the ward—all of them waiting for details of her grand evening.

She sighed. "Did you know taffeta is a summer fabric?"

"No, not at all. Men are not as concerned with how women dress as women are. I thought you looked…well, lovely."

"But not uptown lovely."

"Those women, especially Ava, need a dose of humility. I don't forgive them—any of them—for the way they conducted themselves tonight, but you owe Ava Astor an apology."

"An *apology*? Why? Oh. Because you'll go back if you're invited, won't you?"

"Yes. Jack Astor is a high-stakes poker player. I won a thousand dollars from him and his friends tonight. I'll go back—if I'm invited. That would happen more quickly if you wrote Ava Astor a note."

They rode on in silence.

"I thought the women talked to each other because it was more comfortable to talk to friends rather than to a stranger," Carsie said.

"Those women didn't approve of the way their husbands looked at you. I saw that. They hadn't been given that look by a man in a very long time."

"Did you know those women were going to be…that way?"

"I suspected they might. But I thought you wanted to see how they lived."

Carsie chewed her upper lip while she thought. The cab pulled up to the front of the tenement building, and the driver flipped down the steps and assisted her out.

Rothstein stepped down and took her by the shoulders. "What can I do? You don't fit in up there, Carsie."

"Not yet Arnold." She smiled. "But someday I will, if you'll gamble five hundred dollars of Mr. Astor's money. I'd like to rent a storefront uptown."

LOUIS LEVY completed his apprenticeship at Lord and Taylor on Fourteenth Street in June of 1905, becoming their youngest draper and tailor, hand-making suits for his burgeoning uptown clientele. Louis himself wore a suit to work every day, along with a stiff celluloid collar, a cravat or necktie, and a hat—a straw boater or derby—all of it barely disguising a bony frame still recovering from two years of acute alcohol abuse.

When the Triangle Waist Company expanded, Lilia moved from sweeping chaff on the cutting floor to the ninth floor, where machine operators churned out mass-produced shirtwaists. Thanks to her glasses, she saw well enough to wheel carts of findings from one bank of sewing machines to the next, furnishing thread, buttons, lace trim, and interlining to the girls at the machines so they would not waste time by moving away from their work to get supplies.

ON A fine morning in June, Carsie signed a lease for space on Thirty-eighth Street, using, as a deposit, one hundred of the five hundred dollars Rothstein had loaned her. She scrubbed away decades of coal smoke and street sludge from the front windows and hired a sign painter to letter two lines in an arc:

MODISTE HATS

TO THE TRADE ONLY

She cleaned the walls and painted them sapphire blue, by now her favorite color despite what Ava Astor thought. She washed and polished the floors and lined the front window bays with white satin. She bought display counters and hat stands and forms and trimmings and catalogues with the balance of the money Rothstein had lent her, and the week before *Rosh Hashanah* that year she opened Modiste Hats, near the sweatshops where children made velvet roses. No sooner had she opened than she had to close for a week for the high holy days.

BY AUTUMN of 1905 Aaron and Miriam Bender had fled an insurance fraud indictment brought by The National Life Insurance Company, leaving Chicago by train with the police in pursuit. They arrived in New York, and settled at the new Astoria Hotel on Thirty-third Street. Soon they met with a man named Julian Gerard, a banker and mining promoter with Knickerbocker Trust Company. Gerard lent the Benders money against a gold mine in Death Valley that Aaron Bender had convinced him was a vast source of untapped wealth.

At the beginning of the social season, the Benders threw a reception in their suite at the hotel. Ava Astor included them at her annual Christmas tea.

"FOR THE store," Rothstein said as he slid the gift-wrapped box across the counter toward her. "I hope it will please you." He rocked back on his heels and watched her left the lid off the box. "To keep track of the time," he said. He raised an eyebrow. "Eight golden hours and twenty minutes are quick to become twice that, you know?"

"Thank you, Arnold." She turned the clock around, admiring it from all sides.

"It should bring good luck, I hope…"

"I hope so too."

Rothstein frowned. "What I started to say was, 'I hope to get my loan back soon'."

"As soon as I'm able, Arnold. I haven't forgotten your kindness. And now this—it's, it's very special. Thank you again."

WINTER OF 1906 passed colder than any in the Tenth Ward, even though the landlord had installed indoor plumbing and toilets on every floor, in accordance with a new law. The law also called for the installation of gas lamps in the hallways, and by spring the halls glowed warmly after dark. Tenants decorated the walls of the stairway in some small effort to brighten their surroundings. Spirits in the ward began to lighten.

She tried to ignore what she saw of the Lower East Side now that she had seen better in the Astors' neighborhood. Things were cleaner up there, the buildings, the clothes. The air smelled different on upper Fifth Avenue—almost as though there were more of it, and it seemed easier to breathe.

ILANA LEVINSKY stood in front of Carsie, much as Carsie had stood before Madame Pelletier four years ago.

Carsie studied the girl's hands, trembling visibly in her own. "You are Russian Jew?"

"Yeh. From Kishinev. My family sent me out after the pogrom." Ilana shrugged. "Now, here I am. And I don't know what to do with myself."

Carsie nodded. "And you need a profession, yes? It is different in America than you thought, isn't it? This place is not as lucky as we were told—you have to work harder even than you might have in Russia, but I will teach you what I know. What Madame Pelletier taught me—or rather, what I learned from her. I'm sure I didn't learn everything she had to teach."

MAX SIEGEL took a circuitous route to work each morning—down to Houston from his flat on Second, backtracking to Orchard, south on Orchard to Delancey or Broome or as far down as Grand, if it was a fine day, two blocks east and north again on Essex to the saloon, walking at a casual pace, scanning, searching, clutching the kopek necklace he kept in his coat pocket. In the evenings, unless the weather drove him straight to his flat, he reversed his course, walking down Essex and across so he could walk north on Orchard.

CARSIE PRACTICED her English by reading *The New York World*. The newspaper used easy words and simple emotions to appeal more widely to New York's burgeoning immigrant population. In June, Carsie folded the afternoon edition in her lap to read the latest about the Girl in the Red Velvet Swing, the sensational tale raging all over New York that summer:

> Stanford White, a celebrated architect and womanizer, was buried today at St. James, in Suffolk County. Mr. White, suspected of seducing sixteen-year-old Evelyn Nesbit this spring while she cavorted in the nude on his fabled red velvet swing, was shot four days

ago by Miss Nesbit's new husband, Harry Thaw, of Pittsburgh.

She stared out over Orchard Street at the crowds milling below. Tens of thousands of immigrants had come in the six years since she and Lilia had arrived, many of them settling on the Lower East Side. The overcrowding and piles of muck had grown. She dabbed at perspiration beading on her forehead and studied a man walking north. He looked...no. Impossible. She turned back to the article.

> Miss Nesbit, until last year an actress and artist's model, married Mr. Thaw while she and her mother were in dire financial straits. Mr. Thaw, whose wealth reputedly runs to several million, viewed Miss Nesbit as his virginal bride at the time of their wedding. He did not know of Mr. White's seduction of her, though he knew they were friends.

Carsie sat back in her chair, thinking. Evelyn Nesbit had married for money in order to put food on her table. She supposed a woman could learn to love a man who provided for her after they were married—it happened often in arranged marriages, she had heard.

Her twentieth birthday had passed in November; it was time she married. There seemed no better husband material than Arnold Rothstein. He was an attentive listener, considerate in all things, handsome, and generous with his smile. And he cared for her at least enough to lend her the money to open Modiste Hats.

But even now, Rothstein didn't strike a chord in her when she looked at him. Oh, his smile made her faint, and his eyes— the way he looked at a woman—was five-alarm. Still, there was an ill-defined something about him she thought she should feel that she didn't feel when they were together. Perhaps if they married she might learn to love him.

She mulled the idea. How different life might be to marry wealthy. No more reworking second-hand dresses, or eating lentils and boiled cabbage. And if she had money? Millions, maybe? She would still school the children at the sweatshops. She would keep Modiste Hats. She would give glittery parties for Ava Astor and the others, and she would wear the latest in Paris fashion.

"WHAT WOULD you study?" Carsie asked.

"I haven't decided," Lilia said. "Delivering babies or eye surgery or drug addictions, maybe. Or epidemics, like typhus and scarlet fever."

"No, please, not epidemics. Do us all a favor—we'd worry every day if you worked with people who had such diseases."

"All right, not epidemics. Something useful, anyway. And New York University is so close—I can take a class each term until I'm done. Go when I get off work."

"Lilia! Think! You'll be exhausted at the end of your day— working *and* studying? How could you keep up that pace for long?"

"Carsie, I want to do it. And Louis thinks it's a fine idea. Remember Papa's passion? The Voice of the Pale? Well, mine is to help the people of the Tenth Ward."

Carsie sighed. "I wonder whether you would do better studying something else. What about literature? You could teach. It would take a very long time to get a medical degree one class at a time."

Lilia grinned at her sister—dear Carsie, always the worrier. She took her hand. "But…I have a very long time. Don't I?"

— 25 —

AARON BENDER pushed a back-dated check in the amount of one thousand dollars across the counter to the desk clerk at the Astoria Hotel and held his breath. The check was written on Knickerbocker Bank and Trust. He hoped it would work.

The teller shook his head. "I'm sorry sir; we no longer take checks on this bank. You see…"

Bender heard the desk clerk's apology and explanation, but he knew the reasons. He and the bank's president, Charles Barney, had become friends in the two years the Benders had been back in New York City, and he knew Barney had tried to corner the market on copper, using as much depositor money as he could get his hands on. Even Bender, an improvident man himself, had thought it a reckless idea. And now Knickerbocker Bank and Trust had gone under.

Bender had worked hard on his schemes. Both he and Miriam had cultivated some prominence in New York social circles. They dined at the finest restaurants and with the cream of society. He played poker with Jack Astor and Arnold Rothstein on a regular basis. What were he and Miriam to do now? They had no money.

"…ask you to leave the hotel by this afternoon," the desk clerk said with an oily smile.

THE AKSELRODS planned to celebrate Thanksgiving for the first time in 1907, though it had been a holiday for a number of years, now—a feast to give thanks for what had come to them during the year. The year had been bountiful, indeed. Carsie's millinery business had kept her busy through the selling season that ended with the high holy days, and after that she had enjoyed the lull, using the time to study her English and catch up on the mending and sewing; but while she worked she wondered why Arnold Rothstein hadn't come around as often as he had last spring. She feared he had found someone else, felt it in her bones, knew in her heart that she was not the only woman Rothstein saw. She thought it was because of her night at the Astor house, because she did not know the rules, because she was rude to Ava Astor. Because New York society would not make a place at the table for her.

Her fears were laid to rest when Moishe brought Arnold Rothstein to dinner on Thanksgiving afternoon. Before Rothstein left that evening he asked Carsie to go uptown with him the following Tuesday night to the opening of a new play at the Belasco Theatre.

NOVEMBER 28 was her birthday, and, she hoped, the night Arnold Rothstein would ask her to marry him. He came to call for her in his new Ford two-seater. Lilia thrilled to the sight of the black coupe waiting outside, its brass trim and head-lamps glinting in the gas lights above. The couple left the flat over protestations from Louis about the vehicle's safety, the two of them giggling at reactions to the car from people on every street corner as the Ford bucked and chattered its way up Broadway to the Belasco.

The show, *Rose of the Rancho,* was a bland affair and Rothstein took her home immediately after the curtain. When they pulled up to the front of the tenement building, he thanked her for coming out with him.

She waited for him to ask to see her again.

Nothing.

"Arnold," she smiled up at him. "You don't seem…that is…you don't come around as much as you used to."

"But I always look forward to seeing you. We can't see each other too often, or we'd tire of it, don't you think?"

She saw his point. As it was, she enjoyed their dates, and

perhaps if they went out more frequently they *would* tire of each other's company.

He helped her down from the car and walked her to the door without another word about seeing her again. Then he turned the Ford around in the middle of Orchard Street and headed back uptown.

ON A cold afternoon in February of 1908 Carsie returned home from the shop earlier than usual. Her hats were selling well for spring season—*Gott im himmel,* the number of fabric roses and plumes on them this year! Many of her hat stands had emptied that day. At noon, just as she was about to eat lunch, a woman came in wanting a white felt skimmer. Carsie offered to make one, but she didn't have it available. The woman changed her mind, asking for something dark with white mignonette. Carsie didn't have mignonette on hand, but could get it by late afternoon. The woman had left in a huff.

Carsie finished her lunch, packed her shipments and closed mid-afternoon, hoping for a nap.

A black motor car sat in front of the tenement building. Cars, commonplace uptown, were still a rare sight in the Tenth Ward. The car did not look like Rothsteins's—this one was wider, bulkier looking, not something someone from the Tenth Ward would own. The warders spent their money on food and rent, and seldom was there room enough for a car to negotiate the streets of the Lower East Side. Nor did she recognize it from any of her acquaintances through Modiste.

She climbed the stairs to the flat. The door stood open a crack and noises came from within—men's laughter, drawers banging, furniture being knocked over. Carsie retreated to the street, returning moments later with William Bailey, the same beat cop who had written up her incident with Velvel Kagan six years earlier.

He pushed the door open with his night stick and the two

of them stepped into the flat, taking different directions, Bailey to the back, Carsie to the living room.

Empty. Chairs on their sides, the contents of a hatbox strewn across the floor. She heard noises in the closet, and pointed Bailey to movement in the curtain that covered the closet doorway.

The cop pulled aside the drape, exposing two men rifling through the clothes. "What the hell do you think you are doing in there? Those your clothes?"

"Naw," one of the men said. "But we got a right to be here, don't get snarky." He flashed a badge at Bailey. "Sent over by Mr. Isaac Harris at Triangle. We're here to search, uh…" he consulted a slip of paper in his vest pocket, "Lilia Akselrod's stuff."

Carsie pushed forward. "Why are you searching our things?"

"Who are you to ask?"

"I live here." She reached for a corset the other man had begun to pull apart. "Stop it—that's mine."

He smirked. "Relax, sister. Everybody who works at Triangle Waist Company gets their place searched once in a while. Harris has it done to be sure the girls don't steal from him." He shrugged. "Today this place, tomorrow some other girl's address."

"I KNEW they would come someday, Carsie," Lilia said as she refolded clothing in the drawers of the closet. "They told us to expect it. At work, a watchman stands guard at the door at closing time, and searches our handbags. They poke knitting needles through our hair, hunting for bits that we might have stolen—fabric or lace or a spool of thread we might use here at home."

"But that's monstrous. And they…they don't pay you…"

"Ho," Lilia scoffed. "No, they don't pay us, they pay the contractors who hired us, and the contractors pay us."

"So technically, you still work for Osher Melnick?"

"Yes. Every week Mr. Melnick pays me…probably half of what Harris and Blanck pay him for my work. Harris charges us for our supplies and for the electricity to run his sewing machines, too. And 'rent' for the chairs we sit in thirteen hours a day, six days a week."

"Why haven't you said anything about it until now?"

Lilia shrugged. "That's the way it is all over the city—every shop has contractors who hire girls like me. One of these days, Carsie, the workers will get angry enough to change it. We aren't angry enough yet, I suppose, but I can tell you, it's coming."

"HE'S BUSY," Carsie told Ilana Pekarsky the next day as they worked. "I'm willing to wait—for a while longer. But…"

"Madame, you should look at other men, too, you know. You are…well, you are a very lovely woman, and it would be a shame if Herr Rothstein…"

"I know," Carsie admitted. "If he decided to marry someone else." She looked at Ilana. "Are you seeing anyone?"

SHE HADN'T seen Rothstein since her birthday, in November. He didn't show up again until early June, when he took her to the opening of a new musical revue, *The Ziegfeld Follies*. He didn't pay her much attention that night; his sights set more on the chorines than the woman at his side. That night he treated Carsie in a fashion she thought more sisterly than amorous.

Once again, when they returned to the flat he walked her up the stairs and said goodnight. He paused and removed his hat, cocked an eyebrow, lowered his lids and smiled at her— the shy, bedroom smile he had given her when they first met in front of the Essex Street Market, then spun on his heel and made for the car.

FOR HER birthday, Lilia invited Carsie to lunch at the Astoria Hotel. Neither of them ate out often, seldom uptown. The food was different uptown, and, since the Astor party, every time she ate uptown the food gave Carsie stomach twinges. She chose boiled onions and stewed beef. Lilia liked more adventurous fare and ordered sardines on toast. The dish smelled to Carsie like Fulton Fish Market on a hot day.

A feeling rose in Carsie—a memory she did not want, just yet, to suppress. She was drawn back to a November night eight years ago, when she and Lilia had clutched each other in the coal bin. She looked at her sister across the table, remembering...

But something else was afoot with Lilia that day, Carsie suspected. There was a reason she had asked Carsie to lunch, other than to celebrate her birthday. "Lilia..." she began.

Lilia did not look up.

Carsie continued. "Why, are we here today? Other than my birthday?"

Lilia sighed. "I wanted to talk to you alone, and it's hard, anymore, with others always around in the flat."

"Talk? About what?"

"You. You're twenty-three today."

"Yes, I am. And you're eighteen, soon to be nineteen. A miracle it is for both of us to be sitting here...." She chuckled. "In Mr. Astor's hotel restaurant. My, how things have changed in eight years. From Lucava to...all this." The thought dizzied her.

A familiar-looking woman walked by in a lavender dress. The man behind her paused, swept Carsie and Lilia with a glance, and walked on to be seated with his companion at a table in the center of the room. Carsie gasped.

"What?" Lilia asked.

"Did you not recognize the Benders?"

"Bunk," she said. "Where are they? Can I look?"

"Yeh, they're facing away from us."

"My gosh, it *is* them. Are we going over to say hello?"

"*Gott im himmel*, no." Carsie shivered. "Wonder what they're doing here." She stared at Miriam's lavender dress, remembering the crocheted detail on the cuff, wondering how different life might have been if they had gone to Schenectady with the Benders. She shook her head. "So, what's your news, Lilia? Why are we really out today?"

Lilia grimaced. "I need to know something, Carsie."

"Of course, if I know it. What?"

"Louis and I have waited, Carsie, but we don't want to wait any longer. That is…I need to know if it's all right for me to marry before you do."

"Ah. I guess we both thought Arnold Rothstein would be…but no, not any time soon, is he? So you and Louis are… sure, go ahead. Why wait any longer?"

AARON BENDER had been insolvent for less than an hour when his next scheme struck. He approached each of the men waiting in front of Knickerbocker Bank and Trust on the afternoon the bank failed and gave them his card. Whenever one of the men called, Bender assured his mark that he could get the money out of Knickerbocker, if only they would give him an advance on the amount the mark had lost—a mere five percent of the total for Bender to do the work. Within the day, the Benders had paid their overdue hotel bill, and another two months beyond that. Miriam Bender had been so secure in her husband's ability to con people out of their pocket money that she hadn't bothered to pack.

And when J.P. Morgan effected a market recovery in 1908, Knickerbocker Bank and Trust reopened, depositing the full amount of each customer's money back in their old bank accounts. Bender took credit for his marks' recovery of their money, though he had nothing to do with it. He kept the five percent he made on each one.

LILIA AND Louis Levy married in late March of 1909, in the front room of the flat. Carsie and Lilia had worked for weeks on her wedding gown, made from bolts of new silk and crepe de Chine. Both women agreed they did not want to rework a hand-me-down. This was the beginning of a new life, and Lilia wanted a new dress for it. The sleeves, covered in lace, stood as bouffant as they could make them stand, the waist nipped, the bodice ruched and pleated, the hemline trailed a modest train.

The ceremony began with a simple, lyric beauty: Moishe and Shalva witnessed a hand-decorated *ketubah*, the Jewish marriage contract. The couple stood under a *chuppah* decorated with fabric flowers Carsie could use later on her hats. Lilia circled Louis seven times to signify seven blessings before they took their vows, both of them clearly delighted to be saying the words that bound them together.

They wrapped a glass in a napkin and set it on the floor. Louis hit it with his foot, but it did not break. He stomped harder. Nothing. Again he tried, everyone shouting *"Mazel tov!"* anticipating the glass would break. And again, the glass, its shattering a symbol of the destruction of the Temple or an indication of the shattered world or any one of a number of other icons, did not break. Carsie ran to the kitchen for something more fragile. She grabbed a kerosene globe, wrapped it in a flour sack towel and ran back to the front room to set it on the floor. At last, he broke the glass. But everyone questioned why the ritual goblet hadn't broken on cue.

Carsie had assumed Lilia and Louis would remain in the Orchard Street flat after they married. Their announcement that they had taken a room on Fifth Avenue at Thirteenth Street came as a shock to her. It made sense that they should begin their life together alone, and their work took them farther uptown. Lord & Taylor, where Louis's clientele now sought him out by name, was at Twentieth and Broadway, seven blocks north of their new room. Triangle Waist Company and Lilia's classes at NYU were roughly the same distance south. The couple had almost nothing to begin housekeeping, and little time to appreciate the trifle they had.

Carsie missed her younger sister's company. This was the first time they had separated for more than a few hours, save

Lilia's illness in Trusheny when Carsie was not far off; and Carsie, although she lived in the midst of the most densely crowded square mile on earth there on Orchard Street, was lonely. On an early spring evening she stopped on her way home from work to visit with Louis and Lilia. Leaving the Fifth Avenue flat she spotted Emma Goldman walking toward her.

Emma stopped, studied her, and started on before she stopped again. "Carsie? Carsie Akselrod? Is that you?"

"It is, Emma. How are you? How's life in…your world?"

"Eh, I'm weary. Forty years old, and tired of the fight. Worse than that, I know the struggle has just begun. There's so much to do—the magazine, my speeches, and Ben. You look different, my dear. Grown up."

"Ben? But I thought Alexander Berkman…"

"No, not really. Not since he was released from prison. Prison changes you, I ought to know. He wasn't the same after… well, after he got out. And you? What are you doing now?"

"I have my own millinery business over on Thirty-eighth, and I teach children in the sweatshops."

"Outrageous, that."

"That I teach?"

"That children still work for the sweaters. It must change, Carsie. You are their Jeanne d'Arc—you must take up that task. Free those children."

"But I…"

"I'm off to Alfred Stieglitz's gallery this evening." Emma squinted up at Carsie through her thick glasses. "For the opening of a new show. Will you come? He always invites interesting people, except for Mr. Dreiser, who will inevitably be there. Claims to hate Jews, Dreiser does, except he keeps company with so many of us. Heh heh. You'd fit right in, with your passion and your beauty." Emma Goldman hooked her arm through Carsie's. Together they walked north on Fifth Avenue. "Watch Stieglitz, though, he's a womanizer. Loves women—all kinds of them. Doctor Freud is coming to town, had you heard? Fascinating man…."

The reception looked and felt different from how Carsie supposed an art reception might. She had guessed perhaps punch and cookies would be served at a reception, though she didn't know how, exactly, an uptown art show should look. The walls of Stieglitz's gallery were hung with a row of stark photographs mounted in large white mats. Modern electric lights suspended overhead bathed the walls in a white light. Women in all kinds of dresses—Parisian smocks and robes from exotic countries and straight black gowns that fell from their shoulders—stood among the men. Some wore hats. Many did not.

Emma was right, Carsie thought, this is a most interesting crowd. *I feel more at home with these people than I did at the Astor party, that's certain*, she thought.

A group to her left discussed the Gwangiu uprising, and a clutch of men to her right talked about the push for revolution in Barcelona. Ahead of her two women stared at a photograph of Venice, and mentioned the new Henry James book, *The Italian Hours.*

No, Carsie thought. Wrong again. These are not my people, either. Then she smiled to herself. Unlike the party at the Astors', it hadn't taken all night to discover she didn't belong here. She turned to leave, hoping to slip out before anyone spoke to her.

"Come," Emma said, taking her elbow. "Let me introduce you."

The evening turned into a dizzying slate of names Carsie had heard and read: indeed, Theodore Dreiser invited her to lunch at the Brevoort Hotel on the following day. She declined. With him stood an artist named George Bellows, whose pictures Carsie had seen reproduced in the newspapers. A barefooted woman in a Grecian gown stood nearby; people called her Isadora and complimented her on a recent performance at the Metropolitan Opera House. Lucy Anthony, daughter of the famous suffragette, and painter Robert Henri, clearly sweet on Emma, crowded around.

But it was Stieglitz who scared Carsie, with his intense manner and urgent attentiveness. A gaunt man with an angular face and a bushy moustache, Stieglitz stood too close when he breathed, "You are Jewish, and young, and lovely, Miss Akselrod. May I ask, how young?"

"Alfred," Emma chided. "She's too young, that's how young. What, dear? Twenty or so? To Alfred's forty-four?"

Carsie's heart pounded. It was time to go.

THE ORDER Wanamakers' Department Store placed with Modiste Hats in early August of 1909 enabled Carsie to pay back Arnold Rothstein's loan. She wrote him a note, asking for an appointment on Thursday, just after closing, sending it by messenger to Rothstein's office. When the messenger returned he had an answer: Rothstein would come to Modiste just after five on Thursday afternoon.

Thursday morning she changed clothes three times before she felt her dress was right for her meeting. She swept the shop twice, dusted whenever she didn't have a customer, restocked hats and findings until the place looked as prosperous and professional as any Madison Avenue retail shop.

Closing time approached. Her palms moistened. She sat down to wait. Rothstein pulled up in his Ford shortly after five, and she greeted him at the door.

He stepped in and looked around, nodding, smiling. "Nice," he said. "You've done well, I hear."

"I like to think I have. I got a large order recently and I'm pleased to say I can give you this." She handed him an envelope containing five hundred dollars.

Rothstein counted the money and smirked. "A good beginning. Another payment like this and you'll be clear."

Carsie frowned. "But, that's what you lent me, five hundred."

"Yeh, four years ago. Interest rates being what they are, you owe me another five hundred, wouldn't you say?"

"*Another* five hundred? But you never said anything about…"

"Listen. You wouldn't have been able to get a loan from a bank, so I figure what I'm asking is what you'd have paid on the street for that money."

Her mind raced. "I can't give you any more right now than…maybe another two hundred…" Another two hundred dollars would clean out her bank account. She wouldn't have anything left. "I could let you have the clock back…"

Rothstein growled and punched at the air. "Keep the clock—it was a gift, remember? Two hundred then. Send it by messenger tomorrow. I'll be in my office until one. You're getting a bargain, sister, but you're losing in the long run." He slammed the door on his way out.

On August 13 Carsie read in the *Daily Forward* that Sigmund Freud's visit to New York had included a tour of the Tenth Ward. Two cars had tangled traffic for more than an hour in a freak accident on the new Queensboro Bridge. Arnold Rothstein had married Carolyn Green, an actress.

She dropped the newspaper and clutched her stomach, trying to stop the gnawing feeling that grew there. She understood now what Rothstein had meant at the shop when he said she was losing in the long run. She had lost him and he had made her feel like a fool, paying him an extra two hundred dollars, wiping out her bank account, thinking that by doing it she held onto him.

Now she had no one who might take her out or keep her company or smile that bedroom smile at her. For four years she had waited, always expecting to hear Rothstein ask her to marry him on the next date. Instead, Carolyn Green, an actress, undoubtedly more glamorous, more uptown, a woman who probably knew her way around the Astors' dinner table, had heard the words.

Still, she did not cry. Although she mourned the loss of Rothstein she was happy to see Lilia and Louis wed. With Rothstein she had not found the spark of love that she had seen in Lilia's eyes, hoping only that he would choose her rather than any of the other women she knew he saw in the evenings. He had not and it hurt, but only when she let it. She promised herself that losing the people in her life would not hurt her anymore. She would not think about them, would not let them punish her for caring. She could not bear to feel that ache in her heart one more time, she decided. Not once more. Not ever.

She took little comfort in news that came some months later: Ava Willing Astor had divorced her wealthy husband, the man she called Jack Ass, and sailed for England.

— 26 —

OSHER MELNICK'S former partners, Isaac Harris and Max Blanck, themselves Russian Jews, had arranged the ninth floor of Triangle Waist Company in banks of tables seventy-five feet long with sewing machines on both sides—two hundred forty of them in all. The operators hunched over their machines, breathing in smells of sweat and dust and machine oil, the cadence of the foot pedals pounding.

Harris, an obdurate man, ordered the doors, even the one to the fire escape, locked from the outside during business hours, to keep union organizers out and to prevent the women from stealing or leaving.

As Lilia had predicted, Triangle's employees finally had their fill of low pay, long hours, poor working conditions, and abusive treatment. On November 22, 1909, three days before Thanksgiving, machine operators at Triangle Waist Company refused to begin their shift, shutting down production at the industry's largest sweatshop.

Harris and Blanck were stunned.

More stunning still, the walkout prompted a general strike of twenty thousand garment workers as far south as Philadelphia. A few workers crossed the picket lines at Triangle Waist Company, and for them, Harris and Blanck played phonograph music while they worked, held dance contests, and had lunches brought in.

Much as she and Louis needed the money, Lilia Levy refused to be a scab. Instead, she lettered a sign that read *Living Wages for Women,* and she walked with the strikers even though Louis begged her not to. At first Lilia felt a righteous exhilaration in walking the picket line—the solidarity among the strikers she marched with was buoyant; they knew their cause was just.

Few in New York outside the Tenth Ward took the strikers' demands seriously. Newspapers called them "an army of Amazons," and "petticoated antagonists," "wild with excitement," in "hysterical swarms," referring to the women as having too much time on their hands, as being flippy, flighty, empty-headed girls who "struck against God." Others thought the women wanted to "frolic rather than work," supposing their work got in the way.

Harris brought in thugs who beat the strikers on the picket line outside the Asch Building and hired prostitutes to mix with the picketers so strikers would be mistaken for whores, and bribed police to haul them off to jail. His hoodlums did their work without interference. The police looked the other way for a box of cigars containing a hundred dollar bill.

TRUSHENY WAS as peaceful now as it had been before anything changed, Hod Nakhimov wrote in a letter to Max Siegel. Before the night the Cossack walked into the bar with the girls from Lucava, before Max decided to marry Carsie Akselrod. The people of Trusheny sent their regards...all but Zirl Bakhtin. The bar was fine, and everyone awaited his return—with or without a bride. *Zol zayn mit mazel....*

Max lowered the letter, watching life on Second Avenue from the stoop of his building while he thought. Once again he went through the argument that raged in his head. *He* was the one who permitted the Cossack and the girls to stay that winter. *He* had decided to marry Carsie, and he blamed himself for the mess he'd made. Had he not let Carsie and Lilia leave that morning he would never have lost her to Zirl Bakhtin's scheme. Had he made sure she got to the house of Aiofe Karpin without mishap Carsie would be his wife today. Would have been for nearly ten years, now. They would have children. They would be happy in the peaceful little *shtetl* of Trusheny.

Or, had he planned better how to find her once he got here, looked harder or been a luckier man, they might be happily married, living in his flat, doing things people did in America—going to musical shows, working at their jobs, eating at Katz's after *Shabbat*.

He no longer caught glimpses of her from the back when she paused to cross a street, or through a butcher shop window, or having just stepped into a doorway. No, that was wrong. He *always* saw her on the street, in shop window reflections, or just passing him by without a word. And always it turned out not to be her. His search was useless. He had thought he would find her before now.

Siegel felt alone in America. He had no friends here like the friends who had become his family in Trusheny. He yearned to feel the touch of a woman, and to touch her. He wanted to forget Carsie Akselrod and marry Jenny Goldstein, the widow who lived down the hall. Her husband had died last year of lung cancer, and she could use some help with her four small children. Perhaps one day they might all go back to Trusheny.

ON MONDAY, December 6, Lilia was arrested on the picket line and charged with sexual disorder. Police hauled her from the street in front of Triangle Waist Company directly to Magistrate's Court.

The judge scowled down at her. "Why do you paint yourself up, young woman? What kind of strumpet are you? Officer, wipe that tawdry mess off her face."

"Sir," Lilia said, "I don't paint my face. I never have."

"Don't insult me!" the judge snapped. "I can see from here that you pencil your eyebrows and rouge your lips."

"I don't—"

A bailiff stepped forward, pulling out a linen handkerchief. He wiped at Lilia's lips, her cheeks and eyebrows, and held up a clean, white handkerchief for inspection, proof that Lilia had told the truth.

The magistrate's face flushed in anger. He leaned across the bench and pointed a finger down at her. "Young woman, you dress above your station," he said. "You have no right to do that."

"Sir, I made this dress and my sister made the hat I wear. We do not dress above our station; we save for our clothes and take care of them. Do we not deserve a little of life?"

For her impudence Lilia spent three days in the Tombs.

IN THE months since she read of Rothstein's wedding, Carsie felt the knot in her stomach grow. Her vision clouded. Her thinking slowed. Anger would surge between her shoulder blades, not ebbing until days later. She went to Modiste Hats only a few days a week now, and at irregular hours. Her hair began to gray in a streak at the front, and her eyes took on a vacant fix from lack of sleep.

Shalva watched Carsie's condition worsen during the strike. She would sit by the windows of the Orchard Street flat for hours on end, shouting out nonsense about hat-making and tailoring, words that seemed to well from deep within her. By late December she had not left the flat in a week, had not bathed in two. Mercifully, the weather had turned cold enough that the windows were closed and Carsie could no longer yell out to the people walking below.

Before she left for work one morning Shalva sat across from Carsie and took her hand. Carsie did not move. "Carsie," she ventured. "We need to talk, dear, about Modiste. Have you been up there recently?"

Carsie spoke without turning her gaze from the window. "No, there's no need."

"Don't you think it would do you good to get out?"

"No. Ilana will keep it open."

"But, it's your business, Carsie. You must keep hours. The buyers need to know when they can find you there."

"They don't come around now the strike is on. And after Lilia was jailed I don't feel like going out. It's cold."

"You loved Modiste."

"Not anymore. I don't care about it at all since…" She pulled her hand away from Shalva's. "And neither does anyone else. Besides, it takes more money than I have to keep it open."

"Then we will need to move. Take a cheaper flat. Moishe won't work and you won't either, apparently. I don't make enough at Franck's to support all three of us."

Still Carsie did not take her eyes off the shuffle of the crowds below, people picking their way between piles of sooty snow on the street corners, making their way to jobs uptown or at the wharves. "Fine. Then we move."

"You won't like it."

"There's not much I do like these days, Shalva. Lilia and I supported you—you and Moishe—while you were sick. I suppose you can return the favor."

When the strike ended in January of 1910, Harris called the Triangle Waist Company's employees together to announce that whatever progress other strikers had gained in the walkout—a shorter work week, an end to the subcontracting system, a wage increase, adequate fire escapes, and open doors from the factories to the streets—would not affect his employees. For Triangle Waist Company, nothing had changed.

A few of the women took off their aprons and left without notice. Harris needed machine operators and he needed them fast. He decided Lilia saw well enough with her glasses to operate a sewing machine. He gave her a chair in the light of the Washington Place windows.

She had learned years before to arrive at the shop early enough to avoid the crush of bodies that rushed from the cloak room at the beginning of the morning shift, but her new job meant a longer, messier, day. In her spot near the windows, farthest from any entrance, she was forced to find her way down the row of seventy-five-foot-long tables and into her seat before any of the women farther up the row, or from the row behind her, did. A wicker basket on the floor to her right overflowed with cut pieces of fabric, delicate white lawn waiting to be sewn into shirtwaists. Machine oil dripped onto the floor beneath her feet when the wooden trough above her knees became too full to hold the drippings. Before she left each day, after she had removed her apron, buttoned her coat, and pinned on her hat, she queued up at the door, waiting to squeeze through an opening wide enough for one person at a time, so that the watchman could search her handbag. The process took time, but she made sure she was in line early enough that she was never late for class.

Shalva took a flat at 165½ Mott Street, over the back of a shoe shop. The room looked out onto the yard behind the building, where the shoemaker hung leathers he tanned to use for the more expensive ladies' shoes he made. Between the water pump and the latrine he stored a vat of lime-water, to remove hair from hides, and a lime pit. The flat's rent was rock-bottom. Shalva didn't question why.

When Monk Eastman was jailed in 1904 for robbery, his gang fell apart. Although he tried to resurrect it after his release from Blackwell's Island five years later, members of his gang had joined other gangs or died or found meaningful employment and a quiet happiness in living more humdrum lives. Eastman turned to petty thievery and, like so many others who had been handed a raw deal by life or the law, opium.

Moishe Akselrod, though he no was longer a lieutenant in Monk Eastman's gang, dug in his heels when Eastman's gang disbanded. He refused to take any kind of job. Before she left each morning Moishe took money from Shalva's bag for carfare and lunch. After Shalva was gone for the day, he dabbed on a cinnamon and vanilla solution he had mixed, brushed his suit and buttoned his collar before he went out. He took his morning coffee in a café across Mott Street and then he rode the number five trolley north to lunch uptown with one or another of his friends or a woman he'd met recently named Dody Simms. He sunned himself in Union Square on pleasant afternoons while he played dominoes with the Italians. Near four, he would move to a betting parlor to spend the rest of his day and all of his pocket change.

LILIA WATCHED the ninth floor clock at Triangle Waist Company eagerly on Saturday afternoon. She and Louis had tickets to see Jerome Kern's newest musical revue *La Belle Paree* that evening—a chance to see New York's most talked-about new star, Al Jolson. She knew she should stay home and study. Midterm exams were not far off. And she had begun to read *Crime and Punishment* in Russian, and was enjoying it.

The weather was not really warm enough to go out that evening, but Louis had been given the tickets by Mr. Kern himself, a client of his at the store, so the seats were likely to be good ones. This was their anniversary celebration, marking their second year together, and she had a surprise for Louis— at least she thought she did. She hadn't yet shared her news with Carsie; she wanted to tell her husband first.

ON THE eighth floor of Triangle Waist Company, near four that afternoon, a cutter flipped a cigarette butt into a bin of scraps under a table. The entire bin of fabric ignited.

A PEDDLER pushed his cart under the arch and into Washington Square. He waved to a mounted policeman who rode the bridle path through the park and pulled his jacket around his neck. The sun would set soon, and *damn* it was cold for this time of year. Both men turned in the direction of a sound—a muffled burst from the east side of the square, from a high window in one of the surrounding buildings. A horse reared and bolted. Others looked up to see a puff of smoke eddying from the eighth floor of the Asch Building.

There had been fires in the building before, though it

was known as one of the safest in New York, but the previous blazes had been extinguished without incident. Two of those had been from the Triangle Waist Company, where this one appeared to have started, too. The mounted cop thought little about it other than to find a firebox and ring in the alarm.

The fire spread faster than anyone anticipated it might. One of the cutters tried, in vain, to stanch the blaze by throwing the flaming bin out a window, but it was already too late—flames had moved quickly to other baskets of scraps and caught the cutting table on fire. After one of the cutters alerted Isaac Harris's staff on tenth floor, all of them ran for the stairwell doors and the elevators.

Elevator operators evacuated the administrative staff from tenth floor as the smoke thickened.

Below, people ran toward the building, gathering from all directions. Another bundle flew from a window—this one was human, a young woman.

Sewing machine operators on ninth floor smelled smoke and felt the heat as the fire, fueled by fabric and wicker, wood, paper patterns, and machine oil, roared up from the floor below. The women nearest the doors ran to open them. Others followed. Chairs scraped back, tangling together as the women jumped to their feet, running to escape flames that licked outside the walls of ninth floor. But Isaac Harris had made good on his promise that nothing would change for Triangle workers. The doors to the stairwell had been locked from the outside. Helpless to open the ninth floor doors to the Washington Place stairs, panicked women rang for the elevators or ran to the only window through which they might climb onto the fire escape. And though the window opened, the metal shutter that covered it, too, was locked. The women broke windows and climbed out onto the ledges of ninth floor, their skirts ablaze.

As close to the windows as Lilia sat, she slowly wound her way among the fallen chairs, stumbling and recovering only to trip again as she worked along the seventy-five-foot length of table before she could reach the cloakroom doors or elevators. She caught a foot in an overturned chair and fell, hitting a temple on the flywheel of a sewing machine and knocking her glasses off.

She pulled herself up, untangled her feet from the twist of chairs, and felt around on the floor for her glasses. Blinded now, with the workroom lit only by the setting sun, she did not see that she missed finding them by inches. Blood streamed from a gash on the right side of her head. She reminded herself that she and Carsie had overcome these kinds of ordeals before. They had run. She could get through this, she thought. She could outrun danger again.

FIRE ENGINES pulled pumper trucks to the curb and unfurled hoses. A woman's body fell near the truck, then another and a third. The truck's horses reared away from the flames and dead bodies.

The crowd yelled, "Raise the ladders! In heaven's name, raise the ladders!" But when the ladders extended to their full length, they reached only to the sixth floor. No one had anticipated a fire any higher in a skyscraper.

LILIA HEARD glass shatter and inhaled a cool gust of air an instant before the blow of an explosion knocked her back against a table, heat rippling around her as the fire snatched oxygen from the air to burn hotter still.

Women ran from the newest rush of flame, shrieking.

Choking, Lilia stumbled toward the light of the broken window, falling forward over a body she had not seen in the thick black machine-oil smoke. Struggling to keep her footing she fell again, pushed by others who hurried to the window.

She heard their footsteps miss her head, dodging around her to climb out through the opening, until she felt feet pushing down on her as the women battled each other to get out, standing on her back, weighing on Lilia's lungs, robbing her of air she needed to call out that she lay beneath their feet, her face pressed into the smoldering floor boards. She felt her collarbone snap.

The blaze burned through the floor, set a nearby basket of fabric in flames, and ignited a trough of machine oil close to where Lilia lay.

Black smoke billowed out the window from the oil fire and blew back into the room, filling ninth floor, blinding those who had not yet found the window. Flames advanced from the far wall, driving the women from the elevator shaft and doors toward the windows where the oil fire burned.

Nine stories below, the crowd heard screams of those trapped above, distinct from the noise of fire engines and police patrol wagons clanging toward the corner of Washington Place and Greene Street, where the fires raged on the three top floors of the Asch Building.

AT LAST the pin that held closed the shutters to the fire escape gave way, and ten women zig-zagged their way down the metal stairs, followed by more behind them, and more still when they discovered the elevators had stopped running. A bolt securing the fire escape to the building popped loose. The stairway shook. The women held tight to the hand rail. The fire escape trembled again as more women loaded on.

On eighth floor, flames burned higher. A metal bar fell across the fire escape, preventing the women from running farther down the stairs. They turned to go up, toward tenth floor and perhaps to the roof, but fire raged from the windows above. They were trapped.

More bolts fell from the walls. The metal stairs creaked and groaned, jolted a final time, twisted with the heat of the fire and the weight of so many women on its stairs, sagged toward the street, and fell away from the building. A rain of bodies fell onto the pavement of Greene Street.

LILIA HEARD something crack in her skull when another

worker fell on top of her. The weight overhead became greater as a third woman fell on top of her, Lilia's ribs fracturing under the crush of women stepping on the others, trying to save themselves by getting out onto the fire escape. She understood they did not care who or what they stepped on in their panic. She struggled for air, knowing a vital few breaths might save her, but she could not expand her chest or open her mouth for the smallest gasp.

— 28 —

LATE ON the afternoon of March 25, Moishe had bet on a horse named Devil Fire and awaited the results of the race from Aqueduct when the Triangle blaze began.

Shalva swept up, preparing to close at Franck's.

Carsie had not eaten for three days. She sat at the window of the flat, staring at the lime pit in the back yard while she murmured, "The hats were black at Ascot last year…their brims wider than ever…the hats were black at Ascot last year… their brims wider than ever…"

On his way down Broadway, Louis Levy heard shouts: "Fire at Triangle Waist Company, did you hear?" and, "Big fire at the Asch Building, let's go!" and, "I'm on my way to the fire, down at Washington Square."

He ran to the building, seeing police lower bodies from the upper floors by block and tackle. He lost his hat and his celluloid collar in his struggle to get through the crowd that surrounded the Asch Building. "Lilia! Lilia!" he yelled, as he elbowed his way past curiosity seekers and onlookers clustered at the scene.

When he got to the police line he reached his arms forward, calling out her name again and again until a cop let him through. Wildly, he glanced at the faces of the women who stood nearby, alive but overwhelmed by tragedy. He glanced at the bodies being brought out of the building—fourteen here, nine over there, across Greene Street a line of twenty-some— the bodies lining both sides of the street, their faces unrecognizable, blackened by soot and smoke, charred or bloody or both.

He searched among the injured and those overcome by

228 – *Cynthia Drew*

smoke, who received medical treatment at the scene. "Lilia," he cried out again. No one responded.

He staggered most of the way from Washington Square to Mott Street in tears and stood at the door of the Mott Street flat not remembering if he had knocked. He knocked again. The smell of fire hung in his hair and his clothes. His carefully pomaded hair stood at odd angles to his head, disheveled and matted with ash.

At last Carsie answered the door. She smiled at him wanly but said nothing, turning to climb the stairs, leaving him in the doorway. Louis followed her up to the flat. She sat again in the chair at the window.

"I've come about Lilia," Louis said.

Carsie blinked and gave her head a shake as though she had only then realized he stood there. "Lilia, yes." She frowned at him. "Hello, Louis, why is she not with you?"

"Lilia is… There was a fire at Triangle this afternoon, a bad one…."

"And Lilia?"

"Some jumped. Others fell or were trapped by the flames. It was horrible."

"*Lilia?*"

"Is missing, Carsie. I couldn't find her, anywhere."

Carsie leaned forward, her arms crossed over her stomach. She listed left off the chair as though she might fall, righted, and sat for a moment, staring at the lime pit in the back yard. "She has to be there someplace, Louis."

"Today is our anniversary," he choked. "Two years. And Carsie, I think she is pregnant. She *must* be alive."

She stood and smoothed her dress. "I want to go."

He nodded. "Then come with me. We will find her."

Unaware that they were running, they ran west on Houston to Mercer and north, slowed to a trot when Louis got a stitch in his side, stopped to rest against a building, and ran on to Washington Square.

This is my fault, Carsie thought as they hurried up Mercer. *Lilia must be alive. I took my eye off her, permitted her to move uptown with Louis, and now she is missing. It had been the same the night the Cossacks attacked Papa's print shop in Lucava—I turned my back for one moment on Mama, and she was killed.*

She'd had dreams of that night for a month after it occurred—fiery, ghostly visions that left her only at daybreak. Had Lilia dreamed of this happening? Had she dreamed of a fire licking at her heels? And what if Louis was right—that Lilia was pregnant?

She remembered how she and Lilia had enjoyed going to work at Melnick's when his shop was housed on second floor of the Asch Building. They felt special, somehow, clever even, going to business in a building uptown.

Lilia must not leave me, Carsie prayed. *If she is dead, I will have no one. Everyone in our family would have fallen away. Everyone but me. No. No. NO, that has not happened.*

Carsie and Louis reached the corner of Greene and Washington Place near six p.m. Louis spotted Shalva walking toward them, her mouth agape. "*Mayn Gott,*" Shalva whispered when she reached them. She spread her arms, looking at the scene, her eyes full of horror. "This isn't true. It can't be...is it?"

Again they fought their way through the crowd and again police admitted them behind the barriers to look for Lilia. They consulted lists the ambulance teams had created. Lilia's name wasn't on them. They checked among the women who stood watching. Lilia was not there.

Shalva pointed at a row of the dead, laid out in front of the building. "Did you check the...have you asked whether she is...?"

"No," Carsie said. "Because she's not there."

"But how do you...why are you so sure?"

"Louis thinks she's pregnant, that's why."

Shalva shrugged and turned away. Louis took Carsie by the shoulders. "Carsie, I hate the idea, but if she's...We should begin to look."

"She *isn't dead*, Louis. Don't bother looking. It's a waste of our time."

"Then I'll waste the time. But I have to know." He bent

and worked his way from one to the next of the women who lay in a long row near the entrance to the Asch Building.

Carsie held a handkerchief over her mouth and nose to stifle the smell, the same smell that had filled her head on a night more than eleven years ago, in another world—the smell of fire and burning flesh. She wondered whether the smell would ever leave her now. She had thought America would never have that smell.

LOUIS WORKED his way along, knowing what he looked for: no…and no…and no…and no… Hope built in his heart as he searched the row of bodies…and no, and…

29

SHE LAY with her left leg at an odd angle to her body, her dress bloody at its midsection, her glasses missing. He brushed a lock of hair from her face, reached into the pocket of her apron and pulled out what he knew he would find. Staggered, not wanting to believe what he held, he lifted it for Carsie to see: Lilia's favorite book, Henry James's *Washington Square*. His face contorted.

Carsie collapsed at Lilia's feet. "Lilia!" she screamed. *"Lilia!"*

Clutching the book fiercely, Louis ripped out its pages and threw them at the building, tore at his hair, kicked at the door, and slumped to the pavement next to Lilia's body, sobbing.

Shalva wiped tears from her own face and pulled the two bereft people to their feet. Weaving among the corpses, the three of them worked their way to a bench at the edge of the park.

Carsie shook free of Shalva's grip and turned, stumbling back toward Lilia's body. "I am not leaving. I will stay until they take her."

Shalva followed behind. Louis stood where Shalva had left him, staring numbly at the eerie scene. Search lights snapped on. The work to find bodies in the building continued, the sidewalks littered with corpses waiting for the coroner's wagon. A few had been removed, but a shortage of coffins had slowed the process. Police cordoned off streets around the Asch Building.

The same policemen who had beaten the women during the strike a year and a half before kept sightseers from trampling on the dead bodies. They sent for ambulances to carry away the ones who had survived and lifted those less lucky into coffins—the count, when they had finished that night, the night of March 25, 1911 was one hundred forty-six dead, one missing.

"SHE'S HAD some difficulties. Lost her sister in the fire..." Shalva told Doctor Chertok.

He nodded and pinched the bridge of his nose in thought. "She has neurasthenia," he said.

"But what...she seemed so healthy until we moved to..."

Chertok shook his head. "I see it a lot these days. It's quite common among women her age, actually. Tell me, do you think she has...forgive my asking...has she lain with a man, do you think?"

Shalva chuckled. "No, not Carsie. She waited six years for a man who never loved her."

"Ah," Chertok nodded again. "Then my diagnosis is surely correct. The disease drains a woman of her nervous energy. That is the problem. But that is not the cause. Most often, neurasthenia is brought about by...again, pardon my bluntness...by excessive masturbation. And for that, coupled with her grief, she will need time to heal." He pulled a prescription pad from his bag. "I will leave this—for a tonic. Her stomach acid is out of balance because of the illness. This is for hydrochloric acid to correct the imbalance. Use only a drop of it in a glass of water. Only a drop." He looked again at Carsie—her face ashen, her lips moving, whispering sounds only she understood. He turned to Shalva. "If she does not improve in a month, let me know."

Night fell on the last day of Lilia's *shiva* before the *sheloshim* began, but restrictions made no difference to Carsie; she had no plans to leave the flat. She had not bathed since well before her sister's death.

She sat on her *shiva* stool, holding her stomach, trying to force back the sour taste that welled in her throat; struggling instead to cry for her sister, knowing she should grieve.

Words jumbled together in her head, some of them forcing their way to her lips as syllables or incomplete thoughts she would mouth while she rocked back and forth.

Her stomach gurgled and burned and she sipped at the tonic Doctor Chertok had prescribed. She suspected the tonic kept her awake, but she did not need sleep. Her duty now was to guard the people of the Tenth Ward. At night she laid clutching a butcher knife, listening for the advance of Cossack horses' hooves on Mott Street's cobblestones, the window above her bed open to the sounds outside.

JACOV PEKARSKY had met Ilana Levinsky, an immigrant girl, when she had first come to apprentice with Carsie Akselrod. Pekarsky had fallen in love with her almost at first sight, and asked her to marry him. She did not return his affection, at least not as quickly as he gave it, but she knew she might not have an offer such as his again—a man who owned properties like the building where she worked, someone to whom people paid money every month or suffered consequences. She hoped Pekarsky was kind, because she married him whether he was or not.

He stood at the door of the Mott Street flat, staring at the garbage in the gutter. Feh, he thought, how lucky he was to own property in a block where food wasn't an issue. In his neighborhood, the garment district, all was fur and trucks and fabric and feathers.

A rank odor wafted from the back yard of the Mott Street building. Pekarsky heard voices and walked down the alley that ran along the side, seeing the shoemaker empty his vat of lime-water into the outhouse hole. He could hear the mixture of waste and desiccated lime sizzle from as far away as his side of the fence. Pekarsky shook his head. It was only May—in the heat of summer this whole area would be near unlivable because of the tannery smells.

Living conditions on Mott Street weren't his worry, though. He was here about his storefront on Thirty-eighth

234 – Cynthia Drew

Street. He had tired of people in the retail trades asking where they might find the proprietress of Modiste Hats.

Carsie Akselrod hadn't opened shop for seven months now, and Pekarsky wanted either the rent or his shop back. Two months after they married, he and Ilana loaded the hats and trimmings and threads and forms and stands into bags and stored the bags in the basement of the building. He scraped the words *Modiste Hats, To The Trade Only* from the windows and changed the locks.

He had come to Mott Street only as a courtesy, because his wife had worked with the woman, to bring Carsie Akselrod her Adamantine clock and tell her she no longer needed to bother paying the rent—that he had taken her millinery supplies and her apprentice, and had rented the space to Louis Levy for his tailor shop.

"I leased the shop because you were so far behind on the rent," Louis explained. "I didn't want to see you to lose the space, and I can use it for the custom business I'm starting. When you recover, you can begin again. Ilana stored the things you left behind—she saved everything so it will be there for you when you're ready."

Carsie's lips stopped moving. She regarded him blankly while she backed into the kitchen in short, stilted steps. She dipped a cloth into a pan of water to bathe her face, sighing deeply into the cloth before she smiled up at him. "How are you doing, Louis? How is life without Lilia?"

"Hard," he said. "Every day is hard, knowing she no longer walks the same streets I walk. There were days I did not want to walk those streets either. But the fact is, you do, because there is nothing else."

"That is what I see, Louis. That is *all* I see—simply nothing else."

"But there is, Carsie. There is your life, and your work in the ward, and your hats. For now, that must be enough."

"Can that be enough to make any of this feel...real again?"

"I don't know, but I remember when I was...sick...I knew

I had to do something—not just quit." He took her by the shoulders. "Please, Carsie. You have to try."

IN THE few months Carsie had her back turned on fashion, hats had changed. Brims had moved from wide to nonexistent. Cabbage roses disappeared. The maharaja turban, adorned with a center medallion and a Mephisto feather, had come over from Paris in the latest rage for everything Occidental. New York's uptown clientele clamored for evening turbans to complement the drape of the long silk robes that replaced last year's over-effusive crinolines. The new styles bewildered her. She had to learn once more how to form and decorate the snug new cloches in demand by uptown society that year. She sought out Anya Pelletier, steeling herself for Madame's verbal assaults, only to discover that her old master had returned to Paris the previous year, no longer willing to compete against America's newest millinery rush for ready-made hats.

MOISHE AKSELROD had not come home in three days. On a Thursday evening, when she came in from work to discover Moishe still had not turned up, Shalva moved around the flat silently, her chest heaving with sighs. She picked up an envelope that had arrived in the day's mail and slit the top with a paring knife, dropped the knife and gasped. She turned to Carsie, beaming, holding out a letter and a check for her to see. "Life changes in an instant, doesn't it? Look what came in the post today."

Struggling with a length of gray wool felt gathered in her right hand, the heavy flat-iron in her left, Carsie squinted at the letter. A lock of newly-washed hair flopped over her brow. "What, dear? Read it to me."

"It's from Imperial Bank of Florida—we have won the British Royal Lottery! $115,000! And to prove they are sincere, they have mailed us a check for three thousand dollars, asking us to deposit the check and wire them the same amount to cover the international clearance fees and the cost of wiring our winnings to us, and so forth. Carsie! Our troubles are over! We can move to a better flat!"

"Wait. What? They sent us a check so we can send them the same money? Why didn't they just keep the money in the first place and send us the prize?"

"Because, they say, their records have to show we paid the fees first. They sent us the money, we deposit it and send them the same amount so it looks to their government like we paid those costs up front. After the bookkeeping is square they send us our winnings. *Az me git gelt, nemts*, Carsie." If someone offers you money, take it.

Carsie laid aside the wad of gray felt she wrestled on the ironing board to scrutinize the check, bearing a gold crown in its upper left corner, over which was printed *Imperial Bank of Florida*. The check looked real, but the address for the wire was not in Britain. Instead it was the address of a man who listed himself as the British consul in Philadelphia, a man named Widrow Hempel.

The following day Shalva deposited the check and wired three thousand dollars to consul Hempel. Two weeks later, the check from Imperial Bank of Florida was returned, marked "No Such Institution." Five days later, Knickerbocker Bank and Trust sent her a letter, signed by a man named Maor Fine, insisting she repay the bank for the bounced check.

A week later, Shalva sat in Fine's office, insisting Imperial Bank of Florida *did* exist, and that she would soon be receiving the handsome sum of $115,000. She showed Fine the letter from Widrow Hempel as proof.

"Oh, I see." He sighed and sat back in his chair. "Mrs. Akselrod, Mrs. Akselrod, Mrs. Akselrod," he clucked. "I'm sorry, but I have seen this scam more than once. Did you not wonder why they wanted you to send them the same money they had just sent to you?"

Shalva opened her mouth, her jaw working without saying a word. She remembered Carsie questioning that, and how eager she was to ignore it. "No, I didn't, when I saw the man who wrote to us was the British consul, and the amount of money we stood to gain."

"You have lost a serious sum of Knickerbocker's money, Mrs. Akselrod. You must pay it back."

"But I don't have it yet!" Shalva cried out. "It is coming—from Britain. That takes a while, wouldn't you think? And surely you don't expect me to give you money I sent to someone else?"

"We do. There is no British Royal Lottery, Mrs. Akselrod. You must make good on our loss."

"What about finding Widrow Hempel? He has our money—he can return it to you."

"I can safely say there is no Widrow Hempel, and that whoever he is, he is not the British consul. The man who wrote to you duped you into sending him that money."

"If what you say is right, Mr. Fine, he duped Knickerbocker Bank and Trust into sending him the money."

"Did you deposit the check into your account?"

"Yes, but—"

"And you wrote out the transfer instructions, to be drawn on your account?"

"Well, that was—"

"And Knickerbocker, in good faith, took money *we had put in your account*, and sent it to this...charlatan."

Shalva's job at Franck's did not pay well enough that she could save anything, let alone almost three thousand dollars. Carsie, after her ruinous winter, had no money. The two women appealed to Moishe to do something, but he no longer had the financial contacts he'd fostered during his days with Monk Eastman. Knickerbocker Bank filed suit against Shalva and Moishe Akselrod to cover the fraud.

ALONE IN the flat during the day, Carsie heard things talk to her—the sewing machine squealed, *fail-ure, fail-ure, fail-ure,* when she pumped the pedal. The new white metal radiator, recently installed under the window, thumped, *worth-less, worth-less, worth-less.* She heard people on the street whispering about the Akselrods and how hopeless their lives were, saying things she felt a deep need to defend. She yelled curses out the window, her words falling into the back yard, across the lime-water pit and the outhouse. No one ever passed beneath those windows except the shoemaker, and he ignored her. After a week she stopped talking altogether, knowing her words came out in nonsense syllables.

Her mind raced; she felt helpless to create hats. The few she made emerged as shapeless gray lumps Shalva could not bring herself to wear, never mind deeming them good enough to take to Franck's to sell.

The images in her head returned, scattered here and there in her mind, pictures of the fire and the Cossack horses, sounds of the whip snapping and her mother's screams, the smell of the coal bin, and finally the feel of a penetrating cold that nearly killed her and her sister.

She stayed awake for days at a time, fearing the cockroaches that scuttled in the kitchen and under her bed. She had nightmares when she slept. She lost weight because she was afraid to eat, fearing Shalva tried to poison her. She quit bathing, suspecting the water turned her skin blue. She stared at herself in a mirror, barely able to make out her features in the dusky light of the room, screaming out, "Cry, damn you! Cry!" But no tears came. It was as though her heart was not her own, beating instead inside the Adamantine clock that sat, now, on a shelf in the kitchen.

ILANA PEKARSKY stood at the ironing board in the Mott Street flat, showing Carsie, for the third time, how to block a cloche. Carsie stared vacantly at the form taking shape, steam rising over their heads. "You are too young to stop yet," Ilana lectured while she worked. "Get a grip on yourself, Madame."

Carsie turned away. "Don't call me Madame. I am not Madame to anyone, anymore."

"But you could be...."

"No, I can't. I can't. I can't."

"You can't or you won't?"

"Both," Carsie said. "I won't be Madame to anyone, ever again, even if I could be."

LOUIS PLEADED for Carsie to bathe and eat and brush her teeth for *Shabbat*, for him. After she bathed and washed her hair she ate a boiled egg, and then another with a piece of bread. She slept for an hour while he kept watch to see that the neighbors didn't try to break in as Carsie thought they might. She wakened when he left and did not fall asleep again for three days.

When he came the following week Shalva took him aside. "There is only one answer for her, Louis."

"I think I know what you're going to say," he smirked. "But tell me anyway—let's see if I'm right."

"The only answer is that you marry Carsie—to save her life." Shalva waggled a finger at him. "You should have married her in the first place. The older sister should be married before the younger one, you know? Maybe Lilia would still be alive if you had done the right thing and married Carsie."

"Why would anything Lilia did be different? How do you figure? "

Shalva shrugged. "Eh, she doesn't work so much? She's not at Triangle on Saturday when she should be home studying? Things would be different, that's what I know. Carsie would still have her business. None of us would be down here burning our lungs on the damn lime pit."

Louis snorted in disgust. "Because you think she would still be supporting you and Moishe?"

"When she and Lilia came to America, who gave her a place? Who? Even though she and her sister brought trouble to our family?"

"How did they—"

"Doctor Chertok says she needs time to heal. Faw...heal.

We have no time to heal in this house—all of us need help. Look at me—sweeping floors, sewing until my fingers are bloody." Shalva held up her right hand to Louis, hoping he could see needle cuts on the tips of her fingers. She waved in the direction of Moishe, sprawled on a chair in the kitchen. "Putting up with that *mensch.*"

Moishe burped. He cocked his derby back on his head and glanced sideways at Louis. "So, how's business, my boy? Getting rich, are you?"

"Doing well, thanks. Better even than I had expected I might, for the first year."

Shalva scrubbed socks on a washboard while she spoke. "Your color's good, Louis. You look healthy for a change. Have you saved any money?"

He smiled, knowing where the conversation would go if he let it. "Everything I've made, I've put back into Levy et Cie, Fine Custom Tailoring. But I get along. I stay busy."

Moishe belched again. "She's not stable, Carsie isn't. Needs a firm hand, that girl. You can't let her get out of control."

Out of control? Louis thought the ones out of control were Shalva and Moishe—desperate to be rid of Carsie so they could go back to the life they'd had twelve years ago, before any of this happened.

Between the smell filtering in the window from the back yard and his annoying in-laws, he wanted out of the Mott Street flat. He would have agreed to anything to escape, but theirs was a reasonable request. Marrying Carsie was his duty to Lilia.

30

CARSIE AND Louis were married in Louis's flat to mark Lilia's birthday in January of 1912. Carsie wore a high-necked gown of cream-colored peau de soie, trimmed in Chantilly lace, a dress that set off her simple bouquet of white chrysanthemums, statice, and ostrich feathers. Louis wore a suit of blue serge he had made with the help of his apprentice. Several of their friends attended the ceremony, including Rose Schneidermann and the Pekarskys. Carsie stared numbly at the rabbi through most of the service, remembering three years earlier, when Lilia had stood at Louis's side.

She knew she needed a firm hand right now, and that Louis offered his, but she didn't love him, not like she thought she should love a husband. No lust burned in her for him. She glanced over her shoulder at Ilana Pekarsky and recalled that Ilana hadn't loved Jacov when they married last year. She had hardly known him. At least Carsie had been around Louis for—what?—twelve years now. She remembered Evelyn Nesbit, the Girl in the Red Velvet Swing, a teenager who sacrificed her youth to marry a man twice as old and ten times wealthier. Every man who had ever shown any interest in Carsie hadn't worked out for one reason or another: Max Siegel, Selig Akselrod, Arnold Rothstein.

She had wanted to marry someone who made her pulse race, but she knew most women didn't marry men like that. What was wrong with marrying a man, who had, perhaps, a taste for resilient women and did not depend on their forgiveness? A man who wasn't afraid to marry a girl who made her own money? She looked at Shalva and Moishe. No, not that— Shalva had forgiven her husband too many times, and given

Moishe far too much of her money rather than spending it on herself.

Carsie'd had her fill of uncommon men—Max the cuckold, Selig the numbers runner, Arnold the gambler. *Mayn Gott*, she thought, please, no more of that. And so she recited her vows. Louis broke the glass on the first try.

Shalva and Rose Schneidermann set out the wedding dinner of boiled beef that had been delivered from the Astoria Hotel kitchen, boiled potatoes, cabbage, and kale. Rose had made a cake, decorated with Carsie's trademark purple roses. The guests drank their traditional toasts. They danced and sang—all but Moishe, who sat in a corner, pale and still. The rest of the wedding party ignored him—he often sat mute for hours, they were used to seeing it. They did not realize until a pause in the dancing and toasting that Moishe Akselrod had stopped breathing. No one in the family had noticed.

BOTH OF them giggled at the idea of kissing—it seemed a more familial idea than passionate. Louis untied her corset and pulled off her petticoat. He rubbed her back, reassuring her it was natural to be nervous.

Carsie wished for the night to be over as quickly as possible. Louis told her it would be, all too soon. He ran his hands down her smooth back while she fought to keep her lips from moving, from mouthing words that welled in her throat.

He pulled down her chemise and gently caressed her breasts, laid back and guided her on top of him. Slowly he entered her, and took his hands away, permitting her to move at her own speed. She curled her hips against his, tentatively at first, then grasped his shoulders. She moaned as she pressed herself down against him, his cock fully in her.

He smiled. "Keep moving," he whispered. "I'm almost there."

"You move a little, too," she said.

They rocked gently together, until he rolled her over, tilted her hips up and pulled her to him. They pushed and pushed again before both of them tipped their heads back, gasping. When Louis opened his eyes he saw blood on the sheet beneath her, and he held her all night in his arms.

IN MARCH of 1912, Max Blanck and Isaac Harris were acquitted of wrongful imprisonment at the Triangle Waist Company, absolved of any guilt in the fire. Carsie and Louis were stunned by the news, believing Harris and Blanck would be punished for the unspeakable safety breach against their workers. Louis stayed close by Carsie for the next few days until her mumbling subsided.

> ON LAST Sunday night, 14 April 1912, the weather was fine and cold in the north Atlantic. Captain Smith, having received iceberg warnings via wireless over the last few days, altered the RMS Titanic's course to the south. A message from the steamer Amerika warned that large icebergs lay in the Titanic's path, but the radio operators, paid to relay messages to and from the passengers, were not focused on messages to the bridge.

Carsie looked up from *The New York World*, fighting a wave of nausea. She ate a bite of *matzoh* cracker and turned again to the article.

> At 11:40, whilst about 400 miles south of the Grand Banks of Newfoundland, a large iceberg was spotted directly ahead of the ship. The First Officer, using the tiller to signal apparently thought he gave a hard-starboard order, an abrupt turn to port (left), and adjusted the engines. However, according to eyewitness accounts the order signaled was, instead, full reverse or stop. The iceberg brushed the ship's starboard side (right), buckling the hull in several places and popping out rivets below the waterline. Captain Smith,

244 – *Cynthia Drew*

alerted by the jolt of the impact, ordered a full stop. Shortly after midnight lifeboats were readied and a distress call sent out. Many were rescued in the lifeboats but among those lost at sea were members of New York society's crème de la crème: John Jacob Astor, IV...

She gulped back nausea once more, and thought of a man such as Astor losing his life along with so many others, instead of a death unique to the very rich—a sword fight or a duel perhaps, or...she didn't know what, these days. Rather than anything of a noble sort Astor had died in an accident in the north Atlantic. She remembered him. Astor had been one of those who gave her what Rothstein had called "that look" the night she went to their dinner party. And here he was now, no more than another name in a list.

Gott im himmel, she thought when she heaved her breakfast for the fourth time in a week, if this is the way babies get born it's a miracle there are so many of us walking this earth. She was due in November and though she couldn't hold anything down, she had never felt better.

MAX SIEGEL had married Jenny Goldstein two years ago, and in addition to her four children, they'd had a fifth, a wonderful son named Maurice, he wrote to Hod Nakhimov. How he enjoyed fatherhood!

And Nakhimov wrote back to say that according to what was now local lore, Siegel had known that joy multiple times before he ever left Trusheny. He pleaded for Max to come home, to bring his wife and children and resettle in Russia, but an unnamed pull kept Siegel in New York.

Wherever he went he still looked for Carsie, not having any idea what he would do if he found her, knowing that Jenny made him a good wife—the most kind and caring and kosher of women. He had not loved her when they married, but he supposed he loved her now, in a quiet way that he didn't think would ever approach the yearning he still had for the girl he remembered.

SARIT LILIA Levy slid into the world in late November of 1912, just after Carsie's birthday. She caused her mother no more than a few hours of labor and lost her purple flush within days. She became the perfect baby, in Louis's estimation, a child of the sweetest disposition and most beautiful eyes, fringed, like her mother's with long lashes. Louis spent hours kissing her tiny fingers and toes and twirling her dark curls around her face until she resembled the new doll called Kewpie. The baby made kissing gestures to her father, and it was for him that she smiled her first smile.

For Carsie, the birth of a daughter turned to bitter disappointment in the weeks following the baby's arrival. She had hoped for a boy, as Shalva had when Naomi was born.

The buoyant mood she felt when she was pregnant evaporated within a month, replaced by jealousy of Louis's love for baby Sarit. Carsie wept and did not sleep and argued with Louis over petty differences. Her hands trembled, she mumbled again.

And again, Louis consulted Doctor Chertok, because Louis had, in the months between January and November, come to love Carsie for who she was and how he felt when he was with her: masculine and self-assured. He loved her for those reasons and because she was his darling Lilia's sister and the mother of his beautiful daughter. He wanted her to be happy in the way she was before Sarit came. He did not understand the divide between mother and daughter, nor did he want to distance himself from Sarit. Doctor Chertok prescribed a lithium bromide for Carsie, a sedative, and by January of the following year, when she and Louis celebrated their first anniversary, Carsie had settled into a hypnotic happiness near enough to marital bliss.

When Carsie and Shalva joined him in his business in mid-February of 1913, Louis had the sign on the front of the shop repainted to read "Levy et Cie, Tailors and Milliners." Ilana Pekarsky worked with them part-time, blocking cloches and sitting with Sarit and her own child, a boy named Saul.

Louis's clientele expanded to the limits of two tailors and two milliners, and word of mouth made them prosperous. Their handmade suits and dresses and subtly elegant hats appealed to those who lived in the fine limestone mansions on Fifth Avenue and along the east side of Central Park.

Shalva lent a hand in both the tailoring and hat making, using most of the money she made to pay off the debt she owed to Knickerbocker Bank and Trust. Her position at Levy et Cie did not pay much better than the job at Franck's, but by June of that year she was free of her obligation to the bank. Two years after the bank had first filed suit, they absolved her of the debt and decided not press for her imprisonment on fraud charges.

Though she had despaired of losing Moishe, and had wept over him when he died on Carsie's wedding day, the farther she got from his *tahara* the happier she became.

An article in the *New York World* that July made the Akselrod family feel as though justice had been brought back from its cynical underpinnings:

SOCIETY PATRON AARON BENDER JAILED
WIFE ESCAPES HOURS BEFORE ARREST
LONG-TIME CONFIDENCE ARTIST DEFRAUDED
HUNDREDS NATIONWIDE

Last Thursday night, in a surprise raid on an Astoria Hotel suite, Aaron Bender was arrested for defrauding banks across the nation of more than $4.2 million. His account books, also seized in the raid, show that one elderly man alone was scammed of $80,000. In addition to him, two others lost a total of $43,000. One of them had wired $16,000 over a five-day period to a person claiming to be the British Consul here in the United States on behalf of the British Royal Lottery before a bank teller called police. By the time Bender was apprehended, police and local banks had stopped $4.2 million in fake checks Aaron Bender and his wife, Miriam, had issued in the last two years. Miriam Bender, thought to be in Philadelphia, remains at large although a warrant...

AFTER SARIT was born Carsie found the flat where she and Louis lived cramped. And in January of 1914, shortly after they celebrated their second anniversary, she announced she was pregnant again. She wanted to move.

Louis laid aside his newspaper to turn up the gas lamp. "Move? Why on earth?"

"Reasons," she said. "I have my reasons. Soon there'll be four of us—can you picture four of us in this flat? Anyway, I can't think here—Lilia's ghost keeps me awake."

"Lilia's ghost? I've never seen a ghost here."

"Not a ghost really, just the thought of her. Sleeping in our bed or standing at the stove or sitting there, where you sit now, reading. I see her."

Louis sighed. One more of her odd moods coming, he thought, probably brought on by her pregnancy. Maybe it would pass when she had another baby to distract her. "When did the doctor say you are due?"

"September. I hope it's a boy. Boys have much better... opportunities."

"My prospects were not great, you'll recall."

"Well, we need to think about the future. We have a family now. And a business to worry about."

"I'll worry about the business, Carsie." He smiled. "You worry about taking care of yourself—and our children."

"Don't you think it's time we moved...I don't know...uptown?"

Louis frowned. "We're comfortable here. Why can't we stay put for a while?"

"Our business would be so much better if we lived among

our customers, wouldn't it? If we cultivated a clientele among our neighbors?"

By peculiar chance, Shalva met a man that spring at Levy et Cie when he came in for a fitting on a new cashmere overcoat. She had met a great many men through the business, but this man was different, she thought. He was appealing in a way she had not seen in others. His name was Gaddiel Carmoly, a wealthy Romanian widower who worked as a vice-president with Argonaut Savings Bank, located up near Bonwit Teller on Fifth Avenue.

Carmoly asked her to dinner, but embarrassed by where she lived, Shalva met him after work so that he picked her up at the shop rather than at the Mott Street flat. For the next three months he took her to dinner almost nightly, or to a music hall, or on afternoon outings to the Hudson River Valley in his open 1912 Oldsmobile Autocrat.

He seemed to relish the complexities of life in New York, and took Shalva to places she had never thought to go—to Harlem nightclubs, to Coney Island, and most romantically, to breakfast at four in the morning at Maxim's, where he proposed. He taught her table manners and the tango, and encouraged her to bob her hair.

When they married, Carmoly was shocked at the address Shalva provided to the mover's lorry driver—her address on Mott Street. He had thought she lived on Thirty-eighth, over the shop, rather than in a Bowery room overlooking a lime pit. Still, the idea of marrying a woman from so low a background and educating her to move among New York society amused Carmoly. Shalva took two trunks of clothes, shoes, and hats to the four-story brownstone on East Sixty-sixth Street and left the rest behind, including the chair her parents had given her as a dowry when she married Moishe.

In late June, after a honeymoon week at home on the upper East Side, Carmoly left for his first day back at the bank. The morning was fine and not yet warm, though the promise of a hot afternoon hung in the air. His heart was full of joy—he had done right in marrying Shalva. She would make a good wife; she was tractable and submissive.

Carmoly, though he had the money to afford a driver, thought himself a modern man, and drove himself to work each day. That day, he drove the Oldsmobile, top down. Near the intersection of Fifty-ninth Street and Fifth Avenue, a four-year-old boy carrying a sailboat bolted from his mother's hands into the street, eager to get to the pond in Central Park. He ran in front of Carmoly's car and Carmoly, horrified by the approaching calamity, froze. It never occurred to him to hit the brakes.

The front bumper caught the boy between his head and shoulders and dragged him fifty feet before he fell away into the street. He lay fatally injured in the middle of the street. His mother collapsed in shock nearby. Carmoly's car veered toward the park and up onto the sidewalk before it stopped. Unable to crawl from behind the wheel he stared numbly at the crumpled figure of the boy lying in the street, until a truck came to tow the Oldsmobile.

For the rest of the day Carmoly tried to concentrate on business, knowing Argonaut's president watched him for signs of distraction, but he could not get the image of the twisted, bleeding boy lying in the middle of Fifty-ninth out of his mind. He made mistakes in paperwork, snapped at a long-time customer, and stared into space, seeing the morning's tragedy over and over.

Shalva showed him little sympathy—she had maintained for months that a man of his station should have a driver. Carmoly was as bereft as though the boy had been his own—he could not sleep that night, so haunted was he by what he saw when he closed his eyes.

The following day, Argonaut's president let him know he would be moved to a position of night auditor for the rest of his career if he chose to stay with the bank; that their customers weren't keen on the idea of a reckless driver in charge of their savings accounts.

That evening, Gaddiel Carmoly went to the garage in back of his brownstone, lit a fire under the car, sat down in the driver's seat and waited for the gas tank, located directly under him, to explode.

AFTER THE firemen and officials from the coroner's office left, Shalva found herself widowed once again, this time a woman of means. She inherited the brownstone and all of her husband's wealth, most of which was held at Argonaut Savings Bank. She sat *shmira* throughout the night, praying, never leaving Carmoly's side until he was buried.

During the seven days of *shiva* she murmured the *kaddish* prayer under her breath from the time she sat on her stool in the morning until she left it at night. And when she finished *shiva* she suggested to Carsie that the Levys move into the brownstone to live with her.

Delighted by the opportunity to live uptown, Carsie decided they should come before the birth of their new baby. From the morning the moving truck arrived at the brownstone with the few possessions Carsie and Louis had accumulated, Carsie breathed easier. The house, perfumed by the lilacs that drooped heavy outside the open west windows, was large enough to accommodate Shalva in rooms on the first floor, while she gave two airy bedrooms and a sitting parlor on the second floor to the Levys. It was more space than Carsie had ever lived in, and the few pieces of furniture they had brought from their room on Fifth Avenue looked small and plain next to the grand beds and dressers Gaddiel Carmoly had bought to furnish the second floor. The Levys stored Louis's overstuffed arm chair, their bed and chest, two straight-back chairs, and table in the damp basement.

For Carsie, the best of the move was the sense that she had left Lilia's ghost behind. Louis suspected there would be a price to living with Shalva.

IN JULY, Russia and Austro-Hungary began to squabble and

before the month was out the argument had become the Great War. Once the war started Carsie noticed that trends in hats developed their own military leanings. Tricornes and postillion hats—the tight, tidy numbers recalling gentlemen's military top hats—became popular, having first been adopted by war widows who added black veils at Shalva's suggestion. Uptown women adopted variations on the style. Modiste Hats once again became the craze among New York City's chic. The cloche, that shape that had so baffled Carsie's ability to block almost anything from a length of felt, took on the air of a helmet. Toques, the mushroom shapes that resembled chef's hats, grew taller, worn with high-collared coats in another reflection of military style. And though millinery flourished, hats, in general, grew smaller in scale and less expensive than they had been ten years before.

IN SEPTEMBER, Carsie gave birth to Sophia Yona. She was disappointed to see she had borne another daughter, though both Sophia and her older sister would now have a comfortable place to live and, perhaps, opportunities to match. Louis fawned less over Sophia than he had over Sarit, but Carsie, whose mood remained light only with her daily dose of lithium bromide, scarcely noticed the difference.

— 31 —

ON A mild spring afternoon in 1916, nineteen-year-old Charlie Luciano leaned back against the wall around Central Park and looked down East Sixty-sixth Street. He had been there since noon, jiggling the dice and change in his pockets, pacing, thinking. He had found his place in a gang that would take care of him, he thought, and he planned to do everything he could to earn the trust of his boss, a tough Jew named Arnold Rothstein.

These boys were thorough, but they made it look easy. Luciano liked that. They controlled most of the gambling in the Northeast, as well as liquor distribution and a new operation—car theft. Everything that made big money from Philadelphia north to the border, it seemed to him, was controlled by his gang. The Great War had slowed gambling, but liquor sales were up, and with fewer men around to watch their cars, boosting one of these new sleds was easier than ever. Luciano watched the swells and their dames, trussed up in their cashmere coats and furs, ride north toward the museum and to the shops on the blocks extending south from where he sat.

Luciano had come uptown to collect a debt from Shalva Carmoly, whose first husband, a *faccia de merde* named Moishe, had run up a big bill with his bookie before he had the bad sense to die. Dumb shit, didn't know what kind of dough his little woman could get into, or he would have stuck around to pimp her out.

He was glad when she'd moved out of that hole she'd lived in on Mott. Back then, Luciano had spent endless hours in the café across the street watching her come and go as much as he could before he had to puke from the smells of lime and sulfur and garbage. He was grateful to the ugly banker who married her and moved her up here, and equally gratified that the ugly *finoccio* had killed himself, sparing Luciano the task.

They were milliners, the woman and her sister, at least he thought the other one was a sister, hard-working Jewish *cafona* who lived in the brownstone he was about to visit. Two milliners and a *ruffiano* tailor—an arrogant little prick. Luciano knew the type. He'd worked for a hatter; one of his first jobs here in America. But he didn't think honest work was quite what he wanted to do, so he had begun to line the hat bands with narcotics—moving drugs through customs on the heads of unsuspecting *frocio* like the ones he watched now, or in hat-boxes the customs agents passed without a glance.

That afternoon Luciano felt as lucky as any stiff who walked Millionaires' Row. One way or another, he would go back to the boys in the Tenth Ward with some sort of vig for Akselrod's debt—the money or Shalva Carmoly's head on a stick. *E, chi se ne frega?* he thought. Who gives a damn? Luciano snapped his collar up against a chilly April wind, and, clutching the sweet little bone-handled Mannlicher pistol in his pocket, walked down East Sixty-sixth toward the brownstone.

MAX SIEGEL took his customary long way home, trudging south on Essex, west on Delancey for two blocks and up Orchard Street as he had every day for more than twelve years, searching for her face in shop windows and at intersections and among the women crowded around pushcart vendors. Behind his searching eyes he thought about his life and how he needed a change. He loved his children—well, most of them. Maurice, four now, his beautiful son, showed so much promise—a smart boy and handsome. Jenny's girls, Ethel, Esther, and Bessie, took after their mother—as kind and caring as she was. They would make good wives. But eleven-year-old Ben, Jenny's eldest, would put him in an early grave unless the kid decided to leave the family in the next few years. That had to happen, Siegel thought. Why, just this summer, the boy had tried to set up an extortion racket among street vendors around the Tenth Ward, threatening to burn them out if they didn't pay him protection money. As quickly as Siegel could encourage Ben to go, he wanted him out of the way though he dared not say so to Jenny.

Too, he was tired of being in love with a memory. When he saw something for the first time—a new motor car, say, or a new building taller than the others here in town, he tried to see it through Carsie Akselrod's eyes. Before he formed an opinion of a particular taste—an egg cream or an oyster or any of the other delectables Coney Island offered, for example—he asked himself whether she would like it.

He still thought about her at the holidays, while he watched his own family celebrate. He hoped she had married and had a family of her own to share those occasions. Surely she had found that happiness. And he prayed her children did not cause her the grief Ben caused at home.

He yearned to be free from the image of Carsie's face in front of him and the lock she had on his heart, but he had lost more than fingers and toes in his search for her. He thought perhaps he had lost his mind; she had become as entrenched in his bones as his religion.

LUCIANO TOSSED the pile of betting slips and IOUs on the hall table. "Thirty thou, with the vig," he said.

Shalva riffled through the stack: ten dollars, fifty, a hundred, more than a few for five hundred, each of them marked with the Hebrew initials *mem aleph*. Moishe Akselrod. The slips dated back to just after Monk Eastman was jailed. "I wonder, Mr. Luciano, where you were when Moishe was alive. Why didn't you try to collect this money from him?"

"Mr. Rothstein knew he wasn't good for it." Luciano stepped close, taking her chin in his hand. "And even though your new *cavaliere* ain't around no more, the boss knows you got his cash."

Shalva shook the betting slips in his face. "How do I know

these are real? That you aren't trying to shake me down? Don't forget, Moishe worked for Monk Eastman—I know a gangster when I see one." She studied Luciano for a moment. "And in you, Mr. Luciano, I'm afraid I don't see one." Gently, she removed his hand from her chin and sneered. "Prove to me that these are real, and I'll pay you. If you can't, we're through talking."

Luciano pulled the little Mannlicher pistol from his pocket and pointed it at Shalva. "Then we're through talking. You pay me, or you pay with your…"

Sarit Levy scrambled down the stairs, stopping at the landing to take in the scene in the hallway below. She looked at the pistol and leaned over the railing, her thumb and forefinger pointed at Luciano. "Bang!" she giggled. "Bang, bang! You're dead! You have to fall down, now, mister—you're dead."

Shalva smiled coldly. "She has apparently shot you."

"And I'll shoot you both unless I leave with the money."

"You're not the big wheel you'd like to think you are, Mr. Luciano. My niece used to date Arnold Rothstein—now *there* is a gangster. You? You're a common thug." She pulled a leather-bound book from the table drawer and picked up a pen. "Who do I make the draft to?"

"Was Arnold Rothstein who sent me."

She paused. "Yes, you've made that clear. How much will make him happy?"

Luciano's jaw twitched. "Thirty thousand, I told you. Or you're dead. The kid, too."

Shalva chuckled. "You're not getting thirty thousand and you know it. I'll give you five."

Mute, Sarit sat on the stairs, watching, listening.

Shalva hoped Luciano did not see the pen tremble in her hand. Even five thousand dollars would nearly wipe out what she had in the bank. "I think we both understand that if you shoot me you get nothing, so your threats are pretty hollow, aren't they?" She bent to the book and wrote. "Give Arnold the regards of the Akselrod women, and this." She handed him a check for two thousand dollars. "Tell him if he wants any more he should come ask for it himself, instead of sending one of his goons."

Luciano tucked the check and his gun in his pocket. "Don't you disrespect me, sister."

"Faw, disrespect. At this point, you'd have to work pretty hard to earn my respect." She pointed to the door. "Let yourself out. And don't come back."

Shortly after Luciano had slammed the door behind him, Shalva pulled her coat from the stand and pinned on her hat. She needed to walk. The encounter had scared her; he'd pulled a gun—a gun! This was the Upper East Side; people didn't get guns pulled on them up here. She locked the door from the outside, hoping Sarit would not get into anything while she was gone, and she walked, still trembling. Had Moishe really run up that kind of debt? Or had she paid Luciano almost half of what she had just to get him out of the house?

She had not been curious about her neighborhood, rarely walking more than a block or two in any direction from the house, but the day was warm for April, and she walked quickly, headed north on Fifth Avenue, trying to walk off the humiliation and fear.

At East Seventy-sixth Street she stopped, awestruck by the building on the corner—the Moorish edifice of Temple Beth-El. She climbed the limestone stairs of the synagogue, drawn to its comfort. Stepping through its arches into the vestibule she heard a cantor practicing his antiphonal liturgy at the back of the building.

She moved around a dark bend toward the music, then to the women's section, where she sat, trying to calm her nerves. The dim glow of the place, the mystical music, the cold air of the synagogue, all of it weighed on her almost palpably. She thought about her life—thirty years of it, now—her miserable marriage to Moishe, twelve of those years—yet she still missed him—and her brief, happy time with Gaddiel. A bad man and a good one. She thought about how Carsie and Lilia had come into her life because she had done the right thing in taking them in. She was proud of that. It might be that they had been her salvation.

She had strayed far from her religion, she knew that, and had hardened her heart because it was her only defense against Moishe. Her father would have been mortified if he'd known how she lived.

She was destined to be a widow, she decided, but she would not give in to the seclusion she expected widowhood might bring. She would shepherd her young nieces, teach them how to be good Jews. It was her duty. Her eyes fell on a quote painted above the women's section, a quote from Ruth: *"Wherever you go, I will go. Wherever you lodge, I will lodge. Your people shall be my people, and your God my God. Where you die, I will die, and there I will be buried."*

She stood, shaking with a strength she had not felt before, a sense that the place in the world she had sought for the last sixteen years was right in front of her, as those things usually were. Feeling as though she was lifted up and carried, she walked the ten blocks south to the brownstone.

32

IN FEBRUARY, Ilana Pekarsky announced she was pregnant again. Working even part time would not be possible; the doctor had ordered her to bed. The following month, Louis's cutter quit for a better-paying job closer to his flat in Brooklyn.

"I could be your cutter," Carsie proposed.

Louis said nothing.

"I said, I could be—"

"I heard what you said," he snapped. "Please, Carsie. I have asked you to speak English in the shop. Only English... please."

She paused. "Well?" she went on in English. "What do you think? You could teach me to be your cutter."

Louis sighed and rubbed his forehead. He'd known this conversation was coming since the moment his cutter resigned, and he had dreaded it. "I don't think so, dear," he smiled.

"But you pay a cutter so much more than—"

"I know. And there's a reason I do."

Carsie put on a hat she had finished that morning, mugging in a mirror. "What reason?"

"Because they have families to support."

"But so do we." She put her arms around Louis's neck. "If I cut for you, it keeps the money in the family."

"Cutters are men, aren't they? And I am so happy you aren't a man." He kissed her forehead and pulled her arms away gently.

"Well, yes, most of them *are* men. And don't be coy with me, Louis. Let me try. Teach me."

"*All* of them are men because..." Oh, damn, he thought. He'd wandered into dangerous territory.

She cocked an eyebrow. "Because…?"

He had started the sentence; he supposed she deserved to hear a finish to it. He sighed and plowed ahead. "Because men plan better than women."

She staggered a step and gripped the edge of a glass case. "They *what?*"

"Plan better than women—lay out the pattern pieces more efficiently. It's been studied. Men are more…uh, economical, more methodical, more mechanical."

"Do you really believe that? Do you think there's a man in this city who can decide better how to spread fabric or run that machine back there better than I could?"

"No. Yes. I don't know. Probably. An experienced cutter could, certainly."

"You don't want to pay me what a cutter makes, is that it?"

"Well, of course you already make more than, say, if you worked anywhere else doing the same thing. You have to admit you make handsome money for what you do."

Carsie stamped her foot. "But an extra fifteen or twenty dollars a week would be enough to hire a nanny for the girls, and, when the time comes, to send them to private schools."

"Shalva watches the girls. We don't need a nanny."

"I don't like asking Shalva to do that. Remember, she gave us all shelter when we needed it, and now she's done it again, without a whisper about rent. We can't ask her to watch the children, too. Besides, I'm not sure she won't…that she wouldn't…"

"Wouldn't what?"

Carsie stared out the window at a veil of snow beginning to blanket West Thirty-eighth Street. "Feed them Mrs. Winslow's Tonic, is what. I don't trust her not to do that."

Louis shook his head. It was her own fault. She had become too independent to press for favors. But after all her years in the needle trades and losing her sister to the sweaters, she still did not understand the role of women in this workplace.

Even so, he thought, she had imbued in him the self-confidence he needed for this moment. He straightened and raised his chin as he had seen her do. "Carsie, we are not hiring a nanny, and you are not going to be my cutter. We will hire a man as soon as we can find one, and you can go on with your millinery business, which has become smaller for the loss of Ilana. It is not necessary that you replace her. And I don't want to hear any more about it."

A disagreement of principle with her husband—the very kind of argument she had wanted to avoid in a marriage. The kind of fight she knew would simmer and rekindle to be fought in front of the children. She had seen it in her own parents. She was surprised Louis would argue over anything—he didn't seem the type. She had brought it on herself, she supposed, because she believed in the cause. She wouldn't let it go. The audacity of the idea—that men were worth more than women in the workplace—was intolerable.

Carsie wanted to talk to Emma, but she didn't know how to find her. After she and Louis closed the shop for the day, she pleaded the need to see Mr. Macy about his order, promising to be home before suppertime. She took a Fifth Avenue streetcar south to Twenty-third Street and walked up to Gallery 291. A light burned at the back, and she heard the sound of men's voices—one high and sibilant, another resonant.

"That is not yours to decide, Stieglitz," the high voice cried. "Don't be one of the art boobies."

"But these are so…patriotic, so common. What I hang on these walls *is* mine to decide," Stieglitz boomed. "I'll run this space, thank you. It is as much mine to run as my own life."

"Bravo," Carsie said, stepping into the office. "True conviction."

The two men looked around. Stieglitz smiled, but said nothing. The man to his right flushed red.

Stieglitz stood, offering her his chair, but she shook her head. "I am looking for Emma…Goldman. Do you expect to see her any time soon? Can you give her a note for me?"

Stieglitz scrutinized Carsie: married, shapely, probably a mother from the set of her breasts. Lovely face, Jewish, no doubt. She seemed vaguely familiar. Her dark eyes looked shyly from under the brim of her hat. Still he did not say a word, but volunteered a pencil and a small sheet of paper. He and the man with whom he had argued sat silent until Carsie finished writing her note and folded it in half. "Thank you," she said, handing it to him. "Most kind."

He opened the note and read aloud:

Dear Emma:

I hope this note finds you and finds you well. I would like to talk to you about organizing a demonstration of working women to protest inequality of pay for women in the workplace. It has become an issue in the garment trades, as I am sure you know. Please come to see me at Levy et Cie on West 38th Street, just west of Seventh Avenue.

Fondly,
Carsie Levy

Stieglitz raised an eyebrow and glanced at the man on the opposite side of the desk. "Childe Hassam," he said, indicating his companion. "Paints pictures of flags. Bah."

Hassam pounded the arms of his chair. "They are far more than paintings of flags, Stieglitz. You're being quarrelsome."

"I have had all I want of arguments today, gentlemen," Carsie said, wearily. "I will leave you to it. Thank you, Mr. Stieglitz. I hope to hear from Emma."

Stieglitz turned in his chair, watching as Carsie walked back through the gallery. "And *I* would hope to hear from *you*, Mrs. Levy," he called.

ON THURSDAY of the following week Carsie had gone across town to deliver a hat for a wedding when two women came into Levy et Cie. They browsed the fabrics for a moment before asking Louis if Carsie was available.

"She is out," Louis smiled courteously. "May I help, in her absence?"

"I am Emma Goldman," the woman in spectacles said in Yiddish. "This is Bessie Abramowitz. Carsie asked to see us about…well…" Emma sat in a chair near the dressing room. "Perhaps we will wait for her."

Louis's patronizing smile faded. He had read of Emma Goldman's role as a labor organizer and socialist, though he had not recognized her from her pictures in the newspapers. He suspected the young lady with her was the same seditious sort. He wanted them out of his shop. "She has gone to the Bronx to deliver some things for me," he lied. "She will not be back for some time."

Emma Goldman gave him a short, skeptical nod and stood.

The woman named Bessie Abramowitz stepped forward, a pamphlet in her hand. "She will want to read this, I think. Please tell her we called and we are sorry to have missed her."

Louis watched the two of them cross West Thirty-eighth and head east before he glanced down at the brochure he held, titled *Comparable Worth*. He skimmed the text. Phrases leaped out—"equal pay for equal work," "new costs to society," and "gender-based pay." Garbage, he thought, as he threw the pamphlet in the wastebasket. Socialist garbage. Carsie would never see the pamphlet nor would she hear about Emma Goldman's visit.

Emma and Bessie found Carsie at the corner of West Thirty-eighth and Seventh Avenue as she returned to the shop.

"How was it in the Bronx?" Emma waved as Carsie approached.

"How glad I am to see you!" she greeted Emma. "You got my note?"

"I did. And I thought perhaps you needed to meet my friend Bessie. Her greatest concern is equal pay for women."

"I left a pamphlet at the shop," Bessie said. "I am very happy to meet you—a kindred spirit in our cause, I understand."

"Thank you for coming around to see me. Of all the things I care about it seems that…well, it's not just children who are being victimized by…" She waved a gloved hand around, indicating the buildings that housed sweatshops and showrooms on all corners. She gathered Bessie's hands and Emma's in hers as she spoke, a new zeal in her voice. "Women have been wronged by all this, too—and have been for many years. My sister died in the Triangle fire.…" Carsie caught a tear in her throat. "It must stop."

When the doorbell tinkled at Levy et Cie, Louis came forward to find Carsie rummaging at the front counter. "Hello, my love. Back so soon?"

"Mmmm….I ran into Emma and her friend on the street corner. Where is the pamphlet they gave you?"

"Uh, it's around here somewhere, I'm sure." Louis leafed vaguely through a stack of receipts and orders that lay on the counter.

Carsie searched the tables near the front, checking under the display racks and in the shop windows for a stray piece of paper. Nothing. She turned, scanning the floor, and spotted a folded sheaf in the wastebasket. She stepped closer. The top page read *Comparable Worth.* "You threw it away?"

"You found it?" Louis hurried to her side. "Wonderful. Where was it?"

"In the wastebasket. How do you suppose it got there?"

"It probably fell off the counter…when the door opened."

She looked at him and waited. Then, "Are you sure you didn't toss it after Emma and Bessie left?"

"No, I did not."

"Don't insult me by lying, Louis, please."

Louis dropped into the chair by the dressing room, his hands on his knees. He sat still for some time, blinking but saying nothing. Then he said, "You should know. When I went to work at Lord and Taylor, I lied to them. I told them my accent was Dutch—that I was a Knickerbocker, which, to them, meant I was a blueblood. That's why they hired me as an apprentice."

"Ah," Carsie said. "And that is the reason we don't speak Yiddish in the shop, isn't it?"

"I worked hard building my clientele, Carsie. Too hard to have Emma Goldman come in here asking *in Yiddish* for my wife. Why, if any of my gentlemen from Tammany Hall or uptown had been here—*danken Gott* none of them were—I would have been exposed on the spot." He wiped his upper lip with his pocket square.

"No better than the Benders," she mumbled. The Adamantine clock on the shelf above the counter ticked. Carsie chewed her upper lip, remembering the night Ada Astor had sneered at her for being a Jew. Remembering the afternoon Arnold Rothstein had given her the clock, and how happy she had felt that day—forgiving the world its weaknesses, forgetting everything but her dreams. "But you didn't want to move uptown when I suggested it, even though it would have fit your 'blueblood' image. And when Shalva offered her place, you never said anything about…"

"It seemed less a lie if I didn't really try to live it. Until then it was a harmless story. But now that we do live uptown, and my business is with those kinds of men, I should try to fit in, shouldn't I? If I don't, they won't have anything to do with me."

"So…what does that mean for me, exactly?"

He sighed. How different his life would have been with Lilia. She thought he ruled the world, and he had—her world, anyway. Lilia had worshipped him, and though he knew Carsie cared for him she didn't embrace his thinking as wholeheartedly as Lilia had done.

"What it means, Carsie, is that these men want their women to do what they were meant to do. That is to say…if you are at home, like Shalva is, you care for the children and the house. If you work, you do what your boss says you should do."

Carsie sneered. "Wait a moment. You see yourself as my boss? *Gott im himmel*, Louis, *think*. We lost Lilia to a boss who thought his business was more important than the lives of a hundred and forty-six women. And what about the children? How would you feel if, in a couple of years, we had to send Sarit off to work in a sweatshop, sewing coat linings because we needed money?"

"That would never—"

"Don't say 'never.' If Sarit has to go to work in the sweat-shops how will you feel?"

"I can't imagine…it would be the most terrible thing I could think to happen."

"The bosses around here are ruining us, Louis."

He took Carsie in his arms. "Look, my love, you are a woman, and a smart one. But you are my wife, and that means you should honor my wishes. If you want to look at it that way, then yeh, I'm your boss, though I don't like the term."

Carsie pushed away from him. "I don't accept that, Louis, and if you like, I'll move my business somewhere else to relieve you of that burden."

"You'd do that? Take your business out of here?"

"You sound almost hopeful. Why not? In the extra space, you could stock the Italian fabrics you've been wanting to buy. You may be my husband, Louis, but I see us as equals—two people standing shoulder to shoulder, working toward the same things. That's how it could work if you'll give me the chance."

Louis began to shake. He dabbed again at his upper lip with the pocket square. There was something inherently wrong with what she was telling him—there had to be. "We aren't working toward the same things if you can't follow my thinking, Carsie."

She stared at him again. "Oh? Well, I don't know that your way of thinking is the way I want our girls to live."

Louis leaped to his feet. Her words had hit him as hard as a lead hammer. "Then, until you do," he said, "I can't consider you my wife."

33

DURING THE February thaw, Carsie moved her millinery business to the house. Her lips worked quickly, mumbling while she packed her hat stands and bolts of felt onto the moving lorry. Louis stood at the front of the shop, watching her work, but he did not try to help her.

Her stomach gnawed at her again, and the whispering had resumed. "When the last stitch has been made..." she murmured, wedging in a final box at the side of the moving truck, "the upper square should be folded so to form a triangle, basted through the points...."

Once she unpacked and set up her things in the front parlor, a room the Levy family rarely used, she sent letters to her customers to advise them of her relocation. She fastened a brass plaque below the doorbell of the brownstone that read *"Modiste Hats, Carsie Levy, Proprietress,"* dosed herself with liberal spoonfuls of hydrochloric acid and lithium bromide, and settled in to wait for the uptown ladies to call at her door for hats.

"IT'S NO good, you in the guest room, Louis on the divan in the library," Shalva said.

"I'm sure it isn't doing his back any favors," Carsie said. "But it was his decision, Shalva, not mine. If only he could understand that I am not his enemy."

"This isn't natural. You are a wife—you should be in there doing what wives do. And giving Louis more children while you do it."

"Did you hear me? I said it wasn't my idea to live like this."

"It is your doing, though. Be a good wife, Carsie. He is a

Jewish man and they can be the worst bastards and the most loving husbands in the same night. I ought to know."

"Shalva, it is Louis who has decided to stop honoring our marriage."

"You have to make yourself available for him. He can't... come to you. His pride won't let him."

"Mine won't either. He does not respect women."

Shalva sighed. Persuading these people to be better Jews was harder than she had imagined it might be. She couldn't even get them together. Getting them to *shul* was a long way off. Passover was coming, though. Maybe then she could convince them to take the ten-block walk to the synagogue. Once they did, they would see what had inspired her and strive for *mussar* of their own—the refining of their souls. She was sure of it.

FOUR-YEAR-OLD SARIT stood to the side of her mother's chair, thinking. "Mummy," she smiled up at Carsie. "Do you have more than two fairies in your bosom?"

"What?" Startled at her daughter's question, Carsie looked up from decorating a hat.

Sarit threw her chubby arms across her mother's knees. "Tiny fairies, Mum. Auntie Shalva says you have fairies in your bosom and so does she. And we will have them too, Sophie and me, when we grow up."

"Really? How many fairies do I have, did she say?"

"She said, two. You have two and she has a thousand, she said. But I bet you have more than two. You just can't see them, because they're invisible."

Carsie giggled and hugged her daughter. "She has a thousand and I only have two? So, what do they do, these fairies?"

"They are little Jewish creatures, like Sophie and me. They make everyone happy when they fly out of Auntie Shalva's bosom."

"And they do that when?"

"In the mornings, while she is dressing. Sophie and I go

into her bedroom and kiss her bosom and our kisses turn her Jewish fairies loose. That way we are happy all day."

"PEACE WITHOUT victory, he wants," Shalva said, looking up from her newspaper.

"Mmmm? Who wants?"

"President Wilson. Wants the war to end without anyone calling it a victory. Carsie, that's the way you and Louis should be thinking—no one's winning here. Why don't the two of you declare peace and say you don't agree? Please, for the girls. Peace without victory."

Carsie thought. She could give in; submitting to her husband's will would, in some sense, bring her closer to being the kind of woman one found on the Upper East Side. Submissive creatures who depended on their husbands for their clothes, the food on their tables, the houses they lived in. But no. Her life had not been built that way. Shalva provided the roof, she herself provided the clothes, Louis provided only some of what their family needed, and little in the way of love, these days. She shook her head. "No, I can't. Please understand—in order to have peace without victory Louis would have to...he would have to be a different man."

"...HERE ARE quills, take one or two, and down to make a bed for you." Carsie closed the book of nursery rhymes. "That's all for tonight, I think. Mummy is sleepy."

Sarit sighed. "I love the stories about ducks and rabbits."

"What do we say at bedtime?"

"Remember well, remember right..."

"Goodnight, goodnight..." Carsie prompted. She covered the little girl's shoulders with a comforter.

"Goodnight, goodnight," Sarit yawned. "Mummy, do you think the Catholics will take over the world before my birthday?"

Carsie snorted in surprise. "*What?*"

"Auntie Shalva says Catholics are arming to take over the

world and only Jews can fight them off. I won't even be six until next month—I'm too little to fight anyone."

"I don't think you need to worry about that, sweetheart. No one is going to take over the world."

"But, isn't that what they are fighting about in Europe? Taking over the world?"

"Some of it, yes." Yes, it seemed to Carsie the whole world was angry. She hoped Sarit would never have to fight the fights she had taken on. "I'll make sure no one ever takes over your world."

"So, I can have fairies and ducks and rabbits my whole life if I want?"

"If it's fairies and ducks and rabbits you want, you can have all of them that you can squeeze into a pillowcase, and no one will have the right to take them from you. I promise." She blew a kiss to Sarit from the door. "*Zis chaloymes*," she whispered. Sweet dreams.

SHALVA PRESSED a Passover shopping list into Carsie's hand. "It's not as hard as you're making it out to be," she said. "A few simple rules—just details to remember when you go out to the market."

"But, we never kept kosher when we lived downtown."

"We weren't very good Jews when we lived downtown, were we?"

"No, I suppose not—we were too busy surviving." Carsie brightened. "We celebrated the holidays, though. Even then. Remember?"

"*Oy*. In the most irreverent way, like everyone else did down there—eating and trompsing around playing at the rituals, and I'll tell you why. Because to celebrate the sacred was too...foreign. We ran around acting like Americans—like we were free to observe whatever we wanted to believe or not believe it, if we chose. Well, that isn't who we are." She shook a finger at Carsie. "We should act like Jews."

Gott im himmel, Carsie thought. Had everyone around her

decided to reform at once? There was too much of this go-ing on—people preaching to others how they needed to act: Louis wanting her to be an obedient wife and Shalva insisting she needed to keep kosher. "Do you…" Carsie started. Did she want to know? Yes, she decided, she had to ask. "Shalva, what do you tell the girls during the day—about being Jewish, and about being a woman?"

CARSIE SAT in the library, waiting for Louis to come in after closing his shop. When he walked into the room she stood and closed the door. "We need to talk."

"I'm tired, Carsie. Can it wait?"

"No. No it can't. It's about Shalva and the girls. She is teaching them things I would prefer they not hear."

Louis frowned. "How can that be? Shalva has become the most righteous of women."

Carsie looked out the window. "I wish I could say she is, Louis, but she is not. She is…there was probably some dam-age when she was drinking the tonic. She tells the girls strange things. Like…"

"Like?" He prodded.

"Like, Catholics are arming to take over the world. Like, women should not be allowed to vote or hold political office. Like, Shalva has fairies in her bosom and the girls can only see them by kissing her breasts."

Louis smiled. "Well, I like that one."

"*What?*"

"I'm teasing, Carsie, calm down. I'm sure she means well—there are explanations for these things, certainly."

"I asked her. She said she meant every word, that she wants to teach the girls to be committed Jews and good women." She waited for him to react.

Warning sirens went off in Louis's head. He agreed with Shalva that women would be happier if they were not permit-ted to own land or hold political office or vote. Getting the vote was the first step toward independence from men, and they would be better off if that didn't happen. He knew Carsie's friends believed otherwise. Best to evade this dilemma, he decided. She was offering him a chance to heal their differences—she had come to him for advice. He didn't want to irritate her. "Sarit and Sophia are little girls," he said. "Children believe anything. As they grow up, they decide for themselves what is true. I think we should let Shalva tell fairy tales and rely on Sarit and Sophia to sort the truth out later."

"They are five and four—I think it's time we hire a governess, someone who can teach them properly."

And pay her with what, he thought. Hats? If Carsie wanted the girls tutored, why couldn't she teach them herself while she sat in the parlor waiting on customers to come? She still taught the children in the sweatshops while she bought her millinery supplies from them. Why couldn't she teach her own children? The greater question, he thought, was how did Shalva have a chance to get the girls alone long enough to tell them these things?

LOUIS STRODE along Fifth Avenue, renamed Avenue of the Allies last year in a frenzy of national fervor. This was the first day he had thought warm enough to wear his navy blue wool blazer and gray flannel pants, a new look for menswear. In the past year he had become adept enough at his trade to practice what was known as "rock of eye" tailoring—the ability to adapt a jacket to his customer by an eyeball estimate rather than relying on a measuring tape. He was, at last, the kind of tailor he had set out to be. He hoped to set a trend by strutting his newest creations on the avenue during these fresh spring mornings. Peach-fuzz lined his upper lip in a thin stripe, a semblance of a moustache he thought would look distinguished when it grew in. Good for business.

All along the street automobiles fought for space with streetcars and delivery wagons. He thought about how traffic had changed in the past few years from pedestrian and horse-drawn buggies to automobiles—thousands of them now, it seemed. Mr. Ford had taken a lesson from the sweatshops' assembly lines, assuring a steady stream of motor cars and trucks.

American flags flapped in a warm spring breeze from the fronts of department stores and specialty shops, reminding him of the clever artist named Childe Hassam who painted New York street scenes, an American flag always in the foreground. America had entered the Great War more than a year ago; patriotism ran high in the city.

Louis's chest swelled. He felt an obligation to his country—it had given him everything he could hope for: a fine trade, people who loved him and a home on the Upper East Side, thanks to the bounty of the late Gaddiel Carmoly.

He stopped in front of a storefront Marine recruiting office, looking at the poster in the window. FIRST IN THE FIGHT— ALWAYS FAITHFUL it read. Another called the Marines the Soldiers of the Sea. He had considered joining one of the armed forces, but he knew there was a problem in joining the Marines—he didn't think he could be a soldier of the sea. The very thought of going to sea again made him nauseous.

A young recruiter opening shop for the day touched his fingertips to his hat in a casual salute. "Help you, sir?"

"Soldiers of the Sea?" Louis gulped.

"Yes, sir, we are. Finest fighters in the world."

"I'd like to help, but the sea...I don't do well on the sea."

"Oh." The soldier smiled. "Well, we can find something other than the sea for you to fight on. As a matter of fact, most of our boys are fighting in France right now."

"Ah. I'm somewhat familiar with France."

The recruiter gently nudged Louis inside, talking as he opened the window shades along the front. "I'm sure they could use an extra hand from someone who knows France, sir. And there is no finer feeling than putting on this uniform. If you feel proud of your country now—and I'm sure you do— when you slip into this jacket, why, you'll bust out crying with love for our United States of America."

"The sea…" Louis said, wiping his palms against his flannel pants. "I would have to cross to France on a ship, wouldn't I?"

"The Germans call us Devil Dogs. Let's get you signed up, sir. The war to end all wars, eh? Our boys can finish it."

Louis blotted his brow with a linen pocket square. Had the summer heat begun early? After all, it was only March. He dabbed the handkerchief at his upper lip. What would become of his business if he left to fight in Europe? "A ship would be the only way to get there, of course."

"Take up the sword, sir. Make your family proud. Your country needs you."

Louis considered the recruiter's uniform. The jacket could use some tailoring, a tuck here and there. He felt the fabric. "Wool? You're wearing wool in this heat?"

The recruiter snapped to attention. "I am so proud to wear this jacket I never notice heat." He held out a sheaf of papers. "Would you like to fill in the forms?"

By noon, Louis stood in line at the State Street Depot waiting to get his uniform. He spent the afternoon tailoring it to fit at the shop. He had bought both hats—the broad-brimmed campaign hat and a barracks cap, so that he would not soil the big hat by wearing it when he might wear something more casual. The recruiter had been right—the moment he slipped on the newly-tailored uniform jacket he felt he had found his purpose.

His excitement grew as he walked home with his uniform in a package under his arm, thinking of his future as a Marine. He was sorry his father couldn't see him fit out as a member of the fiercest fighting team in the world, but he hoped Carsie would be proud of him when he announced he was off to fight in France. Certainly when he came home a war hero her respect for him would leave her no choice but to understand the order of things and settle down.

That evening, while Shalva and Carsie finished putting the girls to bed, he dressed in his uniform and campaign hat and sat in the parlor to wait.

Shalva came into the parlor first, faltered a step and fled to the kitchen. She knew, without a word from Louis, what he had done.

Carsie came behind her, talking. "…child is growing so fast I could almost stand there and watch her sprout. She's going to be…" She stopped short in the parlor doorway, her mouth open. "Louis, why on earth are you dressed that way?"

He stood, beaming. "I joined the Marines." He turned, modeling his newly-tailored uniform. "What do you think?"

She felt for the sofa and sat. Surely there were reasons he…she understood why he thought…but why hadn't he… "Did someone talk you into this?"

"I'm finally part of something, Carsie, the Sixth Marines. Black Jack Pershing needs me!"

She jumped to her feet. "Your family needs you more!"

"You and Shalva will keep the shop running—it's for America we do this!"

"But you didn't ask us if we would keep the shop open. You assumed we would, that's all."

"Why wouldn't you do that for me? I'll be home before you know I'm gone."

"And what if something happens, Louis? What if you come home in…pieces? Or you don't come home at all?"

"Nothing will happen. I'm fighting with the Marines, remember? The toughest fighting force in the world."

"Says who? I've seen thugs on the Lower East Side shoot each other point blank in the head over nothing and Cossacks mutilate my parents for the sheer joy of it—I don't think Marines fight like that. They somehow strike me as more civilized." She stood before him, her arms crossed. "What am I to tell the girls?"

"Tell them I will be back before Sophia's birthday."

"Is there any way you can get out of this, Louis?"

He removed his campaign hat, disappointed with her reaction. Lilia would have been proud to see him serve their country. Carsie seemed almost appalled. "No, I can't get out of it. I wouldn't, even if I could."

Carsie shook her head. Had he not learned anything from their ongoing rift? He still did not understand that they could be a fighting force of two against the world, and that she wanted to be consulted about things that shaped that struggle. Things like this. "When do you leave?"

"Early tomorrow."

Carsie took his face in her hands and kissed him tenderly. "Then let yourself out when you leave in the morning. I won't be down to see you off."

34

AFTER BOOT camp, Louis's troop shipped out to France in mid-May. He wrote home:

> I was seasick off and on for three days, but so were some of the others—too many of us to cut us loose from the corps. They need us in the fight and will not dismiss us for our one small frailty. Like the trip you and Lilia and I (along with the "Count and Countess," let's not forget them!) made on the Marseilles so many years ago, this crossing on the USS Mallory (dubbed by some of us the Hell Rolling Mallory) was an undeniable hell for me.
>
> Although the ship moved across the water faster than the freighter, cutting through the waves where the Marseilles had floated up and down on top of them, the Mallory gave us other causes for sickness. The food made me yearn for Shalva's good kosher cooking, and the bed was indescribably hard and lumpy. No, that is wrong. Sleeping in these cots reminds me of the weekend Papa and I spent on the rocky shoreline of Odessa before we joined your caravan to cross the Carpathians.
>
> A spectacular sight greeted the Mallory in the harbor upon our arrival in France: a band playing on deck and airplanes circling overhead. Unfortunately, that excitement soon went away as we got set for our first battle....

He missed Carsie and the girls as much as he missed Shalva's cooking. Now that Shalva had little else to do but clean and cook, she did both with an enthusiasm any man might expect in a spouse.

He hoped his letters would help Carsie realize fully her role as wife and mother, while he fulfilled his as head of their family, enduring hardships so that she and the girls would not. The following week he wrote:

> It began raining here this morning and it is still coming down, so I have time to write a letter and perhaps rest a bit, as I am tired already of war. My uniform is stiff with mud and smells as bad as anything I wore in my worst days as a drunk. The rifle I carry drags behind me more often than it rests on my shoulder, my boots are wet through, and with no chance to dry in this weather my toes have a fungus that does not heal. My helmet is leaden and bows down my head and they gave me a pack, a poncho, and numerous things I don't know how to use, to weigh me down even more...

A letter from Carsie found him in camp nearly a month after she had written it:

> Dearest Louis:
>
> Truly, if our separation was over a simple misunderstanding, things would not be so serious, but there is more to argue for me than just convictions.
>
> When we came to America, Lilia and I, full of hope and struggling for every penny, we were grateful to have what little we could get, no matter what wrongs we had to suffer to get it. But as we grew up, I saw those wrongs could be repaired.
>
> Still, I never found it possible to repair the rift you created between us after you denied me as your wife. I do not complain as the mother of your children,

but as the woman who wants to walk beside you. You will remember that it was not I who refused, not even for a day, to be your wife even after you spoke those words—that it was you who refused me.

So the problem, as I see it, is your insistence to have the last and only word in our family. That has cost you not only my dwindling affections, but your daughters' as well. They do not understand, nor could I explain to them, why you left the three of us with battles to fight on these shores, to let out truths the world waits to hear—that children should not have to work, that women are the equals of men....

Louis wadded her letter and burned it. He had tired of her insistence that she be his equal. Women would never be treated the same as men—men could think better, they made more money, they had greater business acumen than women. It was a shame his children were girls but it was no surprise—Carsie was so headstrong she had undoubtedly determined the sex of their babies even while they were in the womb.

At the end of May, Louis found a paper bag to use as stationery, a pencil, and time enough to write again:

After a night march we stood like a wall against the enemy here at Belleau. Before daylight we lined up and went over a hill toward a thicket of trees, into reach of the Germans' liquid fire spray which turns everything black and chars those unlucky enough to advance the charge. There is something in the whine of a shell that creates a feeling of despair, and the more you hear it the more it affects you. The thunder of the guns on the hills beyond and the poison gas exploding above us are as though some demon hurtles toward you, where, in fact, we know it is German storm troopers. I am wishing wishing wishing for this to be over....

———

LOUIS'S LETTERS home stopped after the one in late May, the one in which his spirits had sounded so low. Shalva watched Carsie slide as she had after Lilia's death—her doses of lithium bromide and hydrochloric acid becoming larger and more frequent.

Shalva took charge of Sarit and Sophie, feeding them, dressing them, seeing them off to school each morning. Carsie's millinery trade dried up again as it had seven years earlier, after Lilia died, and, as then, she mumbled her way through the sticky days of late summer.

In a letter dated July 27, Carsie wrote:

Dear Louis:

I write to share news I do not believe you will have heard on the Western Front—news that should buoy your spirits. It seems we left Russia too soon. Had we stayed (and lived) to see this day we would have stayed forever. You see, I read in the Forward last night that the Czar and his family had been imprisoned after the Bolsheviks took over last year. Of course, the takeover pleased Emma when it occurred, and she prepares even now to return to the Eastern Front as soon as fighting subsides.

But to the news, which is good. A week ago, on July 17, the royal family was led away under the pretext of safety after someone discovered a plot to liberate the Czar. A firing squad waited, and they shot the Czar multiple times in the head and chest.

My papa would have been so happy to see that day! Jews have taken over the administration of the government—why, even Lenin is to some degree a Jew, and we are proud to claim him...

MAX SIEGEL had been a patient man all his life. Before he married Jenny he had endured three empty years in America searching for Carsie. Now he waited for Benny to leave the

house. That could not happen soon enough—the boy had befriended another hooligan named Meyer Lansky, and the two
had formed a club, as boys will, but theirs had an edge Siegel thought dangerous. The two were busy recruiting others
from around the Ward and into Brooklyn to join them. They
had organized the protection racket against the pushcart peddlers, and had started a floating craps game the cops could
never find. They called themselves the Bugs-Meyer Gang.

LOUIS'S COMPANY moved to fill a gap in the French line,
advancing toward the town of Torcy. As he slid along on his
belly, a sniper took one final shot from a nearby tree, hitting him. His fellow soldiers moved on. He hoped a stretcher
bearer would find him, and while he waited he thought of
Lilia and of Sarit and Sophie, and then of his business and his
father, and after those thoughts he felt somewhat better. He
looked at his injury: a flesh wound to his hip.

He applied iodine from his kit to the scrape, and gauze,
then struggled to his feet and began to retreat from the battlefield, stopping occasionally to study the bodies that lay
on the ground. The first was too short, the next too portly,
the third, well, just wrong. Finally he saw a man fallen close
by whose face had been burned black by liquid flame. Gri-
macing, he knelt, swapped his dog tags with those dangling
around the neck of the corpse, pulled photos and letters from
the dead soldier's helmet, and then he walked out of Belleau
Wood.

While he walked he flipped over the dog tags and rifled
through the letters thinking, for a brief moment, about bury-
ing the things and assuming another name. But the pictures of
a woman and two children compelled him to keep the name
as his own. This woman would never see her husband again—
he lay dead on a battlefield in Belleau Wood. She would hear
only that he was missing in action. Louis could use this man's
name just as easily as any other name he might drum up.

The ground had finally dried after the rains and the sun

warmed his shoulders. He walked across pastures dotted with docile black and white cattle, along roads bordering fields green with spring wheat, and through lush vineyards like those he remembered from the train ride across France to Boulogne-sur-Mer when he was seventeen. He walked for three days, taking a shirt from a clothesline here, trousers there, a pair of shoes from the doorway of a house.

He had played at being someone else before, when he lied to Lord and Taylor to get his first job. He could do it again. He would miss Sarit and Sophia, and he would always have the memory of Lilia, but his name now was Tucker Wilson, a man about to get a new destiny.

35

ON AUGUST 30, two days after she had ridden a subway for the first time, an ache between Shalva's shoulder blades began to spread down her back and into her chest. She knew she ran a fever. Her lungs clouded so badly she had difficulty breathing by daybreak on the thirty-first. She discounted her symptoms, thinking them no harsher than what she suffered when she quit Mrs. Winslow's Soothing Syrup years before. If her body could withstand the rigors of opium withdrawal, she thought, she could weather whatever virus she had now.

Wearing a face mask, Doctor Chertok attended her bedside that evening. "It is the Spanish influenza," he confirmed. "You must keep the girls away from her." He looked over his glasses at Carsie. "And try to stay away yourself."

"But who will care for her if I don't?" Carsie cried. "She took us in when we came to America, and again when she moved up here! I cannot desert her now."

"For your own health, stay away," the doctor warned.

For another two days Shalva struggled, trying to breathe, knowing that if she fell asleep she would die. On the morning of September 2, Sarit tugged at her mother's sleeve. "Mum," she said. "Auntie Shalva is sleeping on the floor upstairs, and she's snoring real loud. I patted her face, but she didn't wake up."

Exhausted from the struggle to breathe and her lack of sleep, Shalva had tried not to give in, but her heart, damaged by years of addiction, had been incapable of battling the potent virus.

Carsie sat *shiva* alone for the full seven days. On the eighth she took up her position on the stool again, not knowing what else to do. She had found a mother in Shalva, a sister, a friend, and once again had lost her. Her chest tightened, but tears did not come.

Sarit brought her mother broth and tea and stale toast as she had during the previous week, and fed the same to Sophia. She brushed her mother's hair, her sister's, and her own.

Carsie spoke nothing to her daughters, mumbling only, "...glossy black Japanese straw, this hat, in a pleasing sailor shape...each ruffle is edged with jet spangles...a trimming of hackle feathers and a tail aigrette..." until, on the fifteenth day of her mourning, she stood from the stool, bathed and dressed in clean clothes, and made sure the girls did the same. Still she mumbled.

Chanukah came early that year and had long gone by December 15, when Carsie opened the door to a Western Union runner, who handed her a telegram addressed TO THE FAMILY OF LOUIS LEVY. She moved in staggered steps to the parlor sofa and broke the seal, knowing how the telegram would read:

> THE SECRETARY OF WAR REGRETS TO INFORM YOU THAT CORPORAL LOUIS LEVY WAS KILLED IN A VALIANT FIRE FIGHT AT BELLEAU WOOD ON THE AFTERNOON OF 6 JUNE, 1918. HE LIES BURIED IN THE FIELD CEMETERY LOCATED NEAR THAT BATTLE, IN NORTHERN FRANCE.
> HOLD FAST TO MEMORIES FOR COMFORT...

Carsie dropped the telegram and stood, clutching her stomach, retching, gasping. She had killed him as surely as though she had shot him herself.

She returned to the hallway, staring out the door, still open; the Western Union messenger gone. People moved silently on the sidewalk, their mouths buried behind coat collars so that she could not hear their whispers. Cold wind blew in the trees. She smelled the scent of vodka and a fog of opium and she knew who had come.

She slammed the door, bolting first the lower lock and

then the upper one. She ran to the front windows, securing the latches, pulling down the shades. Shadows moved behind her. A man, perhaps nine feet tall, stepped out of the drawing room and pulled off a skeleton mask. Behind the mask he was clean-shaven, blond, and blue eyed. His eyes stared intently. He locked his thumbs, pointing his index fingers downward. Two bolts of lightning struck the floor on either side of him, blinding her momentarily. His body blurred and vanished.

Screaming, she ran to the kitchen, searching for the paring knife. She checked the back door lock and the windows on that side of the house. Voices swelled around her head in a cascade of languages, laughing, buzzing. She caught sight of herself in the dining room mirror, her face pale against her dark hair. She dropped the knife to cover her ears, the sound of voices deafening now. Her feet went cold, the skin of her hands turned the color of glass. Fire—she needed warmth.

A wail behind her. She spun. Nothing. Someone cried out. Carsie found the knife and walked again to the parlor, guessing why they had come, knowing she could not escape. She read the telegram again. The second time it read:

IN BESSARABIA STANDS JUST ONE TREE,
IMPERIAL BLUE, THE COLOR OF AIR.
A JEWISH PHOENIX TRIUMPHANT REIGNS
OVER RUSSIA'S ROYAL FAMILY THERE.

She smelled smoke and ran for the stairs. A fire on the landing, and how perfect! Its ashes covered her like a triumphant bird. She stretched out her arms, still holding the knife in her right hand, opening her mouth to inhale flames. Her eyes closed, she bowed her head. The fire would take her but she would rise.

"Mummy!" Sarit screamed, her voice high and reed thin, piercing Carsie's perceptions. "Mummy! Stop!"

———

THE FIRE department wound hoses and sorted through the rubble that had been the front staircase.

"Hard to say who set it," the captain said. "Could have been one of the kids, but maybe not. Those little girls ain't strong enough to pull down the paneling, now is they?"

The assistant chief scratched his head. "The mother?"

"Might be, but she's pretty ate up. I don't know if she's got what it takes to strike a match right now."

"Who, then?" The captain looked around the parlor, his eyes falling on a table stacked high with magazines. "Aw, nuts. Looka here." He held the telegram up to the light. "Husband killed in the war it says. Telegram's dated today. Tough break. Explains a lot."

The assistant chief stepped back to survey the damage. "They can use the back stairs for a while—Earl's barricaded these until the woman can get them fixed. Let's leave 'em be. Now's not the time to go calling up Child Welfare to take her girls away. My Pearl would go dotty, too, if she got a telegram like that one."

FROM THE edge of the shaded window, Carsie watched the fire engines pull away. She had beaten them. She was the phoenix triumphant. She felt her power surge. Her hands warmed. The voices faded.

She took down the Adamantine clock from the mantle, the clock Arnold Rothstein had given her, the clock that had stood guard on the shelf above the cash register at the shop. She sat with it in her lap, watching its hands creep imperceptibly—one hour, two, ten. She rose from her chair at daybreak, carried the clock to the kitchen, lifted the heavy meat mallet from the counter with both hands, and brought it down on the clock, shattering the marbleized celluloid with her first blow.

The sounds in her ears swelled once more, gears grinding and laughter, both of those replaced by the beat of wings. From behind her she heard Lilia say, "But…I have a very long

time, don't I?" And her father whispering, "Remember well,
remember right..." And her mother railing, "You know too
little about being a Jew *or* how it feels to starve...." From the
corner of her eye, she caught a swirl of pain and fury, hissing,
wailing.

She turned slowly. Singing drifted from the front hall on
the sweet smell of last night's wood smoke. She took up the
paring knife again and moved toward the music, remembering, remembering, remembering how it felt when she stabbed
the knife into Velvel Kagan's neck—no more difficult than
carving a chicken. How easily his flesh had yielded, how simple it had been to pull down on the blade, how dark the blood
that pooled beneath his body on the kitchen floor. From that
afternoon on, she had understood how effortlessly the Cossacks had killed her parents. She had never cried for losing
Lilia or Shalva. And now she would not cry over the loss of
Louis. She would never permit herself to grieve—her soul had
left her. That had been her punishment for wishing to leave
Lucava, for taking her eye off her mother and Lilia, for killing
Velvel Kagan.

Carsie raised the knife, swinging at the young Cossack who
wielded the whip over her father's head, smelling a fire of lead
type and paper; she thrust the blade at the sweatshop boss
who locked Triangle Waist Company's doors from the outside,
the scent of burning flesh stinging her nose once more; she
slashed at the German who shot Louis in Belleau Wood, the
stink of black powder in her nose.

She looked at the blade of the knife—its cold gleam and
slender shape. Now it would know her blood. She wondered
where best she might make the cut that the blade would not
bend but yield the tender relief of a hurried death. The knife
beckoned a butcher's kiss, longing to feed on her flesh, calling her to the grave. She traced its sharp edge with her thumb.

Her eyes adjusted to the dim hallway and she saw, peering over the stairway barricade, the faces of Sarit and Sophia.

"The firemen are back, Mummy," Sarit rasped, her face wet with tears. "They're in the kitchen."

The firemen ran to the hallway door, ready to retreat if Carsie charged them with the knife. Behind them stood a policeman, braced, his gun drawn.

Doctor Chertok opened his bag and withdrew a paraldehyde sedative. "Have you been taking your lithium bromide, Mrs. Levy?"

Carsie looked away. A gong and discordant flute played a haunting melody in her head.

Chertok turned to the cop. "She has a history of nerves. I think she will be fine after some sleep."

"The girls—they should be moved, don't you think?"

"I think if we took the girls away now she would never recover."

"But they could be in serious danger."

Chertok shrugged. "They're her girls. Let's give her one more chance."

36

ATTORNEY CHARLES Nussbaum pulled his thin coat closed against the late-January freeze and buttoned it to the neck. He checked the address again. It was a little after five o'clock on a Friday afternoon and just beginning to get dark. The address was the house in front of him, an imposing brownstone. He knew the family was Jewish; he hoped he was not intruding on their *Shabbat*. Still, he thought they might welcome him gladly when they heard what he had to tell them. He climbed the steps and rang the bell, tentatively.

A girl of about six opened the door, the daughter of a servant, perhaps, judging from her unkempt appearance. Even though the drapes were drawn, darkening the elegantly furnished drawing room, he could see it needed a good dusting. A smell of wood smoke hung in the air. A carpenter worked on the staircase, replacing decorative pieces.

Nussbaum saw piles of magazines on a corner table, and more stacked on the floor, all of them singed. Afternoon sun bled around the edges of a window shade, lighting dust motes that floated in the air. He suspected something had happened in this house, something he was not prepared for. His visit would not be as simple as he had planned.

As she gulped back the last of a dose of lithium bromide, Carsie halted in the doorway to study the man who stood there leafing through one of her fashion magazines.

He looked up and blushed. "I understand, Madame," he said, "that you are Carsie Levy?" In the dim light he could tell little about her—a Jew, obviously, probably Russian. Pretty, actually, though her hair needed grooming and her dress, well, there was a smell about it.

"Is it a hat you want?" she asked.

"No, no," Nussbaum replied. "I just want to know if you are Mrs. Levy."

"I do not make hats, I design them. Others make them for me."

"Oh, I thought you were the owner of Modiste Hats, the proprietor," Nussbaum said. "Then you are not Mrs. Levy?"

"I am the *proprietress* of Modiste Hats. But I do not own this house." The man stood with his back to the light. She could not see his face, but she could see he needed a tailor. She pursed her lips. "This is the house of my late aunt. If you are not here for a hat, why are you here?"

Nussbaum smiled. "I did not wish to trouble you. I'm a solicitor, and wanted to make sure this was the place I was looking for. Is Mr. Levy at home?"

"Mr. Levy was killed last June. In the war."

"I'm sorry. So very sorry. I know you lost your aunt, too. That is why I am here."

"To extend your condolences, Mr....?"

He handed her a business card. "Charles Nussbaum. Attorney at Law."

"So the card says. Why are you here?"

"Most people call me 'Chat.' A nickname."

"I don't approve of nicknames. Should I show you to the door, or do you have a reason to stay?"

"My firm handled Gaddiel Carmoly's affairs when he died. You will recall Mrs. Carmoly—your aunt—received everything from his estate."

Carsie nodded. "Yes, I remember."

"We received notification from the state of New York that Mrs. Carmoly died in the influenza pandemic."

"In September."

Chat Nussbaum set his briefcase on a stack of magazines and unfastened the lock, withdrawing a file. "Yes. I have a copy of her death certificate. Do you, by chance, have anything that indicates Mr. Levy's death?"

"I have the telegram from the War Department. That's all."

"That's enough, I should think. We can proceed with that, if you'll find it for me."

"Now?"

"I have to do this in the proper order, Mrs. Levy. Now would be fine, if you know where the telegram is."

She crossed the hall to the parlor, retrieved the telegram, and returned to the drawing room, handing it to Nussbaum without a word.

He read the brief message and winced. "My deep condolences. I am happy to see that our men are now out of harm's way over there."

"Indeed. Is that all, Mr. Nussbaum?"

He gave his head a shake. "Not quite. But I think you'll want to sit for what I have to say."

She sighed, staring at him. "I can take bad news standing up these days."

"This news, you'll find, is very much the opposite of bad. Not as good as it might be, as its circumstances come by way of Mrs. Carmoly's death, but you are about to become a wealthy woman, Mrs. Levy."

Carsie's eyes widened. "Go on."

"As I said, Mrs. Carmoly inherited everything when her husband's car exploded. He had no other heirs. Do you know if Mrs. Carmoly had anyone else?"

"Only…ah, let me think. No. There is just me, now. Shalva's father is gone, her husband and the one before him, my sister, my husband, everyone but me. Dead."

Nussbaum nodded. "I noted most of that in the census records. Except for the death of your husband. They have not recorded that yet, of course."

"And how do you see that as fortunate?"

"Since your husband is no longer…well, no longer with us…you are the sole heir to Mrs. Carmoly's estate, Mrs. Levy.

You have this house and all of her bank accounts at your disposal. They are yours when you sign these documents."

Carsie felt for the edge of the sofa as she had the night Louis left for the war and sat. "What does that mean, sir?"

"It means you own this brownstone, and that Mrs. Carmoly's accounts at Argonaut Savings will be assigned to you. Accounts totaling more than five thousand dollars. There is… only one minor problem."

"Yes?"

"The back taxes on the house. But of course, you have more than enough money now to pay those."

"And how much are the taxes, please?"

"After Mr. Carmoly died Mrs. Carmoly did not pay any property taxes. At all." He shrugged. "Probably didn't understand that she was required by law to do that."

"How much, Mr. Nussbaum?"

"Eight hundred ten dollars, Madame."

"Don't call me Madame." She thought. The house and what amounted to a little more than four thousand dollars had been dropped in her lap by this man? Why did it not feel real? Was this a trick? She stood. "Who are you, really?"

He studied her but did not answer.

"Mr. Nussbaum?"

He sighed. "It's true, all of it. I am an attorney with the firm of Wilkinson, Cobb and Field. And you have, indeed, inherited Mrs. Carmoly's estate. But I am not an estate attorney with our firm. I handle the child labor issues before our legislature. I had heard of your work with the children in the sweatshops and when your name came up as Shalva Carmoly's niece, I pleaded with the partners to permit me to call on you—to give you the good news and process the paperwork. I am very much an admirer of yours, Mrs. Levy."

Carsie shook her head and smiled. They might think her crazy, but she was no fool. "My aunt was once tricked by a scheme like this. I think you are not who you say you are."

Nussbaum had suspected things would not go as they normally went with visits like this one, but he did not expect a reaction so peculiar. He did not know how to counter. "How can I prove to you that I am?"

37

SINCE HER husband's prison term had begun, more than five years ago, Miriam Bender had lived in noisy, smelly, cockroach-infested tenements in Philadelphia and here, on the Lower East Side. Aaron had another two years to serve, but the sentence, to Miriam's way of thinking, was more severe for her than for her husband. She was desperate to escape this life.

Philadelphia dock workers had coined a phrase last year: "It's not what you know, it's who you know," and the words rang in her ears. But who did she know who could help her get Aaron out of the Tombs? Who? What would it take? A pardon? Parole? Then she thought of Carolyn Green, Arnold Rothstein's wife, and she knew what needed to be done.

Miriam brushed her lavender dress and the basque-waisted coat and with her last dollar sent a messenger uptown, with an invitation for Carolyn, hoping she would agree to lunch at Café French in the basement of the Brevoort Hotel. She and Carolyn had become casual friends before the war and it was time to renew the friendship.

MAX SIEGEL limped north on Orchard Street after work on Friday, pulling at his beard, mumbling to himself. "A patient man, haven't I always been?" Hadn't he, after all, walked across the entire continent of Europe? Hadn't he spent years behind a bar, serving drinks to *ganovim*—clean shaven, card playing thieves like Arnold Rothstein? Working on *Shabbat*, sometimes until after dark? "But this?" he mumbled. "Too much."

It had taken such a short time for him to lose all hope for his eldest son. He had told Jenny that morning that Ben must leave. Predictably, she said nothing. When Jenny didn't approve of his ideas she stonewalled.

This Bugs-Meyer gang, they were nothing but a band of ruthless hooligans, stealing cars and worse, he feared. What was it he had heard they had decided to call themselves? Murder Incorporated. What the hell kind of crap was that?

He laid part of the blame at Jenny's feet. Spoiled the kid, she had. Ruined him. Gave him money and took food out of her own mouth to put it in his.

Max had trouble thinking of a twelve-year-old boy fending for himself on the streets of the Tenth Ward, but if any kid could, Ben could, the little *goniff.* Maybe he and Jenny could tell the boy the usual—"If you ever need to come home," and so on. Yes, that should do it. If anything scared a boy into staying away, it was the prospect of admitting failure to his parents.

CARSIE SAT at the round table in the corner, amid the stacks of fashion magazines, her arms crossed.

"Of course," Nussbaum smiled. "I remember when it happened. A number of people were gypped out of a lot of money back then. But they caught the con man who sent those letters." He thought a moment. "Mrs. Levy, I think I know how I can prove who I am." He opened his briefcase again, pulled a folder from the bottom and opened it facing her. "This is the first bill I wrote for a federal child labor law."

Carsie read the top sheet. "Yes, in 1916. I remember hoping that would work, but it was too soon, I'm afraid. And the Child Labor Committee lacks—"

Nussbaum nodded. "Lacks almost everything it needs to enforce..." he dug again in his briefcase. "Here, look at these." He spread a pile of photographs on top of a stack of magazines, pictures of children with soot-blackened faces, children working in mills or breathing the foul air in shoe factories. "The law was declared unconstitutional last year, as you know—so I'm revising it now, to see if I can get an amendment passed in the next term."

Carsie tapped the pile of photographs. "I was one of those children, Mr. Nussbaum. My sister also, and my aunt. I have argued long and hard with those who think children that work in factories should not be shown a better life."

"And here you are." Nussbaum smiled, looking around the room. "How few of those children will make it this far?"

"If they do, I pray it is not at the cost my family paid. My sister died in the Triangle fire. Shalva was beaten by her sweater because she was so tired she made mistakes."

"Ah? I'm sorry. I knew you had lost your sister, but I did not know how."

Carsie studied his face, lit by the lamp over the table. He was a pleasant-looking man; that struck her first. His face had no angles—all his features were round and clustered in the center of a large circle of a face: his round blue eyes, and his rosy mouth, and his rounded nose. His glasses too were round, and the ears over which he hooked them as he prepared to work. He stood not quite as tall as she, in a coat too light for this weather. She had not asked him to sit or to shed the coat, and, as she became aware of the temperature in the house now, she realized he was probably more comfortable with it on.

"I should sign your paperwork and let you get home to *Shabbat,* Mr. Nussbaum."

"I'm not worried. *Shabbat* can wait this week."

"But your family—"

He shrugged. "There is no one waiting at my house. I'm single. My parents live in Chicago. I moved here to take this job—it's a wonderful opportunity to do what I believe in." He laid a number of documents in front of her, arraying them left to right, talking as he did so. "But you have your holy day to think about. And daughters who need looking to, I'm sure. I should move this business along rather than taking up your time with my passion." He held out a pen for her signature.

She smiled at him as she took the pen. "No worries on our account either. We are, in this house, atheistical Jews, as

Mr. Churchill called us." She spoke as she signed her name to each of the documents. "Of course, with children of my own, your passion to end child labor is very dear to my heart. I admire your enthusiasm."

"Ah. Thank you for your time. I appreciate the opportunity to meet you and..." he filed the estate folder along with the others in his case. "I wonder, Mrs. Levy, I mean, I realize it is very soon after learning of your husband's death, and mourning that of Mrs. Carmoly. You are still in *sheloshim*, I know, but..."

"I think, Mr. Nussbaum, that I would be pleased to see the outside world again, if that's what you're suggesting."

His round face lit as he smiled. "For dinner then, on Monday?"

FROM THE edge of the window shade Carsie watched Chat Nussbaum walk down the street. The man needed a coat, a tailor and a barber. But he seemed kind enough, and his heart was in the same place as hers.

And his news! In one hour she owned a house and had come into more money than she could conceive of. She flicked the switch on the electric lamp and gathered the girls in the parlor. They ate bread and butter, some salt cod and a piece of cheese. She would go to the market in the morning, after all three of them bathed and put on fresh clothes.

Perhaps she would buy a coat for...Chat. She remembered what it had felt like twenty years ago, when she and Lilia needed coats in Lucava and Mayim Shulman had provided them. She recalled Louis being jailed for stealing a coat when he needed it. She thought about all the coats she had made when she and Lilia first came to America. She looked at the faces of her girls, giggling and whispering at the table, their dark eyes dancing in the glow of the lamp—they would never have to work like that. They would never know such cold as a Russian winter could bring. They would never need coats.

After they ate, she braided ribbons into their hair. She

washed their faces and her own, studying her eyes in the mirror: two rings of dark circles spread from her nose across her cheeks. She had not slept in…how long?

She tucked the girls into their beds, kissed each of them, and whispered, "Remember well, remember right…"

"Goodnight, goodnight…" Sarit yawned.

"Goodnight, goodnight." Sophia echoed.

38

HER FIRST advertisement announcing the reopening of Modiste Hats appeared in the *Jewish Daily Forward* on March 5. She hoped to take advantage of the demand for the showy hats worn at Fifth Avenue's annual Easter Parade. By the end of the month she had orders for twenty hats; the parade would occur in a little more than two weeks. Twenty hats to create— twenty!—along with feeding and nurturing two girls, and lessons to be taught to the children when she went to the sweatshops to buy supplies. She had no time to think about who had died or how recently.

The weather had begun to warm. She found herself walking along Houston Street on a particularly fine afternoon in early April, shopping for millinery supplies and a coat for Chat Nussbaum. Surely now that winter had gone, a bargain might be found among the pushcarts of the coat peddlers.

A man limped to a bench near where she stood, shopping. He lowered himself wearily, rubbing his feet as though they ached, using his right hand, a hand missing the center, fourth and pinky fingers. Aware that she was staring at the man, Carsie looked away, but was compelled by a memory to look again. Though grayer, the man reminded her of Max Siegel. No, she thought, it couldn't be. Max Siegel had all his fingers, and besides, the last she had seen him was in Trusheny almost twenty years ago. The man did not look up from massaging his feet. Carsie fled before he could see her.

SOMETHING ABOUT Arnold Rothstein made other gamblers nervous. Maybe his intellect irritated them, or his well-tailored suits; perhaps it was his free spending. Still, Rothstein held sway among the rich and powerful in New York, both city and state, by connection and bribe. No one could ignore him as a force in the underworld.

"If a girl goes to bed with nine guys," Arnold Rothstein chuckled to "Sport" Sullivan in late August of 1919, "who's going to believe the tenth one's the father?" He tucked a fifty in Sullivan's pocket and sent him to Chicago to talk to the White Sox. The war had been hard on major league baseball—many of its best had left the ball field for a battlefield. Rothstein's book-making business had suffered, and he had just made sure the 1919 World Series fix was in. Sullivan's proposal that he bankroll the fix had been the second approach Rothstein had received that year to make sure the Chicago White Sox lost the series. He figured one offer was as good as the next. He went with the first proposal, knowing that with Sullivan, the fix was in at Tammany Hall, too.

CARSIE SAT at the round table in the parlor, reading the New York World:

> "...testifying before a Grand Jury investigation of the incident, Arnold Rothstein stated he was an innocent businessman intent on clearing his name. Prosecutors could find no evidence linking Rothstein to the affair and he was not indicted. 'The whole thing started when (Abe) Attell and some cheap gamblers decided to frame the Series and make a killing,' Rothstein told the Grand Jury. 'The world knows and my friends know I turned the deal down flat. I was not in on it, and did not bet a cent on the Series after I found out what was under way...'"

The doorbell rang. Carsie sighed and closed the paper. Another customer. She had begun to doubt the wisdom of re-opening Modiste, although the simplicity of hats these days had lightened her load.

A little tulle on a straw or felt silhouette usually pleased her customers these days; the idea was to make colors play against each other, rather than turning out the dull brown toques and navy boaters and big black Merry Widow picture hats that women had worn for so many years. That spring, Carsie's hats had featured lilac tulle over pale blue felt—a combination that gave off an overall opalescent glow, or peach silk ribbon gathered on pink straw, to approximate azalea blossoms.

Carsie gasped and smiled when she saw her visitor. "Emma!" she cried. "How happy I am to see you! Come in!"

Emma Goldman stepped in and looked around. "Life has been good to you, eh, Carsie?"

"At some pretty awful expense, yes. It's been quite a year— I lost both my husband and my aunt last year, and then I lost my mind. I inherited the house from Shalva. But sit—and tell me all. How did you find me? Why have you come? What can I do to help? Would you like tea?"

Emma chuckled. "You have helped already, my dear, by your work with the children. And no tea, no. I found you through your...your friend, Chat Nussbaum."

"Oh yes, of course you would know him. He brought the news that I had inherited the house. That is how we met."

"He is a fine champion for our cause. And it is about the cause that I come. That and to say goodbye."

"Yes, I was sorry to read of the deportation," Carsie said. "Yours and Berkman's."

"Agh! I am like Lenin—past my season and out of fashion. No one believes in doctrine anymore. Truth is, times have changed since the war." She shrugged. "Women will vote in next year's election. And with Chat Nussbaum's help, it won't be long before children will not work in the factories. I came to ask only that you never give in, Carsie. In the face of conflict do not step back. Never let them know when you're afraid."

Her father's words, Carsie remembered. She thought. "What, then, Emma? If anarchy is out of fashion, how do I do that?"

"I think," Emma said, "that I am getting old. I've changed. Maybe the way you're doing it is right—with your teaching. By encouraging people to think for themselves."

SHE RECALLED the year she had spent looking for Arnold Rothstein on Exeter Street: shopping in the same place where they had first met, walking north and south in front of the market waiting to see his face. Now it was in front of a pushcart that she waited, hoping to see the man with two fingers once again. She had decided she would speak to him—what did it matter if he wasn't Max Siegel? She would admit her mistake, offer an apology and move along. But she had to know.

He approached. Carsie's stomach churned, her hands trembled. Her breathing grew shallow—*danken Gott* she had abandoned corsets. Moments like this changed everything if they turned out they way they should, or shouldn't. She watched. He sat on the bench and rubbed his foot. She took a step toward him and stopped, light-headed. He looked up at her, and leaped to his feet.

CHAT NUSSBAUM watched the clock on the afternoon of January 15, 1920. When he was through at work he would go home and warm his *tuchis* with what little whiskey he had left. Prohibition would begin tomorrow, and the merchants had stopped stocking spirits altogether. Nothing was available until someone could find a way around the law. Normally he respected the laws, being an attorney, but the government had some misplaced ideas of how people should live these days.

MIRIAM BENDER did not look at the policeman as she handed Aaron's street clothes over the glass barrier. It had taken everything she had to secure her husband's release—favors called, all their savings and then even more money, wheedled from the women who rolled bandages with her on the Lower East Side.

Five years Aaron had spent in the Tombs for fraud, and his

release, accomplished by a phone call from Arnold Rothstein to "Red Mike" Hylan, the mayor, had finally got it done.

She was grateful to Red Mike and to Arnold Rothstein, and to Carolyn Green, but she fervently hoped Aaron would think of something the minute he hit the pavement, something that would make them comfortable again. She needed clothes and shoes and a decent place to lay her head.

"…SHOULD HAVE known how to look for you—the world passes here. I should have sat on this bench seventeen years ago and let you find me," Max said.

"Seventeen years? You've been in America that long?"

"Looking for you every day. I never gave up."

"Max! Oh, Max, I am so sorry. Please forgive me. After the postman said…"

He sighed. "The postman suffered a beating for what he told you. And for taking your money."

"Our money? But he gave us…let me think—it's been so long. He gave us four hundred rubles."

"I know. He should have given you sixteen hundred. He kept most of it for himself. We found him out the same night, and I went in search of the caravan, and, well, I had the accident with the horse."

"And after that you walked…on your poor feet," she said.

"Eh, I was young. I did not feel it then. Now, I feel my feet all over my body. *Ikh bin an alter shkrab*, Carsie." I'm a worn out old shoe.

She touched his hair, the hair of a man with worries. "And do you have a family?"

He smiled. "Yeh, I do. I have a fine son and I adopted my wife's children—four of them—a boy and three girls."

"*Mazel tov.*"

"Normally you would say that, wouldn't you? But that boy of hers! *Oy gevalt!* He has shown me hell on this side of the grave."

———

THEY MET at the park bench on Thursdays for a year—sometimes moving to Katz's Deli for warmth or shelter from the rain or snow. She told him of her daughters and her business. She talked about losing Lilia in the Triangle fire and of Shalva's addiction to opium because of her sweatshop boss, and about having worked in the sweatshops herself. He talked about his walk across Europe with the *Fusgeyers,* and his trip over, on the *Carpathia's* maiden voyage; of his marriage to Jenny, about the trials he had been through with Ben and his joy at the birth of Maurice.

In late September she told him she was engaged to a wonderful man, a man whose crusade to end child labor in the sweatshops so sweetly agreed with her own efforts to educate those children.

They would talk for an hour each time before Max shuffled west on Houston Street toward Second Avenue and Carsie continued on to the shops and pushcarts to buy millinery supplies.

On the third day of *Rosh Hashanah,* 1920, radicals detonated a wagonload of explosives at the Wall Street offices of J. P. Morgan and Company, killing thirty people and injuring more than one hundred. Anarchy was back in style.

On October 13th, the day after Yom Kippur, she told him about killing Velvel Kagan.

"You have stood at the gates of hell, eh?" he said. He chuckled. "Not to worry, my dear. I believe all hearts have some murder in them. The night you left I truly wanted to kill Zirl Bakhtin. I still believe I would have, if Nakhimov hadn't sent me to find you. To get you back—to give you what was yours. This." He pressed a wad of rubles into her hand. "Use it as a dowry—this is your money."

"But you must keep it, Max! Surely you need it—and I have all the money I can use."

"I don't want it, Carsie. It isn't mine—this money was meant to do something noble. If I keep it, Ben will find it, and nothing decent would happen with it, then."

"Then donate it."

He thought for a moment, and his eyes lit. "Yes," he nodded. "And I know where. When I first came to New York an old Jew picked me up. He took me down here and gave me a bed."

"At the Sheltering Society? That's perfect, Max. They helped us when we got here, too. I'd like to see them get the money."

CHAT NUSSBAUM caught a cab from city hall, headed to the brownstone on East Sixty-sixth mid-afternoon. He had planned to surprise Carsie with the offer of a splendid evening out—he had made three dinner reservations at different restaurants: the Astoria Hotel if she wanted elegance, Delmonico's steakhouse if she craved a good piece of beef, and Romany Marie's for the Russian food and a colorful clientele. And after dinner he had tickets to a movie he thought she would like—Rudolph Valentino's *The Sheik*. Didn't every woman in America swoon when she saw that man?

His cab crept along Houston Street, the cabby jockeying for position in traffic. Nussbaum's thoughts drifted: the child labor law had failed again, and he had begun yet another draft...he yearned to marry and settle down with Carsie and the girls...he looked forward to the evening out. He bolted forward in the seat, staring at a man and woman who sat on a park bench on the sidewalk, holding hands. It couldn't be! The woman lifted her head. It was.

He paced Fifth Avenue after the cab dropped him off, north first, as far as the museum, and again to the brownstone. She had not returned. He walked south, to Ladies' Mile, and back to sit on her steps until she came in. He was in no shape for an evening out after his two-hour constitutional; he was exhausted.

Only one of the three restaurants appealed to Carsie when Nussbaum put the choice to her—Delmonico's. The others? The Astoria, well, no. Too many memories there—of the Benders, of Lilia, of the Astors and their party. And Romany Marie's? No again. The very thought of Russian food in a room full of people who might recognize her—Stieglitz or Dreiser or Childe Hassam—gave her stomach a turn.

The chandeliers at Delmonico's glittered and the waiters moved in quiet grace as they set down her chicken and noodles and refilled her water glass.

"How goes the teaching?" Chat asked.

She chewed thoughtfully. "I enjoy it more than I ever thought I would," she said. "Most of the children are students like I was—they don't care, they don't want to know. Sometimes one of them breaks my heart—they die, they're abused at work and at home, or they come in the dead of winter without coats."

Chat tucked into his steak. "Did I see you on Houston Street this afternoon?"

"Possibly. I was there."

"Mmmm. I thought I saw you talking to a man." He paused to chew. "On a park bench." He wiped the corners of his mouth. "Your hand in his. That was you?"

She dabbed at the corners of her own mouth as Rothstein had taught her to do in polite company. "Yes. He is an old friend from Russia. He has been here quite a while, looking for me. As it turns out I found him—but only just a year ago."

"An old friend, who came here looking for you?"

She smiled across the table at her fiancée. Dear Chat. They would get to know each other in the years to come, but tonight they did not, not yet. He knew so little about her past, whereas Louis had known almost all of it. "He is married now and has four, no, five children," she said. "You should have stopped—I've told him so much about you."

"Still," he raised an eyebrow. "It sounds like more than friendship. It certainly looked like more than that."

"And there was a time when it *was* more than friendship. But it was also more than twenty years ago—in a time before." She shrugged. "He had no one else to marry; I was fifteen years old and orphaned. Stuck in his *shtetl,* until I was put on the Federation caravan, taken to France, and shipped over here. He didn't find out about that until after I was gone, then he followed and got into some trouble before he had traveled twenty miles."

"Carsie," Chat said. He reached for her hand. "I love you. I want to be your husband. But I tell you now, I want to be the only man whose hand you hold. We will, you and I, walk many miles—"

She gasped. "Yes, Chat? Shoulder to shoulder?"

He nodded. "There will be enough bumps without my having to worry about your old boyfriends."

"That's fair. And I think he will understand."

"May I know his name, this unfortunate man who is about to lose you?"

"His name is Max Siegel. He has a son, Ben, who is driving him—"

Nussbaum's head snapped up from his plate. "Yes, I know the boy. And I pity your friend. The kid's nickname is Bugsy and he's as bad as…"

"MAX," CARSIE said, "I have dreamed of this man since I was a child. For the first time I truly want to marry…he has given me back my life."

Max Siegel's heart soared—the release was more than he'd thought he would feel. Then something else washed over him—a wave of regret. He could have been the man Carsie spoke of now, had he been patient. Persistent. He braced his legs and stood, wincing as he put weight on his right foot. "This day had to come. I knew as soon as we found each other that it would." He brushed her cheek with the back of his hand. "I feel better knowing that you are close by in the world again, my dear. Funny, isn't it, how we can shed pieces of ourselves—fingers, toes, hearts—and still our lives are whole? Every time this foot aches it will remind me that you, like the fingers and toes, are lost to me." He took her hand, pressed a small parcel into it and turned, limping west toward Second Avenue.

"Max," Carsie called.

He stopped and turned. "Yeh?"

"Surely we can still be friends?"

He thought for a minute. "No, I don't think so. We would always be looking back. It is what we've done for a year now, when we met to talk. It's time for both of us to move forward. If we tried only to be friends, you and I, there would always be an expectation, wouldn't there?"

She nodded, blinking back tears that stood in her eyelashes. "I suppose."

He walked on.

Slowly, she unwrapped the parcel he had given her and clasped her kopek necklace to her heart. She heard her father whisper, "Remember well, remember right..." She inhaled and blew out, opening her hands in her lap as though she released the memories. The kopek necklace lay in one palm, her linen handkerchief in the other. The agonized faces in her head faded—Mama, Papa, Lilia, Shalva, and Louis—pictures replaced by an image of each in happier times: Mama at the stove making her turnip latkes to please Papa, Papa bent over his type boxes while he set the broadsides, Lilia reading her novels, Shalva *davening* while she prayed, Louis in his tailor shop stroking a finely-crafted tweed jacket.

Tears swelled in her eyes. Again, she closed her hands around her necklace and the linen handkerchief, and she cried.

Author's Notes and Acknowledgements

First, a word about a couple of details mentioned in the book: the Hebrew and Gregorian calendar dates on page one are for reference and sense of place. In Russia, on this date, the Julian calendar was still in use, making the date by Russian reckoning November 16.

Next, Carsie and Lilia Akselrod would indeed have arrived in New York City at Battery Park. The Great Fire at Ellis Island occurred on June 14, 1897, destroying the entire complex, and the facility did not reopen until December 19, 1900. The girls arrived in June of 1900, while Ellis Island was being rebuilt, and would have processed through the Barge Office, located in Battery Park at the southern tip of Manhattan.

MY SINCERE appreciation to Louise Dolson, whose tale of her mother's journey from Russia to the U.S. originally lit my fire to write about the immigrant experience at the turn of the twentieth century on New York City's lower east side.

Thanks too, to the staff at YIVO Institute for Jewish Research; to the kind folks at the Lower East Side Tenement Museum; to my Yiddish master, Rubin Feldstein; and to Valery Bazarov of the Hebrew Immigration Aid Society, for his encouragement and for pointing me to Yaffa Eliach's superb book *There Once was a World*.

Among the hundreds of other resources I used to research while I wrote, I found myself returning to Leon Stein's *The Triangle Fire*, Wendy Gamber's *The Female Economy: The Millinery and Dressmaking Trades, 1860–1930*; Nan Enstad's *Ladies of Labor, Girls of Adventure*, and Carol Ann Bales's *Tales of the Elders*.

Not having written this book in a vacuum, I'm grateful for the guidance and editorial work of my first readers: Nancy Cash, Eileen Elkinson, Lisa Harvey, Joan Medlicott, Celia Miles, Steve Rinsler, Holly Simms, and Peg Steiner. And of course a tip of the hat to my editor and publisher, Susan and John Daniel.

And finally, special thanks to my wonderful sisters: playwright and screenwriter Joan Golden, and Gail Harrison, whose indomitable spirit to the end was my muse. Remember well, remember right...